FAKED PASSPORTS

DENNIS WHEATLEY

DENNIS WHEATLEY

FAKED PASSPORTS

Frontispiece Portrait by
MARK GERSON

Original Illustrations by
JOHN HOLDER

13 043 10 R7

CONTENTS

THE BACKWASH OF THE BOMB

WHEN the first glimmerings of returning consciousness stirred Gregory Sallust's brain the aeroplane was thousands of feet above Northern Germany. He was slumped forward in the bucket seat behind the pilot and for a moment he did not know where he was or what had happened to him. With an effort he raised his hand towards his aching head. The hand hovered uncertainly for a second on a level with his lowered chin; then the plane bumped slightly, jerking him a little, so that the feeble movement was checked and his arm flopped inwards towards his body. His greatcoat had fallen open and his fingers came in contact with the Iron Cross that General Count von Pleisen had pinned upon his breast. It was sticky with the half-congealed blood that had trickled over it from the wound in his shoulder. As his fingers closed over the decoration full consciousness flooded back to him.

It was the night of November the 8th, '39 and after many weary weeks of desperate hazard and anxiety, pitting his wits against the agents of the Gestapo in war-time London, Paris, Holland and Germany, he had that evening at last succeeded in carrying out the immensely important secret mission which had been entrusted to him. As a result of his work the German Army leaders had risen in a determined attempt to throw off the Nazi yoke and create a new, free Germany with which the Democracies might conclude an honourable peace.

There flashed back into Gregory's mind the incredible scene of bloodshed and carnage at which he had been present only a few hours before, when Count von Pleisen, the Military Governor of Berlin, had led his three hundred officers into the great Banqueting Room of the Hotel Adlon to arrest the Sons of Siegfried, a dining-club used as cover by the Inner Gestapo,

1

who were holding their monthly meeting there behind closed doors.

It had been hell incarnate. Six hundred desperate men in one vast room and every one of them blazing away with an automatic or sub-machine-gun. Some of the Gestapo men had reached the telephones and had warned their Headquarters, the Brown-Shirt barracks and other Nazi centres. The Generals had seized the Central Telephone Exchange and the Broadcasting Station. The people had risen and were lynching isolated Nazis in the streets. Artillery had been brought into action and shells were blasting the Nazi strongholds. But the thousands of S.S. and S.A. men had sallied out to give battle and when Gregory left Berlin they still held the central square mile of the city and, from what little he could gather, certain outlying areas as well.

In Munich that night Hitler and many of his principal lieutenants had attended the Anniversary Celebrations of their early *Putsch* with the Nazi Old Guard in the *Buergerbrau Keller.* As the Army chiefs who had planned the revolt could not be in Berlin and Munich on the same night, and considered it more important to secure the Capital, von Pleisen had reluctantly consented to the placing of a bomb to destroy the Fuehrer. But just before Gregory staggered out of the Adlon news had come through that Hitler and his personal *entourage* had left the meeting much earlier than had been expected, so although the bomb had gone off and had wrecked the cellar, killing many of its occupants, he had escaped and was reported to be organizing counter-measures from his special train.

Now the die was cast it was impossible to foretell which side would gain the upper hand. With their Artillery and tanks the Generals *might* succeed in overcoming the thirty thousand armed Nazis who held Berlin for Hitler and raising the Flag of Freedom there; but what of the rest of the country?

As Hitler was still alive and at large the air must be quivering with urgent orders to his *Gauleiters* and Party Chiefs in every corner of the Reich, instructing them to arrest all suspects, to shoot on sight and to exercise the sternest possible repressive measures against all dangerous elements. Those Nazi Party men would act with utter disregard for life or any human sentiment. They had climbed to power by such relentless methods and they would certainly stick at nothing now, knowing that their own lives depended upon the suppression of the rebellion.

The plane roared on into the blackness of the night. Gregory had no memory of having boarded it at the secret landing-ground some fifteen miles outside Berlin but he knew that the figure silhouetted against the lights of the dash-board was Flight-Lieutenant Freddie Charlton, who had flown him to another secret landing-ground north-west of Cologne just a week after the outbreak of war. Fate had ordained that Charlton should also be the pilot on duty that night outside Berlin, standing by to take any British secret agent who needed his services on the long flight home. With a fresh effort Gregory jerked up his head. The sudden movement caused a stab of pain from the wound in his shoulder and he gave a low moan.

"So you've come round?" said Charlton, turning his head.

"Yes," Gregory muttered. "I suppose I fainted from loss of blood soon after we reached the farm-house."

"That's it; and we didn't even try to bring you round. The farmer and I wanted to bathe and bandage that wound of yours but the young woman who was with you wouldn't let us. You were all for taking her back to England with you but she wouldn't go, so you said that in that case you were damned if you'd go either."

"Oh God! Erika—Erika—" Gregory moaned as the airman went on:

"Apparently she felt that she'd never be able to make you leave her once you came round again and she was desperately anxious to have you safely out of it. She insisted that we should bung you in the plane and that I should get off with you while you were still unconscious."

Gregory lurched forward. "Look here, Charlton," he said thickly, "you've got to turn round and take me back. I'm not going home yet—I can't. You must find that farm again and land me. Understand?"

"Sorry; can't be done," Freddie called back with boyish cheerfulness. "I'm the captain of this bus and you're only a passenger. If you've got any complaints you can make them when we land at Heston early in the morning."

"Now, listen." Gregory laid his good hand on Charlton's shoulder. "That girl we left is Erika von Epp or, to give her her married name, the Countess von Osterberg. She's the grandest, bravest thing that ever walked, as well as the loveliest, and I'm not leaving her in the lurch. It's unthinkable!"

"She'll be all right; she said so."

"She won't. You don't understand. She's von Pleisen's niece and she was up to her neck in the conspiracy. If it hadn't been for her I would never have been able to deliver a letter from

3

the Allied statesmen, guaranteeing Germany an honourable peace and a new deal if the Generals would out Hitler and his thugs. Just think . . ."

"I don't care who she is or what she's done," Charlton cut him short. "We're not going back."

"We must! Von Pleisen was a splendid fool. Instead of taking the advice of most of his officers and mowing down the Sons of Siegfried before they had a chance to utter he insisted that they should be given an opportunity to surrender peaceably. Von Pleisen's chivalry cost him his life and gave the Nazis just the breathing space necessary to draw their guns. A lot of them fought their way out of the trap and were able to rally their men. When I left Berlin the streets were running with blood, but it's anybody's battle; and Hitler escaped the bomb in Munich."

Gregory's head was aching dully but his brain was moving now, and he went on speaking slowly but firmly. "If the Gestapo get the upper hand there'll be a more terrible purge than anything that even Nazi Germany has ever witnessed. Every officer who's in this thing, and hundreds of others who are only suspected, will be shot; their families will be proscribed and thrown into concentration-camps. Erika will be right at the top of the list and God knows what those swine have in store for her."

"Easy, easy," Charlton murmured, "you're letting your imagination run away with you."

"I'm not! You *must* believe me! Grauber, the Chief of the Gestapo Foreign Department, U.A.-1, bagged her just before the *Putsch* and it was only by the luck of the devil that she was still alive when I reached and freed her."

"Well, since she *is* free, what are you worrying about?"

"Damn it, man, Grauber's aware of the part she played so he'll put scores of his agents on to hunt her down again. If I can rejoin her there's a sporting chance that I might get her out of the country. If I can't, I could at least shoot her myself, and I'd rather do that than have her fall into his hands; if he gets her he'll kill her by inches. I've *got* to go back—I've definitely *got* to!"

"Now look here, old chap," Charlton turned his head again and spoke in a more reasonable tone, "I *do* understand what you're feeling. You're in love with her. That was as plain as a pike-staff although I only saw the two of you together for a few minutes. Naturally it hurts like hell to have to leave her behind

4

in such a sticky spot, but what the devil could you do, wounded as you are, even if you were able to rejoin her?"

"The wound's not much. Grauber got me in the fleshy part of the shoulder but fortunately there's no bone broken and the bullet went out the other side. I only fainted from loss of blood and I wouldn't have done that if I hadn't had to go on fighting and chasing about all over Berlin for an hour or more after I was hit. It'll be all right in a day or two."

"That's as maybe, but if you want it to heal quickly you'll have to lie up, and you can't do that while searching Berlin for your girl-friend. Another thing: if this Gestapo man you speak of shot you himself he presumably knows who you are."

Gregory started to laugh but choked and began to cough violently. When he got his breath back he replied:

"Know me? By God he does! We've been up against each other for the last two months. He darned nearly murdered me in London and I near as dammit laid him by the heels in Paris about a fortnight ago; but he got away to Holland and the authorities there put him in prison for travelling on a forged passport. Thinking that he was safely out of the way I impersonated him when I did my second trip into Germany and went swaggering round the country as *Herr Gruppenführer* Grauber in the smartest all-black uniform you've ever seen. Lord, how they kowtowed to me! 'Yes, *Herr Gruppenführer.*' 'No, *Herr Gruppenführer.*' 'May it please Your Excellency.' 'Will you honour us by accepting this damned good meal while we sit here and starve?' The poor saps! But Grauber turned up in Munich to spoil my little game. I had the last laugh, though, when I cornered him in a bedroom at the Adlon this evening. My gun was empty so I hurled it in his face and smashed his left eye to pulp."

"Fine!" murmured Charlton. "Fine! But hasn't it occurred to you that Grauber will be a little peeved about losing that eye of his; and that with the whole of the Gestapo behind him it's he would have the last laugh instead of you if I landed you again in this accursed country?"

Gregory straightened himself. His head was clearing with the cool night air and he was feeling distinctly better. "To hell with that! I'm prepared to chance it. If they get me that's my affair; the one thing that I flatly refuse to do is to go back to England while Erika is left to fend for herself in Berlin."

"It's not a matter of your refusing; you have no option. I've made eleven of these secret trips successfully since I set you down outside Cologne two months ago and now I'm well away with this one I'm not going to risk losing one of Britain's planes and, though I sez it as shouldn't, one of her ace pilots by coming down again because you've fallen in love with a German girl." Gregory tried to control the urgency in his voice but every minute the plane was taking him three miles further from Erika. "It's a lot to ask, I know," he said persuasively, "but there's too much trouble going on in Berlin to-night for the anti-aircraft look-outs to be active. They'll all have heard of the Army *Putsch* by now and will probably be fighting among themselves. Anyhow, they'll be far too busy swapping rumours and hanging on for the latest news to bother about checking up on a stray plane."

"Perhaps; but even if I were willing to take you back I couldn't. You remember how we landed outside Cologne—just one window of the farm-house was left uncurtained to light me in. The same drill is followed at the secret landing-ground east of Berlin but those windows are left uncurtained only for a short period on certain nights, and at stated times, by arrangement. There won't be any light showing from the farm-house now—in fact, it won't be showing again until ten o'clock next Sunday; and this is only Wednesday. So you see, it's absolutely impossible for me to attempt another landing there to-night."

"All right, then; land me somewhere else—I don't care where—any place you like so long as it's inside Germany. Then I'll make my own way back to Berlin."

"How the hell can I, with the whole country blacked out? You must see for yourself that without a single thing to guide me in it's a hundred to one that I'd crash the plane on a hillside or in a wood."

"How far d'you reckon we are from Berlin?"

Charlton glanced at his dash-board. "I managed to pick up a few lights way out on our left, through a break in the clouds, a few minutes ago, and as I know this country like the back of my hand I'm certain they were in the town of Brandenburg. In another few moments we shall be passing over the Elbe so we're somewhere about sixty miles due west of Berlin by now."

"That's not so bad." Gregory murmured; "the province of Brandenburg is flattish country, mostly sandy wastes and farmland which is very sparsely populated. With a bit of luck we might find a spot where you could land me without much likelihodo of running into trouble. Be a sportsman and go down low, just to see if you can make out the lie of the land."

6

"No, Sallust; it would be absolutely suicidal. The anti-aircraft people hereabouts haven't had much to do during the first few months of the war so normally they're pretty sleepy but, as you say yourself, they'll be on their toes to-night waiting for the latest news from Berlin; and this is a prohibited area. I never feel safe until I've climbed to over 30,000 and we're miles from that height yet. Even up here, if the Nazis pick up the note of my engine in their listening-posts, they may start blazing off at us. We're still well within range and I happen to know their orders. 'Fire first and ask questions afterwards!' "

Gregory moved uneasily in his seat. Somehow or other he was determined to get back to Berlin. He could, of course, let Freddie Charlton fly him home, lie up for four days and arrange to be flown out again to the secret landing-ground on the following Sunday night but in the meantime anything might happen and the one thought that agitated his now active mind was the awful danger in which his beloved Erika stood. Tonight Berlin was in utter confusion; almost certainly the street-fighting would still be in progress to-morrow. While the Germans were killing one another they would be much too occupied to do any spy-hunting. If only he could return at once he would be able to move about the city freely, for some hours at least, without being called on to produce any papers. While von Pleisen's officers were still holding their own he would be able to get in touch with some of those he had met and, since many of them knew Erika, ascertain through them the most likely places in which to look for her.

On the other hand, if he could get back to Berlin before Monday morning a decision would almost certainly have been reached by then. If the Generals had come out on top there would be nothing for him to worry about; but he was now extremely dubious about their chances, and if the revolt had been suppressed the old Nazi tyranny would be clamped down more firmly than ever before. Storm-Troopers and police would be challenging all who dared to put their noses out of doors, and without papers his arrest would be certain before he had been back in the Capital an hour.

There was no question about it; his only hope of rejoining Erika lay in returning to Berlin while the fighting was still going on. That meant that he must land in Germany again that night, and every mile further that he allowed Charlton to fly him from the Capital would make his task of getting back there more

7

difficult. He began to plead again—urgently—desperately—but Charlton continued adamant in his refusal.

At last Gregory fell silent, but that did not mean that he had abandoned his project. Instead he had begun to contemplate desperate measures—no less than an attempt to render Charlton powerless and take charge of the plane himself.

He felt confident that if he could get control of the plane he knew enough of aircraft to get the machine down without allowing it to plunge headlong to destruction. Landing was another matter. He did not flatter himself for a second that he could perform such an operation successfully when an ace pilot like Charlton declared that in the black-out a crash was inevitable; but modern planes are stoutly built so Gregory was prepared for a crash and to take a chance that if he could bring the plane down slowly with its engine shut off, once it had hit the ground, he would be able to get Charlton and himself clear of it without serious injury.

The idea was semi-suicidal and Gregory realized that it was extremely hard on Charlton that his life and freedom should be jeopardized by such an act; but if the airman would not help him by attempting to land of his own free will he must take the consequences. Gregory had risked his neck too often to worry about himself and now the only thing he cared to live for was Erika von Epp.

Leaning forward he peered down towards the hidden landscape in an attempt to assess the density of the darkness. For a few moments he could see nothing because they were flying high above a heavy cloud-bank, but after a little the clouds broke and far below he caught sight of a few tiny pin-points of light. The German black-out was still far from perfect. In spite of heavy penalties for slackness there had been a natural tendency to be careless about A.R.P. as the only enemy planes which had flown over the country since the outbreak of war had dropped leaflets instead of bombs.

The lights suddenly disappeared again but Gregory reckoned that once below the cloud-bank he would be able to pick up plenty more. The altimeter of the plane would give him his height until he was within a thousand feet of the ground. If he brought the machine down in a long, flat spiral he could watch the lights. If any of them blacked out he would know that the crest of a hill had come between them and him and so he would be able to zoom up again to repeat the process until, with luck,

8

he struck an area of flattish ground on which he could chance a landing with some prospect of not crashing too badly.

The problem was how to overcome the pilot. Had both Gregory's arms been sound he would have flung over Charlton's head the rug in which his own legs were wrapped and pulled him backwards out of his seat. One flick of the controls would be enough to turn the plane's steering gear over to "George", the gyroscopic mechanism which would keep the machine steady while he tied Charlton up. But, wounded as he was, Gregory knew that such a plan was quite impracticable; he hadn't the strength to overcome the airman. The only alternative was to knock Charlton out: a rotten thing to have to do, but once Gregory had made up his mind about a course of action he never allowed sentiment to deter him from his purpose.

Stooping down he began to grope about at his feet in the hope of finding some object with which he could hit the unsuspecting pilot over the back of the head.

Charlton must have sensed something of what had been going on in Gregory's mind. He turned suddenly and said:

"What're you up to?"

"Nothing," muttered Gregory, who, having failed to find on the floor of the plane any object which he might use as a weapon, had pushed back the rug and begun to unlace one of his shoes with the idea of using that. He did not wish to hurt the airman more than necessary and reckoned that a good blow with the heel would be sufficient to stun him temporarily without cutting open his head.

Charlton appeared satisfied but a moment later he swung round again. Gregory had his shoe off and was holding it by the toe, in his right hand, ready to aim his blow.

"Now, look here," Charlton snapped, "no funny business! If you're thinking of trying to land me one with that shoe and taking over the plane you'd better think again. You've got only one good arm and I've got two. What's more, I've got a spanner here. I'm afraid you're so overwrought that you're near as dammit off your rocker; otherwise you'd never contemplate sending us both crashing to our death. If you make one move towards me or the controls of this plane I'll have to knock you senseless!"

The two men stared angrily at each other. Charlton had his jaw thrust out and evidently meant every word he said. Gregory's eyes were narrowed and the white scar of an old

9

wound which caught up his left eyebrow, giving him a slightly Satanic appearance, showed a livid white.

The airman was wondering if it would not be wisest, without further argument, to knock out this maniac who threatened to jeopardize both their lives, and his right hand was already groping for the heavy spanner which lay beside his bucket seat. The lean, sinewy soldier of fortune was coolly assessing his chances in an open attack. They would be much less than if he could have taken the airman by surprise, as at the moment he was very much the weaker of the two; but he believed that he could rely upon his greater experience in scrapping, and the utter ruthlessness with which he always acted if once compelled to enter any fight, to get in one good blow on Charlton's temple before the airman could overpower him.

"If you get hurt you've brought it on yourself," Gregory muttered, glad now to have been relieved from the repugnant act of striking from behind a man whom he would normally have counted a friend.

"For God's sake . . .!" Charlton exclaimed. He was furious with Gregory for placing him in such a situation. Although he had switched the plane's controls over to the gyroscopes he realized the hideous danger of a fight in mid-air which might even temporarily incapacitate him and he was more than a little scared by the gleam in Gregory's eyes.

Suddenly the tension was broken. The steady hum of the engine was abruptly shattered by a sharp report and Gregory saw the livid flash that stabbed the darkness a little ahead of them to their right.

"Hell!" Charlton gasped, swinging round to the controls. "They're on to us!"

As the plane dived steeply another flash appeared away to their left—a third—a fourth. Each was accompanied by a sharp report like the crack of a whip. A German anti-aircraft battery had the plane taped through its sound range-finder and was putting up a barrage all round it; some of the shells exploded like Roman Candles, sending out strings of 'Flaming Onions'. At the sound of the first bang Gregory stuffed his shoe in the pocket of his greatcoat and flung himself backwards, pushing out his feet to support himself as they hurtled downwards.

The bursting shells were now far above them but as the plane rushed towards the earth the pilot and his passenger could see that they were over another large break in the cloud-bank. Pin-points of light showed far away in the darkness below while a

10

little in front the blackness was stabbed repeatedly by bright flashes from the guns of the anti-aircraft battery. They seemed to make its position an almost continuous pool of light, like a baleful furnace flickering unevenly in the surrounding gloom.

Charlton suddenly checked the plane and zoomed up again. The strain was terrific. Gregory was almost shot out of his seat. His heart seemed to leap up into his throat. Now the Germans had got their searchlights going and bright pencils of coloured light cut the sky here and there, sweeping swiftly from side to side in search of the plane.

The machine was on an even keel again, heading southward, and the groups of shell-bursts were well away to their left. For a moment it seemed as though they had got away but, without warning, one of the searchlights, coming up from behind, caught the plane, lighting the roof of the cabin as it passed with the brightness of full day. In a second they had flashed out of it. Charlton banked steeply to the west but two seconds later it was back on to them again. The other beams swung together as though operated by a single hand; the plane was trapped in their blinding glare. The guns of the battery altered their range and sent up another broadside of shells which burst immediately below the aircraft, rocking it from side to side with the violence of a cockle-shell in a tempest.

Getting it into control once more Charlton dived and twisted in a frantic endeavour to get free. Gregory was flung first to one side and then to another; but the searchlights clung to them and, in the fractional intervals between the reports of the bursting shells, there was thud after thud as steel fragments and shrapnel tore the fuselage.

Suddenly the engine stuttered and gave out.

"They've got us!" Gregory cried.

"A piece has penetrated the magneto-box—or else the petrol leads have been torn away!" Charlton yelled above the din.

The plane began to plunge. Charlton managed to right it and for a moment the "Archies" continued to scatter shells all round them. One piece of metal smashed a window but the searchlights still held them and the gunners, seeing that they were now coming down, ceased fire.

In a strange silence which seemed unnatural after the roar of the guns and shells the machine rapidly lost height. The pin-points of light below and the dark land, which they sensed rather than saw, seemed to be rushing up to meet them. The further lights disappeared and Charlton flattened out. For a

11

minute both men held their breath in frightful suspense, knowing that they might be dead before they could count a hundred.
There was a terrific bump; the sound of tearing metal. The
cabin floor lifted beneath their feet and the whole plane turned
right over.

Gregory's head hit the roof of the cabin with a frightful
crack and he was temporarily half-dazed by the blow. Scrambling to his knees he crouched in the dip of the upturned roof,
swaying his aching head from side to side, until he heard
Charlton yelling at him.

The airman had kicked out the fragments of the shattered
window and scrambled through it. He turned now and was
grabbing at Gregory's shoulders. With an effort Gregory
stumbled up, pulled on his shoe, and, aided by Charlton,
wriggled out of the wrecked plane. In the struggle they fell
together in a heap and rolled a few yards down the slope upon
which the plane had come to grief.

When they had checked themselves and blundered, panting,
to their feet Charlton was swearing profusely; but Gregory was
laughing—laughing like hell—positively rocking with Satanic
glee.

"So you had to land me after all, damn you!" he gasped.
"And by refusing to turn round when I asked you, you've
ditched yourself into the bargain."

"You fool!" snarled Charlton. "You suicidal maniac! We'll
be caught inside ten minutes."

"No, we shan't," said Gregory firmly. "It's black as pitch
and we'll find plenty of places in which to hide. This time
to-morrow night we'll be back in Berlin."

"What a hope!" Freddie Charlton was almost stuttering
with rage. "I couldn't move a mile in this accursed country
without arousing suspicion. I can't speak a word of German."

"Don't worry; I'll talk for us both."

"You'll be talking to the Gestapo before you're an hour
older." Charlton jerked his arm out savagely, pointing towards
a cluster of moving lights that had suddenly flashed out less than
a hundred yards away. "Those are the German gunners coming
to take us prisoner."

"The Devil!" exclaimed Gregory. "I thought they were a
couple of miles away. Come on! Run!"

12

CHAPTER II

HUNTED

INSTINCTIVELY, as he began to run, Charlton turned away from the advancing Germans but Gregory grabbed his arm and pulled him sharply to the right.

"This way!" he grunted. "Our best chance is to try to put the crest of the hill between us and them. We'll get a few minute's start while they're examining the wrecked plane."

For a hundred yards they ran on in silence, then Charlton muttered: "How's that wound of yours?"

"Not too good." Gregory panted. "I wrenched it when we crashed and it's started to bleed again, but I reckon I can do about a couple of miles. I wish to God that instead of listening to Erika you'd had the sense to bind it up for me."

"Your girl-friend wouldn't let me," Charlton snapped impatiently. "I told you; her one thought was to have you out of this, and I don't wonder. If you were as dangerous to her as you've been to me she'd have been better off running round with a packet of dynamite in the seat of her drawers."

"Let's save our breath till we're clear of the Troopers," Gregory snapped back. "We'll have plenty of time for mutual recrimination later on."

Charlton accepted the suggestion and they plodded on side by side up the grassy slope. Suddenly a few distant lights came into view, which told them that they had reached its crest. At that moment there was a loud explosion in their rear.

For a second the whole landscape was lit up as brightly as though someone had fired a gargantuan piece of magnesium tape. Both of them automatically halted and looked back. They were just in time to catch the after-glow of the central flash and see a tall column of lurid flame shoot up towards the sky.

"That's the plane," said Charlton bitterly. "Those blasted

13

gunners must have just about reached it. I hope to hell the explosion put paid to some of them."

As he spoke a shot rang out; another; and another. Outlined against the sky they had been sighted in the flash of the explosion. The bullets whistled round them and with a sharp whack one tore through the skirt of Charlton's leather jacket.

Gregory flung himself flat. "You hit?" he called anxiously, as Charlton flopped down beside him.

"No. It was a near thing, though. What filthy luck that we happened to be right on the sky-line just as the plane went up! If we'd crossed the crest a moment earlier or a moment later we might have got away unseen."

"Anyway, we're spotted now and the hunt is up," Gregory muttered, and they began to wriggle quickly forward on their stomachs.

Bullets hummed and whistled through the grass but the flames from the burning plane lit only the slope up which they had come and the far side of the crest was in almost total darkness. The Boches were now firing blind, so there was little chance of their scoring a hit, and when the two fugitives had progressed about twenty yards down the further side of the slope they were sufficiently under cover to be safe again for the moment.

Standing up, they began to run once more and Gregory said: "I suppose you had a time-bomb in the plane?"

"Yes; we always carry one to prevent our aircraft falling into the hands of the enemy if we have to make a forced landing. I pulled out the pin while you were still rolling about the up-turned roof of the cabin."

"Good man! You know, I like you, Charlton; although I'm afraid I haven't given you any cause to fall in love with me. It takes nerve to remember a thing like that just after you've narrowly escaped being shot to hell and breaking your neck into the bargain."

"Thanks." Freddie Charlton's voice was non-committal. "It wasn't your fault that we were shot down, although you were just on the point of behaving like a lunatic. Anyhow, there's no sense in my bearing you any malice about that now. We're in this filthy mess together, so we may as well be pleasant to each other until we're caught and bunged into separate cells."

"That's the idea," Gregory panted; "but with a little luck we'll give these birds the slip yet. Old soldiers never die, you know; they only fade away. I've been in tougher spots than this in my time and I've always succeeded in fading."

"You'll need the fairy's cloak of invisibility and the giant's seven-league boots into the bargain to fade out of this mess, but I give you full marks for guts and optimism."

"Thanks. I——" Gregory's words were cut short by the crack of a single rifle which was instantly followed by an irregular volley. The soldiers had breasted the rise and were spraying the lower ground with random shots in the hope that one of them might find a mark.

"Hell!" Charlton exclaimed. "Can you put on a spurt?"

"Yes," muttered Gregory through his teeth. "Head a bit more to the right! When the plane blew up I spotted a dark patch of woodland over there."

"So did I." Charlton grabbed Gregory's good arm to support his failing strength and they dashed forward together.

The ground beneath their flying feet was still grassland so they were making good going, but as they glanced over their shoulders from time to time they saw from the flashing torches in their rear that the soldiers had spread out into a long line. It was a case of fox and hounds where, although the fox may be the faster, hounds always win in the long run unless the fox can go to earth. If they could not find cover fairly soon the fastest among their pursuers would wear them down and inevitably come up with them.

Two hundred yards further on Charlton stumbled and fell, pitching into a deep ditch. Gregory's wound was paining him again, badly now, and his breath was rasping in his lungs, but he still had all his wits about him. Pulling up just in time he prevented himself from plunging after the airman.

With curses and groans Charlton regained his feet. Gulping for breath they clambered up the further bank of the ditch together to find themselves on a road. It was very dark but ahead of them lay a deeper blackness and on the far side of the road they both stumbled into tree-trunks. They had reached the wood.

Under the branches the blackness was absolutely pitch-dark and, as they blundered on, they were constantly running into trees or bramble bushes. The next few moments were a positive nightmare. Behind them they could hear the staccato orders of the officer who was urging his men after them and the guttural cries of the Germans keeping in touch with one another. Their pursuers were already crossing the ditch and coming up on to the road, yet owing to the density of the wood and their inability to see even a few inches ahead of them the fugitives seemed to have made practically no progress. They were barely twenty yards inside the wood, still panting from their long run, bruised by collisions with trees unseen in the darkness and their hands torn by strands of bramble which clutched at them from every side, when the torches of the soldiers began to flicker upon the trees that lined the roadside.

As they struggled on, sweating and panting, the twigs under their feet seemed to snap with reports like the crackle of musketry and they both felt convinced that the noise would give away their position. One of the soldiers started to shoot again and bullets whined away to their left but on a sharp order from the officer the firing ceased. He did not want his men endangered by their own bullets, which might ricochet off the tree-trunks.

Gasping, bleeding, bruised, almost exhausted, Gregory and Charlton blundered desperately forward, keeping in touch with each other by the noise they were compelled to make in forcing their way through the unseen undergrowth. Gradually the sounds of the pursuit faded in the distance and at last they could hear only the noise of their feet thrashing against the brambles. Instinctively they halted.

"What did I tell you?" chuckled Gregory, after he had had a chance to get his breath. "You were so certain that they'd catch us but we're still free."

"For how long, though?" Charlton muttered gloomily. "I expect they're on their way back to their comfortable beds by now but they'll be out here again first thing in the morning. What's the sense in spending a night in this filthy wood only to be captured to-morrow?"

"We're better off here than we should be in the cells of the local Gestapo. As for to-morrow, we'll see. If only I were fit we'd put a dozen miles between ourselves and this wood before morning. The devil of it is that this wound of mine makes it impossible for me to go much further."

"Is it hurting much?"

"Yes; like hell!" Gregory was leaning against a tree and he drew a hand wearily over his eyes. "If we'd had to run another half-mile I should have fainted again, I think. As it is, I'm about all-in."

"We'd better shake down here for the night, then."

"I suppose we must, although I'm damned if I like it. We're still much too near that road for comfort. I'm good for a last

16

effort but I don't think we'd better risk trying to get deeper into
this wood in the darkness, otherwise we may move round in a
circle and walk right out of it again. Let's look about for a spot
that's clear of these accursed blackberry bushes."

Charlton got out his lighter and flicked it on. The tiny flame
only lit the surounding gloom sufficiently to show his face caked
with sweat and congealed blood where low branches had
scratched it.

"I can improve on that," said Gregory, taking a box of
matches from his pocket. "It's the first time I've had cause to
be thankful that owing to their tax on matches the Nazis don't
allow lighters in their country."

As the match flared they could see that the wood about them
was very dense and the ground almost entirely covered with
undergrowth. Proceeding cautiously they made their way towards a place where the trees were not quite so thick and found
that the break was caused by a shallow gully.

"This'll do," said Gregory; "in fact it'll have to, as the longer
we show a light the greater our danger."

Side by side they sat down in the ditch. It was quite dry
and soft from the accumulation of leaf-mould and leaves which
had covered it through the years. Gregory eased his tired limbs,
propped his back against the bank and produced his cigarettes.
They shielded Charlton's lighter and lit up. As the flame was
flicked out the surounding darkness closed in about them once
more, seeming blacker than ever. After smoking in silence for a
little they recovered somewhat from their exertions and began
to feel the cold. Charlton remarked upon it bitterly.

Gregory grunted. "Well, it's November, remember, and we're
darned lucky that there's no snow. They had snow in the war
zone over a fortnight ago, and that's hundreds of miles further
south than this place. On my last trip into Germany I came
through the Maginot and Siegfried Lines disguised as a German
private, and my God the cold was fierce! This is nothing to it."

Charlton turned his head towards the spot where Gregory's
cigarette glowed in the darkness. "You're the hell of a tiger,
aren't you, making your way through war zones and starting
revolutions and one thing and another!"

"I suppose I am," Gregory grinned. He was feeling better
again now that he could sit still and rest his wounded shoulder.
"It's not that I'm particularly brave—certainly no braver than
an airman like yourself who takes a hellish risk every time he
flies over enemy territory; it's just that I get a lot of kick out of

pitting my wits against those of other people. But, to be quite honest, I never take a chance of getting hurt unless I absolutely have to."

"Nonsense!" Charlton laughed. "What about to-night when you had the bright idea of lamming me over the head with the heel of your shoe in order that you could crash the plane and get back to that girl of yours?"

"Oh well, that was rather different. You were quite right when you said that I was in love with her; and anyone who's in love is crazy."

"That's a good excuse but I've a feeling that you're the sort of chap who would have acted just as crazily if it had been some job of work which you felt you had to get on with, instead of a woman, that made you so anxious to get back to Berlin."

"Perhaps. Just all depends how important the job was; but you can take my word for it in the normal way I'm an extraordinarily cautious person. 'He who fights and runs away'—that's my motto. By sticking to it I've managed to live through the hell of a lot of trouble to the ripe old age of thirty-nine."

"Well done, Methuselah! Then you're fourteen years ahead of me. But I bet I'll never live to make up the leeway—not with this filthy war on."

"Since you feel like that to-night's little affair may yet prove the best thing that could have happened to you. If we *are* caught you'll be interned, and safe for the duration."

"Thanks. But the idea doesn't appeal. I'd rather continue to lend a hand against little old 'Itler. Besides, if we're caught, what about you?"

"Oh, I'll be shot; because I'm not a member of one of the fighting Services but a secret agent."

"Aren't you a bit scared? I mean—our chances don't seem up to much, do they?"

"Frankly, no. We're faced with two major liabilities which are going to make it extremely difficult for us to get clean away. Firstly, my wound, which prevents our travelling swiftly. I'm afraid it's very inflamed and there's no doubt that I ought really to lie up for at least two or three days without moving at all. Then there's the fact that you can't speak German."

"Our clothes are a bit of a give-away, too."

"Yes. At a push I could pass in a crowd, since this is a German officer's greatcoat that I'm wearing; but your leather kit won't be easy to laugh off, as they're certain to be looking for two English airmen. Fortunately, though, they didn't see us at all

18

clearly so they can't issue our descriptions and, of course, they haven't got the faintest idea of the identity of the people in the plane that they shot down."

"Perhaps to-morrow we may run across some farm-labourer whose things I could buy or, if necessary, take off him by force," Charlton suggested.

"Yes; or we may be able to beg, borrow or steal a change of clothing."

"The devil of it is that first thing in the morning those damned soldiers and the police will be beating these woods with bloodhounds."

Gregory shook his head. "No, I don't think so. They'll beat the woods all right, but not with bloodhounds. For a blood-hound to be any help you've got to give it some article of clothing that's been worn by the person you're hunting, so that it can get the scent, and they've got nothing of that kind in their possession. Anyhow, time enough to face to-morrow's troubles when to-morrow comes. Let's try to get some sleep."

They stretched out in the ditch side by side, pillowing their heads on their handkerchiefs spread out over scraped-up piles of leaves. The silence of the wood was broken only by the occasional scurrying of small animals in the undergrowth as they went about their nightly business. Once Gregory spotted a pair of tiny bright eyes gleaming at him out of the blackness but at his first movement the little animal scampered away in quick alarm. The cold was intense and they would have suffered from it severely if both of them had not been very warmly clad. As it was, it kept them from sleep for some time although they buried their hands in their arm-pits and their faces deep in the turned-up collars of their coats; but at last they dropped off from sheer exhaustion.

When they awoke the pale light of the chill November dawn was just filtering through the naked branches of the trees. Cold, cramped and stiff, they sat up to peer about them. From the gully in which they lay they could not see more than a dozen yards in any direction or any sign of a break in the wood.

Charlton shivered and said miserably: "Oh God! Then it *wasn't* a nightmare! We really *were* shot down and are on the run."

Gregory gave an "Ouch!" of pain as he moved. His wound had set stiff during the night and as he lifted his left arm a violent pain ran through his shoulder.

"You've said it!" he replied through gritted teeth. "It's no dream you're having, but a lovely, real-life adventure."

"Adventure be damned! What wouldn't I give for a cup of tea, breakfast and a hot bath!"

"Why not wish for caviare, a suite at the Ritz and Cleopatra smiling at you from a large double-bed, while you're about it?" said Gregory. "You're just as likely to get one as the other."

Standing up, Freddie Charlton stretched himself. His fair, boyish face now showed little of the strain that he had been through the previous night, youth and vitality having quickly restored him to his normal physical well-being, but his grey eyes were anxious as he stared down at Gregory.

"Well? You're the *Fuehrer* in this little show; so you'd better think of something. We can't stay here for ever without food or drink. What d'you suggest that we should do?"

Gregory wriggled a large flask out of his hip-pocket. "He who drinks, dines," he misquoted gravely, "and this is very good brandy-and-water. Take a pull to warm yourself up. It's much too early to expect me to do any thinking yet, though. My brain doesn't start to tick over until after ten and, unless my watch has stopped, it's only about six-thirty; which is a revolting hour for any civilized being to be awake at all."

Freddie looked at Gregory curiously. He was often up at six himself and would long since have broken his neck flying if he had not had his wits about him just as much at that hour as later in the day. He was not certain if Gregory was seeking to impress him, by an apparently casual contempt for the danger they were in, or if he was a lazy, cynical devil who refused to be hurried into action—as was in fact the case—but he refrained from comment.

Having taken a couple of big gulps from the flask he exclaimed: "Ah, that's better!" and, handing it back, went on: "Well, last night we decided that our first job must be to get some other sort of kit by robbing a labourer or a cottage or something, so the sooner we start moving the better."

"That's the idea; but I'm not doing any moving for the time being," Gregory replied. "As you're feeling so energetic, by all means go and have a look round, but for God's sake don't get yourself lost so that you can't find your way back to me! Otherwise, as you can't speak any German, you'll be completely sunk. Incidentally, you might keep a look-out for a pond or a stream where I can bathe this wretched wound of mine before it starts to go gangrenous."

20

"Right," Freddie nodded, and he set off through the trees.

He was away for nearly an hour and when he got back he found that Gregory was sound asleep again. On being woken Gregory explained that he considered that his time was best occupied in getting as much rest as possible. He then inquired the result of Charlton's expedition.

"I've found a stream not very far from here where you can bathe your wound," replied the airman, "but the water is absolutely icy. It sent cold shivers down my spine when I had a dip in it."

"D'you mean you stripped and went in?" Gregory asked, aghast.

"Yes. What is there so surprising about that?"

"Well, cleanliness may be next to godliness, in which case I rank with the Twelve Apostles when I'm leading a normal existence, but if you take my tip you'll go dirty while we're on the run. Nothing is calculated to lower one's powers of mental resistance so much as the immersion of the body in ice-cold water. Still, I suppose you're one of those hardy blokes. You must have missed the radio announcer this morning when you did your daily dozen."

Freddie flushed slightly. "I believe in keeping fit. A chap can't keep fit without regular exercise."

"Rot!" said Gregory. "From my infancy upwards I abhorred all ball-games and for the past twenty years I haven't lifted a finger that I didn't have to, yet my muscles are like whip-cord. If you once start you have to keep it up, young feller; and think of the hours that wastes in a lifetime! If you don't, you suddenly go flabby and are fit for nothing by the time you're my age. But let's skip it. What else did you find?"

"I went back to the road and there's a row of cottages about half a mile along it, to the left, but they're on the far side, on the open grassland, so I didn't dare to go nearer them for fear of being seen."

"How far are we from the road?"

"About 150 yards. After I'd been to the road I worked my way back again to find out how deep the wood was; at a rough guess I should say it's a good mile and a half from here before you come out on the other side."

"What sort of country lies beyond it?"

"There's a big open space with more grassland and a bit of plough, then more woods running up a slope to westwards. Just on the edge of this one, though, there's a fair-sized country-house, so we'd probably be spotted from that if we tried to advance across the open."

"Well, we won't—for to-day, at all events. But we must find a better place than this where we can lie doggo as it's pretty certain they'll send out troops to beat this wood for us. First, though, you'd better lead me to that stream you found."

Gregory got slowly to his feet and together they ploughed their way through the thick undergrowth until they reached a shallow pool formed by a little rippling brook beside which Gregory sat down and Charlton helped him to remove his great-coat. The blood from the wound had dried stiff on his jacket so Freddie had to cut the cloth away with his penknife and the next twenty minutes were exceedingly painful ones for Gregory.

He sat there without uttering a sound while the airman gradually soaked off the pieces of cloth and shirt which had adhered to the wound, bathed it clean with the cool spring-water, bandaged it with the torn-off tail of Gregory's shirt, got the remains of his jacket on again, his greatcoat over it, and made a rough sling out of his own muffler to carry the arm that was affected. By the time he had done Gregory was grey-faced, sweating profusely and near to fainting, but afterwards he sat quite still for about ten minutes, had a cigarette and then de-clared himself ready to set off again.

Freddie Charlton was considerably impressed by Gregory's stoical resistance to the acute agony that he must have suffered. He could not yet make up his mind as to whether he liked him or not, but it was abundantly clear that his lean, cynical com-panion possessed an ample supply of both mental and physical courage and he could not help realizing that he might have been infinitely worse off had he had many other men that he could think of with him in this desperate situation.

Yet it irritated him that Gregory should be taking things so calmly. It was now past eight o'clock so it was quite certain that by this time troops would be on their way from the anti-aircraft camp to search for them, if not already in the wood. To remain where they were would expose them to imminent risk of capture and in any case he did not see how they were to avoid it for long without a change of clothes and food. At the thought of food he realized how hungry he was and said:

"I don't know how you feel but I'm simply starving."

"Let's make for that house you mentioned," replied Gregory, getting to his feet. "November is a poor month to try to live on the land but we might find something edible in the kitchen-garden. Patching up my wound took longer than I bargained for and the search-parties will be after us soon."

"I'm glad you realize that at last," said Freddie stiffly.

"Oh, there'll be time enough to scrounge some sort of breakfast first and to run from the Germans afterwards," Gregory grinned, parodying Drake and the famous game of bowls, as they set off.

Most of the leaves had already fallen from the trees except where they were larch, fir or pine, of which there were a certain number, so they could see a fair way ahead of them when they were standing upright; but the undergrowth was still green and provided excellent cover ready to hand should they encounter anyone. Picking their way between the brambles they moved cautiously forward, keeping their eyes and ears alert for any sound or movement which might indicate the approach of another human being. After half an hour Freddie pointed through the trees to a wooden barn that had just become discernible. With a jerk of his head Gregory indicated that they should incline to the left and they proceeded still more warily until they reached the edge of the wood.

Looking right they could then see a group of buildings which consisted of a small, white, two-storeyed manor-house, probably built in the early part of the last century, and a number of out-buildings. No-one appeared to be about and the whole place lay silent in the cold autumn morning; so Gregory began to lead the way through the fringe of the wood towards it. After a few minutes they came to the back of the nearest barn and, creeping round its side, found that it fronted on a farm-yard. Half a dozen pigs were guzzling in a sty and a troop of long-necked geese were waddling importantly towards a pond. Turning right they passed behind the next barn and found a gate leading into the kitchen-garden. It ran along at the back of the house and was partly orchard so they were able to advance along its far end screened from the windows by the branches of the short fruit-trees.

Gregory gave a grunt of satisfaction on noticing that some late pears still hung among the withered brown leaves and as swiftly as possible they filled their pockets with the fruit. Charlton pulled half a dozen carrots from a near-by bed and Gregory snatched two heads of celery. Suddenly the clatter of a pail being put down somewhere near the house broke the stillness. They started as though electrified and at a quick, almost noiseless run made off into the wood, which ran right up to the end of the garden.

"Pears, celery and raw carrots," Freddie sniffed, as they eased their pace and drew breath. "Not much of a breakfast, is it?"

"Might be a darned sight worse," Gregory replied. "Anyhow, before we think of eating we must try to find a good, snug hide-out. The troops must be beating the wood further in by now and if we don't get to earth soon we'll be captured. Time's getting on; we've got to hurry."

For some time they searched, hoping to come upon a shallow cave or bramble-covered gully in which they might conceal themselves; but without success. The wood was curiously and depressingly uniform. By lying flat they could have hidden themselves in the bushes at almost any spot from a casual wayfarer who passed within a dozen yards, but the cover was insufficient to prevent their being seen by deliberate searchers who came nearer.

"The only thing for it is to get up a tree," said Gregory at last. "That's not going to be easy with one of my arms out of action but we'll manage it somehow."

Swiftly, anxiously, straining their ears for sounds of the beaters, who they felt might advance upon them at any minute now, they examined a number of conifers, since the leaves on the other trees were too few to afford them decent cover, and selected a pine which had three branches coming out from its trunk, all nearly on the same level and about twenty feet from the ground. Climbing it was a muscle-wrenching struggle. But Charlton was six feet one in height and strong; he managed to swing himself up on to a lower branch and to haul Gregory up after him; and by further efforts they succeeded in reaching the higher branches which they had chosen for a roosting-place.

Their perch was far from comfortable and it seemed doubtful if they would be able to maintain their position there for any great length of time, but Gregory insisted that they must do so at least until the search which they felt certain was in progress had passed by them. Having settled themselves in their hiding-place with considerable relief they munched their pears disconsolately and waited in uneasy suspense.

Barely ten minutes later they caught the first sound of the men who had been sent out to hunt them down. Evidently the search had started from the road and was being made with German thoroughness; otherwise it would not have taken so long for the troops to work right through to almost the far extremity of the wood. Occasional calls came floating through the chill silence as the searchers approached and now and then the blast of a whistle by which an officer was evidently directing them; then came the crackling of twigs and the snapping of brambles as the heavy-footed troopers kicked their way through the undergrowth.

Gregory and Charlton remained deadly still, fearful that the faintest movement would draw attention to their hiding-place; since a pine tree, although the best that they could find at that season, does not afford good cover and anyone standing immediately beneath it had only to glance up to see them.

The flat cap of a grey-clad soldier appeared below. He was carrying a rifle with fixed bayonet slung over his shoulder and halted for a moment just under the tree. Suddenly Freddie felt a frantic desire to cough but managed to convert the spasm into a gurgle, which he half-stifled by clapping his hand over his mouth.

With acute anxiety Gregory stared down at the soldier fearing he had heard the noise that Charlton had made. If the man looked up the only possible way of preventing him from giving a triumphant shout, which would bring his comrades running, was to drop right on top of him. The weight of another body falling from twenty feet would smash him to the ground and with luck knock him out. Balancing himself carefully Gregory prepared to make that desperate plunge. His wound was temporarily forgotten in the tenseness of the moment but he was quick to realize that as the soldier's bayonet was sticking up just beside his head anyone who fell upon him from above must inevitably fall on the point of that too. Nevertheless, his decision had been taken instantly, since he felt that he owed it to Charlton to give him this desperate chance of remaining undiscovered and getting away afterwards.

For nearly a minute the man stood there, directly below them, glancing from side to side; then he moved on again, peering right and left into the near-by bushes as he went. Gregory stifled a sigh of relief and, relaxing, leaned back against the tree-trunk.

Gradually the sounds of the search receded and the two fugitives were able to ease their positions; but soon afterwards the searchers reached the edge of the wood and, turning, began to come back. Once again Gregory and Freddie held their breath as they listened to the thrusting of feet through the undergrowth and the occasional calls of one man to another; but by half-past ten silence had fallen once more and it seemed that they had escaped discovery, at least for the time being.

They were more cheerful now as they argued that the gunners who had brought them down could not know that one of them was wounded; having searched the wood thoroughly would have convinced them that the fugitives were no longer there and, assuming them to have got much further afield, they would not bother to search it again. To be on the safe side the fugitives remained up the tree and as time began to hang interminably they endeavoured to pass it more quickly by swapping reminiscences.

Gregory told Charlton the fantastic story of his adventures during the past two months which had culminated in his enabling the German Army leaders to stage a revolt against the Nazis. Freddie listened with amazed attention, not quite knowing whether to believe it all or not; but as he himself had secretly landed Gregory two months earlier outside Cologne and had picked him up again the previous night outside Berlin he had definite evidence that the lean, sinewy man beside him was not entirely romancing.

The airman's own adventures in making his secret night-landings in war-time Germany would have thrilled most people but he felt that they were mere child's-play compared with Gregory's impersonation of a Gestapo Chief and extraordinary series of escapes; besides which, he was a modest person so he said little of them. Perhaps, however, that was partly because his thoughts were centred about a girl, one Angela Fordyce, to whom he had been engaged to be married before the war.

From his description of her it appeared that Angela was the world's prize wonder, but Gregory wrote that down by about one hundred per cent. Privately he decided that she was probably quite a pleasant-looking brunette with reasonably good blue eyes and all the nice, clean, healthy instincts that an English girl should have, without any particular brain or wit; and so, admirably suited as a wife to the tall, grey-eyed, fair-haired young man who sat precariously perched upon the branch next to him.

It seemed, however, that Freddie Charlton had bungled the affair badly. Unlike many men of his kind he had not considered the war a good excuse for rushing into marriage. On the contrary; he maintained that it was damnably unfair to any girl to marry her, and probably land her with a baby, if there were a

26

reasonably good prospect of being killed oneself within the year; particularly when the girl had been brought up expensively and one had no private money of one's own and so could leave her only the pension of a Flight-Lieutenant. In consequence, knowing that she would not agree with him he had taken the quixotic step of writing to her on the outbreak of the war to break off his engagement, without giving any reason.

Not unnaturally, in Gregory's view, Angela had been annoyed and had demanded an explanation, upon which Freddie had made bad worse by writing to say that he had come to the conclusion that they were not suited to each other. On learning of this his best friend, one Bill Burton, had persuaded him that he had acted like a fool and had been extremely unfair both to the girl and to himself. Burton had then gone to see Angela in the hope of straightening the wretched muddle out, only to find that she had left England the day before and that it was therefore impossible for him to execute his pacific mission.

As Angela's father was in the Consular Service his being posted, without warning, to Amsterdam, and her sudden departure with him overseas, was not particularly surprising, but it had had the effect of erecting a new barrier; and, Burton's mission having been sabotaged by fate, Freddie had felt that having made his bed he had better lie on it, so had refrained from writing to her. But he was still sick with the pain he had inflicted on himself and bitterly regretted that he had not written, especially now that it looked likely that he would be interned in Germany for the rest of the war and therefore debarred from any possibility of running into Angela again if she came on a visit to London, when they might perhaps have had an explanation leading to a renewal of their happiness.

Being an eminently practical person and no mean psychologist Gregory forbore from voicing the obvious, meaningless platitudes and, instead, suggested that if only they could succeed in escaping over the frontier into Holland Freddie might see his Angela much sooner than if he had remained in London.

This cheered the airman up considerably and, as it was intended to do, gave him an additional incentive to use every ounce of his resolution in avoiding capture. He remained unaware that, the Dutch frontier being many hundreds of miles distant, Gregory did not mean to try to get out of Germany that way and, in fact, had no intention whatever of attempting to leave Germany at all until he had found Erika von Epp and could take her with him.

They stuck it out up in the tree as long as they could bear the discomfort but by early afternoon their posteriors were so sore from the nobbly branches that they were forced to abandon their hiding-place and come to ground.

Freddie, who found garden-produce most unsatisfactory fare for a November day spent out in the open, suggested that they should pay another visit to the farm-yard for the purpose of stealing a chicken or a goose, which they might later roast over a wood-fire, but Gregory shook his head.

"It's quite on the cards that the people who were hunting us this morning have left a certain number of pickets scattered about the wood, for to-day at all events. If we light a fire the sight of it or the smell of the smoke might give us away; but the idea of roast goose positively makes my mouth water so we'll see what we can do about that to-morrow."

"Good God!" Charlton exclaimed. "We shall freeze in this climate if we have to spend another night without anything warm inside us."

"I'm sorry, old chap, but we've got to stick it. My fault entirely but I daren't move on yet. This shoulder of mine is giving me hell and I'm afraid I'd only pass out on you if I attempted a cross-country march to-night."

Charlton stared at him with sudden concern. "Yes; you're looking pretty flushed; I believe you're running a temperature."

"I am," Gregory replied.

"Then—then perhaps we'd better give ourselves up. I can't possibly look after you properly while we're in hiding like this and your wound will only get worse if it doesn't have skilled attention."

"It's nothing much, you saw that yourself when you bathed it this morning; only a little round hole through the fleshy part of the shoulder. One of the muscles is torn but it'll soon heal up providing I don't exert myself for a day or two. If we can lie doggo in this wood for another forty-eight hours I'll be all right. Anyhow, I'm damned if I'm going to chuck my hand in. Come on, let's try to find a new hide-out while daylight lasts."

About six hundred yards from the house they found a small ravine, which was even more thickly covered with undergrowth than the rest of the wood, where they would be well concealed from anyone who did not walk right on to them, and sitting down in it they made themselves as comfortable as they could. Gregory lay back and closed his eyes in an attempt to sleep but his wound pained him too much and he could only hope that lying still might cause his fever to abate. Charlton sat beside him, miserable and dejected but keeping his ears strained for approaching footsteps so that they should not be caught unawares.

The afternoon drifted by and shadows began to fall. No sound disturbed the stillness and Freddie thought that Gregory was asleep until he roused up and suggested that they might as well make their evening meal. They ate a few more of the pears and some celery but having tried the raw carrots threw them aside as too unpalatable. A swig apiece from Gregory's flask completed the unsatisfactory repast, after which they settled down again into an uneasy silence. The evening seemed interminable as although the November day had drawn to an early close an occasional glance at the luminous dials of their watches showed them that they still had a long time to go before it could be considered night.

Towards nine o'clock Gregory became light-headed and began to mutter to himself in delirium. Freddie was at his wits' end. There was nothing that he could do to aid his companion or allay the evidently rising fever. More than once he contemplated walking to the house and begging the assistance of its inmates but as he could not speak a word of German it was certain that they would telephone at once to the police and his arrest would follow almost immediately. With his fellow-fugitive in such a state he felt that there was little chance of maintaining their freedom for any length of time but he knew how determined Gregory was not to give in while there was the least hope of escape, and now that the possibility of reaching Holland had been dangled before his eyes he was doubly reluctant himself to take any step which would definitely land him in a concentration-camp for the rest of the war.

Towards eleven Gregory ceased his incoherent muttering and dropped into a troubled slumber, so Freddie decided to see that night through and take a fresh decision the following morning. If Gregory were better they could rediscuss the situation but if he were worse there would be nothing for it but to seek help by surrender.

Just as Freddie was settling himself down to sleep he heard footsteps approaching, then voices talking in German. Stiffening in immediate alarm he crouched there in the gully, his heart thudding against his ribs. Peering towards the sound he strained his eyes but in the darkness he could see nothing. The footsteps halted about a dozen yards away and there was further talking. His forehead was suddenly damp with sweat.

As he strove to silence his quickened breathing the awful urge to cough gripped him, as it had up in the tree. Closing his eyes he fought it down, but cramp got him in the leg that was doubled under him and he was forced to move it. The twigs snapped beneath him but just at that moment the rustling in the bushes came once more, and this time it was moving away. After a further five minutes of tense listening he grew calmer and decided that they were safe again. The sweat on his brow was turning icy with the cold. With a heavy sigh he brushed it off and, settling himself, endeavoured to court forgetfulness in sleep.

When he opened his eyes the cold light of a new day showed the trees and brambles rimed in frost. It was a fairy scene but one which filled him only with fresh dismay. He lifted the white-powdered collar of Gregory's greatcoat and saw that the wounded man was pale but breathing evenly. As he sat up he heard a faint noise just behind him.

It came from the direction in which he had heard the Germans speaking in the darkness the night before. Instantly Gregory's suggestion that the gunners might leave pickets posted in the wood flashed into his mind. Swinging round he very cautiously raised his head and peered between the thorny strands of the blackberry bushes.

Something grey caught his eye; it lifted a little and he saw the flat, round brim of a German officer's cap. He tried to duck back; but it was too late. A lean, grey-moustached face had risen above the brambles and a pair of hard blue eyes were staring straight into his. As he instinctively rose to his feet the German stood up and his hand was already on the automatic at his belt.

CHAPTER III

THE COLONEL-BARON VON LUTZ

HAVING only just woken, Charlton's circulation had not yet got going; he was bitterly cold from his night in the woods and his brain was still half-fogged with sleep. In addition, it was now Friday morning and he had not had a proper meal since Wednesday. Yet, in spite of his lowered vitality and half-dazed condition, he realized that the only chance of escaping capture now lay in an immediate attempt to overcome this solitary German. Bracing his muscles and lowering his head he hurled himself forward.

Several feet of brambles separated them. Before Freddie had plunged a couple of paces through the tangle the officer had whipped out his automatic and ejaculated with a threatening scowl:

"Holten Sie da!"

The lean, grey-moustached face of the German showed stern resolution; his blue eyes were cold and commanding; the blue-black steel barrel of the big pistol that was trained so unwaveringly upon Charlton's middle held a threat which he could not ignore. It would have been stark lunacy to force the hand of such a man with such a weapon. Pulling up with a jerk Freddie slowly raised his clenched fists above his head.

As he stared at the German he thought with bitter fury how utterly futile it had been to spend the last thirty miserable hours hiding in the wood only to be caught at last. Evidently Gregory had been quite wrong in his supposition that. having searched the wood without success, the soldiers would conclude that the fugitive airmen had succeeded in getting further afield and abandon the hunt for them there. Obviously the officer who was staring at him so intently could be in the wood only for the purpose of inspecting pickets that he had left posted in it the previous night.

When the German rapped out, *"Was machen Sie hier?"* it conveyed nothing to him; he could only reply:

"Sorry, I don't understand."

"You are English, eh?" exclaimed the officer with evident surprise, and lowering his gun a little he added: "I asked what is it that you do in this place."

He spoke fluent, if ungrammatical, English and his question made Charlton stare, since it showed that he was not, after all, an officer of the anti-aircraft battery and evidently had not heard that two enemy airmen were being sought for in the neighbourhood.

"Perhaps you'll tell us what you're doing here yourself?" said a quiet voice, and swinging round Freddie saw that the sound of talking had wakened Gregory. He was now standing up and stepped out of the gully on to the higher ground at its edge.

The German's blue eyes narrowed in a queer, uneasy look for a second, but he straightened himself and said abruptly: "I own this wood so I haf a very goot right to be here in. What two Englishmen should be making here in time of war is another question and I haf the right to demand the answer."

From where Gregory was standing he could see the officer's rank-badges and a pile of tumbled rugs round his feet. He bowed slightly and his voice held a gentle note of amusement as he said: *"Herr Oberst,* if you own this wood presumably you also own the charming little manor-house just through the trees there? I have no right to question you at all but I confess that I'm extremely curious to know why, instead of sleeping in your own bed, you passed the night in the ditch where you are now standing."

"Enough of this!" said the Colonel, with rising irritation. "You will observe, please, that I am armed while you haf not. Reply instantlich to my question! What do you do here?"

"The same as you, apparently."

"Donnerwetter! I haf a right to camp out if I am wishing," the German snapped. "What else do you think I make but hard sleeping which for a soldier is goot?"

"Why, that you are trying to keep out of the hands of the Gestapo, of course," Gregory grinned.

For a second the Colonel's jaw dropped, then he said harshly: "Absurdity! What makes you that believe?"

"Simply because even the most hardened soldier would not spend a night in the woods at this season of the year if he could

32

sleep in his own comfortable bed. Evidently the *Putsch* was a failure and you're on the run."

"The *Putsch*! What do you know of that?"

"I started it." Gregory pulled back the flap of his greatcoat and displayed the Iron Cross of the First Class which was still pinned upon his chest. "For the part I played General Count von Pleisen honoured me with this. I can only say how immeasurably distressed I am to learn from your presence here, *Herr Oberst,* that the Nazis succeeded in suppressing the rebellion which was to have freed Germany."

The Colonel suddenly put his pistol back in its holster and took a step forward. *"Gott im Himmel!* I thought I haf somewhere seen your face. I was at *der Pleisen Palast* with the comradeship of officers before the *Putsch* when the Count decorated you. Permit that I introduce myself."* Drawing himself up he clicked his heels and bowed sharply from the waist. *"Oberst-Baron von Lutz."*

Gregory imitated the movement and rapped out his name, adding with a wave of his hand: "This is Flight-Lieutenant Charlton. After I'd completed my mission he was to fly me home and we left from a secret air-field, east of Berlin, on the night of the 8th; but we were shot down a couple of miles on the far side of this wood and have been hiding here ever since."

"Ach so! I knew nothing of this as I escape from the Capital only last night."

"Then, I take it that all hope of the *Putsch* succeeding has been abandoned?"

Colonel-Baron von Lutz nodded despondently. "It might haf succeeded if Hitler had been blown up in Munich as was planned, but swiftly it becomes known that he had escape the bomb and all Army leaders outside Berlin postponed action. This makes him free to concentrate his entire effort against those who in the Capital had risen. He sent bombing squadrons against us early yesterday morning which caused many casualties at the Artillery and Tank Depots. Battalions of S.S. and S.A. men were rushed to the city from all quarters of the Reich. By afternoon our situation desperate became. At six o'clock five of our leading Generals haf taken decision to give their brother-officers chances to escape, also to save further slaughter of their men by issuing the 'Cease fire!' order and giving themselves up. I haf the goot fortune to get away by automobile but I walked the last twelve kilometres point to point so that of the local people none should see me to my estate arrive."

"A sad ending to a gallant effort, *Herr Oberst-Baron*," Gregory said, in an attempt to hearten the elderly officer, "but it is only a postponement. Germany will yet throw off the Nazi yoke."

"Most true. But in the meantime the names of all who attacked the Gestapo Chiefs in the Adlon and of many other officers who participated in the revolt will haf been listed. If among the dead their bodies are not found they will be hunted, as the hares, to all corners of the Reich. Few of us who were in the rising of the 8th will live to see the day of freedom."

"As far as you're concerned . . ." Gregory paused to step back and support himself against a tree ". . . since you managed to get this far there's a decent chance that you may be able to remain in hiding until the time when there is a successful revolution."

Von Lutz brushed up his grey moustache. "I shall certainly endeavour to do so; but if the Nazis hunt me out I intend to sell my life very dear."

"It seems that the three of us are in the same boat," Gregory smiled weakly; "although Charlton, here, could surrender peaceably if he wished, since when he was shot down he was acting as an R.A.F. officer on duty."

"Oh, if there's any fighting you can count me in," Freddie shrugged. "I'd rather take a chance with you two now than be starved to death in a prisoners-of-war camp. We couldn't put up much of a fight without arms; but perhaps the Baron could help us there?"

"Yes; arms and food—that's what we need," muttered Gregory. "I'm afraid, though, that in my case I shan't be able to give much of an account of myself for a day or two."

Von Lutz gave him a searching look. "You are pale. And surely those stains under your left arm are dried blood? Are you wounded?"

"I got one through the shoulder during that fight at the Adlon. The wound's not dangerous but it's become inflamed, and I've an idea that I was delirious last night."

"You certainly were," Freddie supplemented. "How're you feeling now?"

"Pretty groggy. I'm still running a temperature."

"For a hunted man that is bad." The Baron's lined face creased into a frown. "We must do what we can for you. The Gestapo had their hands filled yesterday but by now they will on a nation-wide round-up haf started. They may come to make

34

search of my house at any time. But my family and my servants will do all possible to protect me. They will keep look-out while your wound is being made clean. To the house, then, gentlemen!"

"I hate to add to your difficulties, sir," Gregory demurred.

For the first time the lean-faced Prussian aristocrat smiled. "Please. It makes nothing, as by this time there must on my own head be a price. If the coast is a clear one we will soon haf you fixed; also some breakfast which will put the better heart into us all."

As they turned towards the house Freddie saw that Gregory's teeth were chattering and that he stumbled after he had moved a few yards, upon which he jumped to his assistance, realizing that he had managed to carry on his recent conversation only by a terrific effort of will-power and was still in the grip of fever. When they reached the end of the kitchen-garden the Baron signed to them to halt and went forward cautiously on his own. After a moment he beckoned.

"It is goot. A towel hangs from my daughter's window. This signal I haf arranged with her."

They followed him through the orchard and up some steps to a wide verandah at the back of the low white house. Although it was not yet seven o'clock, like all German households that of Colonel-Baron von Lutz was early astir. A plump maid-servant in voluminous petticoats was on her knees polishing the parquet of the room into which he led them. As they entered she scrambled to her feet and bobbed before her master.

"*Kuss die Hand, Herr Oberst-Baron.*"

"*Guten Tag, Lenchen,*" he nodded. "*Frangen Sie die Fräulein Magda hier stimpt, bitte.*"

The maid quickly collected her cleaning things and left the room while Freddie eased Gregory down into a near-by chair. A few moments later the door opened again and a tall girl in her middle-twenties came in. She was good-looking in a hard, healthy way. Her hair was very fair, her eyes china-blue; her skin was good and the colour in her cheeks was natural but, to Freddie, her lips and eyelashes seemed unduly pale as she wore no make-up, and her strong, well-proportioned figure did not show to its best advantage in the ugly ginger-coloured cloth coat-and-skirt that she was wearing.

When she had greeted her father he rapidly explained to her in German the reason for the presence of the two strangers. Freddie could not understand what was said but he caught the phrase, *"Englische Fliege"*, and noticed *Fräulein* Magda's well-cut chin lift a little as she shot a sharp glance of disapproval at him.

He was quick to sense that as a patriotic German girl she did not like the idea of sheltering her country's enemies, but evidently Prussian discipline was maintained in the household and the Baron's wish was law. She said no word of protest but went over to Gregory at once and laid a cool hand on his forehead.

His eyes were now closed and he remained slumped forward in the chair. The father and daughter exchanged a few quick sentences and then the Baron turned to Freddie.

"Your friend ought to bed be put but here it is too dangerous to offer hospitality. My daughter a trained nurse is so she will give goot attention to his wound. After, we will eat, yes; then we must to the woods return."

While Magda went for towels, hot water and bandages Charlton and the Baron partially undressed Gregory, who had now lapsed into semi-consciousness and become delirious again.

When she returned they found that the wound was suppurating badly. The flesh all round it was hot and puffy and when his temperature was taken it registered the Centigrade equivalent of 103.6 Fahrenheit. Having cleaned the wound and applied hot fomentations Magda dressed it with quick, efficient fingers, then directed them in making Gregory as comfortable as possible on a sofa.

Freddie was now seriously alarmed for him but since there was nothing else they could do he allowed his host to lead him into another room. Breakfast had been laid there, and, as they were about to sit down, an elderly woman came bustling in whom von Lutz introduced as his wife.

The *Frau Baronin* was fat, grey-haired and had a rather stupid face which was only relieved by china-blue eyes like her daughter's. She spoke no English and after greeting Charlton with a nervous smile remained silent, her thoughts evidently occupied by acute anxiety about her husband.

Owing to the Baron's having had to spend a night in the woods a special breakfast had been prepared. In addition to the usual cereals there was a roast hare, the tantalizing odour of which made Freddie realize his hunger to such an extent that it was only with difficulty he prevented himself from eating ravenously. Somewhat to his surprise, there was a big pat of fresh butter, but this, von Lutz told him, came from the home-farm. There were also ample supplies of potato-bread and home-made jam. The only weakness in an otherwise excellent meal was the weak coffee-substitute with which they had to wash it down.

During breakfast the Baron explained to Freddie the precautions he had taken to prevent their being surprised. Most of the men from the estate had been called up for the war but he still had half a dozen, over fifty, working on the place as farm-labourers and foresters. On his arrival the night before he had had them aroused from their beds and brought to the house so that he could explain his position to them. All of them came from local families who had served his own for several generations. Such of their younger members as had become influenced by the Nazi doctrines had been conscripted for the Army, but these older men were completely loyal.

On their expressing their willingness to do everything they could to shield him von Lutz had organized them into watches which were to take turns in guarding the approaches to the house. Each man would be carrying a shot-gun during his turn on duty and if cars or any suspicious-looking strangers appeared whoever saw them was to fire off first one barrel of his gun then, after half a minute's interval, the other, as though shooting at a rabbit. The sentries were half a mile away but in the clear country-air the sound of the shots would easily carry that distance and give sufficient time for the fugitives to escape out of the house into the woods again.

Magda had tackled the maid-servants and farm-women, who had all sworn that no questioning would induce them to say that they had seen anything of the Colonel-Baron since he had last been home on leave in the first week of October.

When breakfast was over it was decided that Gregory must be carried out to the woods again and while von Lutz went upstairs to the attic to get an old camp-bed that they could use as a stretcher Magda fed the sick man with some spoonfuls of hot broth. Having fixed up the bed she packed round him all the hot-water bottles that could be found in the house, to keep him as warm as possible, then wrapped him in blankets; after which the Baron and Freddie carried him on the improvised stretcher out through the garden and back to the gully where they had spent the previous night.

By daylight they were able to find a better place in which to conceal themselves than any they had yet discovered. Some twenty yards further into the wood the gully grew deeper; the side of the bank was nearly five feet high and had fallen away leaving a hollow that was overhung by a mass of brambles. They placed Gregory's bed in it and sat down near-by to await events.

Although the pale sunlight of the November morning was now slanting through the leafless branches of the trees it was still very cold. In his pocket Freddie had an old-fashioned revolver, given him by the Baron: the only weapon, apart from sporting guns, that the house contained, but that was not much comfort. It seemed pretty certain that Gestapo agents would visit the house some time during the day. If one of the farm-hands proved unreliable, or one of the women-servants broke down under the questioning which they would have to face, the Nazis would surround the hiding-place and capture was certain. In any case, with the climate against them and a desperately ill man on their hands, Freddie did not see how they could possibly remain at large for long. But he was in this thing and he could only wait, with the best patience he could muster, to see what the day would bring.

CHAPTER IV

"HANDS UP, *HERR OBERST-BARON*!"

WAITING there would have proved an incredibly tedious business had not the Baron proved a most knowledgeable man and a great talker. He had travelled considerably in his time and had friends in many countries so he deplored the post-Great War era in which the policies of most European nations had led to the shutting-off of one from the other.

As he pointed out, previously to 1914 passports had been unknown unless a European was travelling to some semi-barbarous country where he might need official aid in securing means of transport or other assistance. Apart from that, men of every nation had been free to come and go without let or hindrance and could even settle in foreign countries without restriction if they wished.

In France, England, Italy and Scandinavia there had been thousands of Germans earning an honest living and abiding loyally by the laws of the countries that gave them hospitality. This freedom of movement and often permanent interchange of peoples had been enabling the European nations to get to know and appreciate one another's qualities in an ever-increasing degree throughout the whole of the last century. Englishmen had found with some surprise that Frenchmen did not exist solely upon a diet of frogs, and Germans had been able to see for themselves that all Englishwomen did not have flat chests and protruding teeth. Had that state of things continued for another half-century, with facilities for travel becoming ever easier, faster and cheaper, the constant mingling of the nationalities on a friendly footing might well have created a mass goodwill strong enough to prevent any Government from daring to declare war on its neighbours; the more so as, by the fact that there was then no restriction on Germans, English, Americans, Italians or anyone else living in any country that they chose, the whole question of living-room seemed already to have been solved.

That splendid prospect of a possible permanent peace had been shattered by the war of 1914-18; after which both victors and vanquished had been faced by the terrible problem of reconstruction and through huge unemployment figures in their own countries had been compelled to put a bar up against emigration from abroad. That, maintained Colonel-Baron von Lutz, was the root cause of this new struggle in which the major nations were now engaged. Germany was not a rich country compared with many other European states and she had even been robbed of such Colonial possessions as she had had; yet the German race was breeding just as fast as ever. Therefore they must either be given over-seas territory or, better still, be allowed free ingress to other countries for their surplus population; otherwise the standard of life in Germany would become so lowered by more and more people trying to cut a slice off a single loaf that anarchy would inevitably result.

He was not a Nazi and most strongly deprecated Hitler's power politics and disregard of Germany's word pledged by solemn treaty; but he argued that eighty million people, representing one of the most advanced races in the world, could not be expected calmly to sit still and allow themselves to be gradually starved to death. Hence the German people as a whole had become desperate and had allowed Hitler to lead them into the present assault upon the great Democracies.

Charlton, who had done a short course at the College of Imperial Defence, pointed out that the problem of giving Germany back her Colonies was by no means as simple as it looked. Where, he asked, would Britain be now if Germany had not been deprived of her African possessions after the last Great War? In the last half-dozen years Hitler would have established huge arsenals and air-bases in German West, Tanganyika and the Cameroons and would have turned their ports into heavily-fortified lairs for great flotillas of commerce raiders and submarines. The coming of the aeroplane, the increased range of U-boats and fast motorcraft, the destructive power of mines and direct communication by wireless had absolutely revolutionized strategy in the last quarter of a century and would have made such enemy bases a hundred times more potent as factors in the struggle than they were in 1914. With them in her hands Germany would have been able totally to disrupt Britain's sea traffic in both the South Atlantic and the Indian Ocean, cutting her and France off entirely from the Eastern hemisphere in which lay the greater part of both their Empires. In addition Hitler's African bombing squadrons would have had Johannesburg, Cairo, Cape Town and the Suez Canal at their mercy; and any determined attempt to protect these African territories would have necessitated Britain and France detaching so large a proportion of their Air Forces from the main theatre of operations that they could have been left virtually defenceless at home. A *Blitzkrieg* then might even have caused the Democracies to lose the war. Freddie paled with his intensity as he added firmly: "That is why never, never again must Germany be allowed to hold one square mile of African soil."

As a soldier von Lutz readily conceded the terrible threat to the security of the British Empire which would lie in the return of the German Colonies, if Germany had an ambitious or unscrupulous ruler, but he submitted that whatever peace plan was eventually agreed the German people must be given an opportunity for expansion, otherwise such a peace could only be the forerunner of yet a third Great War when there had been a sufficient interval for Germany to pile up yet more armaments. In his view the only permanent solution lay not in giving Germany territories of her own outside the Reich but in once again opening up all countries to all peoples.

While agreeing in theory Charlton suggested that the difficulty would be the different standards of living demanded by different nationalities. The Germans, for example, were used to working much longer hours than the British and the people of many other countries were content to live on a much lower scale than either so far as food and clothing were concerned. Therefore a great influx of foreigners into Britain or the United States would mean huge unemployment among the British or Americans themselves and tend to draw down their scale of living, which they were naturally anxious to protect.

But the Baron did not seem to think that that would necessarily follow. He argued that, on the contrary, if the Trades Unions played their proper part the scale of living in the more prosperous countries could be maintained and that of other countries gradually brought up to it; thereby eventually making life happier and more secure for mankind throughout the whole world.

As they talked on Freddie learned many things about Nazi Germany and was the more readily able to understand why such great numbers of the Germans were behind Hitler—at all

41

events, for the moment—when he heard the Baron describe the drastic changes—many for the better—which the Socialist activities of the National Socialist Party had brought to the German masses. On his asking what proportion of the German people von Lutz thought was really whole-heartedly with the Fuehrer the Baron replied:

"I give you analysis of this question. Ten per cent of the people are very much pro-Nazi and ten per cent of the people are very much anti-Nazi. The other eighty per cent, they haf not the brain to think for theirselves at all. They are led most times by the pro-Nazi Press and believe that Chamberlain deliberately planned their country to encircle. Each time Hitler as a diplomatic triumph gained they haf shouted their heads off in applause. That eighty per cent was right through in favour of the *Anschluss* with Austria; also the annexation of Czechoslovakia and the war with Poland. Now they wait only to cheer for Hitler again if he any spectacular military success over the Allies can make. Against that, they will make cheers for him as long as he makes successes and they get enough to eat; because they do not live happy under the Nazi régime and are called upon many comforts to sacrifice. If things go very bad in Germany during the next few months through the Blockade, or Hitler makes a *Blitzkrieg* which is no goot, that eighty per cent will turn coats in a flash; perhaps set off only by some little thing; but instead of making cheers for him they will be yelling for his head."

At half past twelve Magda came out, bringing with her a welcome hot lunch. Gregory had fallen into a troubled sleep so they did not disturb him but hoped that he would sleep on, as complete rest was what he needed. They ate the meal while she waited with them and when she had gone settled themselves to try to pass a little time by dozing where they sat. At three they roused up again and lit cigarettes.

It was soon afterwards that they distinctly heard two reports echo through the wood, and realized with quick apprehension that one of the sentries had sighted suspicious visitors. From fear that the smell or sight of the smoke might betray them if some of the Gestapo men, who were probably arriving, came out through the back of the house and began poking about on the fringe of the wood, they stubbed out their cigarettes; then crouched down in the gully under cover of the brambles and waited in anxious silence.

For over an hour they remained there listening for the light-

42

est footfalls but nothing stirred in the wood except the occasional flutter of a bird or the scampering of some small animal in the undergrowth. At last, as the shadows were beginning to fall they heard a rustling which gradually grew nearer and, peering through the bushes, von Lutz saw that it was the maid, Lenchen.

She was gathering sticks in her outspread apron and as he watched he saw that she was working her way towards them. Two minutes later, without looking at him, she stooped for some sticks on the edge of the gully and whispered swiftly:

"Do not show yourself, *Heer Oberst-Baron*. Two car-loads of Black Guards arrived at ten past three; they ransacked the house, the barns and the outbuildings, but found nothing. They appeared to be satisfied after they had questioned us, as we all said that we had not seen you since the first week in October, and the cars have just driven off back to Brandenburg; but they have left two of the men behind who are to be billeted in the house in case you should suddenly arrive here. *Fräulein* Magda sent me to tell you this and to explain that she may not be able to bring your *Abendessen* at the usual hour in case they suspect and follow her; but one of us will manage to slip out with cold food for you some time during the evening."

As the girl talked she kept moving, and having delivered her message she began to work her way back to the house, gathering more firewood as she went.

"*Teufel Nochmal!*" exclaimed the Baron, when she had disappeared among the tree-trunks. "This is bad—worse than what I fear." And having explained to Freddie what had happened, he added: "I haf goot reason to expect they visit my house but after they find I am not at home I believe they get out; then we are safe to move ourselves and your friend in bed to put. But now that is not possible."

"It looks as though we'll have to spend another night in the woods, then," Freddie said miserably and, as that seemed the only thing they could do, they resigned themselves to a cold and dreary evening.

At ten o'clock Magda came out to them with a bundle of rugs in which were wrapped a bottle of hock, a thermos-flask full of hot soup and some packets of cold meat, bread and *Appfel-kuchen*. She said that the two Nazis who had billeted themselves in the manor were not unfriendly and appeared to have no suspicion that her father might already have arrived there or be in hiding in the neighbourhood. Nevertheless, they seemed con-

43

fident that sooner or later he would make his way to his own home and had declared their intention of remaining there until he put in an appearance. They had also threatened all the servants with the direst penalties if at any time the Colonel-Baron arrived by stealth and they warned him that Gestapo agents were waiting in the manor for him.

Gregory, who had been sleeping or dozing in a semi-conscious state most of the day, roused up while they were talking and Magda examined his wound by the light of a torch. It showed no sign of improvement and he was still feverish. Now that any hope of getting him properly to bed in the warm house had had to be abandoned they were more anxious than ever about him, but there was little they could do, so having settled him as comfortably as possible Magda gave him some aspirins and, promising to come out again as early as she could the next morning, she left them.

After eating their supper, which to some degree restored their cheerfulness, the Baron and Freddie settled down under their rugs for the night; but it was long before they could get to sleep, as the cold was more bitter than ever and about midnight snow began to fall.

When Freddie woke it was still pitch-dark and glancing at the luminous dial of his watch he saw that it was only a quarter to three. His movement roused von Lutz and for a little time they talked together in low voices. Snow was falling heavily and as Gregory's camp-bed occupied the only sheltered space beneath the bank it had begun to settle on their rugs and faces in a thick white powder.

At last they could bear the cold no longer so decided to walk about in an attempt to restore their circulation. The contents of Gregory's flask had already been used up, but von Lutz had another, which he shared with Freddie as they stumbled up and down a patch of ground that was fairly free from undergrowth.

Their misery and distress during the next four hours were almost indescribable. On two occasions they tried to sleep again but the warmth of their bodies melted the snow which had fallen on their garments so that these had become half-sodden and they found it impossible to remain still for any length of time. In the early hours of the morning their difficulties were further increased by a bout of delirium which seized Gregory in its grip. He was completely off his head and 'fighting the battle in the Adlon' over and over again, shouting curses, threats and warnings interspersed with heart-rending cries that he must save

44

Erika because Grauber would —"*Torture her—torture her—torture her!*"

In the silence of the snow-carpeted wood his agonized shouts seemed so loud that von Lutz feared they might rouse the Gestapo men in the house half a mile away; so he and Charlton had to muffle the injured man's ravings by putting a handkerchief over his mouth and to frustrate his attempts to fling himself about, which would have caused his wound to start bleeding again, by holding him down.

When dawn came they were utterly exhausted. The Baron was grey-faced and heavy-eyed; Freddie had a splitting head and a horrible taste in his mouth; both felt as though they had been up for a week and were so numb from the cold that they feared frost-bite. Gregory had lapsed into unconsciousness again but his head looked like that of a corpse. His cheeks had fallen in and were leaden-coloured under a three days' growth of beard, the skin across his forehead was taut, with little beads of perspiration standing out upon it, and his mouth sagged open as though the muscles of his face had relaxed in death.

At seven o'clock, Magda arrived, bringing breakfast. The previous night her unwelcome guests had said that having nothing to do they did not wish to be called till eight o'clock and she had had food prepared early so that she could get it out of the house before they were about. With hands shaking from the cold her father and Charlton took the welcome bowl of hot stew which she had brought them and the big hunks of bread to dip into it, while she examined Gregory.

After a moment she turned and shrugged her shoulders. "He is much worse and there is nothing I can do. Another night like this and he will die here."

"That must not be allowed," said her father quickly.

She gave him a sullen look. "What does it matter? He is an Englishman."

As she was speaking in German Freddie could not understand what she said but he sensed the gist of her remarks and her hostility.

The Prussian aristocrat's voice was terrifyingly stern as he replied: "Speak only of what you understand, girl. This man risked his life in an attempt to bring about peace and enable us to create a free and better Germany. He is our guest and no effort must be spared or risk remain unrun which will aid his recovery. Go now and send Hans Foldar to me immediately."

"Yes, Father," Magda murmured with sudden meekness, and

45

wrapping her shawls about her she hurried away to do his bidding.

For three quarters of an hour they waited then they heard footfalls crunching the newly-fallen snow. Von Lutz peered out from his hiding-place then stood up to greet a tall, broad-shouldered man of about sixty wearing the top-boots, leather jerkin and fur cap of a forester.

"You sent for me *Herr Oberst-Baron?*" the man inquired in a hoarse voice.

"Yes, Hans. You know the situation I am in and are loyally helping to protect me from the Gestapo. That would get you into serious trouble if it became known, but now I have an even greater service to ask of you; one which would certainly mean death for you if you were caught. If this weather continues—and I fear it will—we can't last long out here in the woods. If we don't die from cold we shall certainly lose our toes and fingers by frost-bite. Moreover, one of these two friends of mine is wounded and may die unless we can get him into shelter. Are you willing to receive myself and these gentlemen in your cottage?"

"Certainly, *Herr Oberst-Baron.* All that I have came from you and your family so it is yours to dispose of."

"Thank you, Hans. I felt certain that I could rely on you, but I should tell you that these two friends of mine are Englishmen; one is an officer of the British Air Force and the wounded man is a British Secret Service agent who is wanted by the Gestapo. They were in the plane which was shot down a few miles from here three nights ago."

"The *Herr Oberst-Baron* knows best. If he thinks it right to protect them that is sufficient for me, too."

"Come, then; let's get the wounded man to your cottage as soon as possible. It's going to be a hard job to carry him all that way but we'll manage it somehow."

The Baron informed Charlton of the arrangement he had made and again using the camp-bed as a stretcher the three of them set off through the woods with the unconscious Gregory. Von Lutz and Freddie carried the bed while Hans picked the easiest way between the snow-covered bushes. It was a two-mile tramp but at last they reached the forester's cottage.

Hans Foldar went in first to prepare his wife. She accepted without argument his decision to shelter their master and his friends and at once they began to plan how best to conceal the fugitives. It was decided that the loft above the kitchen-sitting-room would be the best place and, Gregory having been carried in, after some difficulty they got him and the camp-bed up there. Von Lutz then sent Hans to tell Magda to come to them with linen and bandages as soon as she could slip away from the house without being seen by the Nazis.

Frau Foldar, who was a buxom, middle-aged woman, provided the refugees with a midday meal of vegetable stew and in the early afternoon Magda arrived with the things that her father had sent for. They were then able to undress Gregory, treat his wound with hot fomentations again and put him back in the camp-bed after it had been properly made up with sheets and blankets. Meanwhile Hans brought in straw from his barn to make up two shake-downs in the loft for his master and Charlton.

Gregory's temperature became still higher in the evening and it strained the nerves of those who were with him to listen to his monotonous ravings; but by nine o'clock he had dropped into unconsciousness again. His two companions were then able to relax and settle down to a much more comfortable night than they had known since the abortive *Putsch* on the previous Wednesday.

The next day, Sunday the 12th, proved the crisis in Gregory's illness but by evening his fever had worn itself out and although very weak he regained consciousness for the first time in many hours.

In the days that followed he gradually began to mend. The handsome, hard-faced Magda managed to visit them each morning or afternoon, varying the times of her daily excursions so as not to arouse the suspicion of her unwelcome guests and always approaching the cottage by way of the woods in its rear. As well as treating Gregory's wound she brought parcels of such luxuries as she could acquire locally to supplement the frugal fare which was all that the Foldars could provide. There was no actual shortage of food and, apart from lack of sugar, rationing did not worry them, as the country-people evaded surrendering a considerable proportion of their produce to the authorities; but delicacies were rare and imported foods had entirely disappeared. Magda also brought them what news she could but little was coming through.

Six Nazis had been killed and sixty-three injured by the Munich bomb explosion which, according to an announcement made by Himmler, had been plotted by the British Government the previous August and carried out by British Secret Service agents who had bribed a workman, employed on repairs in the *Bierhaller,* to place the bomb. No-one believed this, as it was generally known that a most terrible purge was taking place throughout the length and breadth of Germany. Every effort was being made to suppress particulars of the military revolt in Berlin spreading to other parts of the Reich but many hundreds of officers, intellectuals and industrialists had been arrested while others had gone into hiding or escaped into neutral countries.

With the Nazis in the house Magda and her mother dared not listen to the foreign broadcasts, since the penalty for being caught was six months in a concentration-camp for the first offence and death for the second, so for most of their news they had to rely on the German stations and such accounts of the war as appeared in the Nazi controlled Press.

The tension with Belgium and Holland had died down and a Foreign Office spokesman had declared that the Reich would respect the neutrality of both countries provided that Britain and France continued to do so.

The German Air Force had become much more active. Reconnaissance squadrons had photographed many British military areas, even in the estuary of the Thames, without opposition; successful raids had been carried out against British shipping and for the first time in the war German airmen had actually dropped bombs on British soil, in the Shetlands.

Time would have hung heavily on their hands had it not been for the magazines which Magda provided, out of which von Lutz read translations to Charlton, and also attempted to teach the young airman German.

Freddie was not a good linguist and he progressed slowly but by the time they had been in the cottage for a fortnight he could speak enough German to ask for anything he wanted and to carry on a halting conversation. Each night he and von Lutz got air and exercise by walking in the woods at the back of the cottage, since after the first few days it became apparent that the Nazis who had been left at the house to await the appearance of the Baron still had no suspicion that he was in the neighbourhood and, after depleting his cellar, went to bed at a regular hour.

By Saturday, the 18th of November. Gregory had recovered sufficiently to be able to get up for the first time and by the following Tuesday he had his arm out of the sling. The wound was only a small one, and once the poison had been checked and the inflammation had gone down it had healed rapidly.

It was during this week-end that they heard the first news of the Czech rebellion. The village schoolmaster had returned from his unit in Prague on special leave, to see his dying mother, and, according to his account, at least twelve, and possibly more, Czech students had been shot by the Gestapo for anti-German demonstrations. Baron von Neurath, as Governor of the Protectorate had ordered the Universities to be closed for three years. Prague was in a state of open revolt when the schoolmaster left and he said that the anti-German feeling was so strong that even before the revolt German soldiers had not been allowed out at night in the city in parties of less than six, for fear of assassination.

The account of conditions there as retailed by Magda reminded Gregory of the state of things in Ireland after the Great War and he recalled the stories that he had heard about British officers, stationed in Dublin, being sandbagged and thrown into the Liffey. That the extremist section of the Irish still bore Britain a bitter grudge was evidenced by the activities of the I.R.A.; out of which the German broadcasts made much capital. It had recently been reported that their fanatics had brought off four successful bomb outrages in the West End of London, and the Nazis were cock-a-hoop about it.

By Thursday, the fifteenth day after he had received his injury, Gregory was able to use his arm again without any danger of the wound's reopening. In himself he was now very fit and for some days he had been able to accompany von Lutz and Charlton on their nightly walk in the woods, which was the only exercise they dared to take and a great relief to them after having been cooped up all day in the loft for fear of running into the two Nazis who were billeted in the manor-house.

On Friday the 24th, the news was by no means so good for the two Englshmen and they had to repress their feelings to the best of their ability as Magda recounted, with a glee that she did not attempt to conceal, the results of Hitler's releasing one of his much-vaunted secret weapons, the magnetic mine.

Apparently the campaign had been launched the previous week-end and twenty-five ships were already reported to have fallen victims to the new weapon. That the majority of them were neutrals did not seem to cause Magda any concern, since like many Germans her theory of warfare was, 'all who are not with us are against us'. In secret Gregory had a certain sympathy for her attitude as it was entirely owing to his own complete unscrupulousness against his enemies that he had survived to the age of thirty-nine.

That Friday Magda also brought news that Himmler had explained the Munich bomb plot. Georg Elser, a thirty-six-year-old workman, had been arrested and had confessed to having planted the bomb at the order of Otto Strasser, a former associate of Hitler's who had turned against him and was now said to be directing the anti-Nazi Black Front from Paris. According to Himmler the British Secret Service was also involved and two of its members, Best and Stevens, had been arrested on the Dutch frontier trying to come into Germany on November the 9th.

As they were said to be attempting to come *into* Germany the day *after* the bomb had exploded this hardly made sense. But the more intelligent Germans had long since given up trying to make sense out of the so often contradictory statements of the Nazi leaders who were obviously using all the influence they had to sway the Fuehrer and the German people in favour of their individual policies.

By the middle of this the third week after the abortive *Putsch* Gregory was beginning to get restive. He pointed out that, grateful as he and Charlton were to von Lutz for concealing them, they could not remain there indefinitely. Every day and every night of his convalescence he had spent hours of misery wondering what had become of Erika. With iron control he had curbed his impatience to be off to Berlin in search of news of her until he should be really fit to face hardships and danger again. Now he grudged every further hour's delay. Freddie, too, had remained inactive only through necessity. The thought that if he could get into Holand he would be able to see Angela and patch up his quarrel with her made him discount the difficulties and perils of such a journey. Only on account of Gregory's state had he refrained from urging an attempt to get out of Germany earlier. Neither disclosed to the other his special reason for being so desperately anxious to set off, but once the subject was broached it was clear that both were in favour of starting at the earliest possible moment.

Von Lutz declared that he intended to stay where he was until the two Nazis had become tired of sitting doing nothing in his house, when he would be able to move to it and remain in hiding in more comfortable quarters; but he expressed his willingness to aid the two Englishmen by every means in his power.

The question was raised and settled on the morning of Sunday, the 26th, and when Magda came to the cottage that afternoon von Lutz discussed the matter with her; upon which it was agreed that she should come to the cottage again that night, after the two Nazis had gone to bed, bringing with her a complete outfit of the Baron's civilian clothes for Charlton, a civilian overcoat for Gregory and a small stock of tinned goods —from a store that had been laid in before the war—to serve as iron rations until the fugitives got well away from the district.

The wintry daylight was already fading by the time Magda left and darkness fell soon after, but they knew that they had to wait for hours yet before it would be safe for her to leave the house with the things she was to bring and make her way back to them by the forest path. Von Lutz drew a rough map of the surrounding country as a guide for them in the first part of their flight but there were no other preparations they could make, and now that they were keyed up to start the time seemed to hang interminably. At last, shortly before midnight, Magda arrived, but she carried no bundle and one glance was enough to show that she was in a state of great distress.

Her father questioned her anxiously but she only stared at him, wild-eyed and speechless. Gregory took her by the arm and shook her. Suddenly she burst into tears and between her sobs the whole sordid story came out. One of the Nazis, a brawny young man named Carl Dietrich, had taken a fancy to her immediately on his arrival at the house and had been paying her the most unwelcome attentions ever since. These had led up to violent scenes in which he had demanded to know how she, the daughter of a traitor colonel, dared to put on airs with a member of the Black Guards, Hitler's chosen legion, picked for their strength and fitness, whom any German girl should be proud to sleep with. She had not told her father this before, for fear of what he might do, but recently, with no-one in the house to whom she could turn for protection, her situation had become desperate; on several occasions during the past week Dietrich had tried to get into her room.

That night he had smashed the lock on the door and forced his way in. Contrary to his expectations, he had not found Magda in bed, but busy packing up the parcel of clothes she meant to bring to the cottage.

For a moment it had seemed that he guessed the purpose of her preparations although she had swiftly assured him that the parcel was intended for a Brandenburg charity organization.

But she had felt it so vital to her father's safety that the Nazi's mind should be immediately and completely diverted from the question of the clothes that instead of calling her mother and the servants to assist her to get him out of her room she had begged him to be quiet so as not to wake them. That was enough to turn his thoughts to his original purpose in breaking in on her and to convince him that her resistance so far had only been feigned. With an ear-to-ear grin he had begun to unbuckle his belt and she had forced herself to allow him to make love to her. After he left her she had not dared to bring the clothes since, if he remembered about them, she would have to produce them the following day and let him see her dispatch them to Brandenburg.

As he listened von Lutz went white with rage and his hands began to tremble. Immediately Magda had finished sobbing out her tale he declared his intention of going up to the house there and then to drag the Nazi from his bed and shoot him.

Gregory, Charlton and, above all, Magda endeavoured to dissuade him from this step which would almost inevitably cost him his own life, but the thought that his daughter had been seduced, against her will, by one of these blackguards made the Prussian nobleman furiously reject any counsel of caution.

It had taken the best part of twenty minutes to piece together Magda's half-incoherent ramblings and get the full story from her. For another quarter of an hour they stood there in the kitchen-sitting-room, wrangling together and trying to turn her outraged father from his purpose, but at last, seeing that the Baron was determined on vengeance, Gregory said with a wry grin:

"All right; since you're absolutely set on it Charlton and I will go with you and we'll settle the two of them. No man who wears the uniform of a Nazi Storm-Trooper is fit to live. You'll then have at least some chance of getting away with us. They probably only have to report to their boss in Brandenburg once a week and if we're lucky we'll have several days' start before it's known that your unwelcome guests have been eliminated."

In spite of Magda's renewed pleading they began to make their preparations. The Baron had his automatic and plenty of ammunition for it; Freddie had the old-fashioned revolver with which von Lutz had furnished him on their first day in the woods together while Gregory was still delirious. In order that they might put up a good fight if their hiding-place were discovered, and they had to resist an attack, four sporting-guns had also been smuggled to it from the manor-house by Hans. Gregory selected one of these and stuffed his pockets full of cartridges.

"Ready?" asked von Lutz impatiently.

The other two nodded, and shaking hands with Hans Foldar and his wife they thanked them most heartily for all that they had done for them. With a brief glance at Magda, who was now weeping on *Frau* Foldar's ample bosom, the Baron threw open the cottage door.

The moon, which was at full that night was hidden by dense banks of cloud so it was dark outside and he stood clearly out-lined against the light within. As he moved towards the open doorway Gregory's quick ears caught the scraping of feet on the garden path. Temporarily blinded by the bright light in the cottage he could see nothing out there in the black night but he felt a sudden apprehension.

Had Carl Dietrich, after all guessed the real use to which the clothes Magda was packing up were to be put? Had he decided that there was plenty of time to take the girl first and catch her father afterwards? Had he *not* gone to bed as she supposed, but roused his companion, lain in wait and followed her out through the woods? Were the two Nazi Storm-Troopers standing there at the bottom of the path, hidden by the darkness, with their automatics already drawn?

Next second he knew. A guttural voice rapped out: "Hands up, *Herr Oberst-Baron*! You are our prisoner."

CHAPTER V

DEATH IN THE FOREST

IT was Gregory who gained thirty seconds' breathing space for his friends. He had been carrying his shot-gun waist-high, at the ready; without an instant's hesitation he loosed off both barrels into the darkness.

The double bang sounded like a thunder-clap as its echo rolled across the still countryside and the bright flash lit the scene as vividly as a streak of lightning. There were not only the two Storm-Troopers whom they expected to see a dozen yards away, but a whole group bunched up round the garden gate; dark figures caught by the flash in the act of drawing their guns as they ran forward.

Had von Lutz fired his automatic, or Charlton the old revolver, it was unlikely, since neither of them could see their target, that their bullets would have hit more than one or, at most, two of the oncoming group. But the wide spread of the shot from Gregory's double-barrelled fowling-piece caused absolute havoc.

Cries, curses, groans rent the night as the tiny pellets zipped into the faces and limbs of the Nazis like the blows from a hundred whips, causing them to reel about in utter confusion.

Within a second of having fired Gregory was back inside the cottage. Von Lutz and Charlton tumbled in beside him and the three of them swung-to the heavy door.

"*Mein Gott!* There are ten or a dozen of them!" gasped the Baron. "And I thought there were only two!"

"Directly Dietrich smelt a rat he must have telephoned for reinforcements from Brandenburg," said Gregory, "but they've got out here mighty quickly."

"Dornitz is much nearer—only three miles away—and he could have got them from the local Nazi headquarters there."

"They came in a motor-truck," added Freddie. "I saw it by

the flash of the shot-gun. It's parked down the road about forty yards away."

As he spoke bullets began to thud into the wood of the cottage door. One of the Nazis was spraying it with a sub-machine-gun which kicked up a hellish clatter. Gregory and von Lutz jumped back towards the fireplace while Freddie sprang in the other direction.

"Keep away from that window!" yelled Gregory; and just as Charlton ducked the hidden glass was shattered by a burst of fire from automatic pistols, the bullets ripping through the curtains.

Magda was standing, white-faced but upright, in a corner. *Frau* Foldar was crouching in a chair near her, weeping into her apron. She knew only too well that having hidden her master now meant certain death for her husband and herself.

"Where's Hans?" asked von Lutz suddenly.

"He—he ran out of the back door just—just after *Herr* Sallust fired," sobbed the distraught wife.

"We'd best try and get out that way, too," cried Gregory above the din, and grabbing Magda by the arm he pulled her down beside him so that they could crawl along the floor under the level of the window through which bullets were still streaming. Charlton and the Colonel seized *Frau* Foldar and between them dragged her after the others.

Gasping with relief they drew themselves upright at the far end of the room and staggered out into the tiny passage. The back door of the cottage stood open, just as Hans had left it in his flight. The passage, which barely held them all was unlit, so from it they could make out faintly the sky-line of the woods and the trunks of the nearest trees.

"Let me go first," said Gregory, thrusting Magda aside and stepping towards the open door, "and for God's sake go quietly!"

Suddenly a flash stabbed the outer darkness and Magda gave a strangled cry. One of the S.S. men had already come round to the back of the cottage and had fired from behind a tree. His bullet had missed Gregory by a fraction of an inch and had caught Magda in the neck. As she fell her father fired over her shoulder at the flash of the Nazi's pistol. He had pressed down his trigger and was emptying the whole contents of his automatic into the open doorway.

Gregory and Charlton had flung themselves flat, dragging *Frau* Foldar with them. Magda, choking blood, had slipped down among them, so von Lutz alone remained a target for the Nazi's fire. One bullet whipped through the skirt of his great-coat, another tore the epaulette on his shoulder, but his escape was miraculous as the burst of shots thudded into the woodwork about him, and a sudden wavering cry from outside, in the dead-silence that followed the burst, told that he had got his man.

Charlton began to drag Magda back into the kitchen-sitting-room but Gregory edged forward again towards the back door. As he did so a tommy-gun opened, sending a stream of lead over his head. Other Nazis had now come round to the back of the cottage and escape that way was impossible.

Turning, he found von Lutz crouching beside him on the floor. The Baron raised his automatic again, fired twice at the flash of the sub-machine-gun, then with his free hand swung-to the door. Springing up, Gregory secured it by thrusting the thick wooden bar home into its socket.

Back in the kitchen they found *Frau* Foldar trying to staunch Magda's wound while Freddie stood helplessly beside her; but the old woman's efforts were of no avail. The bullet had cut Magda's jugular vein; blood poured from it like a river, drenching her clothes and forming great pools upon the floor. She was already dead, having succumbed within thirty seconds of the bullet's hitting her.

Covering her face, the others began a rapid consultation.

"We're trapped!" said Gregory. "No hope of getting alive out of this place either way."

"We will some of these swine to hell send before they get us, though," muttered the Baron grimly.

"If we've got to die anyway, wouldn't it be best to surrender?" asked Charlton.

"What?" exclaimed von Lutz in astonishment; then he added more quietly: "Of course, you can your hand throw in if you wish—but I'll first see them in Hell."

"I wasn't thinking of myself," said Freddie, "but of *Frau* Foldar. If we let them shoot this place to bits she'll probably be killed too, whereas by giving ourselves up we might at least save her life."

The Colonel shrugged. "I apologize. But you shall take my word that noding we can do will make them to spare her, since she shelter us here."

"That's so." Gregory gave a grim chuckle. "You don't know these Nazis, Freddie. my boy. They'd butcher a twelve-year-old child for having given a drink of water to a blind man if he had ever raised a finger against Hitler. Come on, let's get the other shot-guns and see if we can't dust up some of these embryo Himmlers before they rush the place."

For the past two minutes there had been a lull in the firing, only an occasional bullet whacking through the curtains of the window or splintering the woodwork of the door. The cottage consisted of only two rooms and the loft above which had been used by the three fugitives during the past fortnight.

"You two stay here and I'll take the bedroom in case some of them try to get in through the window there," said von Lutz, and he left the others abruptly.

There was only one window in each room and both fronted on the lane; so Gregory felt that they might be able to hold the place for some time if they were careful not to expose themselves unnecessarily, although he knew that sooner or later there could be only one end to such an uneven combat.

"We must try to draw their fire," he said to Freddie. "We'll use that fur-cap that Hans left behind. Put it on the end of that stick and thrust it up under the curtains when I give the word. It will part them just enough to show a streak of light and they'll see the cap outlined against it."

Charlton grabbed the cap and stick and together they crawled across the floor. Gregory put his hand up and felt along the lower part of the window. The Nazis' bullets had shattered the glass leaving only the empty frame. Very cautiously he poked his shot-gun out of one corner and warily raised his head until he could see along the barrel; then he whispered: "Ready now?"

Still kneeling on the floor Freddie thrust up the big fur-cap and parted the curtains a little where they met across the centre of the window. Instantly there was a burst of fire and a hail of shots smacked into the cap, knocking the stick on which it was supported out of his hands.

Gregory had marked the nearest flashes and loosed off both barrels of his gun, hoping for a double. As he ducked back yowls of pain told him that some of his pellets had found a resting-place in human flesh.

A second later the Nazis brought a sub-machine-gun into action. There was a deafening roar as it sent a stream of lead through the empty window-frame; cutting one of the curtains nearly in half so that the torn part sagged down disclosing a large triangle of the lighted room. With extraordinary daring Freddie raised himself until the bullets were zipping only a few inches above his head; then, aiming carefully at the perfect target presented by the flame-spitting barrel of the gun, he let the gunner have two rounds from his revolver. There was a loud cry and the firing ceased.

"Well done! Well done!" murmured Gregory. "But for God's sake don't try any more of those tricks or you'll get yourself shot to pieces."

"What's it matter?" Freddie was crouching on the floor again and turned his head to grin. "We'll be dead anyway within the next half-hour."

Gregory shrugged. "I'm afraid so. Still, we might as well try to hang out as long as we can."

The sound of sharp explosions in the next room told them that von Lutz had come into action and it seemed that the Nazis had turned their attention to the bedroom window. But a moment later bullets descending at a sharp angle began to spatter the floor of the kitchen within a foot of the place where Gregory and Charlton were crouching.

"Hell!" whispered Gregory. "One of them's got up a tree and is firing down on to us. He can see through the rent in the curtain; we must put out that light."

With a swift wriggle he scrambled across the floor and, raising his hand, turned down the oil-lamp that was on the kitchen dresser. Instantly the room was in semi-darkness, lit only by the soft glow of the fire.

The shooting died down again and after a few minutes it ceased altogether. The silence was uncanny after the almost continuous banging of explosions and thudding of bullets that had created pandemonium for the last ten minutes. The Nazis were evidently planning some new form of attack and Gregory anxiously strained his ears for any sounds which might give the first intimation of it.

Suddenly it came: a rush of footsteps at the front of the cottage and a terrific battering upon the door. Freddie was nearest and, turning, he began to fire with his revolver at the panels of the door, hoping that the bullets would go through the wood and wound some of the men who were trying to smash it in.

"That's no good!" yelled Gregory. "Here, give me a hand with this table." Sweeping the things that were on it to the floor they heaved the table over sideways and dragged it up against the door; then hastily stacked up all the furniture they could lay their hands on behind it to form a barricade.

Snatching up his gun Gregory ran back to the window. He meant to lean out, shoot along the side of the house and take the Nazis who were trying to force the door in a flank attack. But the second he raised his head under the tattered curtain the sub-machine-gun was brought into play again; a bullet zipped through his hair and others began to splinter the woodwork of the window-frame.

After three minutes of furious thudding the Nazis gave up their efforts on the door and silence fell once more. This time it continued for much longer and Gregory had a feeling that it forebode yet more serious trouble. A quarter of an hour later he began to hope that he had been wrong and that some of the Nazis had gone to fetch reinforcements. in which case the time had come to attempt a sortie.

He estimated that at least five out of the ten or twelve attackers must have been killed or seriously wounded. If one or two more had been sent off to Dornitz to get help, that considerably reduced the odds. To break out and rush the remainder, who would certainly have been left to watch the exits of the cottage, was a most desperate venture; but even if only one of the besieged party got through that would be better than their all remaining there to be massacred, as they undoubtedly would be in due course, unless they could manage to break out.

Leaving Charlton for a moment he slipped into the bedroom to consult the Baron, but before he had a chance to put up his suggestion he was struck by something peculiar about the atmos-phere of the room. It was not the close fugginess in which Hans Foldar and his wife usually slept. since the window of this room, too, had been smashed to atoms by the Nazis' bullets. It was something else. Gregory sniffed quickly twice—then he knew. It was the faint smell of wood-smoke.

Von Lutz was almost indistinguishable in the darkness but his voice came from near the window.

"How does it go with you?"

"We're still all right. But what are they up to now? Can you smell anything here?"

The Baron drew a long, deep breath through his nostrils and, exhaling it, suddenly exclaimed: *"Himmel, ja!* I haf not notice it before but it comes from the window. I can smell smoke."

"That's it. I had a hope just now that they'd sent to Dornitz for reinforcements and we might stand a chance of breaking through while their numbers were reduced; but my first

59

hunch—that they were planning something pretty nasty for us —was right. They've been collecting wood all this time and now they've fired the place."

As he ceased speaking a faint hissing and crackling caught their ears, proving him to be right. The Nazis had piled up all the loose wood they could find against the blank wall at the bedroom end of the cottage and the bonfire was just beginning to get well alight.

The smell of smoke grew stronger; soon great puffs of it were drifting in through the broken window and the crackling of the flames increased to a low roar. Gregory put his hand on the far wall of the bedroom and withdrew it quickly; the timbers were already scorching to the touch.

There was nothing they could do about it—nothing whatever. They could not get at the blaze to attempt to put it out, while it was still small, and once the flames had eaten their way through the wall it would have much too strong a hold for them to get it under. Even the possibility of delaying its action by throwing buckets of water from the kitchen tank against the threatened wall was denied to them since they were compelled to crawl about the floor; not daring to stand upright in case the Nazis started shooting again through the shattered windows.

Von Lutz began to cough from the acrid smoke which was now filling the room, so Gregory called to him and they both returned to the kitchen. Freddie looked up quickly from where he was kneeling behind the barricade. "They've fired the place, haven't they? There's been a strong smell of smoke for some minutes."

Gregory nodded and the airman went on: "Well, what are we going to do? Break out or stay here to be roasted alive?"

"Break out," said von Lutz; "but not yet—not till the flames haf goot hold. They wil gif us light to see by so we can shoot more of these swines before we ourselves are shot."

"That cuts both ways," Gregory replied promptly. "The brighter the light the easier it will be for them to pick us off from a distance as we come out."

Although his argument for an immediate sortie was sound they still hesitated, knowing that once they were outside with their backs against the flames they would make a perfect target for the sub-machine-guns of their enemies. It was a foregone conclusion that within two minutes of crossing the threshold they would all be dead.

The voice of the flames had swollen to a sudden roar and,

60

now that it had properly caught, the old wooden cottage was going up like tinder. Von Lutz stepped across the narrow passage and opened the door of the bedroom. A great cloud of smoke billowed out, choking and half-blinding him. The far wall was now a solid sheet of flame. Curtains, bedding and draperies had also caught, making glowing red patches in the blackish murk. He hastily thrust the door to again, brushed his hand over his watering eyes and gasped:

"We haf another few moments only—at the most. Let us go now to die like brave men."

Gregory picked up his shot-gun then he smiled at Charlton. "Sorry I let you in for this, Freddie."

Charlton smiled back. "I might just as well die riddled with bullets on the ground as in a plane; and that would have been my end for certain if this filthy war is going on for long."

Frau Foldar was still seated in the corner where Freddie had put her, well out of danger from shots coming through the windows. During the fight she had remained there, wide-eyed, terrified, unspeaking, seeming hardly to understand what was going on. Glancing towards her he said to the others:

"We can't leave her here, although I am afraid having to lug her along with us puts paid to any chance we might have had of getting through by a sudden dash."

"I'll take her," said Gregory and von Lutz simultaneously, but the Baron added:

"This my affair is. She is one of my peoples. Go, please—both of you. Good luck! Make no delay—it is an order."

Gregory did not argue. He knew that whoever led the way would make the target for the first burst of the Nazis' fire, whereas whoever took the old peasant-woman would be screened behind the leaders of the party; so if it could be considered that there was a chance of any of them getting through at all the odds were about even.

Their eyes were smarting from the smoke that now filled the kitchen. The heat was stifling and the fierce crackling of burning wood—much nearer now— showed that the flames had advanced from the bedroom and were already devouring the partition wall beside which they stood.

"Let's go," said Gregory, and they moved out into the tiny corridor which gave out on to the back door. As he lifted his hand to pull back the heavy wooden bolt a fresh burst of shooting suddenly broke out behind the house. Pausing with his hand outstretched he exclaimed: "What the devil's that?"

They listened for a moment but no bullets thudded into the woodwork of the cottage so the Nazis were not now firing at it. What then, they all wondered, could this fresh shooting mean?

"It is Hans!" cried von Lutz, his eyes showing joy and excitement. "I know him forty years. When the Nazis first surprise us and he runs away I am as much ashamed as if I haf run away myself. But I was unjust. Now all is clear. Hans has the goot sense. He knows we cannot hold out here. He rushes his fellow-woodmen to get and they are now the enemy from the rear attacking."

Gregory hesitated no longer. Pulling back the bolt he wrenched open the door and yelled: "Come on, then! Now's the time to give him a hand; we'll save our necks yet."

He dashed from the cottage, the others hard on his heels; Von Lutz and Charlton each grabbing *Frau* Foldar by an arm to support her as they ran. No hail of shots came at them; the Nazis were now fully engaged with the woodmen who had attacked them in the rear. Spurts of flame stabbed the darkness of the woods from half a dozen different directions and the night echoed to the roar of explosions as automatics and shot-guns were pitted against each other.

The glare from the burning cottage lit the scene for some distance but threw up great black shadows here and there so that the ground looked broken and uneven. When Gregory had covered twenty yards he could see vague figures moving among the trees. A splash of flame came from the weapon of the nearest; it was one of the Nazis who had suddenly turned and seen the fugitives rushing from the blazing building. His bullet might have ended Gregory's career had he not at that second tripped and gone crashing headlong over the body of another Nazi who had been shot down earlier in the attack.

For a few moments utter confusion reigned. Von Lutz pistolled the man who had fired at Gregory but others had turned their weapons upon the escaping party. As they crouched together beside Gregory, who was struggling to get back his breath, bullets whistled overhead and scores of pellets from the woodmen's shot-guns rattled on the dry branches and the leaves of the undergrowth. Someone was wailing piteously further in among the trees; a sharp cry told of another who had been hit. The S.S. officer was shouting to his troopers, now caught between two fires, as Gregory, the Baron and Charlton again came into action. Von Lutz was yelling to Hans so that his men should not shoot at them by mistake in the semi-darkness. Then Hans's voice came in the near distance and next moment, crying: "Don't shoot! Don't shoot!" he came blundering through the trees towards them.

"Hans! Hans!" The Baron rose to meet him and grasped his arm. "We should have been dead now but for you; and *Frau* Foldar is here, unhurt, with us."

"Gott Sie dank!" gulped the woodman, stooping to embrace his wife as she struggled up from her knees.

"Quick!" urged Gregory in German, "or they'll get us yet. We shan't be safe until we're deep in the forest."

They all began to run again and did not pause until they had covered another three hundred yards. By that time they were well clear of the flickering glare from the cottage which was now a roaring column of smoke and flame.

"How many men did you bring with you, Hans?" asked von Lutz breathlessly.

"Three only, *Herr Oberst-Baron;* the others lived too far away. But I fear we have lost Joachim; I heard him cry out as though he were badly wounded just before I reached you."

The shooting was still going on a couple of hundred yards to their left as the Baron replied with swift instructions: "Then you must call them off now and if Joachim is still alive get him away somehow between you. He and the other two will be safe from arrest later as the Nazis cannot know who they are, but you and your wife must go into hiding for a time; then, with any luck, the Nazis will believe that both of you were killed when the cottage was attacked and that both your bodies were burned inside it."

"Ja, ja, Herr Oberst-Baron. We shall find shelter and no-one in the district will betray us; but what of you and your friends?"

"We must take care of ourselves. You have done more than enough for us. We are eternally grateful. Go now and get your men away while we create a diversion from this side of the enemy."

"God be with you!" muttered the tall woodman, and with his arm about his wife's shoulders he hurried away through the trees.

"Come!" said von Lutz, breaking into English. "Of these swine there cannot many be left. Let us attack with stealth a final settling to make."

With Charlton and Gregory beside him he crept about a hundred yards until they could see the flashes of the Nazis' pistols more distinctly; then they crouched down behind the undergrowth. Just as they were picking their men the hoot of an owl came from the near distance and the Baron whispered:

"That is Hans; he calls to the others. It's our turn. Make ready? Together now. Fire!"

At his word all three of them squeezed the triggers of their weapons. There was a scream of pain as one of the enemy was hit; but they had now given away their own position and the remaining Nazis turned their fire upon them.

Suddenly von Lutz gave a strangled cry and lurched forward. Gregory was kneeling behind a tree and Freddie had flung himself flat to escape the bullets. Both of them grabbed the Baron's shoulders and pulling him from the bramble patch into which he had fallen head foremost dragged him away from the spot at which the Nazis were still firing.

When they had covered a dozen yards they laid the wounded man down and Gregory made a quick examination of him. The Baron's body had gone limp but owing to the darkness they could not see where he had been hit. Gregory's hand came in contact with blood, warm and sticky, on von Lutz's face. Next moment his fingers found a great rent in the Baron's forehead and he knew that this friend who had stood by them so loyally had been shot through the head and had died instantly.

In the attempt they had been planning to get clear of the Brandenburg district Gregory and Freddie had been counting on von Lutz for advice, clothes and supplies. Now he was dead; and as they lay beside his body they both realized that he could no longer lift a finger to help them. Even poor Magda, who hated the English yet might for her father's sake have rendered them assistance, was now only charred flesh and bone, beyond any further test of divided loyalties. For the first time in many days the fugitives were again alone and on the run in the country of their enemies.

CHAPTER VI

THE HORRIBLE DILEMMA

T HE Nazis continued to fire into the patch of shrub where von Lutz had been killed but it was difficult to estimate how many of them were still in action. Gregory did not think that there could now be more than two or three who had remained unscathed in the attack on the cottage and in the fight against Hans Foldar's woodmen afterwards; but several of the wounded were apparently still capable of using their pistols so even such a depleted force was too large for Charlton and himself to tackle now that the woodmen had withdrawn.

Freddie had raised his revolver again and was drawing a bead on a dark hump from which a flash had just appeared when Gregory checked him.

"Don't fire any more for the present or you'll disclose our new position. Give me a hand here instead and help me to undress the Baron."

"Undress him?" breathed Freddie in a horrified whisper.

"Yes," Gregory whispered back. "Beastly thing to have to do but I want his uniform and I know he wouldn't grudge it to me."

"All right. But what's the idea?"

"I mean to swap clothes with him. The ones I'm wearing were made in Germany so when he's found in them they won't give anything away; while in his colonel's uniform I'll be practically immune from suspicion if only we can get out of this blasted wood and reach a town."

"That's a brain-wave; but better still, dress him up in my Air-Force kit and let me have your civilian clothes."

"No. They have no idea that the two men who were shot down on the night of the 8th are still in the district. If we did as you suggest, directly they found his body the R.A.F. outfit would give away the fact that we took shelter with him, that we've

65

been here all the time and that one of us is trying to make a get-away dressed in his uniform. They'd catch us then before we could cover ten miles."

"They'll catch us anyway if I can't find a change of clothes."

"Not necessarily. One airman looks very like another and at the moment they're not looking for airmen at all. I shall be wearing the Baron's greatcoat so you can have the one I've got on. You'll look like a flyer who's made a false landing and been lent an Army greatcoat on account of the cold."

When they had stripped von Lutz of his outer garments with as little noise as possible Gregory began to change. As they were both slim men of about the same height the Colonel's uniform fitted him fairly decently. He was also able to acquire the dead man's automatic which still had a few rounds in it and one spare clip of unused ammunition. After they had finished the grim business of getting Gregory's garments on to the body Charlton put on the German officer's overcoat in which Gregory had escaped from Berlin.

"I should have thought that by wearing this thing I'm falling between two stools," the airman said in a low voice. "It won't hide the fact that I'm an R.A.F. officer if an inquisitive police-man questions me and asks to see what's underneath it; yet it's enough to damn me utterly if we're caught."

"On the contrary. It will prevent ninety-nine out of every hundred Germans giving you a second glance and in the event of our being cornered, whereas I shall be shot as a spy whatever I am wearing, by retaining your R.A.F. flying-kit under that coat the worst they'll be able to do to you is to send you to a prisoners-of-war camp."

"Perhaps you're right."

"Of course I'm right," Gregory muttered impatiently. "Don't waste any more time in arguing; we haven't got a moment to lose."

"You've thought out a plan, then?"

"I wouldn't say that; it's just a hunch that we might be able to pull a fast one on these swine while they're collecting their wounded. Tread as softly as you can now and follow me."

For some moments now the Nazis had given up sending pot-shots into the wood. Cautiously at first, and then more loudly, they had been calling to one another until, reassured by their continued immunity from attack, they evidently believed that their surviving enemies had given up the fight and made off. The unwounded were now emerging from their hiding-places to give first aid to the wounded and to search for their dead. The woods were silent once more, except for the sound of their voices which came quite clearly and gave a good indication of their positions.

Using extreme caution Gregory and Charlton moved in a wide semi-circle round the area occupied by the Nazis, until they struck the lane on the right-hand side of the cottage and about half a mile from it. The little building was now almost burnt out and the flames had died down, but a red glow from the ashes still lit its surroundings for some distance. At the edge of the wood Gregory paused and pointed. The motor-truck which had brought the S.S. men from Dornitz was still there, parked on the roadside about half-way between the place where they stood and the remains of the cottage.

The wood was higher than the road by about four feet; so having warily tiptoed along, weaving their way in and out among the trees on the top of the bank until they were opposite the truck, they were able to look down into it.

As they paused there, holding their breath, two S.S. men, one of whom held a torch, were just lifting a dead or unconscious companion into the back of the open vehicle, and a minute later the torch moved disclosing the bodies of two other Nazis who had been laid out on its floor-boards. After the third body had been placed beside the others the man with the torch muttered something and set off at a quick walk down the road towards the cottage, leaving his helper—who presumably was the driver—just below the place where Gregory and Charlton were crouching. Lighting a cigarette he remained there, his back towards them, facing his van.

Gregory waited until the first man had climbed the bank and disappeared into the trees further along the road then, clubbing his shot-gun, he rose slowly to his feet. Balancing himself carefully he raised the gun high in the air, leant forward and let the driver have it. The heavy wooden stock hit the Nazi full on the top of the head. He went down like a pole-axed ox, without even a murmur.

"Quick!" Gregory whispered, springing down the bank. "You get the engine going while I heave this tell-tale cargo into the ditch."

As Freddie scrambled up into the driver's seat Gregory seized the nearest body by the boots and, with one violent jerk, dragged it out of the back of the truck. The engine sputtered for a minute, on the bad petrol, then it burst into a steady roar.

Gregory grabbed a handhold, hauled himself up into the body of the van and yelled:

"Go on, man! What the hell are you waiting for?"

"You," Freddie yelled back.

"I'm all right. Drive on, for God's sake, or they'll shoot us as we pass the cottage!"

The truck moved off with a jerk which nearly threw Gregory off his feet. Steadying himself with an effort he got a grip on the second Nazi and, exerting all his strength, bundled him overboard; then lurching towards the third in the wildly-rocking van he pushed him out of the back, gasped with relief and flung himself flat.

Once Freddie had shifted gear their get-away was so swift that the remaining Nazis had not enough time to guess what was happening. No shots came at the truck as it roared past the glowing embers of the cottage and in another moment it was hurtling away at the top of its speed down the road into the darkness.

Three quarters of a mile further on the lane ended, coming out at right-angles into a second-class road. As the headlights glimmered on a wire fence dead ahead Charlton jammed on his brakes and brought the truck to a skidding halt.

"Crossroads; which way do you want me to take?" he sang out.

"Half a minute." Jumping out of the back Gregory scrambled up the bank on the corner to a signpost which he had glimpsed outlined against a break in the clouds where the moonlight was now filtering through and tried to decipher what was written on it. The bank brought his head within a few inches of the lettering and by holding up matches one after the other their light was just sufficient for him to read: "DORNITZ—2 KILOMETRES" on one arm and "GLOINE—$3\frac{1}{2}$ KILOMETRES' on the other.

"Turn left," he shouted as he ran back and jumped up beside Charlton on the driver's seat. "This road will take us to a place called Gloine. Where the devil that is God knows, but anyhow it's in the opposite direction to Dornitz and we daren't run through there in case the police recognize this van and want to know how we got hold of it."

The road was fairly flat and Freddie pushed the lorry along at the top of its speed through the sandy Brandenburg countryside which was broken only here and there by woods and was now, outside the glow of the headlights, hidden by the darkness.

68

Five or six minutes later they rumbled into a straggling township. It was nearly two o'clock in the morning so no one was about, with the exception of a solitary policeman who was standing in the little square beside a memorial to the fallen of the last Great War.

"Drive straight on." muttered Gregory as the lamps of the truck lit a road-sign reading: "GORZKE—10 KILOMETRES" and "WIESENBURG—18 KILOMETRES".

He had never heard of these places either; but the wintry night sky was fairly clear and on their way to Gloine he had had an opportunity to get his bearing from the stars and from what he could recall of the map which von Lutz had drawn for them that evening. He now knew the direction in which they were heading and in any case it would have been madness to pull up and ask a policeman, since as soon as the surviving Nazis could reach a telephone they would report the theft of their truck and send out a general call to have it held up wherever sighted.

"Where are we going?" asked Freddie as they left the last houses of Gloine behind and headed for the open country once more.

"This road heads almost due east, which is a bit of luck for us," Gregory replied. "Sooner or later it must get us to Berlin."

"Berlin?" echoed Freddie. "Are you crazy? That's the last place we want to go to! I thought you meant to head for the Dutch frontier."

"So you're still thinking of that girl of yours, Angela Fordyce, eh? Well, maybe we'll get to Holland and you'll be able to see her yet, but first I want to find out what's happened to Erika."

"But damn it, man! That means running both our heads into the noose. In a place like Berlin we're absolutely certain to be captured. Besides, we *must* make the utmost of our start. Our only chance is to make a dash for the Dutch frontier right away."

"Not necessarily, Freddie. And if I *were* doing any dashing for frontiers I should head for Denmark, which is nearer than Holland by hundreds of miles."

"Well, I'm jolly sorry for you about Erika, and all that, but I don't think you're quite playing the game in boggling our only chance of escape."

"All right, my dear fellow," Gregory shrugged, have it your own way; just pull up and drop me here. I'll make you a present

69

of my half of the van and you can drive straight to The Hague or wherever it is your delightful young woman hangs out."

"But my German's not half good enough yet," exclaimed the exasperated Freddie. "I'd never be able to get all that way on my own."

"Of course you wouldn't, dear boy. I don't suppose this thing's got enough petrol in it to do a hundred kilometres, and there isn't a service station in Germany out of which you could wangle another gallon without me to help you. Even if you succeeded in reaching the frontier you wouldn't stand a dog's chance of getting across it. As it is, we shall have to ditch the truck in half an hour or less because once those swine we left in the wood get to a telephone every policeman in Brandenburg will be on the look-out for it. That's why—putting both our girl-friends entirely out of the question—we should be absolutely mad to try to make a dash for *any* frontier at the moment; and why, even if I were not anxious to find out what has happened to Erika, I should be heading for Berlin."

"I suppose you're right about our having to ditch the van pretty soon," Charlton admitted reluctantly, "but the thought of trying to keep out of trouble in a great city sends cold shivers down my spine."

"Don't let it. There's an old Chinese saying which I've often found to be a very true one. 'When thou wouldst be secret do thy business in a crowd'. If only we can get to Berlin we'll be all right, but the problem is how to get there."

Gorzke proved to be a larger town than Gloine but owing to the late hour it was almost as deserted. They had to pull up for a moment in its central square to find direction signs but on reading them Gregory saw "WIESENBURG—8 KILO-METRES" and under it "BELZIG—19 KILOMETRES". The name Belzig rang a bell in his mind which made him believe that it was on a main-line railway, so he decided to push on towards it.

The road now curved to the south-east but it was a good main-way, wider and with a firmer surface than that upon which they had been before, and they made better going. In this quiet country district they had not so far met a single vehicle and as they bucketed along Gregory was busy calculating distances. He reckoned that by the time they reached Wiesenburg they would have covered about fifteen miles and, as the top speed of the lorry with the handicap of *Ersatz* petrol was in the neigh-bourhood of 30 m.p.h., half an hour would have elapsed between their arrival at that town and their seizure of the lorry from the Nazis.

He had been fairly confident about getting through Gloine and Gorzke without trouble but every moment now increased the likelihood of their being held up. It was not more than twenty minutes' walk from Hans Foldar's cottage to the home of their late friend, Colonel-Baron von Lutz, and it was certain that the manor-house would be on the telephone. If the Nazis had set off for the house at once the police all over the district would now have been warned and be drawing cordons across the roads to catch the stolen truck before it could get further afield. On the other hand, if the Nazis had wasted time in argument or, feeling confident that the vast German police network would easily pick up the fugitives on the following morning, considered it more important to patch up their wounded than to make a dash for the nearest telephone, there was a decent chance that no emergency police-call had yet been sent out.

Gregory said nothing to Charlton but as they approached the first houses of Wiesenburg he braced himself for trouble. Peering out into the darkness ahead and holding the shot-gun that he still had with him ready across his knees he prepared to fight rather than to surrender.

Further into the town a belated roisterer lurched off the pavement and almost under their wheels. For a second Gregory did not realize that the man was a drunk and thought him the leader of an ambush who had jumped out to call on them to halt; but Freddie swerved the van, missing the fellow by inches, and it clattered on.

In the centre of the town a line of light lorries was pulled up at the side of the road and in the half-light they could see that a number of soldiers were gathered about them. Once more Gregory tensed his muscles. Perhaps these men had just been dispatched from a local barracks to bar the road; but when he saw that the lorries were all parked in line he realized that his fears were groundless. The lorries would have been drawn across the road if the men were there to stop them. It was only a company of troops engaged on some ordinary night operation.

As they passed the unit some of the men called a greeting and Gregory sang out cheerfully to them in German in reply, thanking his gods that in the half-darkness they could not see that he was wearing the uniform of a colonel. Another three minutes and they were out of Wiesenburg on the Belzig road.

The tension was over for the moment and Gregory was able

to sit back while the truck rattled on for a few more miles; then he began to peer ahead at both sides of the road as far as he could see in the uncertain light. After another kilometre they came to a wood and Gregory told Charlton to slow down, meanwhile keeping an anxious eye open for any sign of a track that might lead off the road in among the trees. A white gateway loomed up. Leaving his shot-gun on the seat, as he meant from this point to rely on von Lutz's automatic, he jumped down, opened the gate and beckoned to Freddie to drive through.

In the darkness among the trees it was not easy to find the most suitable place to abandon the van; but a few hundred yards up the track they reached a break in the wood which on investigation proved to be a sandy patch sloping downwards at a fairly steep angle.

"This'll do," said Gregory; "we'll ditch the van here. Be careful how you go, though."

Freddie drove over the grassy verge on to the sand and the van bumped its way down until more trees became visible in its headlights. Pulling up he switched off the lights, got out and scrambling up the slope rejoined Gregory.

"It'll be visible from here in daylight, I'm afraid," Gregory said, "but we can't help that; and, with luck, this track may not be much used. There's a sporting chance that no-one'll find it for a day or two and in any case it's well out of the way till to-morrow morning, by which time we shall be miles from here."

"What's the next move?" Freddie asked.

"We've got to foot it into Belzig and I mean to try to get a train to Berlin from there."

Side by side they set off back along the track and took the Belzig road. Half an hour later they reached the outskirts of the town and taking Freddie's arm Gregory whispered to him to go cautiously. Over an hour had elapsed since they had stolen the truck and he felt certain that by now the police in every town for fifty miles around had been notified and would have special patrols out. Two minutes later a match flared a hundred yards ahead and by its glow the vague outline of two men's faces could be seen as they lit cigarettes from it.

Gregory would have bet his last shilling that they were only two of an armed squad which had been posted there to hold up the lorry should it make an appearance. Although they might not regard two pedestrians with suspicion he was extremely anxious to avoid being questioned, so twenty yards further on he silently turned Charlton off the road down a path at right-angles to it which ran along a garden fence. Where the fence ended they turned again and with subdued curses stumbled across some back lots till they reached a group of buildings and a lane, by taking which they arrived back in the main street at a point well beyond the police picket.

It seemed most unlikely that there would be any trains in the middle of the night but Gregory wanted to find out when the first one for Berlin left in the morning, so their next problem was to find the station. The houses were dark and the streets deserted but presently they came upon a man who was lighting his way with a torch, who Gregory felt certain, from his kit, was an A.R.P. warden doing his rounds. Motioning to Charlton to keep in the background Gregory stepped forward and asked the man the way to the station; upon which he civilly directed them and, ten minutes later, they came to the small, open space on the south-eastern edge of the town where the station lay.

As Gregory was now in the uniform of a German colonel he would never have dared to attempt travelling on a train within a hundred miles of the war zone, or anywhere near Germany's frontiers, without the military voucher which anyone in uniform would normally have presented; but as they were right in the centre of Germany and far from any military zone he felt that he might risk trying to buy tickets, like an ordinary civilian, without arousing awkward questions.

Just before they reached the door of the railway-station he touched Charlton on the arm and said: "Now we're for it! But keep a stiff upper lip and forget all the German that you've recently learned. Whatever happens, you're to stay absolutely dumb and not utter a word, even if they speak to you in English, unless I tell you to."

"Right," said Freddie, and pushing open the door they went into the small, dimly-lit station hall.

The booking-office was closed and only two people were in sight; an elderly porter and an officer of the S.S. in a smart black uniform. What this Nazi official was doing there at such an hour Gregory had no idea but he did not by the flicker of an eyelid show his alarm at this inconvenient meeting. Striding up to the porter he said with abrupt authority befitting his rank:

"What time does the next train go to Berlin?"

"Five-twenty," mumbled the porter.

"Is there a waiting-room here where we can sit in comfort?"

The porter jerked his head in the direction of a door leading out of the small hall. "You can wait in there, *Herr Oberst*, but

73

there's no fire." And having given them this depressing information he slouched out on to the platform.

The officer of the S.S. had been eyeing them curiously.
Freddie had on the grey-green officer's greatcoat in which
Gregory had left Berlin but he did not look like a German officer
and he was still wearing his flying-helmet. Lifting his hand in a
casual half-salute the Nazi said to Gregory:

"You are up early, *Herr Oberst.*"

Gregory frowned. "My car broke down just outside the
town—it's this filthy *Ersatz* petrol—otherwise I should have
gone straight through to Berlin by road. As it is, my business is
urgent so I left the chauffeur with the car and walked in to catch
the first train."

"You've over two hours to wait yet," said the Nazi, "and
you'll find it icy-cold in that waiting-room. I think you'd better
come along with me to Party Headquarters."

Gregory remained quite still for a moment, but his brain
was revving over like the engine of a dynamo. Was this a casual
meeting and the Nazi only acting with friendly intentions? or
had this man, after the news of the fray in the woods had been
telephoned through, left his bed for the purpose of picketing the
station and bringing in any suspicious characters who might
have slipped past the police on the main road?

There was nothing suspicious about Gregory himself, since
his uniform, although somewhat mud-stained, was perfect and
his German irreproachable; but Freddie Charlton in his queer
get-up was quite another matter. Flying-officers do not wear
army officer's greatcoats, and if the coat were once undone it
would reveal the service kit of a British Flight-Lieutenant. The
Nazi was alone, so although he was armed there was a fair
chance that the two of them would be able to overcome him
before he could secure help. On the other hand, if they attacked
him and had a fight in the station-hall it was certain that the
porter would hear and report it—which would put an end to any
hope of their being allowed on the Berlin train when it came in.
Yet for what other reason could the Nazi be there at three
o'clock in the morning, if not to bring in suspects? If that was so,
and they once allowed him to take them to the Party Headquarters, Gregory knew that it would mean a firing-squad for
him the following morning.

His hand moved towards his gun.

CHAPTER VII

INVITATION TO THE LION'S DEN

GREGORY had raised his hand only a couple of inches when, evidently entirely unsuspicious of his intention, the S.S. officer produced his cigarette-case with a flourish and flicked it open.

"A cigarette, *Herr Oberst?*" he said, offering the case with a friendly smile.

It was touch and go. In another second Gregory would have whipped out his automatic to hold the Nazi up. As it was, with a polite *"Danke, Herr Ober-Lieutenant,"* he accepted the cigarette, and Charlton, being offered the case, took one too, refraining from speaking but smiling his thanks.

As they lit up the Nazi went on: "It's just as you like. You can remain in the waiting-room if you prefer, but it's devilishly cold in there and you know how late the trains are running these days. I doubt if yours will be in before half past six. I've just finished the job that brought me out to-night but I'm still on duty. At Party Headquarters I could fix you up with a drink and make you quite comfortable in the Mess."

Once more Gregory hesitated. Was this a trap because they were two to one and the Nazi wanted to get them inside quietly without having to risk his life tackling two desperate fugitives? Or was his offer of hospitality genuine?

If the Nazi really had no inkling that they were on the run a refusal of his offer was the very thing best calculated to arouse his suspicions. No-one but a fool, or a man who had something to hide, would willingly kick his heels in an icy station waiting-room for three hours in preference to sitting in a warm Mess. It was a horrible dilemma but Gregory was a shrewd judge of character and the bluff, fair-faced *Ober-Lieutenant* was not the type that makes a good actor; so he was now inclined to think that of the two risks it would be better to enter the lions' den.

But the devil of it was that once they reached the Nazi Mess

Charlton would have to remove his greatcoat and reveal his
R.A.F. service kit. That was the awful snag; but Gregory
decided that there was only one thing for it: to risk his friend's
freedom on a line that he had already thought out for use in an
emergency, and to gamble once again upon the audacity which
had served him so well in the past.

"You are most kind," he said, "and nothing would suit me
better than to doze in one of your arm-chairs for an hour or two.
But I must first ask you if you are willing to take into your
custody a British officer."

Freddie had picked up enough German from von Lutz
during the past two and a half weeks to be able to follow the gist
of the conversation and when he heard Gregory's request he was
utterly staggered. On the face of it Gregory was trying to sell
him out and preserve his own liberty at the price of handing his
friend over to the Nazis. Such an act of treachery seemed too
horrible to contemplate but he felt sure that he had not mis-
understood what Gregory had said. It was only with a great
effort that he had managed to control his feelings and the
muscles of his face while he waited with acute anxiety to see
what would happen next.

"A British officer!" exclaimed the Nazi, suddenly switching
his surprised glance to Charlton. "Is that him there?"

"Yes." Gregory drew calmly on his cigarette. "The cold is
so bitter that we had to provide him with a greatcoat, but he's
still wearing his service uniform underneath it. D'you think
you can find him a cell?"

"Why, certainly, if you wish. But why isn't he in a prisoners-
of-war camp?"

"Because his plane was only shot down early to-night, over
Essen."

"I see. But Essen's a long way away—nearly five hours from
here by road. Why wasn't he interned locally?"

"He was shot down at about nine o'clock," Gregory shrugged,
"and as he was flying a new type of plane the anti-aircraft people
handed him over at once to Intelligence. He's rather an unusual
type for a flying-officer and I think, if he's handled properly, we
may get something out of him. Anyhow, we immediately telephoned Berlin about this new type of machine he was in and it
aroused such interest at the Air Ministry that Marshal Goering
said he would like to see him personally. That meant at once,
of course, and it was not a job that could be passed on to a junior
officer so I set off with him by car straight away."

76

Gregory felt that he had explained away rather neatly the fact of such a high officer as a full colonel being in charge of a single prisoner, and he was gratified to see the immediately favourable reaction which the name of Field-Marshal Goering provoked in the Nazi, who said promptly:

"In that case, *Herr Oberst*, our Party Headquarters are entirely at your disposal. Let us go there at once." Then clicking his heels and bowing sharply from the waist he formally introduced himself: "Wentsich."

Gregory followed suit by barking: "Claus," and added: "My prisoner's name is Rogers—Flight-Lieutenant Rogers."

As they left the station Gregory made Freddie walk in front of him while he talked to the Nazi about the progress of the war. Ten minutes later they entered the main square of the town and after going up a few stone steps passed through a black-out light-lock into the big hallway of a fine old building which had been taken over as the local Nazi headquarters, on Hitler's coming to power.

Gregory looked warily about him, his hand never very far from the butt of his automatic. The *Ober-Lieutenant* of Black Guards had not betrayed the least sign that he suspected them but Gregory still felt that they might be walking straight into a trap. A dozen Storm-Troopers might come running at the *Ober-Lieutenant's* first call but the cynical Englishman meant to see to it that, if that happened, the *Ober-Lieutenant* himself never lived to profit by the results of his strategy.

Except for a couple of clerks working in a downstairs room, the door of which stood open, no-one was about, and the Nazi led the way upstairs without giving the signal that Gregory so much dreaded. But, even now, he feared that they were only being led further into the snare so that there should be no possible chance of their shooting their way out and escaping from the building.

On the first floor the Nazi flung open one half of a tall, carved-wood door which gave on to a handsome *salon* overlooking the square. The room was comfortably furnished. A big china stove was hissing with heat in one corner and on a sideboard stood a fine array of drinks. To Gregory's intense relief the room was unoccupied. It all seemed too good to be true. There must be a snag somewhere.

"Come along in," said the Nazi cheerfully. "What are you going to have?"

Gregory glanced at the bottles and away again. "Hadn't we better see my prisoner locked up first?"

"Need we bother?" the *Ober-Lieutenant* shrugged. "He'll stand no more chance of getting away from you here than he would if he were downstairs in a cell—and very much less than when he was alone with you walking to the station from the place where you left your car. Anyhow, it's so darned cold I expect the poor chap could do with a drink, too."

At last Gregory's fears were set at rest. Things had panned out as he had desperately prayed that they might. He had suggested that Charlton should be locked up only in order that the S.S. man should more readily believe that he was an important prisoner.

"Certainly," he agreed at once. "So long as my prisoner has no chance of getting away I'm perfectly satisfied, and I'm sure he'd like a drink. But he doesn't speak German. Do you speak any English?"

"No; a few words only—but enough to say 'How d'you do', 'Hard luck', 'You will drink, yes?'" Wentsich smiled at Charlton.

At an almost imperceptible nod from Gregory, Freddie said: "Thanks. It's very kind of you; I'd love one."

He had listened with anxious ears to every word that had been said and was now not only reassured about his own position but felt extremely guilty at his unworthy suspicion that Gregory had ever intended to leave him in the lurch. He could only admire the clever ruse by which his fellow-fugitive had accounted for his Air Force uniform and the audacity of this brilliant stroke which had led to their both being received as guests in the comfortable Nazi Party Headquarters—the last place in which their enemies would ever look for them.

When Wentsich had poured the drinks all three of them removed their greatcoats and sat down in deep arm-chairs near the roaring stove. At first the talk turned on the mythical episode of Freddie's having been shot down over Essen the previous evening. Fortunately, as Wentsich spoke very little English, Freddie was not called on to give any details of his forced landing direct, and Gregory rendered what purported to be a translation of the airman's sensations by drawing freely on his own experiences when they had actually been shot down nearly three weeks before. Several British airmen having fallen victims to the Nazis in the interval, and the localities being so widely separated, the *Ober Lieutenant* did not suspect any connection between the two episodes.

Gregory then remarked that Wentsich must find life pretty

boring stationed so far from the war-fronts or any of the great cities; upon which the S.S. man laughed and said:

"In the ordinary way it's pretty quiet here but after the recent *Putsch* we had plenty to occupy us and, as a matter of fact, I had it over the 'phone half an hour before I met you that only to-night half a dozen of our fellows were killed rounding up a traitor-Baron about thirty miles from here."

"The devil!" exclaimed Gregory, swiftly concealing his uneasiness. "I hope they got him."

Wentsich shrugged. "We're not certain yet. The cottage in which he was hiding was burnt to the ground so if he was lying wounded there he was probably roasted to cinders, but he had two or three of his peasants with him and others came on the scene later to try to relieve the cottage when it was attacked. Our people shot several of them but the rest got away by a damned clever trick. In the darkness they managed to get hold of the truck in which our men had come out from Dornitz and they drove off in it. Whether the Baron—who is a colonel, by the way—got away with them we don't know. If he has, I expect we'll run him to earth before he's much older but I doubt if we'll be able to bring any of the peasants to book. They will probably have ditched the van somewhere and made their way back to their own cottages. As the schemozzle took place in darkness our people couldn't identify any of the men who attacked them, so I don't see how we're going to prove which of the 'locals' was in the show and which wasn't; and it's quite certain that all their wives will swear that they were safely in bed at home."

These were really cheering tidings for the fugitives. Not only did it look as though the woodmen who had assisted them so loyally would come out of the affair all right but apparently the Nazis had no idea that the two airmen who had been shot down in the neighbourhood over a fortnight before had had any hand in the matter. Presumably they had both been written off as having managed to escape safely out of the district and, since no description could be circulated of either of them, nobody was bothering to try to trace them up any more.

"Even if life in Belzig is a bit boring at times, though," Wentsich went on, "I'd a darned sight rather be stationed here than in Czechoslovakia."

"Yes. We've been having quite a spot of bother there recently, haven't we?" Gregory murmured. "Apparently, last week they had to shoot twelve students as an example."

"Twelve!" the Nazi laughed. "That was only the start of it. We had to shoot 1,700 of those blasted Czechs to prevent our garrisons from being massacred. Prague was in a state of open revolution last week-end and orders came from the Fuehrer himself that, whatever the effect on neutral opinion, the revolt had to be put down. From what I've heard, it's been absolute hell there."

"Have they succeeded in quelling the rebellion now?"

"Oh, yes. The Gestapo doused the flames all right but there are still plenty of red-hot embers kicking around. The Czechs loathe us Germans to the very guts and neither the troops nor police dare move about the city in squads of less than six after dark, for fear of being sand-bagged or stabbed in the back. Of course, it's those filthy Jews who are at the root of the trouble; Prague simply swarms with them."

Gregory felt that from what he knew of the Czechs they were quite capable of making plenty of trouble for the Germans without any assistance from the Jews, but he was sorry to hear that they had risen in force when the time was not yet ripe and had suffered so severely in consequence. It would have been so much better had they waited until later in the war and made their effort to regain their freedom after Germany had been weakened by the blockade or had suffered some serious reverse. As it was, by the abortive rising they had done little material good either for themselves or for the Allies and it must almost certainly have robbed them of many of their best leaders, which was a tragic business.

Wentsich went on to describe how thousands of Black Guards had been rushed on motor-cycles to the scene of the trouble for the purpose of suppressing the riots and guarding the public buildings. President Hacha had been made a prisoner and was confined to a room in the old castle. The universities, which were such hotbeds of anti-German feeling, had been closed for three years, and in addition to the shooting of 1,700 Czech and Jewish leaders thousands more had been deported for forced labour in Germany.

So accustomed has the mind become to accounts of mass persecution and even slaughter that it is apt no longer to grip the full horror of the facts that lie behind newspaper headlines and such statements as the *Ober-Lieutenant* was making, but Gregory consciously tried to visualize just a fraction of the abysmal woe which must have stricken the Czech people during the last week.

For every one of those 1,700 deaths—loves, friendships and life-long ambitions must have been cut off. All those thousands of men dragged away into exile left behind them distraught families, many of which had now been robbed of all protection or support. Countless parents were mourning the loss of their sons; countless wives and sweethearts weeping for the men who had been torn from them by the brutal agents of the Gestapo; countless children were left fatherless; countless girls and young married women, who had no means of earning their own living, were left at the mercy of any man who would offer them enough money to buy the food they must have to keep the life in their bodies.

In his mind's eye he saw the big blond Storm-Troopers breaking into the houses, beating the Jews with their rubber truncheons, frog-marching the Czechs through the streets into captivity, pulling the prettier girls from their hiding-places in attics and cellars to provide brutal fun in the nearest bedroom while their parents were held prisoner.

It seemed impossible to believe that the big, blond, cheerful Wentsich, who was entertaining them so hospitably, was capable of committing such atrocities; yet Gregory knew that, had the *Ober-Lieutenant* happened to be drafted to Prague in this emergency, he would have acted in exactly the same way as his colleagues.

Perhaps he and his like were not altogether resposible for their actions, owing to the madness which had swept Germany and bound a great proportion of her younger, more virile men to obey any order which came down to them from the criminal lunatic whom they regarded as God and called the Fuehrer. But one thing was certain: even if such men were only partially responsible in the degree of leniency or brutality with which they executed their orders, those orders had been given; and the Monster of Berchtesgaden could not escape the utter condemnation of the whole civilized world for all this incredible suffering and misery which his insane ambition was causing.

"Eh? What was that you were saying about the Finns?" Gregory suddenly roused himself. "So the trouble has flared up again?"

"Yes; only to-day," the *Ober-Lieutenant* nodded. "The Russians accused the Finns of having fired on their troops with artillery, killing an officer and three privates. Molotov has lodged a protest which almost amounts to an ultimatum. He insists that the Finns are threatening Leningrad."

"What nonsense!" Gregory laughed. "The Finnish nation consists of only about four million people, whereas the Soviet's population is somewhere near one hundred and ninety millions. It's absolutely absurd to suggest that a little people like the Finns could possibly threaten the Soviet with its colossal armies and air fleets."

"Anyhow, the Russians are insisting that the Finns should withdraw their troops sixteen miles from their frontier."

"But that's impossible! It would mean their surrendering the Mannerheim Line, and how on earth could they be expected to do that? If they once gave up all the forts and gun-emplacements south of Lake Ladoga—into which they've put every penny they could raise for years—they would leave their principal cities in the south of Finland absolutely unprotected. The Russians have such enormous superiority of numbers that they could just walk in and take them any time they chose."

"If you ask me, that's what they mean to do," Wentsich grinned.

They talked on about the war until well after four in the morning, when the door was flung open and a fat, bald-headed officer stumped into the room. Wentsich immediately rose and clicked his heels, presenting Gregory as Colonel Claus and the prisoner as Flight-Lieutenant Rogers.

The bald man was a major of Storm-Troopers and rapped out his name, Putzleiger, in reply. He seemed to be in a particularly ill temper—perhaps from having had to get up so early in the morning and, since the S.S. and the Reichswehr were always more or less at loggerheads, his temper was not improved by finding an Army Colonel in his Mess.

But immediately he learned that the *Herr Oberst* was on his way to Goering his manner changed entirely; and when Gregory skilfully managed to imply that he knew the Field-Marshal personally the Major became positively gushing. He asked Wentsich if he had rung through to the station to find out for the *Herr Oberst* how late the Berlin train was likely to be.

Wentsich replied that he had not, but that he had intended to do so later on, nearer the time when the train was due.

"Get through at once, then," ordered the Major, and picking up the telephone Wentsich asked the exchange downstairs to put him through to the station.

When he had made the inquiry he turned back to them. "It is the train from Dusseldorf that you would catch, which is due in at five-twenty, but they report that it is nearly two hours late already so I doubt if it will reach Belzig much before seven-thirty."

Gregory knew how the railway services had gone to pieces in war-time Germany so there was nothing unusual about a train running several hours behind schedule when nearing the end of its journey. He just nodded and said:

"Well, it can't be helped. We'll wait here if we may; but the delay is annoying as I am naturally anxious to be able to report with my prisoner to the Field-Marshal as soon as possible."

"Yes," agreed the Major. Then suddenly snapping his fingers he exclaimed: "But I have it! If I had been fully awake I should have thought of it before. The reason I am up so early is that I must see a man in Berlin before he goes on duty this morning. What is to prevent your coming in my car with me?"

As Gregory accepted the offer he felt like laughing; he was so tickled with the idea that an officer of Hitler's Storm-Troopers should actually be providing him with transport back to the Capital which he was so anxious to reach. He had been by no means certain that he would be able to secure accommodation on the train without facing the searching questions of the local railway transport officer and on their arrival in Berlin he knew that at any moment he might be asked to produce identification papers which he had not got. But here was this heaven-sent offer to travel in comfort, and free of charge, with a man whose uniform alone would render Freddie and himself immune from all questioning so long as they were with him.

An orderly appeared with the Major's breakfast and Freddie noticed with interest that in spite of the rationing it consisted of a good-sized gammon-rasher, coffee, rolls, butter and apple *confiture*.

With a wave of his hand the Major instructed the orderly to bring two more breakfasts but his politeness did not extend to waiting for his guests. Tucking a paper napkin into his stiff uniform collar he sat himself down at once and lowering his head began to guzzle as though his very life depended upon the speed with which he consumed his food.

In due course two more gammon-rashers and another jug of *Ersatz* coffee arrived, upon which Gregory gave Freddie a swift look and, tucking his paper serviette into the top of his collar, set-to with a most admirable imitation of the Major's manners, that the airman did his best to follow.

"Aren't you going to join us?" Gregory asked Wentsich with

83

his mouth full of ham and bread-and-butter. But the *Ober-Lieutenant* shook his head.

"I don't go off duty until seven o'clock and I have my breakfast then; but I'll keep you company with another drink in the meantime."

As soon as they had finished breakfast the fat Major stood up and said: "We'll start at once, then I shall have plenty of time to drop you at the Air Ministry before I keep my appointment."

"Danke Schön, Herr Major," Gregory murmured, but he felt no gratitude at all for this new offer; in fact, it perturbed him exceedingly. He had counted on the Major's dropping them 'somewhere in Berlin', which would have left them free to follow their own devices; whereas, now that he intended to set them down at the Air Ministry, it meant that they would at least have to make a pretence of inquiring there for Goering. And once inside the Air Ministry with a British Officer in R.A.F. uniform as his companion, Gregory felt that it might be anything but easy to get out again.

Wentsich rang for the Major's car and, having thanked the *Ober-Lieutenant* for his kindness, they went downstairs out into the still dark street where the car was waiting.

It was not a big car, as the Germans were economizing petrol and, in fact, no cars were on the roads at all now except those in use for the Fighting Services and official business. Nevertheless, they made a steady thirty miles an hour towards Berlin and did even better when they got on to the broad *Autobahn* between Wittenberg and Potsdam. By ten-past six they were running through the suburbs of the Capital and a quarter of an hour later, in the grey light of dawn, the car pulled up in front of the Air Ministry.

Gregory was about to get out when the Major checked him.

"Ein Augenblick," he called. "It is unlikely that the Field-Marshall will be in his office as early as this. Let us inquire, and if he is not you can come on with me and we can have a second breakfast together after I have done my business."

Cursing inwardly, Gregory had smilingly to agree. The Major sent his chauffeur into the building to make the inquiry; the man returned to say that the Field-Marshal had not slept in his flat at the Air Ministry that night and it was not known at what hour he would arrive.

"Perhaps we had better wait," suggested Gregory hopefully, but the Major would not hear of it; insisting that his own business, although important, would take only a few moments, and that it was senseless for the *Herr Oberst* to kick his heels in a waiting-room when he might be doing justice to a meal.

Gregory having agreed to this with another false smile, the car drove on towards the Wannsee quarter and pulled up outside a big private house in a fine residential district. The Major then left them and went inside; but as his chauffeur remained in the car it was impossible for Gregory and Freddie to slip away as they would have liked to have done.

Ten minutes later the Major came out again and beckoned to them from the doorstep. "My business is done," he called, "and my friend invites you both to breakfast; he is anxious to meet the English flying-officer."

There was nothing for it but that they should accept the invitation, so they got out and accompanied the Major into the house. The friend proved to be another officer of Black Guards; a fair, thin paunchy man with almost white eyelashes, whose name was Blauhoff. He spoke English well and, while maintaining a smiling, urbane manner, questioned Charlton exhaustively; not so much upon the British Air Force, about which a flying-officer would naturally be averse to disclosing any details, but regarding events in London and the state of England generally.

Freddie stood up to the ordeal well, as he had an unshakable conviction that Britain would win the war and that the Government was neglecting no possible opportunity to mobilize her resources with speed and efficiency.

In consequence, he came out of the business with credit and the German got little satisfaction from him. Even when Blauhoff made sarcastic remarks about the amazingly poor quality of British propaganda Charlton innocently assured him that although there was certainly a great deal of muddle at the Ministry of Information when it was first started that was only to be expected in a country where propaganda had been deemed quite unnecessary up to the outbreak of the war: and that, in any case, much more competent people were now being given jobs there, as a consequence of which his host could rest assured that in the long run it would function with extreme efficiency.

The talk then turned on Finland and the new crisis that had arisen there. News had just come through that the Finns had offered to withdraw their troops if the Russians would do the same; which demonstrated beyond question the Finns' pacific intentions. But Blauhoff said that he did not think that the Russians would accept the offer. In addition to a withdrawal of the Finnish Army they were demanding the surrender of certain islands in the Gulf of Finland which together with the bases that they had now established on the coast of Estonia would give them control of the whole of the Eastern Baltic; and now that they had decided to exert pressure on Finland again it looked as though they had made up their minds to have what they wanted.

Gregory and Freddie did not like their host at all but they could not quarrel with the breakfast he provided. It was an excellent meal and yet one more demonstration of the fact which Gregory already knew: that, however short of food the German people had to go, the Nazi officials denied themselves nothing.

When they had finished they all left the house together. Blauhoff drove off to his office while Putzleiger insisted upon driving his passengers back to the Air Ministry.

It was now just after eight o'clock and, knowing the early hour at which all Germans start work, Gregory thought it quite possible that Goering had by this time arrived at the Air Ministry; that is, if he was in Berlin at all—a point upon which Gregory was by no means certain.

As they pulled up in front of the big building he extended his hand to the Major and thanking him for his kindness began to wish him a hearty farewell; but the Major would have none of it and insisted on accompanying them into the hallway, where Gregory was forced to make his inquiry for Goering in front of his jovial but infuriatingly persistent escort.

One of the uniformed clerks behind the long 'Inquiry' counter in the big hall informed them that the Field-Marshal had not yet appeared so the Major promptly asked at what time he was expected. An inquiry was put through to one of Goering's secretaries and ten minutes later an answer came down that he would not be at the Ministry at all that day as he was staying at Karinhall. his house outside Berlin, but that anyone who had special business could go there and apply for an interview.

To Gregory's fury Putzleiger immediately said: "Come along, then, I will drive you out to Karinhall; it is no great distance."

"But really, *Herr Major*," Gregory protested, "I don't feel that we can trespass on your time like this."

"Not a bit of it, my dear fellow," came the prompt answer. "Now I'm in Berlin I shall spend the whole day here, but I have nothing at all to do this morning. In being of assistance to you I am serving our great Air Chief, and when you see him you

86

might perhaps—er—casually mention my name in that connection. In any case it would be a pleasure to see you safely to your destination."

In vain Gregory tried to persuade the Major that he had done more than enough for them but he declared that he had never seen Goering's famous mansion, Karinhall, and that this was an excellent opportunity for him to do so. Quite clearly he had no intention of being deprived of it or of this chance of getting his name mentioned to Goering as a zealous Nazi, so yet again Gregory had to give in and they set off in the car once more, this time heading for the northern suburbs of the Capital.

Many of the smaller private traders in Berlin had already been forced to close their shops, which made the outer suburbs more than usually dreary and depressing, but they were soon out in the open country and the bright cold air helped to refresh Gregory and Freddie after the exhausting hours of their sleepless night. By half-past nine they arrived at the gates of the great park which surrounded the country-residence that Goering had turned into a palace, rivalling those of the old kings of Prussia, by the almost limitless outpouring of some of the millions which were his share of the loot that the Nazis had taken from the German nation.

At the gates they were halted by grey-clad members of Goering's special bodyguard and had to undergo a most rigorous questioning, but at last Putzleiger was given a pass for himself, his chauffeur and his car to enter the grounds and Gregory one for Charlton and himself to go up to the house. As an added precaution, apparently to see that none of them left the car while driving through the estate, one of the bodyguard jumped on the running-board to accompany them.

They ran up the mile-long drive and the bodyguard directed the chauffeur to a big car-park at one side of the great mansion. As Putzleiger had not come on business he was told that he could not be allowed inside the house and their escort expressed his intention of accompanying him on a walk round the building; while Gregory and Charlton, having been questioned by yet another official, were directed to cross the great open space in front of the mansion and present their pass to the man on the front door. At last they were able to shake the Major off, and having parted from him with many expressions of goodwill they left the car-park to walk across the open expanse of gravel.

It was the first time for many hours that Gregory and Freddie had been alone and that the airman was able to give expression to the worry he was feeling. As Putzleiger had been present when Gregory had been questioned by the guards on the gate he had had to stick to his story that he was bringing a British Air-officer prisoner whom the Field-Marshal wished to question personally. They could not possibly, therefore, turn round and go out again without entering the building and between the car-park and the front door of the mansion there was no place where they could conceal themselves.

A hundred yards away on the steps of the portico a small group of the grey-clad guards had already noticed them and were eyeing them casually; and Freddie's first swift glance round the grounds had shown him that other guards were posted here and there in positions where they could keep a look-out over the gardens, so it was out of the question to try to run for it; they would be shot before they had covered twenty yards. They could not go back and must go on, but he was grimly antici-pating the moment when they got into the house and were questioned by somebody in authority. Gregory's story about Goering's wishing to see his prisoner would soon be found to be quite untrue and wherever he said that he came from a long-distance telephone call would be quite sufficient to disclose the fact that he was not whom he said he was at all. The fat would then be in the fire with a vengeance.

He glanced anxiously at Gregory, who had lit a cigarette and was walking forward apparently quite unperturbed.

"Well," he asked in an undertone, "what the hell do we do now"

Gregory suddenly turned and grinned at him. "Why, since the Nazis have already provided us with two breakfasts this morning I think it would be a good day to take lunch off Goering."

"Oh, stop fooling!" Freddie muttered angrily. "With all these damned guards about we daren't run for it, and once we're inside this place even your plausible tongue will never get us out."

"It is rather tricky, isn't it," Gregory admitted. "Just the toss of a coin as to whether we come out on our own feet or are carried out feet first. Of course, I could easily have held up old Putzleiger with my gun while you tackled the chauffeur on the way here. On a lonely stretch of road we could have tied them up, rolled them in the ditch and got away with their car."

"Then why in the name of thunder didn't you?"

"Because that wouldn't have enabled me to find out about

Erika or to get out of Germany. We'd only have been on the run again and risking our necks every moment of the day to no particularly good purpose; and it occurred to me that old Putzleiger might be Fate playing into our hands. I think this is the biggest gamble that I've ever taken, but now I'm here, by hook or by crook I mean to see Goering; after that our lives will probably depend upon the quality of the butter that he ate with his breakfast."

CHAPTER VIII

THE WAITING-ROOM OF THE BORGIA

As Gregory and Charlton had been talking they had crossed the open space and were now at the foot of the steps leading up to the great pillared portico. The grey-clad guards did not move forward to question them but the nearest gave the two visitors a long, searching look. It was the quiet, intent gaze that Gregory had noticed at times on the faces of good detectives when for the first time they saw a criminal who had just been arrested. He felt quite certain that the man was specially trained in remembering faces and that if he ever happened to run into Freddie or himself again he would know them instantly.

A uniformed porter was standing just inside the door and an officer of the guard was slowly walking up and down the great marble-tiled hall. Gregory produced his pass and showed it to the porter. The officer turned in his stride, came over, glanced at it and motioned with his hand to a doorway on the right. They walked through it and entered a small office.

A shaven-headed clerk with thick-lensed spectacles was seated there behind a desk and taking Gregory's pass he gave him in exchange a yellow form. Gregory glanced down it and read: "Interview desired with . . . . . . By appointment—or not . . . . . . Name of applicant, rank, etc . . . . . . Business upon which interview is requested."

He took up a pen from the desk and instead of filling up the form simply wrote across it in German:

"If Your Excellency would examine the inscription on the back of the enclosed you will realize that the sender is in possession of information which is of importance to you."

Opening his greatcoat he then unpinned the Iron Cross which General Count von Pleisen had given him and, asking

90

the clerk for an envelope, placed both the decoration and the form inside it. Having sealed the envelope he handed it back and said:

"I shall be grateful if you will have that conveyed to the Field-Marshall."

"The Field-Marshall is extremely busy," replied the clerk officiously; "much too busy to deal personally with officers' grievances; so sending up your decoration won't do you any good."

Gregory suddenly became the autocratic Prussian officer in a manner that positively startled Freddie. He froze the clerk with an icy stare as he snapped: "How dare you assume that I am an officer with a grievance! Obey my order instantly or the Field-Marshal shall hear of this."

The little Jack-in-office wilted visibly, banged a bell-push on his desk and stuttered: "If the *Herr Oberst* will be pleased to wait in the next room an orderly shall take this up at once."

The adjoining room proved to be a very much larger apartment. Its colour scheme was blue and gold; its furnishings were rich and elegant. Wood-fires on open grates—a rarity in Germany—were burning in two big fireplaces; papers, magazines and periodicals were scattered over a number of tables and the room contained between thirty and forty arm-chairs and sofas. There were between a dozen and twenty people already in it, sitting about reading and smoking, so it would have resembled a rich man's club-room had not the company been an extremely mixed one. There were several officers of the *Reichswehr,* Air Force and Black Guards, also a couple of well-dressed civilians; but the presence of three women and a peasant in a leather jacket, together with the way in which they all refrained from speaking to one another and kept a watchful eye upon the door as though expecting to be called at any moment, gave it the atmosphere of a dentist's waiting-room.

Gregory and Charlton selected an unoccupied sofa and sat down. How long they would have to wait they had no idea but it seemed probable that it would be a long time if all the people already gathered there had appointments with the Field-Marshal. For ten minutes Gregory flicked over the pages of "Simplissimus", smiling at the caricatures of Chamberlain, Churchill and John Bull, which were the most prominent feature of Germany's leading comic; then he yawned, moved over to an arm-chair and, stretching out his feet, remarked:

"We may be here for hours yet so I think I'll get some sleep."

"Sleep?" echoed Freddie. "In this state of uncertainty! How *can* you?"

"Why not?" muttered Gregory. "We may be up again all to-night."

"I only hope to God we are!"

"So do I, since if we sleep at all to-night it may be for good. D'you know that little rhyme?

> '*A man's not old when his hair turns grey,*
> *A man's not old when his teeth decay,*
> *But it's time he prepared for his last long sleep*
> *When his mind makes appointments that his body can't keep.*'

Well, thank God, I'm a long way from having got to that stage yet, so when the time comes you can trust me to put up a show all right, but while we're waiting a spot of shut-eye won't do either of us any harm. We'll be all the fresher for it when we lunch with the Field-Marshal."

A major who was seated near-by eyed them curiously, as they were speaking in English, but no-one else took the least notice of them and while Freddie endeavoured to distract his racing thoughts by trying to puzzle out the captions beneath the pictures in a German illustrated-paper Gregory drifted off to sleep.

They did not lunch with Goering. At intervals during the morning many occupants of the room were quietly summoned from the door and had disappeared not to return again, but new arrivals had taken their places and it remained just about as full as when Gregory and Charlton had first entered it. Then, shortly after midday, a portly servant arrived and announced in unctuous tones:

"*Damen und Herren Schaft,* it is His Excellency's pleasure that you should receive his hospitality while you are waiting to be received; but I am asked to remind you that discretion regarding business matters should be observed while you are at table. Please to follow me."

Freddie roused Gregory and with the rest of the waiting company they followed the portly man down a corridor into a large dining-room. Gregory's eye lit with appreciation as it fell upon a long sideboard on which was spread a fine, cold collation and, nudging his friend, he whispered:

"There! What did I tell you? Even if we are not lunching *with* the Field-Marshal we are taking lunch off him."

92

"I wish I could be as certain about dinner," Freddie muttered.

"Oh, we'll probably dine with him personally. You must remember that I haven't had the chance to talk to him yet."

"You lunatic." Freddie suddenly laughed. "I can hardly believe that all this is real, you know. It'd be just like acting in a pantomime except for the kind of nightmare possibilities that lie behind it all."

Gregory grinned. "That's better. Just go on thinking of it that way. In any case, you've got nothing to fear so long as you're inside that uniform. They can only intern you."

"That's all very well, but I'm worried about you."

"Oh, I'm an old soldier. My motto always has been 'Eat, drink and be merry, for to-morrow we die', and those bottles over there look to me like excellent hock. Goering always does his friends well."

Freddie squeezed Gregory's arm. "Well, whatever happens, I'd like to tell you that I'm proud to have known you."

They had been standing a little apart but now they sat down at the long table and proceeded to enjoy the luncheon provided for them. There was very little general conversation, as the butler's reminder that the reasons for this strange company's having been brought together should not be discussed served to make everyone present extremely cautious. Remarks were confined to the barest civilities and as soon as the meal was over they were all shepherded back into the other room.

In spite of his anxiety Freddie was drowsy now; which, quite apart from the fact that he had been up all night, was not to be wondered at, seeing that during luncheon Gregory had deliberately filled him up with Liebfraumilch Kirkenstuck. By half past two quite a number of people who had arrived much later than themselves had been summoned to the presence, so it seemed as though Goering had his day mapped out and might not receive them for some time to come. In consequence, Freddie decided to follow Gregory's example and they both stretched themselves out in arm-chairs, side by side, to get what rest they could.

Coffee and cakes were brought at four o'clock but both Gregory and Charlton refused them and dozed on until after five. People had been coming and going nearly all the afternoon but now the room was almost empty and by six they found themselves alone, which gave Freddie his first chance to speak freely and to ask a question that had been bothering him ever since the morning.

"Why should you be so certain that Goering will see you because you sent up your Iron Cross? He'll probably imagine, as the little clerk said, that you're just an old soldier with a grouse."

"Oh, no, he won't," Gregory smiled. "That Cross is a super visiting-card. You see, every decoration has engraved on its back the name of the man upon whom it is conferred. My Iron Cross has von Pleisen's name on it, and von Pleisen was the head of the anti-Nazi conspiracy that darned nearly put paid to little old 'Itler and all his works, just on three weeks ago. The second Goering sees that name he'll know that whoever has brought the Cross is well worth talking to."

"I get you. Darned good idea, that. But, all the same, isn't there a risk that it will never get further than one of his staff—someone who'll just have us up and question us and once the cat is out of the bag put us through the hoop?"

"No. If that were liable to happen at all it would have happened already. Goering's got that Cross now and he's had it for hours; otherwise we should never have been kept waiting all this time. He has evidently decided to get through his routine work before he turns his attention to the intriguing little mystery as to why von Pleisen's Iron Cross should have been brought to him; but he'll personally see the man who brought it, all right."

"I must say that, in spite of everything, I'm looking forward to meeting him," Freddie remarked. "You see, aircraft has been my passion ever since I was old enough to collect toy aeroplanes and to read the simplest books about flying. In the last war the German pilots put up a magnificent show and, after von Richthofen, Goering was the best man they had, so he's always been one of my heroes. I never have been able to understand how such a brave sportsman got himself mixed up with these dirty, double-crossing Nazis."

"It was through his intense patriotism," Gregory replied quickly. "He absolutely refused to believe that Germany was defeated in the field and still declares that the Army was let down by the home front. After the Armistice he was ordered to surrender the planes of his famous air-circus to the Americans; instead, he gave a farewell party to all his officers at which they burnt their planes and solemnly pledged themselves to devote

94

the rest of their lives to lifting Germany from humiliation to greatness again."

"Yes, I know all that. But why should such people have allied themselves with blackguards like Hitler and Goebbels and Himmler?"

"Goering has never really been in sympathy with Goebbels and Himmler—in fact, they're poison to him—but Hitler is another matter. Say what you like, Hitler has extra-ordinary personal magnetism. In 1922, after having failed to make any headway on his own, Goering heard Hitler speak at Munich. He realized at once that here was a fanatic with all a fanatic's power to influence the masses—a man who was preaching the same doctrine as himself and one whose wild flights of oratory people would listen to, while they only shrugged their shoulders at his reasoned arguments. From that day they joined forces. Hitler did the talking while Goering secured for him his first really influential audiences and spent his own wife's fortune on entertaining for the Party, thereby giving Hitler a back-ground that he had never had before. He is a brilliant organizer and it was he who planned, step by step, Hitler's rise to power. The very fact that the two men are utterly unlike in character makes them a perfect combination and Hitler owes every bit as much to Goering as Goering does to Hitler."

"Is that really so?" Freddie raised an eyebrow. "I thought Goering was just an honest, bluff fellow who had been a bit misled, and, having been the head of Hitlers' personal body-guard in the early days, had risen with him."

"Not a bit of it," Gregory laughed. "Hitler is the visionary —the dreamer of great dreams; but he lacks courage both physically and mentally. He listens first to one man then to another and is always swayed in his opinions by the last-comer. It's absolute torture to him to make decisions. Goering, on the other hand, is a realist—a man of action, with an extraordinary ability to assess values and get right to the root of a matter almost instantly. He is a man of enormous energy and a tireless worker.

"While Hitler has lain in bed at Berchtesgaden—as he does on many a morning—staring out across the Bavarian Alps into a mythical future where by move after move Germany gains sufficient strength to dominate the world, Goering has one by one transformed those dreams of his mythical partner into realities.

"When Hitler came to power in 1933 Germany had not even

an Air Ministry. Goering became Air Minister and immediately formed the Air Sports League for teaching young Germans to fly. Two years later he gave them uniforms and foreign statemen woke up to the fact that without their knowing anything about it Germany had the strongest Air Force in the world—an Air Force that has been a threat to the peace of Europe ever since. All that was done by Goering, secretly, swiftly and with incredible efficiency. He himself is not only an ace airman but a brilliant engineer. There are probably few people in the world who know more about the construction and engines of aircraft than Hermann Goering. He chose the types; he created the factories for the thousand and one parts and products necessary to build and supply this great fighting-arm. Yet at the same time he was acting as Prime Minister of Prussia; re-creating the German army, playing a great part in the diplomatic sphere and doing a hundred other jobs as well."

"Yes," Freddie murmured, "everyone knows that he holds scores of posts and has a different uniform for every day, but I had no idea that he was a really brainy chap; he doesn't look it."

Gregory grinned. "Take a good look at that fine head of his when you see him, and try to recall some of his earlier photographs when he wasn't quite so fat. The weight he's put on makes his appearance deceptive now, but doesn't affect the brains inside the skull. His forehead is not only broad but high and the width of his cranium from ear to ear gives him tremendous driving force for the application of his ideas. Nose, chin, eyes, ears and mouth are all beautifully balanced and any phrenologist will tell you that it is *balance*—which prevents one quality in a man from developing to the detriment of others —plus skull capacity, that is the index of real power."

"Yes, I remember those early photographs but of, course, one has come to regard him since as the fat play-boy of the Nazi Party who loves food and drink and showy splendour."

"He does," Gregory agreed; "and that's why he's far and away the most popular of the Nazi leaders. People like a jovial man who has human qualities and Goering has plenty of them. He's a romantic, too, and was desperately in love with his first wife, the beautiful Karin von Fock, after whom this place is named. Everyone knows that he adores his children and is passionately fond of animals. He has made it a penal offence to destroy many kinds of birds and to ill-treat dogs and horses; yet he is utterly ruthless so far as human life is concerned. In any spot of bother his orders always are, 'Shoot first and inquire afterwards'. In addition to organizing Germany's Five-Year Plan for the reconditioning of every single industry in the country he has organized every *Putsch* and blood-bath for which the Nazis have been responsible. That's why the Germans have nick-named him 'Iron Hermann'."

"What an extraordinary mixture he must be."

"No. It's just that he was born out of his time. He ought to have been a Spanish *conquistador* or a Saracen general like Suliman the Magnificent. They recognized only those who were for their religion or their country, and were capable of the most incredible barbarities against anyone who opposed them. He has the same mentality. Just like them, too, he has a passion for personal adornment and love of surrounding himself with riches and splendour. After all, the gilt and marble of this place is only the modern version of a Borgia's palace and, as you know, beneath such places there were always dungeons, torture-chambers and an execution room."

Freddie Charlton shivered slightly as he glanced round the great apartment with its rich carpet and ornate furnishings. It seemed impossible to believe that perhaps under their very feet there lay cells where men suffered and died; and that before the night was out he and Gregory might be thrown into them. Yet he knew that Gregory was right.

Unnoticed, the door had opened quietly behind them and a voice suddenly said: "His Excellency, the Field-Marshal, will receive the *Herr Oberst* now."

CHAPTER IX

"HE WHO SUPS WITH THE DEVIL NEEDS A LONG SPOON"

T HEY both stood up and Freddie followed Gregory to the door, but the official raised his hand.

"It is only the Colonel whom His Excellency has consented to receive."

Gregory glanced at Freddie and said in English: "He doesn't know anything about you yet, as I didn't wish to confuse the issue by mentioning that I had brought anyone with me. You'd better wait here, I think."

It was the first time since the plane had been shot down nearly three weeks before that the two had been called upon to face the possibility of a permanent separation, and in that instant Freddie really realized how much he had come to admire Gregory and to depend on him. But now that the moment had come when he was to be left alone to face whatever fate had in store for him he did not allow any trace of his apprehension to show. With a calmness that, in turn, won Gregory's admiration he just smiled and said:

"Well, good luck. I'll be seeing you."

Gregory smiled back. "Don't worry about me if I'm a long time—in fact, you can take it that the longer I am the better things will be going."

The official led Gregory across the hall to a lift which rose with the speed of an American installation; then down a corridor and into a room where two of the grey-clad bodyguard were sitting. They immediately stood up and while one said politely, "Permit me to relieve you of your pistol, *Herr Oberst*," the other, murmuring, "You will excuse this formality," slipped his hands under Gregory's armpits, from behind, and down over his pockets to his hips to make sure that he was not carrying any other weapon. He handed over his automatic and submitted smilingly to the swift patting of the expert frisker, then the first man beckoned him to a great pair of double-doors and, tiptoeing forward, gently opened one of them.

Next moment Gregory found himself in Goering's vast, dimly-lit study. The door closed softly behind him and he walked forward across a great empty space of thick pile carpet, vaguely glimpsing the big pictures that adorned the walls—portraits of Frederick the Great, Bismarck, Mussolini, Kaiser Wilhelm II, von Richthofen, the ex-Crown Prince, Napoleon, Balbo and Hitler—but his mind was on the powerful figure at the very end of the room, seated behind a fine table-desk. On it there were no papers; only writing impedimenta and a scribbling-block, flanked by two great silver candelebra holding a forest of tall, lighted, wax candles.

From them came the only light in the great apartment but it threw up the big head, forceful face and enormous shoulders of the Marshal. Behind him there was a panel of flaming red and gold, in the centre of which was suspended a huge executioner's sword—his symbol, since it was he who had reintroduced beheading into Germany as a quick, clean death for those who differed from him in their political opinions.

Gregory had ample time to observe these details as he covered the distance between the door and the desk, but immediately he came sharply to attention in front of it Goering wasted no time.

Displaying the Iron Cross in his hand he said:

"Where did you get this?"

"It was given to me, Excellency, by General Count von Pleisen himself."

"Why?"

"For services rendered, Excellency."

"When?"

"At eight o'clock on the night of November the 8th."

Goering raised an eyebrow. "What service did you render?"

"I brought him the list of the Inner Gestapo, whose duty it is to spy upon the high officers of the Army, and a letter from the Allied statesmen guaranteeing Germany a new deal if the Army leaders would overthrow Hitler and sponsor a freely-elected Government."

"Who are you?"

"My name is Gregory Sallust. I am an ex-officer of the last war, now employed as a British Secret Service agent."

99

"You must know that by making such disclosures to me you have signed your own death warrant."

"Yes, Excellency?"

"Then why do you come here?"

"Because I'm in love."

For a second Goering frowned but Gregory's unwavering gaze held his and he saw that his apparently crazy visitor was, after all, not mad. His face relaxed a trifle as he said:

"Well, why should you virtually throw away your life by coming to me about it?"

"Because, Excellency, I believe you to be the only man in Germany who may be able to give me the information that I am so anxious to have about the woman I care for more than anything in the world."

Goering sat back and thrust his hands into the pockets of his breeches. "Give you information? All I'm going to give you, my rash friend, is a bullet."

"Naturally, Excellency. I am prepared for that. All I ask is that you will be generous enough to give me the information first and the bullet afterwards."

Suddenly Goering laughed. *"Lieber Gott!* You must love this woman pretty desperately."

"I do, Excellency. I have had a most interesting life and, for the times in which we live, a reasonably long one. She is now the only thing that matters to me and if I can find out what has happened to her I am quite prepared to die."

"Mr. Sallust, you are a brave man."

"People have been kind enough to say so, Excellency."

"Very well. Who is this woman?"

"Erika von Epp."

"Who?" Goering jumped to his feet with a swiftness amazing in a man of his bulk. *"Who* did you say?"

It was the decisive moment and Gregory brought all his biggest guns to bear in the attack. "I spoke of that old friend of yours for whom you imported a hundred cases of French champagne free of duty, only just before the war—Cliquet 1928, several bottles of which I enjoyed with her at *Das Kleine Schloss,* in Munich—of the lovely girl for whose sake you protected the Jewish armaments millionaire, Hugo Falkenstein, until he was fool enough to quarrel with Hitler—of the clever woman who was invaluable to you in your secret negotiations with her friends among the Army chiefs—of that amazing Erika who is as brave, as generous and as unscrupulous as yourself; who is more beautiful than either the Dietrich or the Garbo and yet has said that if fate permitted she would divorce the Count von Osterberg in order to become Mrs. Gregory Sallust."

"*So!*" As Goering brought the word out he lowered himself into his chair again. For a moment he sat silent, then his whole manner changed completely. He spoke reminiscently, as one old friend to another. "Life was a hard school for Erika, as it was for all of us *Hochwohlgeboren* Germans after the last war. When Falkenstein died she swore that she would never love again and I would have bet a million on it. Her marriage to von Osterberg was made only to please her father before he died and the Count agreed to give her absolute freedom. If it is true that she is prepared to divorce him and marry you—an Englishman —you must be a very remarkable man."

"As I shall shortly be facing a firing-squad there can be no point in my either concealing or distorting the facts, Excellency."

Goering smiled. "No. From the look of you I should think that you could be the Prince of Liars on occasion, but men like you do not lie on matters like this. So Erika really wanted to marry you? I must say that that fact alone makes me wish to know more about you. Sit down and help yourself to a cigarette."

"Thank you," said Gregory with a relief that he did not show. He felt that now he had succeeded in intriguing the Marshal he had at least cleared the first fence in his audacious plan. The cigarette that he took from the lapis-lazuli box was fat, round and long. The first puff of it told a connoisseur like Gregory that it was made of the very finest Macedonian tobacco. He said appreciatively:

"I haven't had anything so good as this to smoke since I entered Germany when I had to chuck away all I had left of my own Sullivans."

"They still come through," Goering shrugged, "and as the war progresses it will become still easier to obtain them."

"That opinion is not shared in high quarters in London," Gregory remarked amiably. As though he had touched a spring, the Marshal suddenly became alive—dynamic:

"Of course not! They think they've got us with their blockade, don't they? That all they have to do is to sit tight on the Maginot Line and hold the seas and that Germany will gradually be starved into surrender as she was in 1918. But they're wrong. In 1918 Germany and her allies formed one block entirely surrounded by enemy countries with the exception of

101

outlets through Holland, Denmark and Sweden. To-day only
one of Germany's frontiers is definitely closed by an enemy army
—the French frontier from Luxembourg to Basle. From any
other quarters we can draw supplies to supplement the vast
stocks that we laid in before the war and our internal arrangements for making the most of our own resources are infinitely
better, so we can carry on for years; and it is I who tell you this
—I, Hermann Goering who planned it all."

Gregory bowed, feeling it a good sign that the Marshal
seemed so willing to discuss the war, and went on: "Your
amazing organizing abilities are well known, Marshal, to anyone
who is even slightly acquainted with the new Germany; but
what is going to happen when a real war starts?"

"You mean a *Blitzkrieg* or the launching of a campaign on
the lines of the last war entailing the movement of hundreds of
thousands of men?"

"Yes. I can well believe that you have very wisely anticipated your normal requirements in vital commodities for a
number of years and that with the supplies you can acquire
through neutrals you will be able to ensure your population
sufficient food to keep them from open revolt almost indefinitely; but once a total war breaks out you will have to use
millions of gallons of petrol a day to keep your huge air force
in the air and will be called on to replace the enormous wastage
of munitions, tanks. equipment. Are you quite so sure that the
structure won't then crack under the strain?"

Goering smiled grimly. "Like most other people you still
think in terms of 1914-18. But this is a different kind of war and
we hold the trump cards because of our geographical position
and, to be frank, our lack of scruple. If we choose we can carry
the war into Norway, Sweden. Denmark, Holland, Belgium,
Switzerland, Hungary or Rumania, any day we wish, and overrun these countries before the Democracies could possibly
establish defensive fronts in them. That is why all these little
nations must continue to do what we tell them whether they
like it or not. On the other hand, the Democracies cannot attack
us through any of our neutral neighbours, because that would
mean abandoning their high principles. For the same reason
they cannot threaten them and therefore cannot get the assistance out of them that we can."

"I appreciate your frankness, Marshal, in admitting that
Germany is prepared to use methods which are quite obviously
debarred to the Democracies."

102

"Why should I *not* be frank with you? Britain and France can't have it both ways. During the peace they made the League of Nations their instrument—used it in a thousand ways to further their own interests under the guise of securing the so-called rights of the small nations. Now there is war how can they throw overboard the League and all the commitments with which it has landed them? In consequence the Democracies fight with one hand tied behind their backs whereas we, who have never pretended to have any other aim but to secure for Germany her rightful place in the world, fight with both hands free."

"That, admittedly, gives you a big advantage for the time being," Gregory nodded, "but in the event of a great land offensive the whole situation might change entirely."

"Who said there would ever be a great land offensive? The Democracies do not wish to repeat the blood-baths of the Somme and Paschendaele so they certainly will not attack our Western Wall—which is infinitely stronger than any of our defensive lines in the last war. And where else can they attack us? Nowhere; without infringing the neutrality of one of the small nations and thereby having world opinion swing against them. They won't do that, so it's up to us; and it might suit us best to remain on the defensive while we develop the resources of our neighbours until the point is reached where we are entirely independent of the outside world."

"Fortunately—or unfortunately, as the case may prove—I gather that some of your more impatient colleagues are not in agreement with such a policy?" Gregory replied.

"No," Goering admitted angrily. 'The fools cannot see that, given a little time, Germany will be in just as strong a position as if the Reich extended from the northern coast of Norway to the Black Sea—and that, mark you, without the unnecessary sacrifice of a single man or plane. These neutrals, countries which comprise by far the largest part of Europe, dare not resist any reasonable demand that we choose to make; and what more could we possibly ask? To march into them would only mean the destruction of their economic systems; whereas while we refrain from waging war upon them their industries remain going concerns which are being used for the benefit of the Reich."

It was grand strategy upon the Napoleonic scale, and Gregory admitted to himself the sense and force of the Marshal's argument but he was given little time to ponder it as Goering went on almost at once, with a change of tone:

"But we're not here to discuss the European situation. Tell me as briefly as you can what you've been doing in Germany."

Gregory very wisely refrained from saying that it would take the whole evening to do justice to the full story of his adventures, but he was an excellent *raconteur* and he meant to attempt the game by which Scheherazade, in the Arabian Nights, managed to postpone her execution from day to day believing that although he had no chance of keeping Goering amused for a thousand and one evenings his tale would still be incomplete when the Marshal's next appointment was due and he would reprieve his audacious visitor until after at least one more session—or perhaps two—by which time it was unlikely that he would be quite so fixed in his determination to have the story-teller shot. In consequence Gregory started at the first week of the war when as an old soldier he had been desperately anxious to get back into the Army but found himself unable to do so owing to his being over the age limit for a new commission or even acceptance as a private.

That won Goering's sympathy at once and he listened intently as Gregory spoke of the joy, at such a time of dejection, with which he had accepted the most unexpected offer of a secret mission that would enable him to serve his country. He told the story of his first secret visit to Germany, his meeting with Erika von Epp and his escape only to be interned in Holland, with such vividness that Goering alternately bellowed with laughter as he heard of the impudent tricks by which Gregory had escaped arrest or nodded with the appreciation of one brave man for another as he learned how Gregory had shot his way out of the traps which the Gestapo had set for him.

By the time Gregory had reached the point in his adventures where he found himself caught and about to be murdered by Marxists in the East End of London there was quite a pile of cigarette butts in the big ash-tray; yet Goering remained enthralled and with obvious annoyance drew a telephone receiver from a hidden ledge under his desk in answer to a low buzzing.

"What's that?" he said. "A quarter past eight? *Gott im Himmel!* They have been waiting dinner for me for a quarter of an hour? All right. Tell them that I am still in conference. Lay places for two in the private dining-room, bring cocktails now and have dinner ready in a quarter of an hour."

104

Replacing the receiver he looked across at Gregory. "I have guests, but this house is always full of people and for once they must do without me—at all events till later. I wouldn't, for anything in the world, miss hearing the rest of your extraordinary exploits. You must dine with me."

Gregory hid his inward satisfaction as he bowed his thanks. One really long, uninterrupted session with Goering was even better than several short ones between which the mood of his dynamic listener might change, and already he felt confident that he had the situation so well in hand that the unpleasant subject of shooting parties would not be raised again. He was conceited enough to look forward to the expression on Freddie Charlton's face when the airman learned that Goering had actually abandoned his guests to entertain him privately and he hoped that Freddie was not feeling the suspense of his long wait too badly. If Goering was the sportsman Gregory believed him to be they would both be given a safe conduct out of Germany and, if Erika was still alive, be able to take her with them.

Champagne-cocktails were brought by a white-coated barman who mixed them as required on a trolley that he had wheeled in. "Don't take any notice of that fellow," said Goering, tossing off the first, "but go on with your story. He's a deaf-mute—that's why I gave him his job."

In the next quarter of an hour Gregory got as far as his departure for Paris in search of Madame Dubois and they sank three champagne-cocktails apiece; then a butler appeared and announced that His Excellency was served. Goering jumped up and with a purposeful stride led the way across the corridor to a small private dining-room that was furnished in red and gold.

"What will you drink?" he asked at once. "Champagne or hock?"

"If I were dining with anyone else I'd say champagne but with you I would prefer to drink hock."

With a shrewd glance at his guest Goering said: "I see you're a connoisseur," and turning to the butler he ordered: "Have a couple of bottles of my Marcobrunner Cabinet 1900 sent up."

"1900!" murmured Gregory. "By Jove! I didn't know that there were any 1900 hocks still in existence."

Goering had already started on the *hors d'œuvre*. "I have a little, and it's remarkable how these great wines last. The smaller ones would have turned to dish-water years ago but this is still perfect—marvellous."

"I remember drinking some of the famous '68's when I was a boy and although they were then over forty years old they hadn't turned a hair. My father had some of the '68 Schloss Johannesburg."

"Beautiful—beautiful; I, too. remember drinking that classic vintage when I was a boy. There are no wines in the world to touch our great German wines."

"There I thoroughly agree with you," Gregory smiled, "and the proof of the pudding is in the eating. People talk about burgundy as the king of wines but I've never heard of anyone paying more than two pounds for a classic burgundy, yet one must pay six pounds a bottle if one wants the very finest hock."

The bulky Marshal preened himself as though he, instead of Charlemagne, was personally responsible for the creation of the great vineyards on the Rhine. "Six pounds——" he said, "I'd pay ten to anybody who could find me more of some of the rarities I've got."

When the bottles of Marcobrunner arrived Gregory noticed that they bore the supreme honour paid only to superlative products of the vineyards—which is very rarely seen outside Germany or even in it—gold foil under their capsules, covering the whole of their long necks. When his glass had been filled he sniffed the wine and sipped it slowly. It was a dark golden colour and almost as heavy as Tokay with that wonderful flavour of subdued richness that only great age can give to a wine which has been sweet as honey when young.

"Don't play with it, man—drink it!" said Goering genially. "There's plenty more in the bottles." He took two big mouthfuls, rinsing it round his mouth with delight. "That's the way to get the real flavour of a wine."

"Since we have a bottle apiece I promise you I won't leave a sip in mine," Gregory assured him with a smile; "I was only prolonging this amazing treat. There's nothing I can say about the wine; it is beyond all praise."

"Good. Now, don't take any notice of the servants but go on with your story."

While the rich courses came and went Gregory described his second war-time visit to Germany and the meal was finished before he had reached the point where Hans Foldar's cottage was attacked. The two bottles were now empty of their priceless contents and for the first time in many minutes Goering interrupted to ask:

"Will you have cognac or kirsch?"

106

'Kirsch, thanks," said Gregory at once. He did not doubt that the Marshal's cognac was of the same regal quality as his hock but he knew that the Germans had the extraordinary habit of icing fine brandy—which in his opinion entirely ruined its flavour—and old kirsch being a liqueur in which rich Germans specialize he thought it a safer and more interesting bet.

"Right, then." Goering stood up. "We'll move back to the other room and drink our liqueurs there."

When they reached his splendid sanctum he took up a position in front of the mantelpiece with his legs splayed wide apart and his hands thrust deep into his breeches pockets. "Go on," he said. "How did you manage to get that colonel's uniform and make your way back to Berlin?"

As Gregory told him he frowned when he heard of von Lutz's death, for he had known and liked the Baron; but he laughed uproariously when he heard how *Ober-Lieutenant* Wentsich and Major Putzleiger had assisted in getting the fugitives safely out of the district in which they were being hunted.

"And now," said Gregory when he had finished his story, "as Erika is such an old friend of yours I feel sure you must know what has happened to her. Is she alive or dead?"

"Alive."

"Thank God for that. Is she in prison?"

"No." Goering grinned. "Directly the *Putsch* failed she had the impudence to come straight to me. I ought to have had her shot—she deserved it; but—you know what she is—she talked me into getting her safely out of the country to Finland. She has relatives living in Helsinki—the von Kobenthals."

"You did? Well done! I had an idea that she'd come to you and I felt certain that if she did you'd help her."

"Why? There'd have been hell to pay if the *Fuehrer* had heard that I let her go. And think of the capital that might have been made out of such a story if Himmler or von Ribbentrop had got to hear of it! Those who are not for us are against us. Death is their portion, and at my hands they get it; old friends or new—it is all the same. The enemies of the Party are my enemies. She's an enemy of the Party and what induced me to spare her I can't think."

"I can. And it wasn't sentiment." The champagne-cocktails, the potent old hock and the kirsch that he was drinking had given Gregory complete self-confidence, so he added: "You've

107

had too many of your old friends shot for anyone to believe that you would allow sentiment to sway you."

"What was it, then?"

"Your genius for statecraft. You still talk about the Party as though it were a single entity—just as Stalin still talks of himself as a Communist, although he's nothing of the kind. You know as well as I do that there are now two Parties in Germany. You, von Raeder and the Generals are now at daggers drawn with von Ribbentrop, Himmler and the pro-Russians; while Hitler, whose opinions are taken one day from one group and another day from the other, gradually shrinks into the background."

"Do you dare to insinuate that I am conspiring against my *Fuehrer?*" Goering's big face was black and threatening.

"No. I believe that you are loyal to him but that circumstances are proving too strong for you. Every day Hitler becomes more and more of a cipher. While he sits there brooding in Berchtesgaden, constantly vacillating, utterly unable to make up his mind which of half a dozen policies he ought to follow whole-heartedly, you have found yourself forced to take an ever greater degree of power into your own hands."

Goering sighed. "There may be something in that, but I'm no traitor."

"I didn't suggest that you were; and there would be no cause for you to be if, as in the old days, Hitler's advisers were united; but now that they have split into two almost equally powerful camps you feel that in protecting yourself you're protecting Germany. You need all the support you can get to counter the moves of your enemies and to strengthen your hand for the day when the great show-down comes. That's why you spared Erika. Consciously or subconsciously you knew that she would be on your side and that as she is a woman of immense influence she could be useful."

"*Gott im Himmel,* Sallust! You're right—although I hate to have to admit it. For a foreigner you know a lot about us."

"Perhaps I know a little more than most foreigners, but not much. You forget that owing to your Press here being controlled the German people know very little of what goes on behind the scenes; in England we have our sources of information and all the broader issues are freely published. It's common knowledge in every English village that you and von Ribbentrop are at each other's throats over this Russian business."

The rich wines and subtle liqueur had also loosened Goering's tongue. "That madman!" he exclaimed, suddenly giving way to furious rage. "Think what he has done—think! —*think!* He has lost us Italy, Spain, Japan—and for what? These filthy Russian murderers who do nothing but stab us in the back; who can't send us one-tenth of the supplies they promised, as anyone who had travelled on their railways—let alone seen our secret-service reports—must have known. And look at the Baltic! Think of the disgrace, the loss of prestige in Germany's having to withdraw her communities that have been settled in the Baltic ports for centuries. And now this lunatic is urging Adolph to stage a *Blitzkrieg*. I only managed to stop that attack on Holland—planned for the end of last month— at the very last moment. What the hell do we want to attack Holland for—or any other neutral country—when, as I said only before dinner, we already have all these little peoples in the bag?

"And think of launching a *Blitzkrieg* at *this* time of year! I've a handful of ace pilots whom I can use for raids on English shipping, because they've done commercial flying over the North Sea for years, but in winter conditions most of my boys would lose themselves before they got half-way to London. It's crazy even to contemplate such a thing before the spring, and even then, it's taking a hellish gamble with my air force."

"I know," Gregory agreed. "Your game is to keep your air force intact as a constant threat which can be directed against any quarter—just as we kept our Grand Fleet intact in the last war. By risking it in a major action you've got everything to lose and nothing to gain."

"Of course. But people like von Ribbentrop don't know the first thing about grand strategy. He doesn't even know his own damned job; yet the fool must interfere with mine and constantly reiterate: 'We've got the finest air force in the world so why shouldn't we use it?'"

"Well, sooner or later you'll . . ." Gregory broke off short as the low buzzer sounded, and striding to his desk Goering picked up the telephone from the ledge under it.

"Hullo . . . what's that? . . . They have . . . Well, tell the Soviet Ambassador from me that they'll get more than they bargained for if the Finns call their bluff. Telephone that through at once and urge that no further step should be taken until he has seen me, and make an appointment for His Excellency to call on me at my flat in the Air Ministry as early as possible tomorrow morning."

He slammed down the receiver and turned back with a scowl to Gregory. "More trouble. The Russians have just broken off the broadcast of a musical programme to make a special announcement denouncing their seven-year-old non-aggression pact with Finland."

"That's bad," said Gregory. "D'you think they really mean business?"

"I'm afraid so. And Finland is another sphere of German influence. There are many Germans settled there. It will be a further blow to our prestige if we have to bring them home. I must think now what I can do to counteract this new aggravation with which von Ribbentrop's pro-Russian policy has landed us."

He strode up and down the room for a moment, then suddenly moved over to a bell and pressed it. He now showed not the least trace that he had drunk anything stronger than water as he spoke with abrupt detachment:

"Our talk has been most interesting but I can't give you any more of my time. I've told you what you want to know about Erika and, of course, it's quite impossible for me to release you, but I'm sure that you'll meet your end like a brave man."

For once in his life Gregory was taken utterly by surprise. When he first entered that room a little before seven o'clock he knew quite well that the odds were on his being sent out of it again within a few moments, straight down to the cells, and that his death would almost inevitably follow within a matter of hours. But every moment that he managed to remain there it had seemed that the odds of his eventually walking out of the room a free man had risen, until once he had got Goering interested in his story he considered that the chances were a good three to one in his favour. On his being asked to dine, which would give him at least another hour alone with the Marshal, he had felt confident that he was safe, apart from one chance in fifty that he might slip up in some unforeseen manner which would anger or insult his host. When dinner was done he had believed that even that last fence was safely past. They had drunk as much as would have put most ordinary men under the table, but they were both hardened drinkers so they could stand it, though it had loosened their tongues, filled them with well-being and created an atmosphere in which they had been talking and laughing as freely as if they were old friends. Before the

110

telephone rang Gregory would have bet all Lombard Street to a china orange that he would leave the Marshal not only with a safe conduct for Charlton and himself in his pocket but also with facilities to rejoin Erika if he wished to do so.

"Well?" asked Goering sharply. "What are you staring at?"

"You," said Gregory. "You can't really mean that you're going to have me shot after . . ."

The door at the far end of the room opened. Two of the grey guards stepped inside and came sharply to attention.

Goering shrugged. "Of course I am. What else did you expect? You're a very dangerous man and on your own confession you have committed enough acts against the German Reich to justify any court in condemning you to death a dozen times."

"I realize that," said Gregory swiftly, "but all's fair in love and war. The only difference between us as soldiers of fortune is that you're the greater and have been responsible for more deaths in the service of your country than I have in the service of mine. I confess that I'd hoped that once we had drunk wine together you'd let that weigh more with you than the fact that I've killed a dozen or so of your people. After all, with a world war on, what do a few lives matter between men like us whether they are lost on the battlefield or anywhere else?"

"They do not matter at all." Goering drew quickly on his cigarette. "But what *does* matter is that I should have talked to you so freely. Surely you don't think that I'd have done so if I'd had the least intention of allowing you to live?" With a swift gesture of his hand he signed to the guards to come forward.

CHAPTER X

GRAND STRATEGY

GREGORY now knew that he had been a fool to allow that rich wine and Goering's confidences to lull him into a false sense of security. Had 'Iron Hermann' drunk twice as much it would still not have deflected his judgment or influenced in the least any decision that he had already taken.

This was only one more proof of what Gregory himself had told Freddie Charlton earlier in the evening. Goering had a type of mentality no longer understood in civilized countries; the power to enjoy one moment and work the next without allowing his relations in one sphere to affect those in the other, although this division of his waking hours into watertight compartments often produced results which any modern person would stigmatize as utterly barbaric. Like a prince of the Renaissance he could derive enormous pleasure in supping with an amusing companion and experience the most friendly feelings for him, yet send the same man to torture and death an hour later because it seemed expedient to do so, and go to bed thinking of neither one act nor the other but of what he meant to do to-morrow.

The guards were already striding down the long room. Gregory knew that he had not a second to lose and that any form of pleading was utterly useless. He cursed himself for a brainless fool for having wasted all these precious hours when he had had Goering on his own and might have thrown out a dozen hints of secret knowledge which would have intrigued the Marshal so that, at worst, he would have been put in cold storage for the night or until Goering could spare the time to give him a second interview. As it was, like any cocksure boy who had pulled off a cheap triumph he had been content to drink and laugh and boast about his own adventures.

His thoughts raced furiously, flashing one after the other

through his mind with the speed of lightning, as was always the case when he was faced with a great emergency; yet it was not until the two guards came stiffly to attention, one on either side of him, that he spoke again.

"All right; just as you wish. I'll leave you to tackle the problem of Finland on your own, then."

Goering's jaw dropped at this supreme impertinence. "Finland?" he said. "What the hell do you know about Finland?"

"More than you do," lied Gregory with amazing calmness.

"D'you think they'll fight?" asked the Marshal with sudden interest.

"Yes—if they're properly handled."

"What do you mean by that?"

Gregory shrugged. "Send these men away and I'll tell you."

"If this is just an excuse to delay your execution and waste my time I'll give orders that you're to be made to rue the day you were born before you're finally shot."

"That's a deal. If I can prove to you that I'm worth listening to I get a straight bullet, but if you consider that I've wasted your time you hand me over to your thugs to do what they like with me."

"Do you understand what you may be letting yourself in for?"

"I've got a pretty shrewd idea."

Goering signed to the guards. "You may go. Now, Sallust, I'm ready to let you teach one of the leading statesmen of Europe his business—if you can."

Gregory relaxed, physically but not mentally. He knew that he was up against it as he had never been in his life before. Helping himself to another of the big Turkish cigarettes, he said: "May I have a map of Europe and another drink?"

"Certainly." The Marshal reached behind him and pressed a bell; then in six strides he crossed the room and flicked a switch which released a square of gorgeous tapestry. It whipped up on guides, disappearing through a slit at the top of the panel, to disclose a great map of Europe lit by concealed lighting. As he stepped back the white-clad, deaf-mute barman appeared wheeling in his trolley, which held the same array of bottles with the addition of a magnum of champagne in an ice-bucket.

"What would you like?" Goering asked; but his voice was no longer cordial. The question was put with the curt formality that he might have used when asking a clerk if a telegram had

113

been dispatched. He no longer showed the least trace of the alcohol he had drunk and his eyes were hard as he moved over to the trolley with brisk efficiency.

"Champagne, please," said Gregory, and at a sign from Goering the deaf-mute opened the magnum. As soon as two goblets had been filled he signed to the man again to leave them and turned back to Gregory.

"Now let's hear what you've got to say about Finland."

Gregory took a drink, set down his glass and began to speak with a clarity and rapidity that made it very difficult to interrupt him. "You know what happened to Russia after the last world war. Four years of revolution and civil war devastated the country from end to end. When the Reds at last succeeded in suppressing the Whites so much blood had been spilled that Russia was utterly exhausted. Her whole social structure was in ruins; added to which, the Bolsheviks had not a friend in the world who would assist them with loans or trade or technical experts to help them bring order out of chaos. After their defeat in the Polish campaign of 1920 they abandoned all idea of trying to carry Communism across Europe by fire and sword. The only thing they could do was to crawl back into their own kennel, lick their wounds, clean it up as best they could and endeavour to keep themselves free of further quarrels. The one thing they needed was peace—peace internal and external; not five years of peace but fifty; a solid half-century of peace during which they could exploit the vast resources of their enormous territories—in the same way that the Americans exploited the United States in the '60's and '70's of the last century—so that in time they might become as rich as the United States and as independent.

"From 1920 on they realized that they had everything to lose by risking further wars. The only thing that they had to fear was an attack while they were still devoting all their energies to the construction of the new Russia. In consequence, the whole of Russian strategy, directed by Marshal Voroshilov, has since then been based upon the defensive; in the belief that Russia might be called upon to resist aggression herself but would never never, *never* become an aggressor."

"Yes, yes, I know all that," Goering broke in impatiently.

"Of course you do; but I must state the basic facts if I am to tell you anything," Gregory replied, quite unperturbed, and he rapidly continued. "After the World War Germany also was left exhausted and disorganized, but owing to the fact that she

114

was far in advance of Russia before the World War opened she was able to recover much more quickly. With the coming to power of the National Socialist Party Germany began to grow strong again. By 1935 it was obvious to every thinking man that in a few more years she would once more constitute a threat to the peace of Europe; and such people began to ask themselves what form that threat would take.

"Would Germany endeavour to revenge herself for her defeat by entering into another death-struggle with the Western Powers or would she march East into Poland, Czechoslovakia and the Ukraine? Nobody knew for certain, but the Nazi leaders made it abundantly clear, by the Anti-Comintern Pact and practically every speech they made, that they considered Bolshevism as their implacable enemy.

"Stalin has no reason whatever to love Britain, France or Italy but he had no reason to fear an attack from any of them. In any case, they were too far removed from Russia's frontiers to cause him a moment's worry. Japan might give him a certain amount of trouble, but only in the Far East, and every other nation was either too weak or too remote to constitute a serious menace, with the one exception of Germany.

"Hitler had written in *Mein Kampf* that Germany should turn her eyes eastward, to the great cornlands and oil-wells of the Ukraine and Caucasus. Hitler had gained power and with every week he was growing stronger. Right up to the summer of 1939 Stalin must have regarded Germany as the one and only enemy really to be feared. Germany alone was in a position to nullify his twenty years of peaceful reconstruction and bring his whole régime crashing about his ears at any time she chose to launch her land, sea and air forces against him."

"I know, I know," Goering frowned. "This is all elementary, but the Russo-German Pact of last August altered the whole situation."

"No," Gregory declared emphatically. "That is my whole point. In all essentials Russia's situation is exactly the same as it was this time last year. Use large maps, as the Duke of Wellington used to say. Don't think of this year or the next but regard the matter in terms of long-scale policy. The Russo-German pact has altered nothing. If it has I challenge you to prove it."

Goering shrugged. "While I don't say that I, personally, was in favour of it you can't deny that we have received certain definite benefits by our alliance with Russia. By keeping her

115

from a tie-up with the Democracies we have only to wage war on one front instead of on two. Now that the Polish campaign is over we can concentrate the whole of our air effort against the West instead of having to detach large forces to protect Berlin. Even if we haven't succeeded in drawing Russia into the war on our side, by making her a friendly neutral we've ensured that she won't come in against us."

"*Have* you ensured that? How much faith do you put in the word of Joseph Stalin?"

"Not much; but it is not in his interest now to reverse his policy and deliberately stab us in the back."

"Not for the moment, perhaps; but say the war takes a fresh turn? I don't have to tell *you* how easily pacts can be torn up when they are signed by certain people and it suits those people to scrap them. I consider that it's quite a possibility that Russia may turn against you—unless, of course, you can keep her occupied."

"Eh?" Goering's alert mind instantly picked up the hint. Gregory was literally talking for his life and now knowing that he had won a point in at last arousing the Marshal's interest he went on quickly:

"I'll come to that later. What else do you reckon that you've got out of this tie-up with the Bolsheviks?"

"We can draw on them for foodstuffs and later when we have reorganized their railways we shall be able to obtain almost unlimited supplies of raw materials which will nullify the British blockade."

Gregory shook his head. "I don't believe that. You're getting a certain amount of stuff, of course—Stalin has to put up some sort of a show—but his industrial system is still so ill-organized that he has a perfectly good excuse for not helping you to any appreciable extent. And even if you send hundreds of experts there their efforts will deliberately be sabotaged—for the simple reason that Stalin does not mean you to win this war."

"What grounds have you for saying that?"

"Simply that from his point of view this war is only an episode—a struggle in which he does not wish to be concerned. It may prove either inconvenient or useful to him, according to how he plays his cards in his long-term policy for the reconstruction of Russia; which is the only thing that really interests him."

"And what do you deduce from this?"

"That the Russo-German friendship pact is not worth the

paper it is written on; it was just one of Stalin's cards and a very high one. He still regards Germany as his only really dangerous, potential enemy. If she emerges from the present struggle victorious his situation will be worse than ever. You know Hitler's technique. With the Western Powers disposed of he might suddenly decide to rescue the German-speaking population of South Russia from Russian oppression. Then Stalin would have to face the might of Germany on his own, but . . ."

"Why, then, did he not go in with the Western Powers when he had the chance?" Goering interrupted.

"Firstly, because he didn't want to go to war at all if he could avoid it, and if he'd gone in with the Western Powers he'd obviously have had to resist an invasion once the German armies had overrun Poland. Secondly, he considered that the Allies were quite capable of coming out on top without his assistance. Thirdly, if he'd lined up with the Democracies he would have had to continue to observe the covenant of the League of Nations, which would have tied his hands in the Baltic."

"Ha, ha! I wondered when all this rigmarole was going to get us to Finland."

"We're doing very nicely and we shall be there in a moment. In the meantime I hope I've made it clear that Stalin had nothing to gain and everything to lose by coming in with the Democracies. He simply gambled on the fact—very shrewdly, in my view—that, whether they won or not, by keeping out he would be able to strengthen his hand against Germany.

"So far he hasn't done too badly, either." Gregory pointed. "Just look at the map. As his share of the swag you had to let him have half Poland. That enables him to build a Maginot Line there 400 miles in advance of his old frontier, which will make it infinitely more difficult for you should you ever contemplate marching into the Ukraine. Then where are your other natural bases for an invasion of Russia? Obviously the most suitable are Lithuania, Latvia and Estonia; all small countries, quite unable to resist any pressure exerted by a big neighbour, and all having considerable German populations. By one of your propaganda campaigns such as you used with the Sudeten Germans in Czechoslovakia you might easily have found it necessary to establish yourselves as the protector of these little neutrals and have established bases in them; but by his pact with you Stalin has been able to forestall you there, and it is he who has done this instead of you. Now where is the only

117

remaining jumping-off place which you still might use for an attack on European Russia?"

"Finland," murmured Goering, "Finland."

"Of course. The Finnish frontier is only twenty miles from Leningrad. During the last war you trained a battalion of Finns who afterwards officered the Finnish Army in the War of Independence. You also sent von der Goltz and German troops there to help fight the Bolsheviks. Finland is therefore definitely pro-German and extremely anti-Russian.

"In the event of Germany's emerging from this war still unbroken she might at any time form a secret alliance with Finland. The Mannerheim Line is quite strong enough to resist an attack until Germany could land a considerable expeditionary force in the Finnish ports to reinforce it. People are laughing about the recent Moscow broadcast in which the Russians declared that the Finns were threatening them. On the face of it, the suggestion that a nation of four million people can threaten one of a hundred and eighty millions is laughable: but when we get down to the real root of the matter it is not laughable at all. The Kremlin obviously cannot announce the fact, but what they really mean is that at some future date four million Finns *backed by eighty million Germans* might constitute a threat to Russia, and of such a combination they have every reason to be very frightened indeed."

Goering's impatient scowl had disappeared and he refilled both their glasses as Gregory went on:

"I haven't seen the English papers but I can give a pretty shrewd guess about the sort of stuff that many of them contain. They're saying: 'Now Stalin has at last come out in his true colours and shown himself for the brigand that he is. All his talk about preserving peace because it is the workers who suffer most in any war was mere eyewash. He doesn't give a damn about the workers and has revived all the old imperialistic aims of the Tsars. He's out for conquest and the rotten swine means to grab everything he can while the rest of us have got our hands full.'"

"That's right," Goering nodded. "I see a summary of everything appearing in your papers and that is the line most of them take."

"Well, they're off the mark. Stalin may be a thug but he's not an imperialist. He would still prefer to have peace if he could get what he wants without war—and he's been successful so far—but it's absolutely vital to him that if Russia is to be

118

secured from *German* aggression in the future he should close all her western approaches now, while he's got the chance. We may dislike Stalin and be sorry for these small neutrals whom he's blackmailing but we can't blame him, because it's his job to put the interests of Russia before everything else."

"You think, then, that, if he can't get what he's after by threats, he really means to invade Finland?"

"I'm certain of it; because for the moment you can't possibly afford to scrap the Russo-German Pact and send aid to the Finns. If he waits, some major change in the international situation—a sudden peace move, perhaps—might rob him of his one great opportunity to bar that vulnerable north-western gate. Therefore he must act at once—and by that I mean within the next few weeks."

"Why? Climatic conditions?"

"Yes. The lakes and swamps make Finland's eastern frontier almost impassable from April till November, and from February to April the snow is so deep that major operations are impossible; whereas from the end of November up till the end of January the lakes are frozen over and the ice thick enough to carry transport but there is still insufficient snow to prove a serious obstacle. That is why, having gobbled up Lithuania, Latvia and Estonia, Stalin had to wait until now before he could bring real pressure to bear on Finland. If he waits until January it will be too late to launch an offensive with any hope of a quick break through, and if he waits until next November he may have lost his chance for good and all."

"Yes, yes; you're right about that. But do you think the Finns will fight?"

"God knows. They're a brave people but their numbers are so small and the weight of the Russian tanks and bombers that can be brought against them is tremendous. If they do fight they risk utter annihilation and the destruction of every town in the country, but it is certainly to your interest that they should do so."

"Not necessarily. Personally, I have always been for curbing the power of the Bolsheviks, and if Russia secures her bases in Finland either by threats or by overrunning the country it will be another blow to German prestige in the Baltic. On the other hand, if Russia starts even a minor war it will make it much more difficult for her to fulfil her obligations to us and we don't wish to give her any further excuse for delaying the supplies of material that she's promised. If the Finns give in we get our supplies; if they fight—well . . ." Goering shrugged.

"Listen." Gregory set down his glass with a bang. "You're not going to get those supplies—or, anyway, nothing like the quantity you have been led to believe—so you might as well count that out. I tell you Stalin doesn't mean to help Germany win the war; therefore you'd be mad to allow him to get away with the rape of Finland if you can possibly prevent it."

"I'm doing what I can to persuade Russia to moderate her demands. You heard me say that I intend to see the Soviet Ambassador to-morrow morning."

"That's not enough. You're in no position to exert any pressure on the Kremlin so they won't take the least notice of you. Your game is to tackle this job from the other end and to persuade the Finns to tell the Russians to go to Hell."

"To do so would be to go against the *Fuehrer's* policy. If it leaked out that I had privately been in communication with the Finnish Government there would be the very devil to pay."

"Perhaps. But there are ways and means of ensuring that it doesn't leak out—and, anyhow, I'm not concerned with the *Fuehrer's* policy. He thinks that he is going to win this war, doesn't he? But you don't."

Goering smiled. "As I'm talking to a man who is already as good as dead I don't mind admitting that I think it unlikely. If we had attacked France and Britain right away we might have pulled it off, but I was overruled about that; the others insisted that once the Polish business was a *fait accompli* the Western Powers would throw in their hand. But when I say I think it unlikely that we shall win I do not at all mean that we shall necessarily lose, because, as I've told you, Germany can hold out against the blockade indefinitely."

"Right. Let's assume, then, that this year, next year or in five years' time, when everybody is thoroughly fed up, there will be a peace by negotiation. Germany may still be strong enough to insist on retaining her Austrian, Czechoslovakian and Polish territories; but is that enough? She will still be fenced-in by customs barriers and emigration restrictions. You may be quite certain that Britain and France will not give up any of their Colonies, and if you go on sinking neutral shipping as you have been doing Germans aren't going to find a ready welcome if they try to settle in other countries. It'll take you a few years to recover from the war. Then you'll be faced again with the same old problem; the inevitable pressure of Germany's virile population will force her leaders to seek a new outlet."

"Yes," Goering nodded. "The Democracies sneer at our claim for *Lebensraum*, but they have no right to do so. We Germans cannot be bottled-up indefinitely and this question must be faced, if not at the peace conference then a few years later, when the distress of war has once more faded from the public mind."

"Good. Then what are you going to do—have a third crack at Britain and France? That's not going to get you anywhere, because if the peace is one of negotiation Europe will remain an armed camp. But why should you when, if you could get the Ukraine, South Russia down to the Black Sea and a free hand to develop the resources of Asiatic Russia, you'd have an empire equal in its potentialities to the British or the French? Stalin is the bad boy of the family—nobody loves old 'Joe'—so we're not going to his assistance, particularly after the help he is assumed to have given you against us in this present war. Obviously, then, Germany's future lies in the East."

"Exactly what I have always maintained."

"Like Stalin, then, you must forget the present and adopt a long-term policy. I think it's very doubtful if the Democracies will ever agree to make a peace with Hitler; they have no faith whatever in his word. But he's as good as said himself that he would be prepared to go into retirement if it were for the good of the Reich. Your situation is very different. You are the most popular of the Nazi leaders in Germany and, in spite of the war, your stock still stands pretty high in Britain. Clearly, therefore, if there is a negotiated peace while the Nazis are still in control of Germany you will be the new leader of the German nation."

"Only with the *Fuehrer's* consent and approval."

"Yes, yes; but we can take that for granted. Internal and external pressure will be too great for him to resist. My point is that you should not wait until supreme power is placed in your hands—possibly at some extremely difficult moment—but must make up your mind *now* what your policy is going to be when power comes to you, and shape events as far as possible so that conditions will be favourable for you to carry that policy out."

Goering took a long drink and stared at Gregory. "Why the Hell do I allow you to talk to me like this?"

"Because you're not the fat, jolly fool that it suits you to let the masses think you, but one of the greatest statesmen in Europe; and you know that I'm talking sound sense."

"Go on, then. What do you suggest that I should do?"

"Your long-term policy is an invasion of Russia three years after you have been able to secure a negotiated peace. Finland is your last stronghold in the Northern Baltic. As long as Finnish independence is maintained there is always an opening for you to negotiate a secret alliance with the Finns. Use Finland as your base and strike right down at Moscow. That is why Finnish independence must be maintained at all costs and, rather than that she should give a single base to Russia, by hook or by crook you've got to persuade her to fight."

"That's easier said than done. As I've already told you, I dare not enter into secret negotiation with the Finnish Government and from all I've heard it looks as if they'll give in rather than fight."

Gregory emptied his second goblet of champagne. He was feeling pretty good again now as he said: "I think you'll admit that I've managed to interest you on the subject of Finland, so can I take it that I shall not be handed over to the gentlemen downstairs who beat people with steel rods?"

"Yes. You've won your wager," Goering nodded, "but don't get any idea that I mean to let you go; you'll still have to face a firing-squad."

"Have I convinced you that it is in Germany's interests that Finland should resist Russia's demands?"

"Yes, and I admit that your long-term policy for Germany and the world offers the best hope of permanent peace that has ever been devised."

"Are you, then, prepared to lead Germany on this new and glorious destiny?"

"If I could do so without disloyalty to my *Fuehrer*."

"Good. Then let us discuss it further."

"It would be useless to do so. Our talk has clarified my ideas on the subject and many of your views are in line with those that I've held for a long time, but the plan breaks down at its very outset because the Finns dare not resist."

"If I could produce a method by which you might induce them to do so, would you give me my life?"

"No." Goering turned away. "I've talked much too freely for that. I'm sorry on personal grounds, but I never allow such things to influence my decisions. Nothing you can say now will save you from a bullet."

CHAPTER XI

FAKED PASSPORTS

GREGORY remained quite silent for a moment, studying the heavy, forceful face in front of him. It was serene but implacable. There was nothing cruel about it, nothing evil. It was fat with good-living, like those of the later Caesars and, like the best of them, still handsome in its rugged strength. The eyes, too, were quick with understanding and intelligence.

Hours earlier that evening when Gregory had first entered the great, silent apartment in which they stood he had believed that if he could once intrigue Goering with the story of his adventures his life would be safe. He had done so and they had dined together like the best of friends, yet he had lost that round.

Afterwards he had still believed that he might save his neck if he proved clever enough to clarify the Marshal's ideas upon the European situation by putting forward possibilities with a bluntness that few Germans would have dared to use. He had done so; and to such a degree that he might, perhaps, even have altered the whole course of events in Europe for the next fifty years by influencing Goering's decisions through the ambitious plans he had laid before him. But he had lost that round as well.

What was there left? An appeal to sentiment was utterly useless. Goering moved through life as a super-battleship ploughs the seas; he allowed nothing to deflect him from his course once he had set it, and all lesser vessels were forced to give way before his relentless progress. Having once decided that Gregory knew too much to be allowed to live, what possible argument could make him go back on his decision? He liked brave people and if he would not spare Gregory when he had shown himself to be a man of courage he would only treat him with contempt if he started to beg for mercy.

Gregory knew that he was up against the toughest proposition that he had ever encountered; but he felt no malice. Goering was an opponent worthy of his steel. If the sands of his life were really running out at last he could console himself with the thought that he had failed only because he had tried to move a mountain. It was no disgrace to have broken oneself against the implacable 'Iron Hermann'.

With a little shrug he said: "Well, I suppose we might as well finish the magnum."

"Certainly." Goering refilled the champagne goblets for the third time and replaced the big bottle in its ice-bucket. "I don't feel in a mood for company this evening so I shan't go down and join my guests now. I shall set to work on this Russian business; but there's no immediate hurry, as I never go to bed before two in the morning."

"Good. In that case I may be able to help you."

Goering grinned. "I was thinking of my interview with the Soviet Ambassador tomorrow; and although you're a very clever fellow, Sallust, I don't see how you can help me to bring pressure to bear on the Kremlin."

"No. Nobody can help you there. I meant my scheme for persuading the Finns to resist Russia's demand."

"But you ask your life for that, and as I don't think it possible, I'm not playing."

"You can't say whether it's possible or not until you've heard it."

"In my view, whatever your scheme might be, the general situation would make it impossible of application; because we are no better placed to exert pressure on the Finns than we are on the Russians."

"I don't agree; and since you won't pay me for it I'll give it to you for nothing."

"Why should you?"

"Oh, I owe you something for having made the last evening of my life such an interesting one; and when I get to Hell I'll make even Satan's mouth water by a description of that bottle of Marcobrunner Cabinet 1900 you gave me for dinner."

"All right, go ahead if you wish."

"Tell me first what you know about the U.S.S.R. The German Secret Service is pretty good and a précis of all essential reports come to you. Russia is a closed book to most of us. Some people believe her to be the same old Russia of the Tsarist days; slow-moving, inefficient, with bribery and corruption rife everywhere; almost unlimited man-power still, of course, but not the organization to operate one-tenth of it effectively. Other people believe that Russia has undergone a real rebirth; that her soldiers are now educated men, clean, efficient, proud of their country; and that Voroshilov has forged a weapon in the Soviet armies and air force which is the most powerful fighting-machine in the world. Few people can know the real truth but you must have a very shrewd idea of it."

"The first is the case." Goering lit a cigarette and drew heavily upon it. "Russia remains unchanged in all essentials. They are a lazy, shiftless lot and are always saying, '*Nichevo, nichevo!*'—never do to-day what you can put off till to-morrow— just as they used to say in the past. Apart from a few people in the Polit Bureau, the Organizational Bureau and the Secretariat there is hardly a Russian that can't be bought. Their Air Force *is* big—very big. That is why if the Soviet had tied up with the Democracies it might have done considerable damage in Berlin during the first few weeks of the war. Numbers cannot possibly be ignored in such matters and the Soviet pilots are brave men, as they proved in Spain. But aircraft types get out of date more quickly than any other arm. The Soviet Air Force reached its peak as a weapon three years ago and plane for plane the Russians wouldn't stand a dog's chance against any of the more modern types that we or the Western Powers now have."

Gregory nodded. "I thought as much. How about the army?"

"There are two armies in Russia. The Army proper is very big in numbers but is composed mainly of conscripts who are ill-armed, ill-officered and ill-fed. They're not even up to the standard of the reserve battalions of Moujiks which the Tsar sent against us in 1915. None of these units is equipped with the most modern weapons—apart from tanks—because the Kremlin has always been afraid of an Army *Putsch*. Stalin has deliber- ately starved the Army proper of equipment, to ensure his own political battalions having at least a great superiority of weapon- power over the ordinary troops if it ever came to a show-down with the Generals.

"Those political battalions form an army in themselves but a much smaller one, numbering some 300,000 men. Every man in them is a Communist Party member admitted only after the severest tests—in the same way as our S.S. men here. They have the best of everything—food, quarters, women—and would fight tooth and nail to protect the Government that ensures them these privileges. They are commanded by Budenny, who is

125

Voroshilov's most trusted man, and both are completely loyal to the Kremlin."

Gregory swallowed another couple of mouthfuls of the iced champagne. "I take it, then, that the Kremlin would not risk sending its political battalions against the Finns but would use the main army which you say is in such poor condition?"

"Naturally. They will rely on sheer weight of numbers to smash the Mannerheim Line because it doesn't matter how many of their conscripts they kill; whereas large losses among their crack political troops would leave the Kremlin Government exposed to the danger of an internal revolution."

"Do you think such mass attacks by inferior troops will be sufficient to overcome the Finnish resistance within—say—a month?"

"I doubt it; because it is not only the troops that are of such poor quality; they will be worse led than any other army in Europe."

"Do you mean because Stalin has bumped off so many of his best officers in these constant purges since the Tukachevsky conspiracy of 1937?"

Goering nodded. "It's been infinitely worse than most people suppose. There's no doubt that Stalin nipped the Tukaschevsky conspiracy only just in time. Nearly every officer of importance was involved in it and the Ogpu have been tracing them up ever since. During the last two years he has liquidated 75 out of 80 members of the Supreme War Council, 13 out of 19 Army commanders and 195 Divisional commanders. Altogether they have murdered 350 odd generals, but even that is not the worst of it. Over 30,000 officers of all ranks have been slaughtered."

"Thirty thousand!" Gregory exclaimed.

"Yes. That means that hardly an officer above the rank of major has been spared and practically all their qualified staff officers have been eliminated. Men who were captains last year are now commanding divisions and sergeants have become company commanders overnight. The Navy and the Air Force have suffered equally in proportion. The result is bound to be absolute chaos when the Soviet forces are called on to undertake a full-scale campaign."

"You have, of course, irrefutable proof of this in your Secret Service files?" Gregory asked.

"Certainly. We have far too many agents operating in Russia for them all to be mistaken."

126

"How much of this do you think the Finns know?"

"A little, perhaps; but not very much compared with ourselves. Finland is a small country and her resources are limited. For every agent the Finns have working in Russia we probably have a hundred."

"Good. Now, what you've told me more than confirms my own suspicions, and this is the plan I had in mind. Get the facts from Berlin and sit up all night compiling a full report upon the Soviet Army and Air Force, backed by all the available evidence."

A quick smile lit Goering's eyes. "I see the idea! You're suggesting that I should tip off the Finnish Government that the main Red Army is only cardboard."

"Exactly. There can be no doubt that Marshal Mannerheim would rather fight than give in and from what we know of the Finnish War of Independence I'm certain that most of the Finns are with him. But the Government is the snag. Politicians are not soldiers; the thought of their cities lying in ruins and their women and children being bombed to Hell makes them prepared to go to almost any lengths rather than go to war. If only you can convince the Finnish Cabinet that their country will not be overrun immediately and that in spite of Russia's numerical superiority there's a good chance of their being able to hold out until other countries and the February snows come to their assistance, you'll have done the trick—you'll have saved Finland as a possible base for future German operations when the present war is over."

Goering shook his head. "I believe it could be done; but one thing makes such a course impossible. To convince them that the reports are genuine I should have to send a personal emissary with full authority to let the Finns know that, whatever Germany's ostensible attitude may be, I am behind them. That would mean going behind the *Fuehrer's* back. Himmler's agents are everywhere, even in the highest offices of the Government. There are very few people indeed that even I can absolutely trust, and those few are marked men. If one of them disappeared Himmler would send out a general call through his Foreign Department, U.A.-1. Every Gestapo agent outside Germany would be turned on to hunt for my man; his presence in Helsinki would be discovered and reported, and that alone would be sufficient to give away the fact that I had been trying to double-cross von Ribbentrop. I'm not frightened of him—I can take care of myself and I'm a much bigger man than he is—

127

but there would be hell to pay, and I'm not ready for a show-down with him yet."

"I feared the problem of a suitable emissary would prove a knotty one," Gregory nodded; "because anyone you send on such a mission must be a man of some standing, otherwise the Finns might become suspicious and get it into their heads that he was not sent by you at all. But surely you can find some aristocrat—an Army man for preference—who is outside politics—someone important enough to impress the Finns and at the same time a man whom you could completely trust—someone, for example, like our late friend, Colonel-Baron von Lutz?"

In spite of its size the room was now blue with the smoke of innumerable cigarettes, yet Goering lit another and puffed upon it. "Yes, someone like that," he murmured. "Von Lutz would have been just the man, but he's dead; and unfortunately, where a month ago I could have found a dozen like him who would have done equally well, they were all either killed or have gone into hiding as a result of the Army *Putsch*."

Gregory smiled. "Then it seems there's nothing else for it. If you're to pull this job off—and you must, for the sake of your own future and that of Germany—you'll just have to send me."

"You?" Goering exclaimed.

"Yes; why not?" Gregory grinned now that he had whipped the cover from the life-boat which he had been secretly fashioning for himself during the last few moments, and hurried on: "Nobody knows that the Baron is dead. He might have been burnt in that cottage last night or he might have escaped. Even if the S.S. men find his body in the woods the news of his death will never get as far as Finland, because he wasn't important enough for it to be reported to the Gestapo agents there. I'm wearing his clothes at the moment and although our faces weren't alike our build was much the same. I am a born impostor, and as I spent the best part of three weeks in hiding with the Baron I know all about his family and his whole history. All you have to do is to furnish me with a passport in the Baron's name and an aeroplane. Haven't you realized yet that I can be darned useful to you alive whereas I'll be no good to anybody once I'm dead?"

Goering began to pace rapidly up and down. "That's all very well, but how do I know that I can trust you? You're an Englishman. Why should you offer to work for Germany? To save your life, you may say; but I should not believe that. You are not the kind of man who betrays his country."

"To do as I suggest would not be betraying my country," said Gregory swiftly. "In this instance the interests of Britain and Germany are identical. Britain has always championed the small nations so she would naturally be anxious that the Finns should retain their independence. Further: if Russia's demands are resisted, and she is compelled to fight for what she wants, that will give her an even better excuse than any she has at present for delaying in sending supplies to Germany. That is the price—a very small one, in my opinion—which you must pay if you are to save Finland as a possible base for future operations. But I'm concerned with this war, not the next; and by providing Russia with a spot of bother, so that she is less able to help you, I'm assisting my own country. As far as the future is concerned, I don't see why the Western Powers should object to Germany's compensating herself for her lack of colonies by absorbing Southern Russia and making Asiatic Russia a German protectorate."

"Ha! And what about the right of self-determination that you English talk so much about. You would say we were enslaving the Russians—or some such nonsense."

"The population of Central and North-Eastern Asia is no more Russian than that of India is English or that of Senegal French. I don't think that question would arise, providing you allowed the true Russians to retain self-government in their own original Muscovite territories. What really matters is that the German race would no longer menace future peace if it had sufficient room in which to spread. Given Russia's vast Asiatic lands in addition to the Reich, Germany could afford to give up Czechoslovakia and Poland as she would still have about one-fifth of the world's land-surface—more than enough room for her surplus population. With such an area to administer and develop she need never again come into collision with the Western Powers over the colonial question and there might at last be some real hope of peace in our time. I would not dream of undertaking this mission if I were not convinced that in serving you I should also be serving Britain."

"Yes, yes. If we had the Ukraine, the Caucasus and all Asiatic Russia our problem would be solved for good. But if you wouldn't double-cross me with your own people you might with the Gestapo. How am I to know that you'd not take any papers I gave you straight to Himmler?"

"I should have thought you had a perfect guarantee against that."

"Guarantee? What d'you mean?"

Gregory shrugged. "What am I doing here? Why did I put my neck in a noose by coming to see you? Only because I was desperately anxious to find out what had happened to Erika."

"Of course—of course."

"And now you've told me that she's in Finland, isn't her presence there the best guarantee you could possibly have that the one thing I'm anxious to do is to get to Finland myself so that I can join her?"

"That's true. Yes, I believe you're honest. But it's a hellish risk." Goering's voice still held doubt as he began to pace swiftly up and down again. "Say you slip up and are caught by Himmler's agents, with those papers on you?"

Gregory's pulses were racing. He knew that he was on the very verge of victory. If he could storm the last redoubt of Goering's resistance by yet one more reasoned argument his case would be won; he and Charlton would walk out of Karinhall free men and with facilities for escaping out of Germany. Nerving himself for a final effort he swilled down the last of his champagne, and said earnestly:

"Listen. What have you to fear? In serving you I serve my country. I have the strongest possible personal motive for wanting to go to Finland, because it is only by doing so that I can rejoin the woman I love. If I do slip up, that will be tough luck on me, but there'll be no come-back whatsoever so far as you're concerned. There would be if I were really Colonel-Baron von Lutz or any other German that you might choose to send. But I'm not a German; I'm a British secret agent, and any rigorous examination would prove that. I'm the one and only man you *can* send with complete safety, because if I'm caught you could deny all knowledge of me—swear I'd stolen the papers—and everybody would believe you."

"By God, you're right!" Goering swung round. "Very well —I'll send you to Finland."

Even the masterly control with which Gregory was usually able to hide his true feelings was not proof against the glint of triumph which leapt into his eyes. To conceal it he bent forward and helped himself to another of the fat cigarettes. As he lit it, with his eyes cast down towards its tip, he could feel his heart thumping a rhythm in his chest. "I've won! I've won!

130

I've won!" But all he said as he flicked out the match was: "Good. How soon can I start?"

Goering had suddenly become a different man. All trace of the indecision so foreign to his nature had left him. With his dark eyes fixed on Gregory he said rapidly: "Now that the crisis is on every hour is of importance. You will leave the moment we have the papers ready. I shall send you in one of my private planes. I can trust my own pilots and one of them will not be missed while away on a twenty-four-hour trip."

"He'll have to observe the usual formalities when we land at the Helsinki air-port, though," Gregory remarked, "and he might easily be recognized. I should think it's a hundred to one that Himmler has planted one of his spies among the personnel there."

"That's true," Goering frowned.

"Don't worry about that. You let me have the plane and I'll provide the pilot."

"Ah! You mean the fellow downstairs? I'd forgotten all about him. Is he a good man—competent to fly a Messerschmitt —and would he also be willing to go to Finland?"

"He's one of the best pilots in the R.A.F. and he'll fly anything anywhere rather than be interned in Germany for the duration of the war."

"He won't bring my plane back, though."

"No. You can hardly expect him to do that. But what the hell does one plane matter on a job like this?"

"Nothing at all. But no comment would be aroused among the Finns if a German pilot in a German plane just flew in and out to drop you there; whereas a British pilot arriving with a German officer in a German plane would cause every tongue to wag."

"I agree. But in any case I couldn't go in uniform. You'll have to let me have a suit of civilian clothes and you could easily provide me with a double set of papers; one faked British passport in my own name for me to show on landing at the air-port and one passport in the name of Colonel-Baron von Lutz for presentation to the people at the Finnish Foreign Office. I should then be a British subject arriving with a British pilot."

"But what about the plane?"

"Don't let's use a Messerschmitt. You must have some foreign make in your private fleet that might quite as naturally be flown by a British instead of a German pilot. All we'd have to do then is to paint out the German markings and substitute the British circles for the German crosses."

Suddenly Goering began to laugh uproariously, his fat body shaking like a jelly.

"What's bitten you?" Gregory inquired.

"I was just thinking," the Marshal wheezed, "what a grand joke it would be if I gave you the little plane with which Voroshilov presented me when I made my trip to Russia."

Gregory laughed too, but shook his head. "Russian makes are rare, if non-existent, in Britain. An Italian or a Dutch make would be much better."

Goering nodded. "I have a four-seater Belgian Sabina which would do admirably. It is their fastest type and fitted with de-icing apparatus. I'll let you have that. And now to work."

Although it was well after midnight, within a few moments the big apartment became a hive of activity. Half a dozen officers, forming Goering's confidential secretariat, were summoned and to each the Marshal gave brief, clear instructions.

Three were dispatched to Berlin; one to the Foreign Office to arrange about the passports, and the other two to collect files from the Air Ministry and the War Office respectively. A fourth was ordered to find Gregory a complete change of clothes. A fifth was told to give immediate instructions for the alterations of the markings on the Belgian plane, then to collect Charlton and work out with him, from the latest weather reports and maps of the Baltic, the navigation details of a flight to Finland; while the sixth was sent running to bring all the available reports on Russia from Goering's private files.

The man who was going to the Foreign Office fetched a camera and photographed Gregory, both in uniform and in a borrowed civilian overcoat, for the two passports. Then two clerks brought in a typewriter on a wheeled desk. Immediately the reports arrived Goering flung off his coat and sitting down, in his shirt-sleeves, at his big table he began to dictate.

As Gregory stood behind him, reading snatches of the reports over the Marshal's shoulder, he was filled with amazement and admiration at the spectacle of the man who had created the new Germany exercising his extraordinary brain. Every now and again Goering mopped the perspiration from his broad forehead as he sweated out the alcohol that he had drunk—and was still drinking, for the deaf-mute barman had appeared again and had opened another magnum of champagne. With pauses of only a moment the Marshal was absorbing whole pages of typescript with a sponge-like rapidity and condensing them into brief paragraphs. He missed nothing of importance and his words poured out in a swift, unhesitating flow. The typist's fingers positively flew over the keys as he took the dictation, and the other man who had come in with him constantly prepared fresh foolscap paper and carbons so that there should be the least possible delay in changing sheets at the end of each page.

Gregory very soon realized that there were not going to be any half-measures about the report. Goering was giving an abbreviated but detailed account of the whole building-up of the Red Army. He seemed to know the personal history of every general of importance, the state of moral of every army corps and the positions they now occupied.

At half past two in the morning the first of the three officers who had been sent to Berlin arrived back with another mass of papers. Soon afterwards his colleague who had visited the War Office came in with yet more files. They remained there sorting them as though their very lives depended on it; scanning sheet after sheet and pulling out only those of importance for the Marshal's perusal. "Keep that," or "Scrap that," was all Goering said after a second's glance at each paper that was handed to him.

By four o'clock he had turned his attention to the Soviet Air Force and was giving detail after detail about the various types of Russian planes, their speed, their numbers, their positions; then he passed to bombs, personnel, flight efficiency, petrol reserves, capacity of training-centres.

At a little before five the man who had been to the Foreign Office came in. He had with him the passport for Colonel-Baron von Lutz, but they were still busy faking the British passport in the name of Gregory Sallust and he said that it would be sent out to Karinhall by six o'clock.

With him he also brought a fresh pile of papers and shortly after his arrival Goering turned from the subject of the Air Force to the Russian political scene. Each of the sixteen commissars, who between them made up the three committees which rule Russia, was given a long paragraph—bribable or unbribable, married or single, private life, antecedents, secret vices—everything which might assist a foreign Power in shaping its policy towards these men should they suddenly come into special prominence.

133

At ten minutes past six Goering suddenly pushed back his chair and stood up. The job was done.

In one Herculean effort, which would have taken most men weeks of hard, conscientious preparation, he had compiled a document of 126 foolscap sheets which would give the Finns every vital fact that Germany knew about Russia and would show Russia's weakness.

For a few moments he sat quite still, while the officers withdrew their depleted files, then he dictated a letter which ran:

> "*Karinhall,*
> "*November 28th, 1939.*
> "*The bearer of this is my friend, Colonel-Baron von Lutz. The Baron will hand to you a document of the first importance. With the information therein, for which I personally vouch, the Finnish Government will realize that they have little to fear from an attack by Russia.*
>
> "*At the moment Germany is in no position to make an official pronouncement but I cannot too strongly stress our hope that the Finnish Government will resist the Russian demands, with the knowledge that time is on their side and that in secret I shall do everything possible to assist them.*"

The speed-typist and his assistant left the room. Goering signed the letter, took the top copy of the report and three sheafs of original documents from the piles that his *aides-de-camp* had sorted out, thrust them into a large stout envelope and handed the whole bundle to Gregory with von Pleisen's Iron Cross, as he said:

"The letter has no superscription but you will take it to Monsieur Grado Wuolijoki—Monsieur Wuo-li-joki—at the Finnish Foreign Office. He is of German extraction, on his mother's side, and my personal friend. He will see that these papers reach the right quarter."

Gregory removed the letter, which he folded and put in his pocket as he wished to keep it handy so that he could destroy it at once in the event of any accident by which the plane might be forced down while still over Germany.

"I understand," he said. "That was a marvellous night's work you put in and I'm certain that you'll never regret it. By the bye, I suppose you can let me have some money? As the Colonel-Baron and your secret representative I should naturally put up at the best hotel when I reach Helsinki."

134

Actually, he still had nearly £300 on him, being the balance of the 5,000 marks that Sir Pellinore Gwaine-Cust had given him before his first trip into Germany, but Gregory had always believed in 'spoiling the Egyptians' and saw no reason why the Nazis should not pay his expenses in Finland.

Goering nodded. "Certainly. I like my people to put up a good show." As he spoke he walked over to a large painting of Napoleon Bonaparte which was opposite his desk and, feeling behind the edge of its gilt frame, twisted a concealed knob to a combination that he evidently carried in his mind. The picture and its frame swung noiselessly outward revealing an enormous wall-safe, with many shelves and compartments, to the six-inch-thick steel door of which the picture was affixed.

Picking up a fat packet of bank-notes from one of the shelves he began to count them, but at that moment the telephone buzzer sounded. Thrusting the packet into Gregory's hands the Marshal said impatiently: "Here! Take 3,000 marks from this. That should be enough and give you a good margin to bribe your way into the Finnish Foreign Office quickly if the small people show any signs of keeping you waiting."

"Thanks." The packet consisted of 100-mark notes and Gregory counted himself off thirty from it while Goering carried on a quick conversation at the telephone. As Gregory was holding the bundle he felt an uneven strip across its bottom and turning it over he saw that some very thin, folded sheets of paper were wedged under the thick rubber band which held the notes together. The sheets were so thin that he could see the typescript through the top one. It might be just a check list of the numbers of the notes. On the other hand, it might be something of importance which had got caught in the rubber band by mistake. Anything coming out of Goering's private safe was worth investigation and the Marshal still had his back turned at the telephone. Gregory knew that if he stole the 'flimsies', and they were missed immediately, his life would once more be forfeit, but the temptation to find out what the typescript was proved irresistible. Slipping it from under the rubber band he swiftly pushed it in his pocket; then, so that he should not have to hand the bundle back he replaced it on the shelf of the safe from which it had been taken.

The Marshal finished his telephoning, turned round, gave a glance at the notes Gregory still held in his hand and swung the safe door shut again. He was no longer perspiring and looked as fresh as if he had slept the night through.

135

"We'll have some breakfast now," he smiled, "then I'll snatch a couple of hours' sleep before I see the Soviet Ambassador."

In the private dining-room breakfast had already been prepared; real coffee, crisp white rolls, fresh butter, eggs, fish, sausage and cheese. As he sat down Goering's personality changed again, and it was impossible to believe that he was the same person who had been working so furiously all through the night. He talked, like any country gentleman entertaining a guest, of the wild life on his estate, and mentioned quite casually that he meant to get back from Berlin by midday to join the guns as he had a shooting-party staying in the house.

When the meal was done he summoned the *aide-de-camp* who had been charged with providing a change of clothes for Gregory and told him to see that his guest had everything he needed until he could start on his journey. Then, as they went out into the corridor he shook Gregory warmly by the hand.

"Good luck, my dear fellow. It's been a pleasure to see you here and when the war is over you must come and stay. We'll kill some more bottles of Marcobrunner, and I really *can* offer you some excellent shooting."

"Thanks. I've enjoyed myself enormously," Gregory said politely, and was inwardly tickled by the fantastic idea which flashed into his mind—that possibly his host expected him to write a bread-and-butter letter. Obviously the Marshal had completely forgotten for the time being that at just about that hour his guest would have been led out to die at his orders had it not been for that guest's own wits and determination to save himself.

The A.D.C. took Gregory to a suite where he bathed, shaved and changed. He retained his own shoes and took the opportunity to slip the typescript he had stolen into the false sole of one of them, where he still had most of the money he had brought into Germany. He then rejoined the A.D.C., who led him downstairs and through a long corridor to an underground aerodrome.

Charlton was there, haggard and weary-eyed. He had been given dinner, but after that the poor fellow had been left all night in the waiting-room and owing to his acute anxiety he had not been able to get one wink of sleep. Yet when he saw Gregory he smiled and nodded cheerfully towards the Belgian plane which now carried the red, white and blue British circles.

"Nice little bus, isn't she?"

"Yes," Gregory nodded. "The Marshal's giving it to us as a parting present. I managed to entertain him rather well at dinner last night."

Freddie grunted. "You might at least have sent down to let me know that things were all right. I suppose for the last eight hours you've been sleeping your head off?"

"Not all the time. As a matter of fact, the Marshal kept me up pretty late but he was so hospitable that I found it a little difficult to get away."

"You old devil!" Freddie laughed. "Anyhow. I'm mighty glad to see you—er—looking so fresh," he added as an afterthought.

"Thanks. I'm sorry you had such a dull time last night, but I see you've had a shave so I take it they looked after you this morning?"

"Oh, yes; they couldn't have been nicer—bath, slap-up breakfast, everything—they even produced a change of underclothes when I hinted that mine were due for the long service medal."

"Good! And the Air Officer gave you all the particulars you require for our flight to Finland?"

"Yes. I've got it all here." Freddie held up a small, fat wallet. "And orders have been telephoned through to Anti-Aircraft Headquarters that they're not to interfere with a small Belgian Sabina plane bearing British markings which will be flying over North-Eastern Germany for a special purpose."

"Yes. I fixed that with the Marshal. So long as you stick to the route you've been given we're ensured a clear run out of the country."

The plane had been fuelled to capacity as it was desirable to avoid any questioning which might have arisen by breaking their journey at air-ports along the route, but with only two people on board, instead of the four for which it was built, the Sabina was easily capable of carrying enough petrol for a 700-mile non-stop flight. Directly it was reported ready Gregory and Freddie got into it.

Gregory put his big packet of papers on his knees and felt in his pocket to make quite certain that his two passports and Goering's letter were there all right. The head mechanic signalled to Freddie and the engine sprang to sudden life, making a deafening roar in the underground air-port. They waved good-bye to the Air Officer and mechanics, then the plane ran smoothly up the long slope out into the daylight and across the grass. A moment later it was in the air.

"So you've got us out—and the gift of a plane into the bargain," Freddie said, the moment he had taken off. "You certainly are a wizard."

"No—just a worker," Gregory replied. "And, my God, it was a fight! I had to wrestle with Satan in person for about five hours and work for another six, so I'm about all-in. I'll tell you the story later but I've been through the hell of a strain and I'm going to try to get some sleep now."

He closed his eyes and lay back in the comfortable passenger-seat beside the pilot. It was not until ten minutes later that he suddenly noticed how cold it had become, and opening his eyes again he saw that the altimeter registered 8,000 feet.

"It's darned cold up here," he remarked. "Surely we don't need to fly as high as this?"

"Oh, yes, we do," Freddie grinned. "I'm going much higher —as high as the plane will take us without our conking out through lack of oxygen."

"But why?" Gregory protested. "You've got your route and the anti-aircraft people have been told to let us through."

"Yes; but that's only along a lane over North-Eastern Germany."

"Naturally—since we're going to Finland."

"Finland?" gasped Freddie. "Surely you didn't really mean to go there?"

Gregory sat up with a jerk. "Of course. I've been entrusted with a special mission by Goering so I've got no option."

"Good God, you *are* crazy! Finland? My foot! Thanks a lot for the plane, but now I've got it I'm going home!"

CHAPTER XII

THE RED MENACE

GREGORY closed his eyes and sighed. After having worn down
the most dynamic man in Europe by hours of skilful flattery,
well-timed bullying and reasoned argument, it seemed a bit
hard that, tired out as he was, he should now be called upon to
cope with his pleasant but pigheaded young friend.

Experience had taught him that the better the quality of
the drink the less likelihood of a head the following morning,
but even with the very best of liquor quantity will tell, and he
now had a first-class hang-over. Breakfast and a bath had only
stalled off the evil hour. His brain had begun to feel like cotton-
wool, his eyes were heavy and he had a rotten taste in his mouth,
but it was mental exhaustion, much more than the alcohol he
had drunk, which had got him down. Moreover, he was a night-
bird by nature and always at his very worst in the morning,
when most other people were setting off to tackle the day's work;
yet the effort had to be made, so he said slowly:

"Why not Holland, as that girl of yours is there?"

"I'd make it Holland," Charlton said sharply, "but for two
reasons. Firstly, as a British Air Force officer the Dutch would
intern me the moment I landed. Secondly, it's my duty to report
to my C.O. at the earliest possible opportunity—and if you've
forgotten *your* duty I haven't forgotten mine."

"Oh, Freddie, you make me tired," said Gregory wearily.
"D'you honestly think I'm the sort of chap who would sell
myself to the enemy and that I've taken on this job to help the
Nazis win the ruddy war?"

"No—no, of course not. I didn't mean that really; but when
you said you were doing the job for Goering what the hell else
was a fellow to think?"

"Thanks for the somewhat dubious vote of confidence. Now,
listen to me. I'm going to give you two very good reasons why

139

you're not going home before you've flown me to Finland. After that you can do as you damned well choose. The Finns won't intern you, because at the moment they're much too occupied with their own affairs to bother their heads about minor infringements of their neutrality; so if you don't want to stay you can buy a suit of civilian clothes, and it shouldn't be difficult for you to get a ship home from one of the Norwegian ports."

"Why should I do that, which might mean weeks of delay, when I've got a perfectly good plane?"

"You haven't got a plane. Goering gave this plane to me. But for goodness' sake don't let's wrangle about side issues. The situation is this. Russia has demanded that Finland shall give her bases and receive garrisons of Red troops. If Finland agrees, she will never again be in a position to fight Russia and will be reduced to the state of a Russian province. That has got to be stopped somehow."

"I suppose you think you're such a hell of a guy that directly the Soviet agents report your arrival in Helsinki Stalin will get a fit of the jitters and throw his hand in?"

"Don't be facetious, Freddie, or keep interrupting me. What I *can* do is to persuade the Finns to fight. I've got here the whole low-down on the Red Army and Air Force, showing their real weakness. Once the Finns see these papers they'll realize that they've got a sporting chance."

"What, a mere handful of them against fifteen million armed Reds?"

"Yes. I don't suggest that they can march on Moscow but I do believe they can hold out until help reaches them from the other Scandinavian countries or the Allies.

"I don't suppose you know much about Finland, Freddie—few English people do. The Finns are grand fighters; they showed that in their War of Independence when with little else than shot-guns the Finnish farmers drove thousands of Red guards out of their country and at last made it their own. The state of education and civilization in Finland is very high indeed. They are individualists in the best sense and have a passionate love of freedom. After a hundred years of Tsarist tyranny they managed to throw off the Russian yoke; for the past twenty years they have enjoyed real liberty, living in peace and well-being. Now their liberty is threatened again.

"Think of those Finnish families, living just as our own people do at home; well-fed, well-clothed, enjoying their sport, books, music, cinemas; able to do and say just what they like without any dread of secret police spying upon them and dragging them off to prison or execution. Then think of what we know of Russia—the dirt, the poverty, the forced labour, the constant fear of husbands and wives that they may be separated over-night—never to see each other again—or one of them arrested on a false charge and condemned without even a hearing by some secret tribunal. The Finns are a little people but they are decent folk; they represent everything for which Britain and France are fighting. How can we allow them to be made slaves again when we have a chance to save them?"

The plane was still climbing and Gregory paused for a moment to glance at Freddie's set face, then he went on evenly: "That is my first reason—a sentimental one, perhaps. Now listen to my second. It is the thing that you yourself spoke of just now—our duty. It's our duty to help win this war. If we can help more by temporarily abandoning routine and acting on our own, common sense tells us we should do so. Remember Nelson putting his blind eye to the telescope? Well, we're not even ignoring the orders of our superiors; just remaining a few days longer than is strictly necessary on the list of 'missing', that's all. Germany is getting supplies from Russia; not in great quantity, perhaps, but you can bet that she's getting the things she needs most urgently—even if they come through on a hay-cart. If Russia has to fight Finland she'll have to give first place to her own war and the supply of vital war materials which she sends to Germany will dry up. If we can get the Finns to fight we shall indirectly have extended the blockade along another fifth of Germany's frontiers, and that's as good as a major victory. Therefore you can serve your country infinitely better by taking me to Finland than you can by going home to report for routine duty."

Freddie had straightened out and the compass showed that he was heading not north-east but west—for England; so Gregory threw his last reserves into the battle by continuing: "Then I want you to think of the future for a moment. What is Russia's real game? I talked to Goering for hours last night and I meant a lot of the things I said but others were so much hot air. The original programme of the Bolsheviks was world revolution, and they established the Comintern which financed subversive activities in every country with a view to carrying it out. But Lenin found the job too much for him. Russia was in such a ghastly state that he couldn't pull it together without securing help from the outside world; so he announced the

N.E.P.—New Economic Plan—by which the Bolsheviks pro-
claimed that they had altered their policy. Private internal
trading was to be allowed again and the Soviet was prepared to
recognize capitalistic governments in other countries and to live
in peace with them. From that time onward the Comintern
faded into the background. Nevertheless, Lenin made it
abundantly clear that the N.E.P. was only a means to an end.
He said in public speeches before his death that once Russia
was on her feet again they must revert to their original policy
and endeavour to bring about world revolution by any means
in their power, including conquest by the Red armies.

"Twenty years have elapsed since then. Russia is much
stronger now. In recent times the Comintern has become active
again and Stalin is beginning to show his hand. By his advance
into Poland and his peaceful penetration into Lithuania, Latvia
and Estonia he has already gobbled up millions of people and
barred his western gates against any future attack by Germany.
He hopes to give Germany enough food to keep her fighting for
years, which may weaken us to near breaking point and weaken
Germany to such an extent that when she does collapse the whole
of middle-Europe will fall into a state of anarchy. Then will
come Stalin's day and the Bolsheviks will march in there. France
was on the verge of a Communist revolution just before the
Spanish war broke out in 1936. The Marxists may fly their Red
flags in Calais and we should be in no state to stop them. With
strikes at home and the whole force of Red subversive propaganda turned against us, impossible as it may seem now, we, too,
might go Red and find ourselves the slaves of Moscow.

"It's up to us to try to avert such a peril by every means in
our power. If we can occupy Russia with Finland and divert
vital supplies from Germany we shall weaken Germany so that
we are more quickly able to win our own war and yet leave her
sufficiently strong to act as a bulwark against Russia. By inducing Finland to fight we shall also weaken Russia and—with
luck—her slow, lumbering growth into a world-menace will be
set back for years to come. Finland will be fighting Britain's
fight and the frontier of Christian civilization—the right of
every man, woman and child to justice, toleration and freedom
—to-day lies not in the west, Freddie, but *north-east,* on the
Mannerheim Line."

Freddie Charlton pressed his right foot down on his rudder-
bar, bringing the plane round in a beautiful curve. "You're
right," he said. "I'm afraid I don't know much about such

things and I've never quite looked at it that way before. You must be very tired, old boy; get some sleep. I'll take you to Helsinki."

"Thanks, old chap. I knew you'd understand directly I explained things; and even if we fail in our attempt I'm sure you'll never regret your decision." At last Gregory was able to relax and a few minutes later he was sound asleep.

As there was no longer any necessity for flying at a high altitude Freddie brought the plane down to 3,000 feet and headed for Danzig. The day was fine, and now that his wretched night was temporarily forgotten he was thoroughly enjoying being in the air again after his enforced three weeks on the ground.

On picking up Danzig he descended to 1,000 feet so that the German controls there could check him out of the country and report to Goering. Below him as he passed over the harbour he could see the tangled wreckage on the Westernplat Peninsula where the Polish garrison had held out so gallantly under a devastating bombardment from the German ships and shore batteries. Altering his course twenty degrees nearer to north he crossed the great, 150-mile-long bay west of Königsberg, picked up Libau on the Latvian coast, followed the coast-line for a while and thence flew over the Estonian islands.

The land below him had been snow-covered for the last three hundred miles of his journey and he had to go up to 6,000 feet to get out of a snow-storm over the Gulf of Finland but at a little after eleven o'clock he made a perfect landing on the hard-rolled snow of the Helsinki air-port.

In spite of the bumping the plane had got over the islands Gregory had slept for the whole of the four hours of the journey. Even the landing did not wake him, and Freddie had to shake him by the shoulder as the officials at the air-port came across to the plane. Once awake he declared himself much refreshed and having first established his British nationality by the production of the faked British passport he began to talk to the Finnish officials in voluble German, as they were more fluent in that language. His story was that they had flown direct from England with papers of the utmost urgency for the British Legation and that it was for that reason he had been given an R.A.F. pilot to bring him over.

The Sabina not being a war-plane, the question of interning it did not arise; but normally there might have been difficulties about Freddie. As it was, the Finns were all so concerned by the abnormal conditions created by the crisis, and the additional air-traffic which was constantly coming and going as a result of it, that Gregory had no difficulty in persuading them that Freddie's case was quite exceptional and that he should be allowed to retain his liberty—for the time being, at all events. A friendly official secured a taxi for them and, Gregory having directed the driver to take them to the best hotel, they drove through the suburbs to the centre of the town.

The driver set them down at the Hotel Kamp. Immediately Gregory entered it he pushed his way through the crowded hall to the porter's desk and got the man there to turn up two telephone numbers for him: that of the Finnish Foreign Office and that of the von Kobenthals. There were queues of waiting people before each telephone booth but Gregory got hold of the head porter and simply asked how much he wanted for ten minutes' use of the line in his office. The matter was soon concluded and the moment Gregory was alone he rang up the von Kobenthals' number.

To his immense satisfaction he learned that although Erika was not in she was still staying with the von Kobenthals, so he left no message but in the highest spirits hung up again and turned his attention to Monsieur Wuolijoki. The Foreign Office proved more difficult and it was a little time before he could get a connection; but after a short wait he got through to Monsieur Wuolijoki, and, announcing himself as Colonel-Baron von Lutz who had just arrived in Helsinki from Germany on urgent business, secured an appointment for three o'clock that afternoon. Both love and war seemed to be going splendidly and he left the office beaming.

Recrossing the hall, with Freddie beside him, he tackled a fair man at the reception-desk about rooms. It transpired that the hotel was very full owing to the crisis, but on Gregory's producing a fat wad of German bank-notes the clerk said that he could let them have a reservation which had only just been cancelled, if they did not mind sharing a double-room on the sixth floor. Gregory booked it at once and, since he had been checked in on the British passport by the air-port police, signed the register in his own name. He then changed some of his German *Reichmarks* into Finnish currency and told the clerk that they were going out to do some shopping as owing to a mishap they had lost their luggage. Goering's report and the mass of original papers that were with it formed much too large a packet to carry about conveniently so he handed it across the

144

desk and added: "While I am out I shall be glad if you will take charge of this and put it in the hotel safe."

"Certainly, sir," the fair man smiled. "I'll give you a receipt for it."

"Thanks," said Gregory as he took the slip. "I shall be wanting it again after lunch but it's very important that the greatest care should be taken of it. You're not to give it to anyone on *any* pretext, even if they produce this receipt, but keep it until I ask you personally for it."

As they stood there the sole possessions of the two Englishmen consisted of the few things that they carried in their pockets, so they went out to buy a couple of suitcases and various articles which would enable them to live for the next few days like civilized beings; including civilian clothes for Freddie, to make him less conspicuous and, above all, furs; as although they moved briskly they were already feeling the intense cold of the Finnish capital.

The Boulevard, which constitutes the principal shopping centre of Helsinki, was unusually crowded. The newspaper vendors were doing terrific business and on every corner there were knots of fur-clad people discussing the all-important question, "Shall we or shall we not be at war with Russia this time to-morrow?" Everywhere, too, there were squads of voluntary workers sandbagging the prinicpal buildings or frantically working upon air-raid shelters; but the normal life of the city was still going on. Every shop was open and doing a brisk business. With his excellent mastery of German, English and French Gregory found no difficulty whatever in getting the articles he required. The assistants in the shops were equally friendly whether they believed him to be German or British. Their enemy was Russia and their one question to every customer—whatever his nationality—was: "Do you think we are going to fight?"

In view of Russia's huge air force and the fact that the Finns could hardly expect any protection at all from their own tiny air-fleet, they were remarkably cheerful and the two Englishmen very soon saw that, whatever the view of the Finnish Government might be, the Finnish people—almost to a man—were prepared to take anything that was coming to them rather than surrender to the Bolsheviks.

With what was left of his own money and the 3,000 marks for which he had stung Goering Gregory had brought nearly £600 out of Germany, and furs are amazingly cheap in Finland so they had ample funds to buy the best of everything they wanted.

Helsinki has three harbours, the southernmost of which, overlooked by the unpretentious ex-Imperial Palace of the Tsars and the gilded, onion-shaped domes of the big Russian Church, is a great market. To it boats come from all parts, laden mainly with fish and farm-produce, but along the quays there are many stalls for every kind of merchandise. On this Tuesday morning an unusual number of people had flocked into the town to get the latest news so the harbour market was doing a roaring business and it was there that Gregory and Freddie completed their purchases, returning to the hotel just after one o'clock with two large suitcases stuffed full of parcels.

Just as they were moving towards the lift Gregory noticed a pretty dark-haired girl standing at the entrance to the lounge. A moment later Freddie also saw her and, dropping his suitcase, positively leapt forward.

"Angela!" he cried. "Darling! What in the world are you doing here?"

For a second the girl's face remained strained and uncertain, but ignoring the people who were talking excitedly all around them Freddie seized her in his arms, and Gregory saw by the sudden change in her expression to overwhelming happiness that for her the huge crowd no longer existed. Quietly picking up Freddie's suitcase he stepped, smiling, into the lift and left them to it.

When he got up to his room he unpacked his parcels and had a wash at the fixed basin. It then occurred to him to have a look at the typescript which he had stolen from under the bundle of notes out of Goering's safe, and removing his shoe he drew the pages out from the false sole. The script consisted of six folded sheets of transparent paper, all of which were almost entirely covered with close type. It was a carbon copy and evidently the original had been done by an amateur as there were many typing errors and crossings-out. Gregory deduced that whoever had typed it had been unused to such work and did not wish to have to do it a second time but wanted as many copies as possible. It was in German and headed: *"ARRANGE-MENTS FOR THE NEXT FAMILY-DAY"*.

Gregory read the first page and it appeared to consist of somebody's scheme to hold a big family meeting which was to include the discussion of certain business plans.

Many relatives were mentioned, mostly by their Christian

names, and none of these conveyed anything to Gregory. There was no date on it and no signature at its end. The script was thumbed and dirty so he was inclined to think that it had been got out by some old gentleman who was a remote relative of Goering's and who at some time or other had wished to rope in the now famous 'Hermann' for some big social gathering that he was planning.

It seemed that he had risked his neck for a document which had no political significance whatever, so with considerable disappointment he folded it and put it back into his shoe for further examination when he had more leisure. He had only just re-laced his shoe when Freddie came bursting into the room. His face was flushed, his eyes shining.

"Isn't it marvellous?" he cried. "Angela's here! That was her I ran into downstairs a few minutes ago."

"I had a sort of suspicion that it might be," Gregory smiled, "and I gather it didn't take you long to make up your quarrel either."

"Quarrel?" Freddie repeated with surprise. "Oh, we never quarrelled really—we've always loved each other."

"Splendid. Anyhow, I thought she looked a most lovely person and I'm more happy for you than I can possibly say, Freddie. But what's she doing in Helsinki?"

"Her father was transferred from our Consulate at Amsterdam to our Consulate here a fortnight ago. Apparently the pressure of work here has been increasing ever since the war started so Mr. Fordyce was sent out to lend a hand. He's a widower, you know, so wherever he goes Angela always goes too, to look after him. They want us both to lunch with them. If it's O.K. by you, I said we'd meet them downstairs in about ten minutes' time."

Gregory laughed. "I shall be delighted to lunch if they won't mind my slipping away immediately afterwards. I've got an appointment with a man at the Finnish Foreign Office for three o'clock."

"Oh, no, that'll be all right." Freddie dived at his suitcase. "I must get some of these parcels unpacked so that I can have a wash and change into my new clothes; then we'll get down to the lounge again."

Downstairs they found that the Fordyces had secured a table and were with difficulty retaining two empty chairs for their guests as the lounge was absolutely packed with people. Half the population of Helsinki seemed to have assembled there to see as many of their acquaintances as possible and discuss the latest rumours.

While Freddie made the introductions Gregory was smilingly taking in the father and daughter. M . Fordyce was a tallish man still in his early forties and as yet had not a single grey hair on his dark, smooth head. His double-breasted lounge-suit was of grey Glenurquhart tweed and he was unmistakably English. Angela was even prettier than Gregory had supposed from his first glimpse of her. Like her father she was dark and had blue eyes, a combination which suggested a touch of Irish blood in the family, but her skin was of that smooth whiteness which is spoken of as magnolia blossom and sometimes found in a special type of dark beauty. Gregory noticed that she used very little make-up and thought that just a touch more colour on her lips and cheeks would have made her still lovelier; for her eyes, however, nature could not have been improved upon, as she had long, dark, curling lashes.

After a glass of *aquavit* they went into the crowded dining-room and enjoyed an excellent meal. The smoked salmon—which is as cheap in Finland as herrings are in England—was, curiously enough, not of such good quality as that usually served in London; but the mussel soup was delicious, as the mussels—in which the Finnish coast abounds—had not been out of the sea for more than an hour. Stuffed pike, cooked over a wood-fire, followed and afterwards Gregory and Freddie tried their first bear steaks. Ordinarily, bear meat is inclined to be tough but this had been treated with oil—in the same way as the Italians prepare a tournado—and the meat had a distinctive, rather pleasant flavour of its own. To celebrate Freddie's and Angela's unexpected reunion Mr. Fordyce stood them champagne, and they finished up with a good selection of cheeses and Turkish coffee.

As they were celebrating the meal was naturally a gay one but most of the faces about them were grave and anxious owing to the crisis. Many of the women in the room were quite good-looking but very few of them had on any make-up; the lack of which left their faces curiously colourless compared with the usual restaurant crowd in London, and Freddie remarked upon the fact.

"My dear," Angela laughed, "didn't you know that for a girl to paint her face is the one deadly sin in Finland? That's why I make up so little here. The tarts use cosmetics as a badge of their profession but even they use only as little as possible—

148

just enough to show that they are tarts—otherwise they would never be able to attract the better class of men."

"I see," Gregory smiled across at her. "I thought it must be because they were rather puritanical, the old Protestant strain coming out. The Finns are said to be rather like the Scots in many ways, I believe, and nothing is more dreary than a Sunday in Scotland. They are Protestants, aren't they?"

"Yes, Lutherans," Fordyce volunteered. " And, curiously enough, Christianity was brought to them by an Englishman. King Eric the IXth of Sweden undertook, in 1157, a crusade to convert the heathen Finns, and with him he took his English chaplain, Bishop Henry of Upsala, who baptized the population *en masse*. The unfortunate Henry was assassinated the following year; but he evidently made himself popular with the Finns, as they canonized him and made him their patron saint.

"You're right about the Finns having much in common with the Scots, too. They're thrifty, hard-working people with a passion for education and the same sort of dogged courage which has made the Scots such splendid pioneers all over the world. The Finns are also great travellers; but as they have no Colonies to settle in, all their more adventurous young men become sailors and they serve principally in British and American ships."

Gregory nodded. "I imagine it's the long winter nights which make people in the northern countries like Scotland and Scandinavia so keen on education—plenty of time for reading— and once people get interested in books they almost always educate themselves."

"Yes. They are terrific readers. You've only got to look at the bookshops here to see that. Practically every worth-while book that comes out is translated into Finnish, and a bookseller was telling me the other day that the editions they print are very often as large as those printed in England; which is absolutely staggering considering the relative smallness of the population."

"This business of make-up, then," Freddie brought the conversation back, "is, I suppose, due to the same sort of strict morality that the Church of Scotland enforces so far as it can?"

"Oh, no. It's not that they're the least straight-laced," Angela hastened to assure him. "In fact, women are remarkably free here and the Finns have a passionate belief in the equality of the sexes. They were the first people to give women the vote; and if a servant-girl here has an illegitimate child nobody thinks

149

any the worse of her; she just stay; on in her job and the child is adopted into the family."

Glancing at his watch Gregory saw that it was nearly half past two, and he wanted to be in plenty of time for his appointment at the Finnish Foreign Office so he stood up and excused himself.

Having collected his furs from the cloakroom he thrust his way through the jam of people in the hall to the desk and said to the fair-haired clerk who had booked him in: "I want those papers back now that I gave you just before midday to put in the hotel safe."

The fair man looked at him in blank surprise. "But you sent for them yourself—half an hour ago, sir." He reached into a drawer and produced a chit. "We have your signature for them."

CHAPTER XIII

THE BEAUTIFUL ERIKA VON EPP

I TOLD you not to give that packet to *anyone*—on *any* pretext," Gregory snarled, the second he could give expression to his amazement and anger.

The clerk gave back before his angry scowl. "But, sir, you said you would be wanting the packet again after lunch and I thought . . ."

"But you say you gave it to someone half an hour ago. It would then have been barely two o'clock."

"In Helsinki many people lunch at midday, sir, and would have finished by then. I thought you were busy, perhaps, and so had sent your friend to collect your parcel."

"If I had, he would have produced the receipt you gave me; and I still have it here. What have you to say to that?"

"Only, sir, that visitors are often careless and mislay the receipts we give them. We consider it quite satisfactory if instead of the original receipt we have the visitor's signature for anything deposited. And here is yours." The clerk extended the slip of paper again.

Gregory glanced at it. "That's not my signature."

"Well, it's very like it, sir." The man shrugged apologetically and pointed to the place in the visitor's book where Gregory himself had written his name earlier that day. The forgery would not have been passed by a bank but it was a pretty fair imitation, and as Gregory stared at the fair, blue-eyed, bespectacled clerk he suddenly formed a very shrewd suspicion as to what had occurred.

The man behind the desk might be of Finnish nationality but he was certainly not one hundred per cent. Finnish. The Finns have no blood ties with other Scandinavian peoples—they are a race apart—and the only nation to which they are allied by blood and language is Hungary, for over a thousand years ago a colony of Finns migrated into middle-Europe and settled round Lake Balaton. The Finns are of two main types—the Karelians, who come from the North and the East and are a gay, pleasure-loving people, and the Tavastlanders, from the South and the West, who provide the more sober element—but neither has any resemblance to the Teutons; whereas the clerk's square head and thick neck betrayed his German origin.

That, almost certainly, was the key to what had transpired. The fellow was either a German or had relatives in Germany, which enabled the Gestapo agents in Helsinki to exert pressure on him. As part of his secret duties he had evidently reported that an Englishman had lodged a packet of important papers with him. The member of the Gestapo to whom he reported had then copied Gregory's signature out of the visitors' book and made the clerk hand over the packet.

Gregory knew that he could create a fuss, send for the manager, threaten to sue the hotel and call in the police; but none of these things would get back his vitally-important papers. He swiftly made up his mind that he would try to get the clerk sacked later, if he had time to spare, as the man was dangerous; but there was not a second to lose now. With the smallest possible delay he must try to get on the track of whoever had stolen the packet.

"What was the name of the man to whom you gave my papers?" he asked quickly.

"I don't know, sir."

"Is he staying in the hotel?"

"Oh, no."

"But you knew him?"

"Yes. He has been in here several times in the last two days."

"D'you know where he lives?"

The clerk smiled blandly, with almost open insolence. "No, sir, I haven't the least idea."

"All right. Describe him to me," Gregory snapped. "And remember this: the packet was such a big one that somebody must have noticed you handing it across the counter, and one of the porters would certainly have seen the man walk out with it. I'll have every person in the hotel questioned and if I find that you've lied to me about his description I'll have you put in prison for aiding and abetting a theft. *Now, then!*"

The clerk wilted slightly as he protested. "But I wouldn't dream of lying to you, sir, and the management will be most distressed about this unfortunate occurrence. The man said

152

you had sent him for the packet and produced your signature, otherwise I should never have given it to him. He was a big man, very strong, I should say, but rather fat. He had fair hair, cut like a brush in front."

"A German?"

"I couldn't say, sir, but he spoke to me in English and I thought he might be Scandinavian or Dutch. He had a heavy, pasty face, spoke in a shrill voice and was wearing a black patch over his left eye.

It was all Gregory could do to suppress an exclamation. The description exactly fitted his old enemy, *Herr Gruppen-führer* Grauber, the chief of the Gestapo Foreign Department, U.A.-1. What was Grauber doing in Finland? But that was easy. Grauber had his spies and agents in every capital and, naturally, now that Finland had become the new storm-centre of the war the Gestapo agents there would be working overtime. Grauber must have come to superintend their activities in person. He had probably walked into the hotel a little before two o'clock, glanced down the visitors' book and seen Gregory's name there. On questioning the clerk he would have learned about the packet that had been deposited and immediately decided that, whatever the papers were, they were very well worth getting hold of if they belonged to Gregory Sallust. With the clerk's connivance it had been a simple matter to copy the signature from the visitors' book and secure the packet.

By giving a correct description of Grauber the clerk had cleared himself of all but suspicion of complicity, while definitely confirming Gregory's conviction as to the manner in which the papers had been stolen. The fact that Grauber had obtained them under false pretences was of no immediate help, as with the Finnish crisis at its height it would take hours—if not days—to get a warrant for his arrest.

Without another word to the clerk Gregory turned abruptly away. It was unlikely that he would be able to get hold of Monsieur Wuolijoki before three o'clock, but Erika must have been in Helsinki for the last three weeks and through her connections among the German colony she would be certain to know something of Gestapo activities in the Finnish capital.

Crossing to the hall-porter, he gave him another lavish tip for the use of the telephone in his office and rang up the von Kobenthals. When he had asked for the Countess von Osterberg he was told to hold the line and a moment later a low, husky voice, that made his hand tremble as he held the receiver, said:

153

"Hallo? Who is that?"

"Colonel-Baron von Lutz," Gregory replied.

There was a little pause and then her voice came again. "I know your name, of course, *Herr Oberst-Baron,* but I don't think we have met. What can I do for you?"

"Oh, but we *have* met." Gregory allowed a smile to creep into his voice. "I last saw you at a farm-house outside Berlin, on the night of November the 8th."

There was a little gasp! then a swift whisper. "Gregory, is it you? It *must* be you. Oh, darling!"

"Hush!" Gregory whispered back. "For God's sake be careful. Can I come up and see you right away?"

"Yes, yes, at once—instantly."

"It is Colonel-Baron von Lutz speaking. You will remember that, won't you? I'll be with you within a quarter of an hour."

Replacing the receiver, Gregory pushed his way through the crush back to the crowded dining-room where the Fordyces and Freddie were sitting.

"Is anything wrong?" Mr. Fordyce inquired, on seeing Gregory's anxious face.

"Yes." Gregory bent down and lowered his voice. "A Gestapo agent has made off with my papers."

"How damnable! Was there anything very important amongst them?"

"They may make the difference between peace and war here in the next twenty-four hours."

Fordyce stood up quickly. "Is there anything that I can do to help? An introduction to the Chief of Police? I'll take you round to him personally if you like."

Gregory shook his head. "No; thanks all the same. We mustn't involve you in this owing to your official position. My situation is a very complicated one. Freddie will tell you all about it. Fortunately I know the man who stole them; he's an old enemy of mine named *Gruppenführer* Grauber, so I've at least got that to start with."

"What, the chap you told me all about?" Freddie exclaimed. "The fellow whose eye you bashed in on the night of the Army *Putsch* in Berlin?"

"Yes, that's the man. I must fly now and pull every gun I know to get possession of those papers again before Grauber can send them out of the country."

"When can we expect you back?" asked Freddie.

"I can't say for certain, but I'll try to return between five and

154

six. Still, don't bother about me. You're out of all this now and it's your own affair if you stay here or make arrangements for getting back to England."

"Good lord, no! I'm not quitting at this stage," Freddie announced quickly, "and I'll be standing by to give you a hand any time you want one."

"Thanks, Freddie, thanks. I'm glad you feel that way, because the chances are that I'll need all the unofficial help that I can get."

With a nod Gregory hurried away. The porter got him a taxi and he drove through the cold, sunny streets lined with their snow-covered buildings to the address of the von Kobenthals. It proved to be a long, low house standing in its own grounds, above one of the many bays along the shore, with a fine view of the scores of little islands which fringe the coast-line of South Finland.

He gave the name of Colonel-Baron von Lutz to a trim maid, who was evidently expecting him for she led the way straight across the hall to a comfortable sitting-room that over-looked the sea. Erika was waiting near the window, her eyes fixed on the door, waiting for him.

Inside the room he paused, drinking in once more all the perfection of her loveliness; her golden hair, her widely-spaced, deep-blue eyes, her generous mouth, the regal carriage of her head, her slim, beautifully-moulded figure. He knew that she was twenty-eight, but, in spite of her hard youth when half Germany was starving and the life of intrigue she had led since, she did not look a day over twenty-five. She was one of the very few German women he had ever known who had both the taste to dress well and the courage to ignore Nazi convention, which decrees that women's duty is to be useful rather than decorative. She was dressed very simply now but not a hair of her head was out of place and she carried herself with the air of a princess.

For a long moment they stood gazing at each other. The door closed behind Gregory; then without a word she was in his arms. They clung together as though they would never let each other go; not kissing, but cheek to cheek, straining together in a fast embrace. Suddenly Erika gulped and began to cry.

"Darling," Gregory murmured. "Darling, what is it? We're together again now."

"I know," she echoed, "I know. But it's too much; I can't bear it."

155

He laughed gently. "But, dearest, I've never seen you cry before."

"I—I haven't cried for years. I'm hard as nails—you know I am—at least, I was before I met you. I despise women who cry, but this—oh, I can't believe it's true." She dug her pointed nails into his shoulders.

"Yes, it's true, my sweet." He began to kiss her very tenderly; then with increasing passion until their mouths were locked in a long, breathless kiss.

Ten minutes later she was curled up on his knees in an arm-chair listening as he began to tell her how he had found out where she was and how he had managed to reach Finland himself. He left all details till later, giving her only the bare facts of how he had been shot down on his way out of Germany the night they had parted . . . taken refuge in the woods . . . managed to get back to Berlin to look for her . . . seen Goering . . . become the Marshal's secret emissary . . . and had his papers stolen by Grauber less than an hour before.

When he had done, he said: "Now where d'you think Grauber will have taken that packet? To the German Legation?"

She shook her golden head. "No. Goering has too many friends there, so Grauber wouldn't trust those papers to the Legation safe."

"Wait a minute," Gregory interrupted. "He can have no idea—thank God!—where I got all that stuff. My letter of introduction from Goering is still in my pocket so the Marshal's not involved. Grauber will assume that I managed to get back to Berlin and stole those papers somehow."

"Good. I'm glad for Hermann's sake that Grauber doesn't know the part he played. He's quite capable of looking after himself but it's better that he should choose his own time to have a row with von Ribbentrop on the question of major policy."

"That's exactly what he said to me himself."

"But what about the report? Won't that give things away?"

"No. I might have drafted that myself or it might have been compiled for me by a high-up German official in the pay of the British. Grauber will know that I couldn't have stolen all those documents without some sort of inside help. The thing is—what will he do now he's got them?"

"It's difficult to say," Erika replied thoughtfully. "There's no point in his sending them back to Berlin unless he can find out where you got them. That would simply be sending coals to Newcastle. He certainly won't hand them over to the Finnish Government, because he is Himmler's man and Himmler and von Ribbentrop are hand-in-glove. Von Ribbentrop naturally wants Finland to accede to Russia's demands without fighting so that there should be no further excuse for Russia's delaying supplies which he is counting on from her. Grauber won't pass the papers to the Soviet Legation here, either; there would be no point in doing that and it would only show how much we know of Russia's real weakness. As far as I can see, he will simply put them in his own safe at Gestapo headquarters."

"They have a headquarters here, then?"

Erika smiled, showing her small, even, white teeth. "Is there a capital in the world where the Gestapo have not got a head-quarters? Their H.Q. is a fair-sized private house in the north-eastern suburbs of the city. It's almost country out there and I suppose that's why they chose it; they didn't want too many people constantly watching their comings and goings. Every German in Helsinki knows it, though."

"Well, it's one of the things I wanted to know and it looks as if our chance of getting back my packet is by robbing the safe there."

"That's easier said than done."

"Don't I know it, darling. D'you think we could get any help from the Finns?"

"It all depends. To whom was your letter of introduction from Goering addressed?"

"It's not addressed to anyone but he told me to present it to *Monsieur* Wuolijoki, at the Finnish Foreign Office."

"Oh, Wuolijoki—he's a grand little man; I've met him at parties several times during the last few weeks. He's very pro-German; but by that I mean he's pro my kind of German—not Hitler's."

"Yes, I gathered that from Goering. But what matters now is—do you think he's the sort of chap who would be prepared to risk his job by adopting very unorthodox methods in the service of his country?"

"I don't know. But these Finns are extraordinarily patriotic. Both Germans and British consider themselves patriotic people but I don't think either of us has this love for our country so deeply in us as the Finns. Perhaps it's because they have only had theirs as a free people for such a little time. Every one of the men whom I have talked to these last few days says he would

157

much rather fight than give in to Russia; and by that they don't mean fight as our peoples would—with a good chance of coming back alive or, if they're wounded, being evacuated to a comfortable hospital where they'll have every attention until they're well again. By fight they really mean *go out and die*; because even the most optimistic of them know that Finland can't possibly stand up to a Russia's weight of numbers. They're openly making bets with each other as to how many Russians each of them will kill before he is killed himself."

Gregory remained silent for a moment. By his impostures in England, France and Germany he had caused the death of numerous innocent people, through no fault of his own. It was just his luck that he had managed to get away whereas they had been caught and had died as a result of their association with him; yet he had left a scarlet trail of blood behind him. Now he was an impostor once more, posing as Colonel-Baron von Lutz; and to what end? To plunge a whole nation into war when perhaps the wholesale suffering and death which war would inevitably bring might possibly be avoided.

He sighed. "Poor fellows, it's pretty frightful for them, isn't it? And it makes me feel an utter swine to think that it's my job to try to persuade their Government to take the step which will make their sacrifice necessary, when their lives would at least be safe if they gave Russia what she wants."

Erika shook her head. "They don't want their lives at such a price; and I believe they're right about that. It's not only the dishonour they would feel in having given up everything that they've worked for these last twenty years; they know that once they allowed the Reds through the Mannerheim Line no-one's life or liberty would be safe in Finland. All the writers, the officers, the capitalists, the deputies and the leaders of Finnish thought would be shot. The Universities and schools would be closed; there would be riots among the students and the Red Guards would shoot them down. Then Stalin would conscript the leaderless masses for forced labour and transport them into the depths of Russia. It would be the same frightful business of race extermination as is now going on in Poland. In five years' time there wouldn't be a Finn left in Finland."

"No. I suppose that's true," Gregory agreed, "and rioting wouldn't do them any good once the Reds were in here. If they're going to fight they must fight now. Holding the Mannerheim Line is the only chance they've got. If only they had an

Air Force as good as their Army—small as it is—I'd be a bit happier about things, though."

"Yes. That'll be the worst part—the bombing. But the women here seem as brave as the men, and they've made up their minds to face it."

"We'll pray they don't have to. After all, everybody thought that the Germans would bomb London the first day of the war; but they didn't; they haven't bombed it yet. There's just a chance that Stalin may not be altogether indifferent to world opinion and may refrain from using his Air Force on that account. But let's get back to Wuolijoki. I've got an appointment with him at three o'clock—as von Lutz, of course—so I'll keep it, present Goering's letter, tell him what's happened and ask his help."

"If you're going to ask him for any assistance which might prejudice his official position I think you'd better see him here. Even walls have ears, as they say, and I doubt if the Finnish Foreign Office is any exception."

"My clever sweetheart," he kissed the backs of her fingers one by one, "how right you are. And even if there's no leakage to the outside world, we don't want to compromise Wuolijoki with his own people should he be game to help us. D'you think you could persuade him to come out here?"

Erika released herself from his embrace, stood up, smoothed out her skirt and walked over to the telephone. "I'll try," she smiled.

It took her a quarter of an hour to get through but at last she was connected with Wuolijoki and told him that the person with whom he had an appointment at three o'clock was with her. For special reasons, which she could not explain, it was highly desirable that the interview should take place in private so, she asked, could he come out to the von Kobenthals'?

Wuolijoki said that he was frantically busy but that if the matter was really urgent he would endeavour to do so about tea-time. Erika assured him that it was of the utmost importance and begged him to come out at once, but the best he could do was to promise that he would definitely call between four and half-past. She then hung up.

She had hardly told Gregory the result of her conversation when they both caught the sound of a low, distant murmur like the rushing of a great wind. "Planes!" exclaimed Gregory, and they both ran to the window.

As they reached it the murmur increased to a thunderous

roar and, staring out over the snow-covered islands of the bay up into the pale-blue sky, they saw scores of black dots which within a few seconds took shape as great black war-planes rushing towards them. It was squadron after squadron of the Red Air Force coming up across the Gulf of Finland from their new bases in Estonia, less than fifty miles away.

CHAPTER XIV

TO SINGE THE GESTAPO'S BEARD

GRABBING Erika's arm as the leading planes hurtled low over-head, Gregory ran her towards the door. "Quick!" he cried, as he flung it open. "Where's the cellar?"

"It's only a demonstration," she protested, pulling back. "We should have been certain to have heard of it if war had been declared."

"It may be a demonstration with bombs," he said grimly. "Nobody ever declares war these days, so we're not taking any chances. If I were manning a machine-gun I'd stay above-ground and see the fun but only fools risk their necks when they're powerless to help with any form of retaliation. If we're wounded we'll only make more work for the ambulance men. Come on! Where's that cellar?"

"You're right." Erika had to shout to ensure herself being heard above the din that the planes were now making as they circled within a hundred feet of the roof-tops. "This way. The von Kobenthals have converted one of the rooms in the base-ment into an air-raid shelter."

She led him downstairs and along a corridor to a room, the ceiling of which had been shored up with big baulks of timber and its windows, only half of which were above ground-level, were protected with sand-bags. A fat woman—obviously the cook—was sitting there knitting and the maid who had let Gregory in was with her. The von Kobenthals were out, and two days before they had packed their two children and governess off to Sweden; but it soon transpired that a third maid was somewhere in the house, so forbidding Erika and the others to leave the room Gregory went up to look for her.

He found the girl in the back-garden, hands on hips, calmly staring up at the great black planes which might discharge their deadly cargoes at any moment; but she understood German and on Gregory's ordering her into the house she reluctantly accompanied him down to the basement.

Erika had turned on a wireless and had managed to pick up some dance-music which partially drowned the deep booming note of the planes. They sat there for some twenty minutes, but no bombs fell and, as the Finnish anti-aircraft squads kept their heads, no guns opened fire. Then the booming ceased and they knew that the Red air-armada had gone home after only showing itself as a ghastly threat to the people of Helsinki.

Upstairs in the sitting-room again Gregory found that it was only a little after three o'clock so there was still at least an hour to wait before Wuolijoki could be expected. There was nothing that he could do in the meantime so he and Erika were free to curl up on the sofa and glory in the joy of being together again while, in snatches of talk that were interspersed with frequent kisses, they exchanged particulars of what had befallen them during the time they had been separated. At four o'clock he reluctantly released her so that she could go and tidy her hair before Wuolijoki put in an appearance.

Soon after tea had been brought in Wuolijoki arrived. He was a small, dark man, only a few years older than Gregory; his eyes were black and quick with a humorous twinkle in them and as he spoke he used his hands all the time to gesture, like a Frenchman.

Erika introduced Gregory as *Oberst-Baron* von Lutz. Gregory clicked his heels and bowed in the approved manner; he then presented his letter of introduction from Goering.

Wuolijoki read it through carefully and handed it back. "May I see your passport, *Herr Oberst-Baron?*" he inquired. blandly.

"Certainly." Gregory produced the German one that had been made out for him.

Wuolijoki flicked through it and returned it as he said: "That is all in order. Welcome to Finland, Baron. How did you leave our good friend the Marshal?"

"Well but worried," Gregory replied. "He is entirely satisfied as to the progress that Germany's war effort is making but he is gravely concerned for Finland."

"Ah," Wuolijoki shot out his hands, "our dilemma is a terrible one indeed but it is good to know that we have the sympathy of the Marshal and all those sound elements which he represents in the new Germany. Where is this document, mentioned in the letter, which he states will be of such great assistance to us?"

"At the moment I believe that it's in the safe at the Helsinki Gestapo headquarters."

"But was it wise to leave it there? Unfortunately all Germans are not as yourselves and it is in the interests of the von Ribbentrop party that we should give way to Russia."

"I didn't leave it there," Gregory confessed. "I meant to bring it to you personally this afternoon but it was stolen from me at about two o'clock. It's for that reason we asked you to come here. I wanted to ask you outside the Foreign Office if you could give me your assistance to get it back."

Wuolijoki gasped; bowed to Erika as she handed him a glass of milkless tea with lemon and sugar, sat down and said: "What a blow! This is a major calamity. Do you know what was in the document?"

"Yes. It's quite impossible for me to remember all the details with which it is packed, because it took Marshal Goering nearly six hours to dictate, but I was with him the whole time so I can give you a general résumé of its contents." Gregory then proceeded to describe Goering's Herculean effort and ended up by relating how the package had been stolen from him by Grauber that morning.

"Why should a Gestapo agent steal a German officer's papers?" asked Wuolijoki; and Gregory knew that he was on difficult ground. It had been essential to use his fake British passport at the air-port, otherwise he would have been faced with all sorts of awkward questions as to why he had arrived in the company of an R.A.F. pilot; and, in case of a check-up by the police, to use it again at the hotel afterwards. But on no account must Wuolijoki be allowed to suspect that the Colonel-Baron was really an Englishman, for the Finnish diplomat would then never believe that he had come from Goering and, owing to his extreme pro-German feelings, would change at once from a potential friend to a dangerous enemy. But Gregory was prepared for such a question and replied calmly:

"Because he knows that I was one of the officers concerned in the recent Army *Putsch*. It was for that reason Marshal Goering chose me as his messenger. I have been in hiding on my estate in Brandenburg for the past three weeks so I'm no longer on the Army register and am presumed either to be dead or to have escaped abroad. Therefore the Marshal was able to send me out of the country without arousing the suspicion which would have attached to the sudden disappearance of one of his own staff."

The Finnish diplomat appeared satisfied as he said: "I suppose this man, Grauber, got on to you when you checked in at the air-port? The Gestapo would almost certainly have one of their spies among our officials there."

"No. We thought of that, and to evade such a possibility the Marshal gave me a faked British passport and a British prisoner-of-war pilot, who agreed, as the price of his liberty, to bring me over. He also provided us with a Belgian plane. Grauber got on to me at the Hotel Kamp because I am posing there as a British subject."

Gregory lit a cigarette and puffed it with considerable satisfaction. He felt that he had very neatly circumvented a nasty snag which might have arisen at any time if Wuolijoki had happened to hear that a man answering the description of Colonel-Baron von Lutz had arrived in Finland on a British passport and accompanied by a British flying-officer.

"The Cabinet are sitting now," said Wuolijoki suddenly. "They have been in almost perpetual session for the last three days but they will take their final decision to-night. Our great patriot, Marshal Mannerheim, is urging them to fight and the people are behind him; but the Government still hesitate. They are afraid not for themselves but of the terrible responsibility that will rest upon their shoulders if our women and children are massacred and our towns and villages devastated by Russian bombs. I fear that the Red Air-Force demonstration over Helsinki an hour ago will seriously have weakened the moderates among them, who may now go over to the 'peace-at-any-price' party."

"It's by no means certain that there will be air-raids in the event of war," Gregory argued. "We Germans have so far refrained from bombing London."

"That is true. And I think that in any case the Cabinet would decide to fight if only they could be certain that the Red Army will not overrun the country in the course of a few days. Marshal Mannerheim declares that he can hold his line, but if he's wrong it would be pointless for us to call upon our people to sacrifice their lives."

"You agree, though, that you would be justified in doing so if the line could be held?"

"Certainly. If we could prevent a Russian break-through for a month there would be a real hope of saving our country.

Norway and Sweden know that we shall be fighting their battle as well as our own and even if they do not openly declare against Russia they will send us munitions, planes and volunteers. Every country in the world will recognize that we are championing the ideals of Christian civilization against the evils of atheistic tyranny and they will send us aid of some kind or other. But meanwhile we shall be as David before Goliath, with only the courage of our own little army to throw into the scale against the enormous weight of the Russian masses."

"Marshal Goering's report on the state of the Red Army will convince even your most pessimistic Ministers that Finland can hold out for a month on her own; I'm certain of it," Gregory said swiftly.

"In that case it is vital that we should get it back; but how do you propose that I should help you?"

"Could you find some pretext for your police to raid the Gestapo Headquarters?"

"Wuolijoki shook his head. "This is a free country, my friend—not Russia; we do not use such methods here."

"But if the fate of Finland depends upon it," urged Erika. "After all, it is not like asking you to raid the German Legation, which might create an international incident."

The little man turned quickly towards her. "True, *Frau Gräfin*. We have no official knowledge that the Gestapo have a Headquarters here at all; it is a private house out in the suburbs, leased by a German citizen. But that does not alter the position. Private property here is sacred whether owned by a Finn or a foreigner."

"If I attempted to burgle the place on my own," Gregory said, "I shouldn't stand a dog's chance; and even if I could get as far as the safe, I have only the most rudimentary knowledge of safe-breaking. That's why our only hope is a raid which will keep the occupants of the place busy while somebody who understands such things tackles the safe. I take it that unofficially you would raise no objection if I organized such a raid privately?"

"Ah; that is a different matter."

"If there is any excitement out there are the police likely to come on the scene quickly?"

"No, no. It is quite distant from the centre of the city. Your only danger of that kind would be from a solitary patrolling policeman."

"Good. Could you provide me with bombs and a safe-breaker?"

Wuolijoki raised his eyebrows. "The use of bombs might cause loss of life. It seems that you are prepared to go to any lengths, Baron?"

"Certainly; for your sake as well as mine, since the independence of Finland is at stake. I shall need incendiary-bombs to cause a fire which will keep Grauber and his people occupied while the safe-breaking is going on."

"I must warn you that our police would take a very serious view of such methods, but I could certainly get you a couple of bombs."

"How about a safe-breaker? Your police must know of a man who would be prepared to take on the job if his immunity were guaranteed. He would have to speak German, English, or French, though, so that I could tell him what I wanted done."

Wuolijoki nodded. "That is more difficult, as no immunity could be granted; but a friend of mine in the police might know a safe-breaker who would risk a prison-sentence in the service of his country."

"How about the lay-out of the house? Do you happen to know it?"

"No; but I could easily find someone who does. At what time do you propose to make your raid?"

"The sooner the better; it's dark already. The time must depend upon how long it will take you get me my bombs, my safe-breaker and a rough plan of the house."

Wuolijoki glanced at his watch. "It is now ten past five. Three hours should be enough. Shall we say nine o'clock? I will return here then with all that is necessary." As he spoke he stood up, kissed Erika's hand and shook hands with Gregory. "Forgive me if I leave you now, but my own work is overwhelming and this business gives me many additional things that must be done. Till nine o'clock, then."

When the diplomat had gone Gregory smiled at Erika. "Well, that's that; we're on the move again, thank goodness."

She took his arm and drew him down beside her. "Yes, darling, I know; but the risk you're taking is terrible. There will be at least a dozen Gestapo men in that place—probably more—and they'll all be armed."

"Yes; it's going to be tough work," he agreed. "But it won't be worse than the Adlon on the night of November the 8th, and I'll have the advantage of surprise. They won't be expecting anything of this kind in law-abiding Helsinki and I promise you, sweet, I won't take any risk that's not absolutely necessary; I never do."

"But if you have to kill anybody you may get into frightful trouble. The Finns have an enormous respect for their own law and I doubt if even the knowledge that you had killed a man in their interests would influence a Finnish court in your favour."

"Well, let's not think of the Vistula until we're over the Rhine," Gregory smiled.

"But the Rhine in this case is about as deadly as it possibly could be. Oh, my darling, I can't bear to think of you risking your life again within a few hours after your return to me; and to go into that place alone is like a soldier attacking a machine-gun nest single-handed."

"I'm not going in alone. I'm certain that I can count on at least one fellow to go in with me." Gregory disentangled himself again, and added: "May I use your telephone?"

"Of course."

"Thanks." He went over, and getting through to Freddie at the Hotel Kamp asked him to come out to the von Kobenthals' house at once.

While they were waiting for him the von Kobenthals came in. Fredeline von Kobenthal—Erika's cousin as it transpired—was a pretty, but rather stupid-looking blonde of about thirty; and Oscar, her husband, a well-set-up, fair, blue-eyed, moustached man of about the same age. He had always been anti-nazi and had been wise enough to get his money out of Germany and settle in Finland several years before, while von Hindenburg was still President and Hitler only a menacing figure upon the political horizon.

With the hospitality customary among Germans of good family they greeted *Oberst-Baron* von Lutz most charmingly and expressed their hope that he would make his home with them during his stay in Helsinki.

Gregory accepted with spontaneous gratitude although, privately, he doubted if events would enable him to make much use of their invitation. Von Kobenthal got on the telephone at once and gave instructions at the hotel that Gregory's things should be packed and brought out there as soon as possible.

They had hardly settled the matter when Charlton was announced, and Gregory introduced him as the British officer who had regained his liberty by agreeing to fly him secretly to

Finland. At first the von Kobenthals were distinctly cold in
their reception of Freddie, as their country was at war with his,
but they gradually thawed out when they found that their new
acquaintance, the *Oberst-Baron,* whom they had instantly
accepted as one of themselves, had made a friend of the young
airman.

It was a tricky business but Gregory managed it well, and
Freddie played up splendidly to the leads he was given. As soon
as he could Gregory switched the conversation to the Finnish
crisis. Having explained that although Germany and England
were at war it was to their common interest that Finland should
resist Russia, he disclosed to the von Kobenthals—who knew
Goering—the reason for his presence in Finland and the
extremely difficult situation which had arisen as the result of
the loss of his papers. Then he went on to outline his plans for
a raid on the Gestapo Headquarters that night.

When he had finished, his secret hopes were gratified as von
Kobenthal said at once: "I'm heart and soul with the Finns;
they're splendid people and have been extraordinarily kind to
my wife and myself since we've made our home here. They've
got to fight unless they want to be exterminated, and as you're
acting for Goering that's quite enough for me; I'll come with
you."

Freddie then took his cue and said in halting German: "I'm
not interested in Field-Marshal Goering but I'd do anything
to give these poor wretched Finns a hand, and since my country
is fighting to maintain the rights of small nations, in this particular case our interests, so far as I can see, are identical. You
can count me in too."

It was an amazing situation that a German and an Englishman, and an Englishman who was posing as a German, should
be quite prepared to forget that their countries were in a death-
grapple for world supremacy and make common cause for what
they all considered to be right to the extent of risking their lives
in the same venture; but the crisis was having an extraordinary
effect on the psychology of everyone in the Finnish capital and
by the time champagne-cocktails had been served they were all
talking together as though no state of war had ever existed
between Germany and Britain.

Dinner would have been a gay affair had it not been for the
undercurrent of fear for their men which tugged at the heart-
strings of the two women, but they both did their best to hide

their anxiety and the party was still busy with coffee and liqueurs when Wuolijoki was announced.

With him he had brought a little wizened individual with shaggy hair who smiled politely at everybody in a rather embarrassed way.

The Finnish diplomat was an old friend of the von Kobenthals so Charlton was the only member of the company unknown to him. Erika performed the introductions and informed him at once that everyone there knew about the projected raid. Wuolijoki returned Freddie's smile with a frigid bow but he accepted the story that the British airman had earned his freedom from a prisoners-of-war camp by flying Gregory to Finland and made no comment on the Englishman's willingness to co-operate with the Germans in their anti-Gestapo activities. He then presented his small companion as Mr. Suki, a gentleman with very extensive knowledge of safes and a particular aptitude for dealing with combination-locks.

Mr. Suki nodded to them with a rather sheepish grin and gratefully accepted the drink that von Kobenthal poured out for him, as Wuolijoki hurried on:

"There has been a major development since I was here this afternoon. The 'peace' party in the Cabinet have gained the upper hand and have now agreed to all the Russian demands with the exception of two."

"That means giving up the Mannerheim Line, then," Erika said quickly.

"Yes, *Frau Gräfin*. We shall be delivering ourselves, naked and bound, into the hands of the Bolsheviks unless something can be done in the next few hours. For that reason the matter of securing Field-Marshal Goering's report now becomes of the greatest urgency. It is the last hope by which Field-Marshal Mannerheim might yet induce the Government to reconsider their decision and make a stand." Wuolijoki turned to Gregory. "You are still determined to make this attempt, *Herr Oberst-Baron*?"

Gregory nodded. "Yes. And these two gentlemen have volunteered to come with me."

"Good. I had hoped that you might secure private help, since it is impossible for me to give you any officially. You realize, of course, that this whole affair is illegal and that if you are caught you will be answerable for your actions to the Finnish law?"

"Yes, we know that."

"For that reason I am most anxious that there should be no shooting if it can possibly be avoided. I have brought two bombs, one explosive and the other incendiary. It is to be hoped that they will be sufficient to distract all the occupants of the house while you are at work. If not, you must try to hold up anyone who interrupts you until you have finished, and the more deadly your weapons the more likely a successful hold-up without bloodshed will be. To help you in this I have brought you two of our *Suma* automatic rifles which fire twenty-five rounds a minute and, of course, if you *are* compelled to fight they will give you a much better chance of escaping alive than if you were armed only with pistols."

"That was a grand thought. Did you manage to secure a plan of the house?"

"Yes." Wuolijoki drew a paper from his pocket and spread it out. "The house, as you will see, stands in its own grounds with a drive up to its front but with one of its sides abutting on a lane. The whole garden is surrounded by a wall but, fortunately, out there in the suburbs there will be few people about at this hour of night, so you should have no difficulty in getting in, unseen, over it. The front room on the lane side of the house is used as a dining-room. Behind it are the kitchens. The front room on the garden side of the house is used as an office. The room behind it is a private office also used for conferences, and it is there that you will find the safe."

"All right," said Gregory, taking charge. "Then I shall place the bombs in the lane so that their explosion, which should blow a hole in the wall and set fire to it, will bring everybody running to that side of the house. If they can't get in unseen at the gate, the rest of the party will come in over the front wall the moment the first bomb goes off and break open a window of the back room on the garden side. I shall rejoin them directly I have placed the bombs. Mr. Suki and I will then enter the house and while he works on the safe I will hold the door with one of the sub-machine-guns. In the meantime the other two will remain in the garden to deal with anybody who comes round the house and protect our retreat. Is that all clear?"

"It will not do," Wuolijoki shook his head. "If you place the bombs in the lane they may injure or kill some innocent person who is passing at the time."

"They must be on that side of the house," Gregory insisted, "in order to draw its occupants in that direction and give us a

170

free field on entering the back room; otherwise we should be compelled to start a shooting match at once."

"I think Fredeline and I could help you there," Erika said, glancing at her cousin.

"No, no," von Kobenthal protested. "Neither of you must be mixed up in this."

"Oh, I'm not suggesting that we should play any part in the burglary or run any risk," Erika smiled, "but we could stand in the lane about a hundred yards on either side of the bomb, or far enough away to be out of danger; then if either of us saw anyone coming along at the critical moment we could engage them in conversation and keep them with us until the bomb had gone off. We could pretend that we had lost our way—or anything."

"Excellent, *Frau Gräfin*, excellent!" Wuolijoki cried. "In that case the plan is good. Let us set off. I have my car outside so I can drop some of you there and I will wait near-by so that there will be no delay in the Colonel-Baron's handing the packet to me if he can manage to get it."

"We shall want a second car in any case," von Kobenthal said, "as we ought to have at least one in which we can make a quick get-away." He glanced at his wife. "We'll take ours, dearest, and you had better drive. You can park it at the entrance to the lane, stand a few yards from it in case you have to delay a pedestrian for a few moments, then get back into the driver's seat immediately the bomb has exploded."

"Oh, Oscar," she laughed, "how thrilling! It's almost like a gangster film, isn't it?"

"I wish we *were* only making a film," said Erika soberly as she looked across at Gregory.

They filed out, put on their furs, distributed the weapons and bombs and entered the two cars. Twenty-five minutes later the cars entered a long, lonely road right on the outskirts of the city and drew up a hundred yards short of the house. It was pitch-dark, as a black-out rehearsal was in progress—a piece of unexpected luck which cheered Gregory enormously, since he knew that it would make it much easier for them to get in and out over the garden-wall without being spotted by a patrolling policeman or some civic-minded citizen; which was a part of the operation that had been worrying him considerably.

Gregory, Charlton, von Kobenthal and Suki got out, and Wuolijoki turned his car round; while Fredeline von Kobenthal drove hers on, with Erika in it, to the corner of the lane. The raiding-party then made an inspection of the front wall, with the aid of a small torch which Suki carried hung round his neck so that when it was on he could work by its light with both hands free.

The wall was broken only by a single gateway, and this was of solid wood. They tried it, but it was locked, and a long bell-pull that hung beside it indicated that anyone who wanted to get in had to ring for the porter. Gregory directed the other three to climb in over the wall at its furthest point from the lane, where it adjoined another property, and leaving them with a whispered "Good luck", went along to the corner, where he found Erika waiting for him near Fredeline's parked car.

With Erika beside him he proceeded along the lane until they reached the side of the house, which was blank except for its kitchen-entrance. He set down the two bombs and the rifle that he was carrying and took her in his arms. They clung together for a moment. then she drew herself from his embrace and disappeared down the lane in the darkness.

There was a drift of snow against the wall. Gregory dug down into it for a couple of feet, put the bombs up against the brickwork in the bottom of the hole he had made and released the springs which Wuolijoki had told him would cause them to detonate in sixty seconds. He then began rapidly to tread the snow back on top of them with his foot, knowing that the firmer he could embed them the more shattering the explosion would be. For forty seconds he worked like a maniac, piling up the snow and stamping it down; then, snatching up his automatic rifle, he ran for his life.

CHAPTER XV

HERR GRUPPENFÜHRER GRAUBER
WINS A TRICK

STUMBLING, with every ounce of speed he could muster, through the darkness and the heavy snow that clogged his steps, Gregory had barely covered fifty yards when there was a crash like a six-inch gun behind him, a reverberating roar and the sound of tumbling bricks and mortar. Turning his head he was just in time to glimpse a lurid sheet of flame that seemed to leap right up the wall of the house and, in its glare, he saw a score of brickbats hurtling towards him.

Next second he had flung himself flat in the drift of snow under the wall of the lane, escaping the pieces of flying brick except for one that caught him on his right foot, which was still outside the shelter angle. Jumping up again, he ran on past Fredeline von Kobenthal, who was standing on the corner, and round it, down the main street, to the extremity of the front garden. The garden wall was not a high one. Slipping one arm through the sling of his automatic rifle he ran up the slope of snow at the foot of the wall, jumped, grabbed at its top, hauled himself up and wriggled over.

On the far side he landed among some snow-covered bushes. Forcing his way through them he found a path and ran along it down the side of the house. As he ran he heard the shouts of its inmates which told him that, as he had planned, the explosion had thrown them all into confusion. Next moment he was brought up sharp by a swift challenge; but it came from von Kobenthal, who had the other automatic rifle. He was covering his two companions further along as they worked on the window.

"Good man. Stay where you are," panted Gregory. "Don't expose yourself more than necessary—get behind a tree or something—and if anyone else comes from this direction don't challenge but fire right away. Put a couple of rounds over their heads to check them."

Leaving von Kobenthal groping through the darkness in search of suitable cover, Gregory hurried on. Just as he reached the other two Suki got the window open. At the same instant an electric burglar-alarm began to ring with a deafening clatter.

"Find some cover if you can, Freddie," Gregory shouted, "and fire at anyone who comes round from the back of the house. Two rounds over their heads and the next at the flash of their pistols if they attack you."

As Charlton moved off, drawing his revolver and a pistol that von Kobenthal had lent him, Suki got the inner window open and Gregory thrust in his hand, pulling the black-out curtains aside. The room was brightly lit but empty. He could hear the shouting in the house plainly now; a first-class rumpus was in progress. Grabbing the window-sill he hoisted himself up and over it.

There were two doors to the room. One led on to the passage, and somebody had left it half-open after dashing out, as was evident from a freshly-lit cigarette, the smoke of which was curling up from an ash-tray on a table-desk near the window. The other led to the room at the front of the house. Gregory saw that the key was in its lock, and tiptoeing over, turned it.

As Suki came in through the window Gregory reached the passage door. This also had a key in it, but on its outer side. Swiftly transfering it to the inner side of the door Gregory locked that too.

"Quick!" he whispered to Suki in German. "We must barricade ourselves in"; and between them they dragged the heavy desk up against the passage door. It was the only large piece of furniture that the room contained, so Gregory muttered: "Get busy on the safe; I'll see to the other door"; then, exerting all his strength he carried three tall, thin steel filing-cabinets across and set them against it.

The safe was a large affair which stood in a corner of the room, between its two windows, one of which looked out on to the back garden and the other—through which Gregory and Suki had come—on to the side-garden. As was to be expected in any Gestapo office, the safe had a combination lock, but it was not of the most modern type and after a swift preliminary examination Suki declared that he thought he could deal with it. While Gregory piled up all the chairs and other odd pieces of furniture that he could find in jumbled barricades against the

174

two doors Suki began to operate with swift, deft fingers on the combination lock, listening to the fall of the tumblers with each turn that he gave it.

Having completed the barricades Gregory switched out the lights so that if the Germans came round to the back of the house, broke open the window there and pulled aside the curtains he should not present an immediate target. The room was now in darkness except for the thin pencil of light shining from the torch hung round Suki's neck on to the lock; where, his small wizened face set and concentrated, he worked with frantic speed.

There was no more that Gregory could do and he crouched near the safe-breaker with his rifle at the ready, listening to the noises that percolated from the other part of the house. The shouting had now subsided and he could catch only the sound of loud, guttural voices which came to him muffled by the distance. The burglar-alarm had ceased to ring, petering out in a spasmodic jingle soon after he had fixed the barricades. Since nobody had tried to get into the room as a result of the clamour he decided that all the windows on the ground-floor, and the doors, were probably wired by the same system, and that the Nazis believed that the alarm had been set ringing by the explosion on the far side of the house. But another noise had now taken the place of the shrill ringing; it was a low, angry roar, and Gregory knew that his incendiary-bomb was doing its work in the breach that the explosive-bomb had made. The house was on fire.

He wondered anxiously if Wuolijoki had judged the size of the bomb correctly. Their objective had been to start a fire which would keep the Gestapo men occupied for a quarter of an hour or so but which, with the help of a fire-engine, could be put out. But if the bomb was too big the fire would get too great a hold to be dealt with, in which case the Nazis would abandon the fight and come running to the other rooms to save their papers and belongings before the flames spread to the rest of the house.

Suddenly the handle of the door to the passage rattled. There was a pause. It rattled again. Someone outside was shaking the door impatiently. Gregory remained as still as a mouse. Suki's fingers continued to flicker over the combination-lock; his head was bent down towards it as he listened to the clicking which was almost inaudible except to anyone with his supernormal hearing. There was a sharp knock on the door and

175

a voice said: *"Hier ist Schumacher. Lassen Sie mich hinein Kommen."*

On receiving no reply the man moved away. Gregory could hear his heavy footsteps as he marched down the hall. A moment later the knob of the other door rattled. On finding that also locked the man called out in a surprised voice:

"Grauber, sind Sie dort?" And once more getting no response, he moved away from that door too.

Gregory crouched there, with his automatic rifle at the ready, praying for time. Once they started to batter in the doors the noise might be too great for Suki to catch the sound of the falling tumblers any more and all chance of getting the safe opened would be lost. Turning to the little man he whispered urgently: "How are you going?"

"Fine," Suki nodded. "I'm nearly through; another few moments."

As he spoke feet sounded in the passage again. There was a murmur of quick, angry voices; then a heavy rapping on the door.

"Wer ist da?" cried an impatient voice, which Gregory recognized as that of Grauber. *"Offen Sie sofort!"*

There was another brief pause, the mutter of voices again, then a heavy body crashed against the door in an endeavour to burst it open. The woodwork strained but did not give, as the lock was a stout one and still held. Ten seconds' silence followed, then a series of deafening reports. Someone outside was blowing the lock off with an automatic.

Gregory's lips tightened. He had hoped to get through with the business and away before the arrival of the fire-brigade or police so as to avoid any risk of running up against the Finnish authorities. The fire-engine had not yet arrived or he would have heard the clanging of its bells. Wuolijoki had assured him that it would take the best part of a quarter of an hour to get out to this remote district so he reckoned that there were still some minutes to go before it could come on the scene. But one or two patrolling policemen must have heard the bomb go off, and if they had already reached the house the sound of the shots was certain to arouse their unwelcome curiosity.

The roar of the explosions had hardly subsided when heavy bodies came crashing at the door once more. The lock was shattered but the big desk still held the door in position. After a few moments of frantic banging, as the men outside tried to

176

force it, they gave up and there was another muttered consultation.

Thump! Bang! Crash! A sudden assault had been launched without warning against the door leading to the front office. It strained and groaned but the weighty filing-cases prevented its being forced open. The din was still going on when there came the sound of splintering glass on Gregory's right. A second party had gone out of the house with the intention of coming in through the window that overlooked the back garden.

Poor Suki now stood with a look of despair on his face and his hands dangling by his sides. It was impossible for him to continue his operations in such a hellish clatter. Gregory knew that the doors were safe for the moment but he watched the window like a lynx. A second later the inner panes were shattered and came tinkling to the floor. In the faint glow from Suki's torch Gregory saw the black-out curtain suddenly twitch, as a hand grasped it from outside, and knew that he must wait no longer. He was within a couple of feet of the window; aiming a few inches below the place where the curtain was caught up, he fired.

There was an agonizing scream and the curtain went quite smooth again, with nothing to show what had happened except for a little round hole in it about six inches above the window-sill. At the sound of the shot the banging on the office door ceased abruptly; Suki instantly got busy again in a silence broken only by the distant roaring of the fire yet pregnant with alarming possibilities.

Gregory crouched low beneath the level of the window-sill, expecting a volley of shots to crash through the black-out curtain at any second. Suki in his corner was safe from any blind volley directed at the window and could not be hit through it, unless somebody outside got right up against the house and fired in at a sharp angle.

Suddenly two shots in quick succession sounded outside. Gregory could not tell if it was von Kobenthal or Charlton, but evidently the Nazis were now attempting to get round to the side-window of the room and had come up against one of his' two friends.

There was another silence of perhaps a minute. He looked anxiously at Suki. At that very second the little man gave a chuckle of delight and swung the safe-door open. Shuffling swiftly towards him on his knees Gregory followed with acute anxiety the safe-breaker's little torch as it flickered over the safe's contents. Was his packet there, or had they risked their lives for nothing?

With frantic speed he began to tumble out bundles of documents, letters, cash-box. scattering them all over the floor; then he tried the drawers below the main compartment. His packet was lying in the second. Grabbing it up with a sudden surge of elation he thrust it under his furs and wedged it so that it could not slip down, above the belt that held his fur-coat tightly in to his body.

He had hardly done so when pandemonium broke loose. A volley of shots thudded through the black-out curtain; the sound of more shots came from outside in the garden; and at the same moment, as though they had been waiting for a signal, a third party of Nazis launched themselves in a fresh attack on the passage door.

Gregory let fly at the black-out curtain which was now riddled with small holes. As he emptied the contents of his automatic rifle into it another cry rang out, showing that his blind fire had accounted for at least one more victim.

Ramming home another clip of cartridges he swivelled round to the door that was creaking and groaning under the weight of the bodies that were being hurled against it. Suki had switched out his torch, so the corner in which they crouched was now in thick shadow. It was that which had saved Gregory from a bullet in the back; for the body of the room was still faintly lit, and the light, now Suki's torch was out, came from the passage door, showing that it had at last been forced. It was open about three inches, and the black splodge that broke the line of light about half-way up was a hand which had been thrust through the opening, gripping an automatic.

The pistol flashed three times, sending pot-shots in various directions. Gregory raised his rifle and, firing at the flashes, sent three shots back. There was a yell as the man at the door was hit and the tearing of wood as one of the bullets grazed the door-frame. Bullets were still streaking through the window and volley after volley sounded from the side of the house. A long wail of pain came, showing that somebody out there had also been hit.

Springing up Gregory grabbed Suki by the arm. "Now we've got what we came for we must get out of here."

As they ran to the side-window the outline of a head suddenly appeared above the sill. Gregory raised his rifle but a voice cried: "Don't shoot! It's Freddie"; and Charlton began to heave himself up through the window.

"Don't come in, you fool!" Gregory yelled. "We've got the goods—now we must make our get-away."

"You can't," panted Freddie. "They're too many for us—came round both sides and caught us between two fires. Von Kobenthal's hit. We'll have to try to hold this room."

He was half in the window, half out, when he gave a sudden "Ouch!" of pain and fell back into the garden.

"Oh God!" groaned Gregory. "He's hit!" And he blazed off over the sill from which Freddie had fallen. There was a rush of feet; then a crackle of answering shots which drove him back from the side-window.

With Suki beside him he took up his old position in the corner by the safe, cursing his luck that they had not been able to get it open a few minutes earlier. They might have escaped then; now they were trapped.

Bullets were whistling through both windows and the pounding on the door continued with increased ferocity. Gregory fired another burst at it, hoping that his bullets would pass between the legs of the chairs he had piled on top of the desk and penetrate the panels. For a moment the din ceased, but it was renewed almost instantly. Someone began firing from the partly-open door again, scattering bullets all over the room in the semi-darkness. Suki gave a piercing screech and grabbed his leg where one of the stray shots had caught him in the thigh. Gregory fired at the flashes in the doorway. His trigger-finger was pressed down, but after two shots the rifle went silent; he had come to the end of his reserve clip of ammunition and Wuolijoki had given him only one spare, as he had never visualized the possibility of the raiders having to fight a pitched battle.

The room was now full of acrid smoke; their eyes smarted from it and the stink of it was strong in their nostrils. Suddenly a whistle blew, the firing outside ceased and Gregory wondered anxiously what new menace this portended. Throwing down his empty rifle he thrust his hand under his furs to get the automatic which he was carrying in his hip-pocket.

At that instant there came the crash of falling furniture. Three of the Nazis had hurled themselves against the door with such force that the chairs had fallen from the top of the desk as it was jolted back. One man pitched head-foremost through the now half-open door, the other two tumbled over him into the room; a fourth switched on the lights.

Gregory's fingers had only just found the butt of his automatic and owing to the heavy clothes that he was wearing he could not draw it swiftly. Jerking away his hand he grabbed up his rifle to club it. Except for the fog of cartridge-smoke the room was now bright as day.

The two Nazis who had forced their way in had drawn their pistols and had Gregory covered, when a high-pitched shout came from the passage:

"Don't kill that man! I want him!" And Grauber lumbered through the doorway.

The Nazis put up their guns. Both of them were hefty, bullet-headed men. The third, who had fallen by the desk, was now on his feet again and the fourth followed Grauber into the room.

Suki was lying groaning in the corner clutching his wounded thigh from which the blood ebbed slowly. Gregory had only just grasped his rifle. He was on his feet but had no time to draw himself erect before the two leading Nazis came at him with a rush. He dodged a blow that one aimed at his head, but the other kicked him in the ribs and sent him spinning sideways. He managed to land his foot in one fellow's groin as he went over, and the man gave a howl of agony, but next moment he was on the floor and the other three Strong-Arm men had flung themselves on top of him.

The breath was driven out of his body. He was kneed, kicked and pummelled until, incapable of further resistance, he was lugged to his feet with his hands twisted behind him and found himself looking into Grauber's face.

Herr Gruppenführer Grauber had never been a handsome man at the best of times. He was strong but paunchy and his bull neck rose to a cannon-ball head with fair hair, cut *en brosse*. His face was pasty and his eyes had been a muddy, nondescript colour under his almost-white eyelashes; but now there was only one of them. Gregory himself had bashed out the other with the butt-end of an automatic and the wound was covered by a large black patch. After one glance at the safe Grauber advanced on Gregory with a mincing step.

"*So!* Mr. Sallust," he said in his high falsetto, "you're up to your old tricks and you thought you'd rob me. But it is not so easy to break into a Gestapo Headquarters."

With a swift, catlike movement he wrenched open Gregory's furs and ramming his hand inside drew out the big packet.

"Thank you," he smiled. "Now we will find out the name of the traitor in Berlin who gave you these. Take him down to the cellar, men. I'm sure my ingenuity will be sufficient to make him talk."

CHAPTER XVI

A QUESTION OF IDENTITY

GREGORY had an excellent memory. He did not need to be reminded of what Grauber had done with the lighted end of a cigar to poor old Tom Archer's eyes, only six weeks before, on his secret visit to London. He recalled, too, with the utmost vividness the acid-bath in the secret Gestapo Headquarters in Hampstead and the frightful death which Grauber's lieutenant, Karl, had inflicted upon the unfortunate Jacob Rosenbaum. No-one had better reason than himself to know that the Gestapo were every bit as merciless outside Germany as in it if they once got an enemy into their clutches.

With racing brain he endeavoured to assess his own chances. Now that the firing had ceased and he had not rejoined Wuolijoki the diplomat would know that the attempted burglary had failed and would assume the raiding party to be wounded or dead. Wuolijoki had made it quite clear that, anxious as he was to have Goering's report for submission to his Government, his official position made it impossible for him to play any part in this legal affair. Finland was not only at peace with Germany but in the Finnish War of Independence Germany had been her sole ally. For twenty years the relations between the two countries had been excellent—right up to the time of the Russo-German alliance in the previous August—and, in spite of that, were still good. They might be most seriously damaged by a Finnish Foreign Office official's participating in what amounted to be a gangster-raid on the Helsinki Gestapo Headquarters. Gregory felt that he could not possibly count on any help from Wuolijoki.

Erika and Fredeline von Kobenthal would still be waiting anxiously outside. But what could they do apart from endeavouring to comfort each other for the non-reappearance of their men out of the desperate shooting-affray which they must have heard? Other people, too, must have heard the shooting, even in such a sparsely-populated neighbourhood. The fire was still roaring, so by this time quite a crowd must have gathered outside; but during the hectic quarter of an hour which had elapsed since the bombs went off Gregory had not heard the clanging of the fire-engine bell, so he felt certain that the fire-brigade had not yet got out there.

What would happen when the fire-brigade did turn up, or when the police, some of whom must be on the premises by now, began to ask questions? The local civilians would certainly tell them about the shooting. Grauber would satisfy their inquiries by saying that a gang of bandits had attacked the place and been driven off; upon which it was unlikely that further inquiries would be made until the morning; and Gregory had good reason to believe that by the morning he would have cashed in his cheques after a lingering and most painful death.

As two of the Nazis began to drag him towards the door a third said: "Is it safe to put him in the cellar, Chief? They haven't got the fire under yet."

Grauber's one eye narrowed and Gregory saw his last hopes fading as the Gestapo Chief considered the best means of preventing any interference between himself and his prisoner. "True," he said; "and the fire-brigade may be arriving at any moment. Go and get Flugel."

As they waited there Grauber filled in the time by getting a little of his own back on the enemy who had caused him such acute mental and bodily distress. While the two Nazis held Gregory upright the *Gruppenführer* swung his fist and caught him a smashing blow in the middle of the face. His upper lip was cut against his teeth, his nose began to bleed and the pain from it caused the water to start to his eyes and run down his cheeks.

"How do you like that, Mr. Sallust?" Grauber asked in his thin, piping voice. "It is only one-thousandth part of what is coming to you."

He swung his fist again, this time hitting Gregory not on the chin but just below it so that his collar-stud was driven home, like a small hammer, on to his Adam's apple. The pain was excruciating and by reflex action Gregory immediately began to vomit.

Gregory knew both these blows and had used them himself upon occasion; one to make a man cry, the other to make him sick; and in his pain-racked mind he wondered what the Gestapo Chief would deal out to him next. Perhaps he would put on one of the leather gloves that still lay on the desk and strike him a glancing blow across the cheek, which Gregory very well knew, by the sharp drag of leather on skin, would lay his face open from the corner of his eyebrow to his chin; but he was saved from that by the appearance of a short, gorilla-like man who had the look of a professional wrestler.

"Well, Flugel?" Grauber turned to him. "How are you doing?"

"We're getting the fire under, Chief. Good thing we had those chemical extinguishers; but we had no chance to fetch them from the bedrooms until we'd mopped up the men outside. A crowd has collected out in the street, but so far only three policemen have put in an appearance. I told them that we'd been attacked by Jewish Communists who had made their escape into the darkness after an exchange of shots. As all the Finns loathe Communists they seemed to think it a pity that we hadn't killed some of them, and now they're helping our fellows to put out the fire."

At that moment they all caught the sound of a clanging bell and shouting from the street as the fire-engine drove up.

"They'll be coming through the house in a minute," Grauber said quickly. "We don't want them to see that we've taken any prisoners so we'd better not take this man out through the hall." He nodded at the two men who were holding Gregory. "Get him out through the window and take him down to the shed at the bottom of the garden. No-one is going to look down there for the people who attacked us. Take his little friend who forced the safe with him, and if either of them starts to shout bang them over the head. But don't kill the Englishman; I'll attend to him myself later."

Gregory knew that it was no use trying to argue. If he attempted a big bluff, that they had better be careful, as friends of his in Helsinki knew where he had gone and would come in force to rescue him if he did not return to them by eleven o'clock, Grauber would first laugh at the threat and would then probably kill him on the spot in case there was some truth in his assertion.

The two Nazis marched Gregory towards the back window; a third hauled the groaning Suki to his feet. Gregory could hear the firemen stamping into the front hall now; but he dared not shout for help as it would only have resulted in his being knocked out.

Suddenly a head appeared in the window at the side of the

house and a gruff voice said in German, with a heavy Finnish accent: "What's going on here?"

The whole party turned to stare as a police captain hoisted himself up over the sill and slid into the room. To Gregory's unutterable relief he was followed by Wuolijoki; and more men came crowding in behind them. The Finnish diplomat had arrived with a squad of police.

As Grauber recognized the officer's uniform his manner changed instantly; he became again the urbane, plausible, mild-mannered business man which was his usual pose when outside Germany.

"Ah! How timely your arrival, *Herr Hauptman*!" he smiled. "We have been attacked by Jewish Communists; they placed a bomb at the far side of the house which has partly shattered it and started a fire. While we were trying to put it out they broke open our safe to steal important papers which are the property of the German Government."

"That's a lie," Gregory interrupted. "You were not attacked by Communists and we did not come here to steal papers that are the property of the German Government."

Grauber ignored him and hurried on: "Fortunately, we discovered them before they managed to get away; but they fired on us, wounding a number of our men, and in self-defence we were compelled to fire back. Some of them are out in the grounds, but these two we took prisoner here."

"Those papers that you are holding," declared Gregory impressively, "are the property of His Britannic Majesty; you secured them this morning, under false pretences, from the management of the Hotel Kamp with whom they had been lodged for safe-keeping. I came to demand them back and you and your men fired upon me and my friends without warning."

The story was thin—thin as tissue-paper—since it did not account for the bomb or the looted safe and the presence of Suki, who was known to the Finnish police as a safe-breaker. Yet, while he could not say that the papers had been given to him by Marshal Goering, by dragging in the British Government he gave himself at least some sort of title to them, and he knew that the Finns would think twice before allowing British official documents to remain in German hands after an allegation that they had been stolen. Moreover, it was just the cue that Wuolijoki needed.

Stepping forward the little man extended his hand abruptly to Grauber. "I am an official of the Finnish Foreign Office.

185

Those papers will be safe in my keeping until such time as this dispute has been settled and we have ascertained to whom they rightly belong. Kindly hand them over to me."

"I protest," exclaimed Grauber swiftly. "In the name of the German Government, of which I am a high officer, I demand the right to retain this packet."

"As a representative of His Britannic Majesty's Government I demand that it should be handed back to me," Gregory declared with equal force.

"You see?" Wuolijoki shrugged his shoulders and looked from one to the other. "The only possible course is that I, as a neutral, should take charge of it until the question of their ownership is settled."

"No," said Grauber. "I don't know you; I refuse to give these papers up."

"I know the gentleman all right," said the police captain; "he is Monsieur Wuolijoki, of the Finnish Foreign Office. There's been quite enough trouble here to-night already. You'd better do as he suggests."

"And if I resist?" Grauber's face went deadly white and his hand moved towards the pocket into which he had slipped his automatic.

"Then we'll have to take them from you." The captain jerked his head over his shoulder. "I've got six men here and there are plenty more outside. You'll find yourselves in grave trouble if you resist the police. Now then, hand those papers over!"

As Grauber reluctantly extended the packet to Wuolijoki Gregory sighed with relief. Goering's report would be laid before Field-Marshal Mannerheim in less than an hour. He had fulfilled his mission after all.

The police captain glanced towards the two Nazis who were holding Gregory. "Release that man."

Grauber stepped forward. "I will not allow this. He is a bandit; he broke into this house; he fired upon my friends. It is monstrous that he should be allowed to go free."

"Easy, easy," replied the officer. "Who said he was to be allowed to go? I'm taking him *and* the whole lot of you to police headquarters; and you'll remain there until we get to the bottom of this affair."

"*What?*" From deadly white Grauber's face suddenly became crimson as the blood rushed into it. "You mean to arrest me and my friends? What about the fire? And look; this room that has

186

been half-wrecked—all my papers scattered about the floor."

"That's all right. The fire-brigade will deal with the fire and I shall leave a couple of my men on guard here. Nobody will interfere with your papers."

"But many of them are secret documents."

"I can't help that. There was shooting on both sides, so all of you are coming with me."

Gregory had the greatest possible difficulty in suppressing a grin. His only regret, apart from his anxiety as to what had happened to Freddie and von Kobenthal, was that he had not had time to destroy Grauber's papers once the safe was open; but he felt certain that Wuolijoki would have the good sense to get one of the Finnish Secret Service people out there in order to go through them during the night.

The police captain suddenly stepped towards Grauber and laid a hand on the pocket that bulged with his automatic. "I'll relieve you of this for the time being," he said, and signed to his men, who collected the pistols of the other Nazis.

The whole party was then led across the hall, out of the front door and through the garden, to the street where, in a space that had been cleared of a curious and growing crowd, two police-vans were waiting. Another squad of police was sent in to collect the Nazis who were still dealing with the fire and to search for others in the house and grounds. Meanwhile the first batch of prisoners was sorted out.

Grauber and his men were put into one van, and Gregory and Suki into the other. As he stepped into it Gregory was immensely relieved to find Charlton and von Kobenthal there. Freddie was only just recovering from a blow from a pistol-butt which had caught him on the back of the head as he was standing at the window and had temporarily knocked him unconscious; but von Kobenthal was wounded both in the shoulder and in the right arm.

They had barely exchanged greetings when the torch of the policeman who was lifting Gregory into the van shifted, revealing Erika further inside it. Caution demanded that she should conceal her elation in front of the policeman but she could not altogether repress the look of joy which suddenly suffused her face as she saw Gregory alive and unharmed, and immediately the van doors were closed she flung herself into his arms.

"What on earth are you doing here, my pet?" Gregory whispered as the van jolted into motion.

"I was caught by a civilian," she answered quickly, "a man

187

who entered the lane from my end just before the bomb went off. I stopped him and pretended I had lost my way, just as we arranged. Then the explosion occurred and he thought that I must have had something to do with it, so in spite of my protests he hung on to me until the police turned up. But what does it matter—what does *anything* matter except that you're alive and safe? My heart nearly choked me with every shot that was fired."

Gregory grinned into the darkness of the speeding van as he held her tight. "Yes. It was a pretty tough business and I was lucky to come out of it better than the rest. But we got the packet all right; Wuolijoki has it now, so it's on it's way to Mannerheim."

"Oh, splendid, darling—splendid! Did you see Grauber?"

"Did I not!" Gregory could still taste the salt blood that had been running from his nose. "The swine cornered me and I'm afraid I won't be much to look at for the next few days, darling, but the police arrested him and all his boy-friends as well as us and they're on the way to police headquarters in another van."

"How about Fredeline?" Erika suddenly asked; and von Kobenthal answered out of the darkness:

"She got away all right; I saw her standing among the crowd as I was led out. She saw me, too, so—thank God—she knows that I'm not dead."

"What d'you think they'll do to us?" Freddie inquired.

"Nothing," said Erika promptly. "Wuolijoki will fix it somehow so that we're released to-morrow morning."

At police headquarters the wounded were helped out and the little party was put into a bleak waiting-room furnished with pitch-pine. A large stove roared in the corner and the heat was almost unbearable after the intense cold outside. The police captain came in to take their names. Erika, Charlton, von Kobenthal and Suki gave theirs without hesitation, but Gregory found himself in a most disagreeable quandary. As he had claimed to be a representative of the British Government the officer would think it extremely strange if he gave the name of von Lutz; yet if he gave that of Gregory Sallust the British Legation in Helsinki would equally disclaim all knowledge of him. However, it didn't much matter what the police thought, so long as Wuolijoki was not given the least reason to suppose that there was anything phony about Marshal Goering's emissary. Wuolijoki would have assumed, Gregory felt certain, that he had only claimed to be British in front of Grauber as a ruse to contest the true ownership of the papers and provide a reason for their being given into a neutral's keeping. The diplomat would expect Gregory to disclose his German identity once he was out of Grauber's presence, so after having pretended for a moment not to have heard the officer's question Gregory gave his name as Colonel-Baron von Lutz. The captain blinked, but he was a stolid man; he made no comment and went off to make his report, leaving two policemen with them.

A few minutes after he had gone a doctor came in to make a first examination of the wounds of von Kobenthal and Suki. He declared that none of the injuries was serious, and having applied first-aid dressings, said that he would later attend to them properly. Twenty minutes elapsed; then the party was led along a passage to the room of the Chief of Police. The officer who had arrested them was with him.

The Chief of Police was a grizzled-haired man with a sweeping moustache. He spoke in German, telling them all to be seated. He then signed to the captain and the men who had brought them to leave the room and, when the door was closed, said abruptly: "I don't pretend to know what lies at the bottom of this affair but I have received a note from *Monsieur* Wuolijoki asking me to give you every consideration possible. In consequence, if you are prepared to pledge me your word that you will not attempt to escape I shall not put you in cells for the night."

They all voiced their agreement to his proposal and he went on:

"That is satisfactory, because as two of you are wounded they would normally be sent to the infirmary; but owing to the crisis every hospital in Helsinki has now been evacuated in case of an unprovoked air-attack. We wish to keep every bed free; but I can give you a room where beds will be made up for you and those of you who are unwounded can then look after the others."

"I am quite prepared to act as nurse," Erika volunteered.

The police chief nodded. "In that case you can remain with your friends, *Frau Gräfin;* otherwise I was going to provide you with separate accommodation." He pressed a buzzer on his desk and a police orderly appeared. Having thanked the Chief of Police for his courtesy they said good-night and filed out into the passage.

The orderly led them up to the fourth floor and into a room which looked as though it was used as a lounge by some of the Finnish detectives. It had a large table, numerous chairs

189

and three sofas. The doctor rejoined them a few minutes later, bringing with him two more orderlies who carried piles of bedding.

Von Kobenthal and Suki were helped to undress and their wounds were properly bathed and bandaged while Gregory washed the blood from his bruised face. One bullet had gone through the fleshy part of von Kobenthal's arm and the other was lodged in his shoulder. Extracting it was a painful business but he stood it well and they then got him into a bed that had been made up on one of the sofas. Suki's wound was only a long cut where a bullet had grazed the upper part of his thigh and he declared himself quite comfortable when they had tucked him up in a second bed. Three others were then made up, one on the remaining sofa for Erika and two on the floor for the unwounded men; after which the doctor and the orderlies departed, locking the door behind them.

Gregory dimmed the light so that the wounded men should have a better chance of getting off to sleep; then he sat himself down beside Erika on her sofa and told her in a low voice the details of what had occurred inside the Gestapo Headquarters.

When he had done she smiled, and said: "Well, thank God that's over, and I feel sure we'll all be free to-morrow. It's rotten luck, though, that we should have to spend the first night of our reunion like this."

Gregory felt as badly about it as she did but they tried to console themselves with the thought that they were at least together again, and after a while he urged her to lie down and get some sleep. But she would not hear of it, as she meant to look after von Kobenthal and Suki through the night and the doctor had left with her various items, such as Veganin tablets to give the men if they were in pain and barley-water for them to drink if they were thirsty.

For a time the two of them sat silent in order to give the others a chance to get off to sleep; then, when snores told them that their object was accomplished, they lay down together and exchanged more detailed accounts of all that had happened to them during the three weeks they had been separated.

At seven o'clock police orderlies came in to rouse them. A police matron appeared, who took charge of Erika and led her away to the women's section where she was able to have a steambath and tidy herself; while the orderlies took Gregory and Freddie to the men's baths where they had their first experience of the national manner in which the Finns cleanse themselves.

190

They stripped, and, instead of an ordinary bath, were led into a steam-room where the temperature was very high and they sweated profusely. Afterwards they were given large towels with which to rub themselves down and were lent razors so that they could shave.

On returning to their room they found Erika washing the two wounded men and, in due course, a good, plain breakfast for all five of them was brought up. The doctor appeared at nine o'clock and after examining the two invalids he reported that the wounds were clean and that both were doing well. Suki's wound was so slight that the doctor measured him for crutches and said that he would be able to get up the following day.

The doctor having gone Gregory insisted that Erika should get some sleep and Freddie said that Gregory ought to do so too, volunteering to look after the other two while they slept; but they did not get very long, as at half past ten Fredeline von Kobenthal was shown in, having obtained permission to see her husband.

When she had fussed over Oscar and assured herself that they were being well looked after she told them that in spite of the fact that the Finns still remained outwardly calm the underlying feeling that in a few hours the crisis would reach a head was stronger than ever. From an early hour that Wednesday morning—long before the late winter dawn—everybody in Helsinki had been out and about making feverish preparations against the Russian onslaught, as rumour now had it that the Finnish Government had definitely determined to resist; which looked as though Goering's report was having due effect.

Fredeline was allowed to stay for an hour and, being satisfied that her husband was not dangerously wounded and that they would all be released quite shortly, she amused them with her chatter. Soon after she had gone a midday meal was served, but no official came up to see them so they remained in ignorance as to how their case was being regarded, until Wuolijoki was shown in at half past four. He looked extremely worried and when they questioned him he said at once:

"After seeing the report Marshal Mannerheim determined to make the strongest possible stand and early this morning he submitted his views, together with the report, to the Cabinet, who are still considering their decision. But I did not come about that." He turned his glance on Gregory. "I wish to know who you are?"

191

Gregory stimulated blank surprise. "But I told you yesterday, I am Colonel-Baron von Lutz."

"I'm not quite satisfied about that."

"Really!" Gregory shrugged. "My credentials are all in order. You saw both my passport and the letter from Field-Marshal Goering, so what possible reason can you have for suddenly questioning my identity?"

"But you had two passports," Wuolijoki persisted; "the German one which you showed me, and a British passport—in the name of Mr. Gregory Sallust—which you presented on your arrival at the air-port here. Then, last night in front of me you claimed that you were acting on behalf of the British Government."

"True. But I couldn't possibly admit, in front of members of the Gestapo, that I was acting on behalf of Field-Marshal Goering. I had to lay some claim to the papers—and that seemed to me as good as any."

"It is curious, to say the least of it, that you should have arrived here piloted by a British Air Force officer."

"Flight-Lieutenant Charlton agreed to fly me to Helsinki as the price of his liberty. I *told* you that yesterday."

"Perhaps. But having carried out his part of the bargain why should he involve himself further in your affairs? He is an Englishman; while you say that you are a German. England and Germany are at war. It is not natural that two enemies should agree to risk their lives together in the way that you two did last night."

"It was my idea entirely," Freddie volunteered. "I simply couldn't resist the chance of having a cut at some of those swine in the Gestapo."

"Well—we shall see," Wuolijoki said non-committally; and Gregory did not like his tone at all.

Although he did not show it he had an unpleasant premonition that he might soon find himself in very serious trouble. This impostor business was a great game so long as nobody could check up on one, but in order to keep Goering out of it he had had to play a dual rôle in Finland—landing there as an Englishman so that the Gestapo should not suspect that he had come from Germany, then posing as a German so that Wuolijoki should readily accept him as Goering's envoy. He remembered Goering's telling him that Wuolijoki was half-German, through his mother, which accounted for the fact that the diplomat was distinctly anti-British in his outlook. He had accepted Freddie without open hostility the night before, evidently considering him as no more than a pawn in the game, but if he once secured definite proof that Gregory was also an Englishman the fat would be in the fire. He would regard himself as having been tricked, start looking for hidden motives which did not exist and probably withdraw any protection he was at present prepared to give them, and on which their fate now hung, on account of his inbred enmity for the British.

"I take it we can rely on you to get us out of this?" Gregory said with an assurance he no longer felt; and he waited with acute anxiety for the Finnish diplomat's answer.

CHAPTER XVII

THE TRIALS OF AN IMPOSTOR

WUOLIJOKI regarded Gregory with a distrustful stare as he replied: "The present situation is none of my seeking. The last thing I wished was that a shooting affray should result from your suggestion of burgling the Gestapo Headquarters. Now, unfortunately, the matter has become a diplomatic incident. The German Minister here made the strongest possible protest to my Government this morning about the arrest of the Gestapo men, and since it cannot be concealed that your party were the aggressors we have been compelled to release them; whereas you people must remain under arrest."

"D'you mean that the Finnish police are going to bring charges against us?" Erika asked indignantly.

Wuolijoki looked uncomfortable. "*Frau Gräfin,* it is true that I sponsored this venture unofficially and even assisted it by supplying bombs and the best arms to utilize in a hold-up; but I *did* warn all concerned that in the event of any shooting your friends would be held responsible by the Finnish law. In the fight last night four Gestapo men were wounded—one of them very seriously. God knows, I did not wish to bring the police into this affair but after the shooting had been going on for a few minutes I realized that the only way to get your friends out of the place alive was to have them arrested; so I went off in my car and collected a squad of police from the nearest station."

"Yes; you certainly saved our lives," Gregory agreed. "But what is to happen now? You know as well as I do the reason why we raided the place. Through the raid you were enabled to secure those documents which are so vital to Finland and which will be of inestimable value to her if she decides to defend herself. Surely you don't propose to abandon us after we have rendered your country such a signal service?"

"First I must know if you are, in fact, Colonel-Baron von

Lutz or Mr. Gregory Sallust, and an inquiry is in process which I trust will reveal your true identity. When I have that information I shall know how to act."

'Here are these damnably awkward suspicions cropping up again,' thought Gregory uneasily. 'Perhaps if I test out the fellow's reactions to the possibility that I might be one of the British he appears to hate so much, we'll learn a little more where we stand.' So he shrugged and said: "Just supposing that on some trumped-up evidence you did decide that I was an Englishman, what difference would that make? It was I who got Marshal Goering's report to Finland for you, and that's the only thing that really matters."

"Not at all!" Wuolijoki gestured violently. "Whether you're a German or an Englishman makes a great deal of difference. If you are a German you have acted with me in good faith and there can be no reason to doubt that those documents are genuine. In that case I shall feel a definite obligation to get you out of this trouble. I cannot alter the Finnish law but I could arrange for the Finnish police to connive at your escape."

"Thank you; that is no less than what I expected," Gregory said quietly, but the half-German Finn ignored his interruption and hurried on:

"If, on the other hand, you are an Englishman you have lied to me for some reason best known to yourself. It may be that you are an *agent provocateur* and that all those documents which you brought to Finland were forged with the object of inducing Finland to go to war as a pawn in the game that the Western Powers are playing—caring nothing for her, but just so that Russia should be distracted from sending supplies to Germany for a few weeks. If they are forgeries the details in them can no longer be facts culled from an authoritative source. If we act upon them, and they are incorrect, thousands of Finnish soldiers may lose their lives in consequence of alterations in our strategy. In such a case you will have acted as the betrayer of my country, instead of as its friend, and I shall not lift one finger to avert such consequences as may come to you as a result of the affair last night."

Before Gregory could speak again Wuolijoki bowed to Erika and, turning sharply on his heel, left the room.

"Are you an Englishman?" von Kobenthal suddenly asked from his bed.

"Yes," Gregory replied frankly. "I'm sorry I had to deceive you about that; but the whole situation was so damnably

195

complicated and my one anxiety was that Wuolijoki should have no reason to question the authenticity of the report; otherwise he would never have supplied us with bombs last night—and without bombs we should have been powerless to pull the job off."

"The report we risked our lives for was faked, then," said von Kobenthal bitterly. "You swine!"

"Good God, no!" Gregory took no notice of the abusive epithet. "I give you my word of honour that every one of those documents is absolutely genuine. We flew direct to Helsinki with them from Karinhall."

Freddie nodded. "That's so. I'll give you my word on that as well."

Von Kobenthal frowned. "You expect me to believe that Goering would trust an Englishman with such a mission?"

"You don't understand, Oscar," Erika hurried into the breach. "Mr. Sallust is an English agent but he has proved himself our friend. It was he who made possible the Army *Putsch* of November the 8th, and Uncle Jocheim decorated him with the Iron Cross for his services. Goering knew that he was an Englishman but also knew that he could be trusted."

"I see," said von Kobenthal slowly. "Well, I suppose if von Pleisen decorated him he *must* be one of us. It seems a queer business, though, that we should be hand-in-glove with an Englishman when our two countries are at war."

"No queerer than that you should have consented to go in with Charlton, here, last night," Gregory pointed out.

"No; but the whole thing was arranged so swiftly that there wasn't much time to think about it then."

"Our interests were entirely indentical; you *must* agree about that."

"Yes, that's true; but since you *are* an Englishman, what's going to happen if Wuolijoki finds that out? The whole report will be discredited as a fake and we'll have landed ourselves in a pretty mess for nothing."

Gregory smiled. "Oh, no. If the report had been faked they would have discovered that before now. You can bet that the Finnish Secret Service were working on it all last night and all to-day. They must have quite a bit of information about Russia themselves. The report will check with that and amplify it; whereas if there are lots of discrepancies and improbabilities in it the Finns would know that it was a fake—even if Goering had

196

handed it to them himself. No. We've done our job, all right, and the report will do its work."

"In that case we haven't much to worry about," said Freddie optimistically. "Directly Wuolijoki is convinced that the report is genuine he'll become friendly again and get us all out of here."

"That's the spirit, Freddie, my boy!" Gregory patted him on the back. He was by no means certain that Charlton's reasoning was logical, as it failed to take into account Wuolijoki's extremely anti-British bias, which Gregory now considered to be their gravest danger; but he welcomed the cheery confidence of the airman, whose whole personality seemed to have changed since the day before when he had so unexpectedly found his Angela. All through their time in Germany he had been suspicious, difficult and pessimistic, whereas for the last twenty-four hours he had been willing, easy and amazingly cheerful; so the last thing Gregory wished to do was to damp his new-found optimism. For the morale of the whole party, too, it was much better that they should no longer dwell upon Wuolijoki's change of attitude—at least, until they had some more definite reason to fear that it might bring serious consequences on themselves. He therefore loudly declared that Freddie was right, and proceeded to change the conversation.

Dinner-time came at last and, shortly afterwards, the doctor appeared to have another look at his patients. With him he brought a pair of crutches for Suki and the news that the United States had offered to arbitrate in the Russo-Finnish dispute.

The day had been one of great strain in the Finnish capital, so the doctor told them. Everywhere the whole population had been working frantically on last-minute preparations to face the onslaught of their giant antagonist; evacuating children, sand-bagging buildings, preparing yet more and more beds in the buildings that had been taken over as temporary hospitals. All the younger men of the nation had been mobilized for weeks and were already at their war stations on the Mannerheim Line and along the chain of lakes and canals which form the Russo-Finnish frontier north of Lake Ladoga; but in the last few days many more classes had been called up. The streets were full of middle-aged reservists going off to join their units while men of any age up to seventy—and older—were drilling in the fire-fighting and ambulance squads against the possibility of devastating air-attack.

That was the great danger. The Finnish Air Force was

absolutely negligible compared to the thousands of planes which the Russians could put into the air. Unlike London at the beginning of the war, Helsinki had no balloon-barrage and very few anti-aircraft guns for its defence, yet, according to the doctor, the people were wonderfully calm in spite of the great danger which threatened them and which they could do so very little to avert if it were once launched for their destruction. The women were proving as brave as the men and doing men's work; filling the sand-bags, digging air-raid trenches and taking over a thousand and one jobs so that their men-folk could don their uniforms and go to the front. Nevertheless, that Wednesday had been one of terrible tension and the news of the American offer of mediation had been received with inexpressible relief.

America, the doctor went on, had always had especially friendly feelings towards his country because Finland was the only European nation which had honoured its debt and paid up in full the American loan made in the last Great War. True, the loan was not a very large one, but the thought that a small country that was by no means rich should have managed to meet its obligation, when other much wealthier and more powerful countries had failed, had appealed to American sentiment. The American people were passionate believers in democracy, too, so it was certain that they would not let Finland down. If the United States mediated, Finland might have to accommodate Russia on certain points—such as demilitarizing some of her island fortresses, giving trade concessions and allowing the Russians access to her ice-free port of Petsamo in the far North—but the great American people would see to it that Finnish independence was preserved.

"I wouldn't count too much on that," Gregory advised him. "I'm sure that the American statesmen would like to help you, and also many of the more cultured Americans, but unfortunately the fate of Europe means very little to the millions who live in the Middle West. In spite of papers and radio the bulk of them are still much more remote from world affairs than most of us are apt to imagine. They've known one war in their lifetimes and they can't see any earthly reason why they should be dragged into another, just because what they regard as a lot of lunatics five thousand miles away from them have started to slit one another's throats; and no political party dare go against them, for fear of losing votes at the next election."

"That I do not believe," said the doctor; "and if Russia refuses the just settlement which President Roosevelt will

198

propose, the Americans will be so indignant that they will make our cause their cause and send us arms and supplies."

"I trust you're right," replied Gregory slowly. He felt that now the United States had made this offer of mediation it indirectly involved them to the extent that the Finns would be even more ready to fight, believing that they had America behind them, should the Russians refuse a settlement of arbitration; and anything which even partially relieved him of the awful responsibility of inducing this little nation to resist its giant neighbour by force of arms came as a great comfort at the moment.

When the doctor had hurried away to assist in the preparations against air-attack which were still going forward, it was decided that in order that all of them could get some sleep that night Erika, Gregory and Freddie should take watches of three hours each, in case their two wounded companions needed anything, while the others slept. Erika took the first watch, from ten o'clock until one, Gregory took the second, from one till four, and Freddie the third, from four till seven.

Soon after seven o'clock the orderlies arrived and escorted the unwounded members of the party, together with Suki on his crutches, to the steam-baths; and on her return Erika set about washing von Kobenthal. Breakfast was brought up for them at eight, and a few moments later, while one orderly was still setting it out on the table, the other, who had temporarily left the room, suddenly came dashing back into it.

He spoke rapidly to his companion in Finnish, who thereupon turned to the prisoners and said in German: "It has come. We are at war. At eight o'clock the Russians launched a full-scale attack on the Mannerheim Line."

"But I thought America was going to mediate," Gregory exclaimed.

The man shook his head. "That was last night. Before our Government even had time to accept the offer the Russians broke off diplomatic relations as a result of the strong Note which we sent earlier in the day." Picking up his tray the man hurried from the room.

"It looks as though Goering's report did the trick after all, then," Freddie remarked cheerfully.

Gregory nodded. "Yes. It must have been that which caused the Finns to send the strong Note that the orderly spoke of. The Government was definitely for giving in after the Russian air-demonstration here on Tuesday. The report must have

199

changed their views and—and been the means of making them dig their toes in."

For once in his life Gregory seemed stupefied and sat gloomily silent, thinking of the weight of woe which he had been responsible for bringing on that small and gallant people; but Erika guessed what was in his thoughts and, taking his hand, said gently:

"*Liebchen,* which would you rather do if you were a Finn? Go out and die for what you believe is right—as they are going to do—or, if we had been able to get married, see our property confiscated and us separated, with you working as a slave in the Russian mines of the Urals or the Don Basin, and me being sweated in some factory where in my off-time I was the plaything of the Russian overseers?"

He shrugged. "You needn't ask, darling; you know the answer."

"Well, cheer up, then! However much misery may come to Finland as a result of this war, you have done right; not only just acted in what you considered to be the best interests of your own country but right as a man in giving the Finns the opportunity to do what you would do yourself."

Breakfast was a depressing meal, as although with their knowledge of the contents of Goering's report they had all felt confident the night before that Finland could hold the Mannerheim Line until help reached her, they now began to have uncomfortable doubts about it. Was the Finnish Army really as good—small though it was—as people had been led to believe? And were the Russian masses really so ill-trained and ill-equipped apart from their great fleets of unwieldy tanks? Were the forts of the Mannerheim Line really of the strength that had been claimed for them? Or had that just been bluff on the Finns' part and were they in fact, like the Czech "Maginot Line", just concrete emplacements, many of which had no guns in them? What effect would the terrific Russian air-armada have on the campaign? Would it play the same part as the German Air Force had played in Poland—harrying communications, blasting bridges, railways and crossroads—so that the Finnish rear became utterly disorganized and neither supplies nor reserves could be got up? Then, even if the Soviet Army was of poor quality it would come pouring through the Mannerheim Line because the Finns no longer had the ammunition to drive it back?

Suki was the only cheerful member of the party. Although

he was an habitual criminal and safe-breaker by profession he had never in his life killed a man or harmed a fly; yet he had boasted to his friends that if there were a war he would kill a dozen Russians and he was anxious to get on with the business. He was already hopping round on crutches and his wound was so slight that it would be completely healed in the course of the next few days, but he feared that on account of his participation in the episode with the Gestapo the authorities might detain him instead of letting him rush off at once to join up.

At a few minutes past nine Wuolijoki came in. He seemed in a great hurry and, having bowed coldly to them, said abruptly: "You will have heard that the die is cast. Finland is now at war with Russia. My country needs every able man. Suki, are you willing to serve?"

"Why, yes, sir, yes," little Suki exclaimed. "I have promised my wife that I will kill a dozen Russians."

"Very good. You were unarmed the other night so we know that you played no part in the shooting. Under an emergency decree we have power to release all prisoners who are held only on minor charges. You are free."

Suki began to express his gratitude, but Wuolijoki cut him short and turned to Erika. "There is no proof, *Frau Gräfin*, that you actually participated in Tuesday night's affair. Therefore we do not intend to hold you any longer."

Transferring his glance to von Kobenthal, he went on: "That you were concerned in the shooting I have little doubt but I am convinced that you acted from the highest motives and with an entirely unselfish desire to serve Finland, the country of your adoption. I am having you transferred to a private nursing-home. Charges will be officially preferred against you but I shall arrange that when your wounds are healed you will disappear, so that you will never have to answer them."

Von Kobenthal nodded. "That's very kind of you, Wuolijoki. I hope, though, that you'll also exert your influence to assist these other gentlemen. I'd take my oath on it that they acted from the same motive as myself."

Wuolijoki ignored the remark and, opening the door, said abruptly to Erika: "You are free, *Frau Gräfin*, you will please to go."

She glanced at Gregory and Freddie, and shook her head. "I'm not going until I know what you propose to do with these two friends of mine."

201

"As you will," he replied stiffly. "In that case all three of you will come downstairs with me."

Giving them only the barest opportunity to say good-bye to von Kobenthal and Suki, the diplomat hustled them out into the passage. Two orderlies who were waiting there escorted them down to the ground floor and Wuolijoki led them into a room where the heavily-moustached Chief of Police was standing.

Closing the door behind him, Wuolijoki looked at Gregory and said: "We have satisfied ourselves about you now. Inquiries made through the German Ministry here yesterday resulted in a cable which came in early this morning. It states that the body of Colonel-Baron von Lutz was found in the woods near his home on November the 27th, the day following a shooting affray with some Nazi officials who were endeavouring to arrest him. You are therefore an impostor. You are not German at all, but British. Your friend is also British. He presents himself as an Air Force officer but—whatever he is—he has aided and abetted you in your activities as a secret agent. Both of you are British spies."

"I deny that," Gregory protested hotly. "But in any case your own Intelligence Department must by now have informed you that the report was genuine. It's an invaluable document upon which you can act with every confidence and *we* brought it to Finland for you—so what the hell would it matter even if we were British?"

Wuolijoki's German blood was very evident as he snapped: "If you had been Germans you would have observed my wishes and not fired on other Germans, but only held them up. Now it is clear that, being British, as your country is at war with Germany you deliberately took the opportunity to fire on your enemies. You have committed an act of war in a neutral country, and for that you are to be held accountable to the Finnish law."

As Wuolijoki stepped back the Police Chief stepped forward. He produced a paper and addressed them:

"Four German citizens resident in Helsinki were wounded in an unprovoked attack which you made on the premises they occupy on the night of November the 28th, and one has since died of his wounds. It is my duty to arrest you both upon charges of arson, armed assault and murder."

CHAPTER XVIII

WANTED FOR MURDER

Murder! The blood drained from Erika's face. This was far worse than anything she had anticipated and it seemed that nothing could be done about it; yet Gregory made a last, very able effort to maintain his imposture, knowing that their only chance of reprieve from having to stand their trial now lay in shaking his accusers' belief that he was British. Turning to Wuolijoki he said in a most reasonable voice:

"Honestly, you're making a big mistake. My letter of personal introduction from Marshal Goering clearly states that I am Colonel-Baron von Lutz. If the . . ."

"The letter must have been stolen," Wuolijoki interrupted.

"On the contrary. I can prove that it was not," Gregory declared sharply. "Your cable says that my body was found on November the 27th, yet the Marshal's letter is dated the 28th, proving conclusively that I was still alive the day after the Gestapo believed me dead. That they should have taken the body of a man found on my estate for myself is not surprising; because, as I told you, I have been listed as either dead or missing for the past three weeks."

While Gregory was speaking he had produced Goering's letter again in triumphant proof of his assertion but Wuolijoki waved it impatiently aside. "That will not do. We have other evidence, besides the cable, that you are an impostor."

He signed to the Police Chief, who abruptly pulled open a door behind him, and Erika's heart missed a beat as Grauber marched heavily into the room.

"Can you identify this man, *Herr Grupenführer*?" the Police Chief asked, pointing to Gregory.

"Certainly," Grauber piped in his thin falsetto. "His name is Gregory Sallust and he is a most dangerous British *agent provocateur*. He has twice been secretly into Germany since the

203

outbreak of war and on each occasion he has been responsible for the deaths of a number of my compatriots. It is he who was the leader of the murderous assault upon myself and my colleagues on Tuesday night. We have already made an official request that he should be tried for murder under the Finnish law and if that request is not acceded to I shall apply for an extradition warrant so that he can be executed for his crimes in Germany."

Gregory saw that the game was up but he meant to go down fighting so he snapped back: "And I shall request the British Legation here to apply for an extradition warrant against you, *Herr Gruppenführer* Grauber, for the murder of Thomas Archer on the night of October the 7th, in Hampstead, London."

The Chief of Police turned to Grauber. "The matter of extradition warrants can be gone into later. At the moment it is my province to attend only to the case in hand; and you may rest assured that this man and his companion will be brought to trial for murder here."

Wuolijoki scowled at Gregory: "So at last you admit . . ." he began; but his sentence was abrupty cut short by a loud, thin wail and suddenly the hideous warbling of air-raid sirens broke out all over the city. Next moment a deep booming note became perceptible which, in a few seconds, increased to a thunderous roar.

"The Russians!" exclaimed Wuolijoki. "The Russians!"

Grauber went as white as a sheet and began to tremble. Gregory suddenly remembered that although the German was unquestionably brave in other ways he had an absolute terror of air-raids. They caught the sound of a distant explosion—another—and another—nearer now—until a giant crash seemed to rock the whole building. Outside whistles were blowing and people shouting. The Police Chief pressed a buzzer on his desk and an orderly came running into the room.

"Quick!" cried the Police Chief above the din. "Take all these people down to the air-raid shelter." He glanced swiftly round at the others and added: "I must see that my men are at their stations. We will conclude this business later." In three strides he was at the door and out of it.

The orderly beckoned to the rest of the party to follow him. They filed out down the passage, through the main hall that was seething with hurrying policemen, and downstairs to the basement. As more bombs crashed into the street above the man flung open a door and motioned them to enter a big empty cellar that had been fitted up as an air-raid shelter.

In his anxiety to reach the safest place in the building Grauber had been pressing on the orderly's heels from the moment they had left the Police Chief's room; now, pushing past the man, he ran to a far corner and leaned against the wall for support; his plump face was grey and sweat streamed down it.

Wuolijoki followed Grauber into the cellar. He was calm but puffing heavily upon a cigarette he had just lit. The others filed behind him. The orderly slammed the door after them but did not lock it, as in his hurry to attend to his duties the Police Chief had given no instructions that the party were to be detained as prisoners.

Overhead the roar of the planes had intensified as squadron after squadron came into action circling over the almost defence-less city and discharging their deadly cargoes. Now and again between the crump of the bombs they caught the sound of a series of whip-like cracks as the few anti-aircraft batteries opened against the planes, but the crashes of the bombs succeeded one another with terrifying swiftness.

Gregory waited until the orderly had had ample time to get upstairs again; then he said loudly to Wuolijoki: "Our parole automatically ended when we were charged with murder. We're going now and you'd better not try to stop us."

"Dont be a fool!" Wuolijoki snapped. "This building is strong enough to resist anything except a direct hit. Even if you could get past the police upstairs once out in the street you'd be blown to pieces."

"Perhaps. I'll chance that." Gregory smiled at Erika. "They've nothing on you, darling, so you'd better stay here. Come on, Freddie."

Grauber was too overcome by his own fears to attempt to stop them, but he screamed above the din: "I'll get you! I'll get you yet."

Gregory turned at the door and shouted back: "It's lucky for you I haven't got a gun on me or I'd shoot you where you stand, you white-livered slug."

Wuolijoki made a move to follow them and call for help but Freddie roughly pushed him aside. "Stay where you are, little man," he cried, "or you'll be sorry you ever met us. You can't expect us to stay here and be hanged because we shot a few Gestapo swine to get you that report."

"That's the stuff to give 'em, Freddie," Gregory muttered.

205

He had the door open and was peering down the passage to see that the coast was clear when he found Erika beside him.

"I'm going with you," she said. "I *must;* otherwise God knows when I shall see you again."

It was no time to start an argument and Gregory knew that Erika could be as pigheaded as a mule. The bombing had eased a little in the immediate neighbourhood and he felt confident that if they could get clear of the police headquarters they would soon find equally good shelter elsewhere.

Wuolijoki stood there scowling but impotent. He realized that it was two strong, desperate men against one small one and a snivelling, crepitating lump of fear, so he made no further effort to stop them as they slipped out into the passage.

Having locked the door behind them Gregory abandoned all precautions and taking Erika by the arm walked forward with a quick, confident step. On the stairs they almost collided with a policeman who was clutching a fire-hatchet, but the man took no notice of them and hurried past, intent upon his own urgent business. Up in the front hall the crowd of police had disappeared. There was only a sergeant there and he was gabbling furiously into a desk telephone. He never even looked up as they marched out.

On the doorstep Gregory paused. Across the road a building was in flames. Further along a block of flats was a smoking ruin; in front of it lay piles of debris that had fallen into the road completely obscuring the pavement for about a hundred yards. An ambulance came clanging down the street and the little crowd of fire-fighters who were busy opposite began to carry screaming, wounded people out to it.

"Come on," said Gregory, and with Erika beside him he ran down the steps and along the street towards a big square of sand-bags which bore a placard that he guessed to be the Finnish equivalent of A.R.P. Shelter.

As they ran the planes were still circling low over the house-tops; some were machine-gunning the Red Cross workers in the streets. Further away in the direction of the harbour bombs were still detonating with a horrid crump every few seconds. Great clouds of black smoke were pouring up into the sky from a number of burning buildings. A one-decker bus came career-ing down the street with another fire-fighting squad in it. There was a burst of machine-gun fire from a swooping plane; the driver was riddled with bullets and slumped over his wheel;

the bus, now out of control, suddenly swerved, mounted the pavement and crashed through a shop window.

They were half-way to the shelter when a woman staggered out of a house just in front of them, carrying a little girl. The child's left foot hung half severed from the leg which was mutilated and bleeding, with only a rough tourniquet twisted above the calf to check the flow of blood. The woman seemed dazed and panic-stricken so Gregory snatched the child while Erika and Freddie seized the woman by the arms and they all dashed on together. Machine-gun bullets spattered the pavement but they reached the shelter in safety.

The shelter was a converted street-lavatory so running water was available and a young doctor with several amateur assistants was rendering first-aid to each casualty as it was brought in. Gregory passed the poor little girl to him and the mother was taken over to be treated for shock by a grey-haired, uniformed woman whose fine face radiated calmness and courage.

For a quarter of an hour they remained with the little crowd in the shelter while the earth shook and trembled. They found their nerves difficult to control and instinctively ducked at each explosion, but Gregory knew that they were safe down there and he tried to reassure them. He pointed out that the really frightening thing about air-raids was the possibility of being terribly wounded by a piece of bomb, falling masonry or a splinter from an anti-aircraft shell, so that one might die in frightful agony; whereas once one was in a proper shelter there was nothing whatever to be afraid of. Either they would emerge perfectly sound in wind and limb or, if a bomb had got their names on it, they would never know what hit them but be killed instantly by the explosion or concussion.

Erika realized that he was right, but to her the most appalling thing about the devilish business, apart from seeing the casualties brought in, was the noise. The crack-crack-crack of the guns and bombs was positively ear-splitting and although she tried to shut it out by pressing her hands over her ears each detonation seemed like a sledge-hammer blow on her reeling brain.

At last the din lessened. Bombs ceased falling, the droning of aircraft overhead faded, the fire of the anti-aircraft batteries died down and after an anxious wait of ten minutes the sirens warbled the "All Clear". The raid was over and the still dazed party staggered up into the street.

"D'you know where the British Consulate is?" Freddie asked Erika at once.

"Why?" She looked at him a little vaguely. "Do you want to go there?"

"Yes. I've been worrying myself stiff all this time about my fiancée, Angela Fordyce. It's pretty certain that she'll have been there with her father."

"The police will be much too busy to worry about us for the next hour or two," Gregory declared, "so there's no point in our splitting up. We'll go to the Consulate with Freddie."

"All right," Erika agreed, "it's not far from here," and they set off towards the harbour.

Great columns of black smoke were still rising from a dozen different points in the city. Here and there the snow in the streets was stained with blood where some unfortunate had been caught by a flying fragment of bomb or a piece of anti-aircraft shell. Stretcher-parties were hurrying hither and thither while civilians were now coming up out of cellars and air-raid shelters to fill the streets once more and lend a hand if they could, or stare dumbly at the shattered buildings.

It was twenty-five to eleven when they reached the British Consulate and on Charlton's sending up his name a message came down from Mr. Fordyce that he would see them at once. They were shown up to a pleasant room overlooking the snow-covered garden at the back of the house and found the dark, pale-faced Angela with her father.

Just as Freddie's one thought during the raid had been anxiety for her, so hers had been anxiety for him, and both were unutterably relieved to find that the other had escaped unharmed. While he was still holding her hands and staring at her as though he could never take his eyes off her face Gregory introduced Erika to Fordyce and told him as briefly as possible what had happened to them.

By the time Gregory had finished his recital Fordyce looked very grave. "I'm afraid you can't stay here," he said slowly. "You see, in the eyes of the Finnish authorities you're criminals, and although Freddie and yourself are both British subjects you're both accountable to the Finnish law while you are in this country. The best I can do for you is to get the Legation lawyer to take up your case and give you all the legal assistance possible."

Gregory smiled. "It's very kind of you, sir, but I hope that won't be necessary. I'm not proposing to stay here to stand my trial. Now the Finns have got their hands full there's a very good chance that we'll manage to get out of Finland; and, as a matter of fact, we shouldn't have embarrassed you with our presence here at all if it hadn't been for Freddie's anxiety about Angela."

"Yes; I quite see that," Fordyce replied uneasily. "But it may not be so easy to get out of Finland as you think. I haven't been here very long, as you know, but long enough to realize that the Finns have a remarkable capacity for keeping their heads. The air-raid was pretty shattering, but even so, I think you'll find they'll endeavour to carry on normal police activities to the best of their ability. It's hardly likely that you'll be able to find a ship which is sailing in the next few hours, and anyway you have no visa to leave the country; so I doubt if you'll get past the port officials. By to-morrow, if not this afternoon, they'll all have been notified that you are wanted by the police and will have been told to keep a look-out for you."

"That's true," Gregory agreed, "but we arrived by plane and our machine is still at the air-port, so if we drive out there at once I think we ought to be able to get away in that. Owing to the raid it's certain that there will be a great evacuation from Helsinki and I doubt if they'll bother neutrals who wish to get out quickly about such formalities as visas."

Freddie and Angela had been talking together in low voices on the sofa but they had followed what Gregory said, and Freddie suddenly turned to Fordyce. "Now the Russians have shown their hand, and that they're out for wholesale murder, this morning's raid may have been the first but it certainly won't be the last. I want you to let me take Angela with me."

Fordyce considered for a moment. "Yes. We must certainly expect other raids now and I'm very anxious that Angela should leave the country as soon as possible. What do you feel about it, my dear?"

She hesitated. "I should hate to leave you, Daddy, at a time like this."

"I'm sure you would, darling. But think of the strain that your presence here is going to be on me if you remain. In every raid I shall be terrified—not for myself, I hope—but certainly for you; whereas if I only know that you are safely out of it my mind will be at rest and I shall be able to do my job much more efficiently."

"Do you really mean that, Daddy?"

"Of course I do, my dear. Try and put yourself in my shoes

for a moment. If I had no duties which necessitated my remaining here, would you rather have me out of it or prefer me to stay and keep you company for the purely selfish reason that you like to have me with you?"

"You know I'd want you to go."

"Then since you have no duties here I think you should accept Freddie's offer. I know that I can trust you to him, and if by any chance he is caught before he gets out of the country the Finnish police have nothing against you; so you might be of great use to him by getting in touch with me and letting me know as soon as possible what has happened. Where do you propose to fly to, Mr. Sallust?"

"Stockholm," replied Gregory. "It's less than three hundred miles from here and if we can get off by two o'clock we should be there in time for tea. Freddie can then overhaul the plane and see if he considers it up to flying standard for flying home tomorrow. If not, we'll go on by the Imperial Airways service which I understand has started up again."

Mr. Fordyce nodded and looked at Angela. "In that case, darling, you'd better pack at once. The whole essence of the plan is that the plane should leave before the Finnish authorities have had time to turn their attention to civil matters and notify the air-port people that Freddie and Mr. Sallust are wanted for murder."

"You *will* be as quick as you can, won't you?" Gregory added. "Just one suit-case should be enough as I have plenty of money on me and we can get anything else you want in Stockholm."

"I'll be moderate—just a dressing-case," Angela smiled at him, and kissing her father quickly on the forehead she hurried from the room.

When she had gone Erika said: "I'm sure your daughter will be perfectly safe with Flight-Lieutenant Charlton, Mr. Fordyce, but in case she's air-sick or anything it may comfort you to know that she'll have another woman with her—I'm going too."

"Do you mean, darling, that you'll come to England with me?" Gregory exclaimed.

She shook her head. "No, I don't say that. I wouldn't when you wanted me to before because my country was still at war with England and, although I hate the Nazis, I felt that I ought to stay in Germany and see the business through. The situation hasn't changed materially since; but there's no point in my remaining in Helsinki to be bombed, and I want to be with you as long as possible, so I'll come to Stockholm."

Gregory gave a rueful grin. "I was afraid the conclusion I jumped to was too good to be true, and in any case I meant to insist on your leaving Helsinki with us; but the situation *has* changed since I last tried to persuade you to come to England with me. Then you were in Germany and thought it your duty to stay there, but you had to leave it in order to escape being arrested and executed."

"Yes," she said quickly. "But I went to Finland which, as far as we're concerned, is neutral; and Sweden, too, is neutral, so for me to go there is very different from my going to live in England, my country's enemy." And Gregory saw that it was no use pressing her for the moment.

While they had been talking Fordyce had pressed a bell and given an order to a servant, who now brought in a bowl of biscuits and a decanter, the contents of which Gregory took to be sherry, but as Fordyce poured the wine into the glasses he said:

"One of the amenities of being stationed in the Nordic countries is that one gets such excellent Madeira—a wine we very rarely see at home."

Gregory sipped from his glass and smiled appreciatively. "You're right. This is grand stuff. I wonder why it is that although such quantities of Madeira were drunk in England in Victorian times it has now been practically relegated to the kitchen."

Fordyce shrugged. "Heaven knows. People hardly ever offer sherry in these parts, but the countries round the Baltic take nine-tenths of the Madeira that is vintaged every year, including all the finest. They'll pay up to £160 a butt for some of the rich dessert wines and, although I don't know much about such things, I'm told that's big money."

They talked for a little of the possible effects of the Russo-Finnish War upon the international situation; then Angela rejoined them, looking very pretty in her tweeds and furs and carrying only a bulging dressing-case.

Fordyce had already ordered his car to take them to the airport and he accompanied them downstairs to the front door. The father and daughter were devoted to each other but with the usual British dislike of any display of sentiment their parting was almost as brief as though Angela had been going out shopping. Fordyce shook hands with the others, wishing them the best of luck, and the car drove off.

211

Gregory felt that for Freddie and himself to call at the hotel and attempt to collect their belongings was much too risky. It was a bore to have to abandon the things they had bought on the Tuesday morning but they were still wearing their furs and the other items were of no great consequence. What did perturb him, however, was that the police had disarmed them both when they had been arrested. It had become second nature to him to carry a weapon when travelling anywhere outside Britain; so he asked the chauffeur to drive them to a gunsmith's where, by pulling a bluff that they were neutral Englishmen who were proceeding into Russia on Finland's business, he succeeded in persuading the shopman to sell him two Luger automatics, spare clips and a hundred rounds of ammunition, without a permit.

Having divided the spoils with Freddie they drove on to the von Kobenthals'. Fredeline was out so Erika left a note for her and ran upstairs to get her passport and pack a bag. Into it she crammed the most useful things that came ready to hand, stuffed a flask of brandy and her own small pistol into the pockets of her furs and was back in the car within fifteen minutes.

They had left the Consulate at about eleven-thirty but it was now after half-past twelve, and they were still some distance from the air-port when the sirens began to wail again. The Finnish chauffeur drove on for another half-mile until he reached a large stone building, the entrance to which was heavily sandbagged; then turning to Gregory, who was seated beside him, he said calmly, in excellent English:

"I think perhaps we'd better get out here."

As they left the car the horrid droning of the enemy planes reached them again and looking up they saw scores of black specks coming up from the east in the bright, cold, winter sky. On the doorstep the chauffeur paused for a moment to look at them and said:

"The swine! If only we had a few planes ourselves—we'd show them."

"You will have soon," Gregory strove to reassure him. "If only Marshal Mannerheim can manage to hold his line for a week or two it's quite certain that help will be sent." Upon which they hurried inside.

The big building was a school and as they entered it the last of the children from the classrooms were filing down to the basement under the care of their teachers.

Downstairs the party from the car found that there was a large underground swimming-bath which had been emptied and about 150 children were gathered there. When the last of them had filed in they all lined up without crowding or excitement and evidently by a prearranged plan. It was a mixed school and while each teacher remained with his or her own class the headmaster took up his position near the diving-board and spoke to the children in Finnish.

The first bombs began to fall and their explosions could be heard quite clearly down there in the basement. Some of the children jerked spasmodically at each detonation, but at a signal from the master they began to sing and the thin childish voices were lifted in what the chauffeur told them was the Finnish battle-song by the national poet, Runeberg. He said that the Russians would not allow it to be sung in the days when the Czars were the masters of Finland, and gave them a rough translation of the first verse which ran:

"Sons of a race whose blood was shed
On Nerva's field, on Poland's sand; at Leipzig
Lutzen's dark hills under
Not yet is Finland's manhood dead.
With foeman's blood a field may still be tinted red.
All rest, all peace, away be gone!
The tempest loosens; the lightning's flash;
And o'er the field the cannon thunders.
Rank upon rank, march on, march on!"

At first the singing was faltering and uncertain but soon it swelled to a great volume of sound and Gregory Sallust, who was a hard man, felt himself touched to the very heart by so fine a demonstration of childish faith and courage; when he glanced at Erika he saw that she was openly crying. The hellish battle above continued and at times they could even hear the scream of the bombs as they hurtled earthwards.

Suddenly there was an ear-splitting roar as a bomb hit the building. One corner of the ceiling of the swimming-bath seemed to dissolve in a great puff of smoke, rubble, dust and flame, obscuring the children who were nearest to it.

While the women teachers gathered their charges to them and endeavoured to still their frightened cries the men, with Gregory's party, thrust their way among them until they reached the great pile of debris under which some of the children had

213

been buried. Above them now gaped a great hole, through which they could see the open sky and the black murder planes circling in it with the shells from the few anti-aircraft batteries breaking like white puff-balls here and there among them.

Fortunately the bulk of the fallen masonry had landed on the broad platform that ran round the edge of the bath and comparatively little had crashed into it where the children were standing. With frantic energy, careless of bleeding hands, the rescuers dragged aside the great lumps of brick and stone until they could get at the poor mangled, bleeding little bodies. Six children had been crushed to death and another fifteen injured.

Those still living were carried through into an underground gymnasium near-by which had already been fitted up as a first-aid station. By the time the rescuers had all the wounded children clear the teachers had stilled the panic of the others by the courage and calmness of their own example and the head-master was driving fear from their minds by making them use their bodies in swift, rhythmatical physical jerks. The sound of the explosions gradually lessened and at twenty-past one the "All Clear" again sounded.

Gregory's party went upstairs with a number of other civilians who had taken refuge in the building. They found the car undamaged except for one smashed window which had been broken by a splinter and, getting into it, they drove on to the air-port which they reached ten minutes later. As they descended from the car an official came to meet them, and smiling at him Gregory said at once:

"We're a party of neutrals. Now things are getting so hot here we've decided to go away at once; so we're leaving in the Sabina plane in which my friend and I arrived here on Tuesday morning."

The official shook his head. "I'm sorry, sir: the Russians are shooting down any plane that goes up. Instructions have been given that for the present no planes are to leave the air-port."

CHAPTER XIX

THE UNDREAMED-OF TRAP

"Oh, come!" Gregory protested. "They won't interfere with us; our plane is a Belgian make and it has the British markings. The Russians won't fire on a neutral."

"I'm afraid you're wrong there," grunted the official. "That's just what they have been doing. They shot down two Swedish planes and a Dutchman this morning."

"Were they civil planes or owned by volunteers who had offered their services to Finland in the event of war?"

"Civil planes, sir. Two were caught in the first raid at nine-twenty-five. They had just taken off and were flying south when they ran right into the Russians coming up across the Gulf; the other was shot down as it was coming in and about to make a landing on the air-port at about ten minutes to one."

"But why; Russia is not at war with Sweden or Holland?"

The official shrugged. "You've seen what they've done in the city, sir, and most people would tell you it's because they're a lot of cut-throats who delight in murder; but if you want my honest opinion it's because these Russians are an ignorant lot: they don't know the markings of one country from those of another and they're not taking any chances. They regard any plane that's not one of their own makes as a potential enemy and shoot it down."

"That's pretty rough on the civilian pilots and their passengers; but the sky's clear now and I don't suppose there'll be another raid for a few hours, at any rate, so I think we'll chance it and get out while the going's good."

"I'm sorry, but that's impossible. As I've told you, the air-port's closed until further orders and no planes of any kind are to be allowed off the ground."

Gregory was getting worried, but he tried not to show it as he said: "That's all very well as a precautionary measure; and it's only right that every pilot should be warned what he may be letting himself in for if he goes up; but once you've issued the warning it's the pilot's own responsibility."

"Oh, no, it's not," the official disagreed quickly. "Finland is responsible for the safety of neutrals as long as they're flying over her territory. If we had a decent Air Force we should be able to protect them from attack. As we haven't, the only thing we *can* do is to protect them against themselves by refusing to allow them to go up. It wasn't our fault that those three were shot down this morning but we shall have the job of explaining to their Governments how it came about and, naturally, we don't want to explain any more such incidents if we can possibly avoid it."

"What are you going to do if I insist on going up?" Gregory hazarded.

"The air-port police would prevent your taking off, sir, and I'm sure you don't want to give us any unnecessary trouble when we have so much on our hands already."

"Of course not," Gregory agreed. "But is there anyone else that I can see—someone from whom I might be able to obtain a special permit?"

"There's no-one out here at the port who has the power to grant you that and I doubt if you'll get one anyway; but if you're determined to try the only person who could give you one is the Chief of Police."

"Thank you," said Gregory thoughtfully; "thank you very much."

The others had been standing near him and they all turned away towards the waiting car. Freddie's German was good enough for him to have followed the conversation and he muttered to Gregory: "What the hell do we do now? They may not lift the ban on neutral planes leaving for several days and, even if they do so to-morrow, by that time the air-port police will have been informed that a murder warrant is out against us."

"How much petrol was there left in the tanks when we landed?" Gregory asked. "Enough to get us to Stockholm?"

"I should think so. Anyhow, there's ample to get us across the Gulf to the Estonian coast and we'd be better off there than we are in Finland; but, as a matter of fact, I told them to fill her up. Why d'you ask?"

"Because," said Gregory slowly, "unless we want to be hanged we'll have to return here after dark, get into the air-port by coming across the fields, run the plane out of its hangar ourselves and take off. With all the snow about would you be able to take off at night without assistance from the ground-men?"

"Oh, yes. I've had so much experience of night-flying that I could manage quite easily. The snow doesn't make any difference in places where they're used to it because they have proper arrangements for rolling it solid so that the wheels of the planes don't get clogged. The difficulty will be to get the plane out of the hangar without being spotted."

" I know. It'll be a tricky job and we may have to sand-bag one of the watchmen. We won't have any time to examine the plane either, so if they haven't filled her up and she runs out of fuel we may all find a watery death in the Gulf of Finland."

"No. I'm sure there's enough juice in her to get us over to Estonia; once we're in the air I can soon see what we've got and let you know if we can risk making the full trip to Stockholm."

"That's what we'll do, then. But where the devil can we go in the meantime? In these parts it's dark at this season by half-past three so fortunately we haven't got very long to wait, but it's only just on two o'clock. If we hang around here we may arouse the suspicions of the air-port people. On the other hand, if we drive back to the centre of the town we may be spotted by Grauber or one of these law-abiding Finns who want to put ropes around our necks."

"Ask the chauffeur," Freddie suggested. "He may know of a small hotel or café in the suburbs where we're not likely to run into anyone who would recognize us while we shelter from this freezing cold for a bit."

There is nothing like a danger shared for the swift ripening of friendship between strangers and having just passed through an air-raid with the Finn, who had proved himself a stout fellow throughout, Gregory felt that he could risk being more frank with him than he would ordinarily have been with someone that he had never seen until two hours before; so he said to the man:

"Look here, we're in a spot of trouble. The air-port has been closed till after dark, because the Russians are shooting down every plane that goes up, but we don't want to go back to the centre of the town in the meantime because, between ourselves, my friend and I had a slight difference of opinion on Tuesday night with the police. That's one of reasons that Mr. Fordyce wanted to see us out of Helsinki as soon as possible. Can you

217

suggest anywhere not too far from the air-port where we could lie up for an hour or two?"

The chauffeur grinned. As his master had told him to drive the two Englishmen to the air-port and young Miss Fordyce was going with them, he felt what was actually a quite groundless confidence that they could not be wanted for any very desperate crime; so he replied at once: "My home's only about a couple of miles from here; it's quite a small place, but if you'd care to wait there you'd be very welcome."

Nothing could have suited the fugitives better. Having thanked the chauffeur they gladly accepted his offer, got back into the car and drove away.

Gregory learned that the chauffeur's name was Aimo Loumkoski, and that his excellent colloquial English had been acquired as third engineer on a British tramp steamer in which he had spent the best part of four years; but he declared that the sea was a hard life and he had been glad to leave it when he married.

His home proved to be one of a row of small, two-storeyed timber houses in a suburban street. He took them inside and introduced them to his wife: a good-looking woman of about thirty, with fair hair and rosy cheeks whose face, owing to the Finnish prejudice against make-up of any kind, was entirely innocent of powder and shone as though it had been deliberately polished. She spoke a little English and in spite of their protests she insisted on bustling into her spotless kitchen to prepare hot coffee for them; which among the Finns is a much more popular drink than tea.

While she was getting the coffee they talked with Loumkoski about the prospects of the war. He was over forty but expected to be called to the colours any day, as although the Finnish regular army is almost negligible, every Finn is trained in the militia, and for many weeks all the younger classes had already been called up to man the fighting positions in the Mannerheim Line. Loumkoski said that they felt confident that they could hold the line for a month and that Viborg would not fall before Christmas at the earliest; but after that it might be difficult to hang on unless they received foreign help.

He thought it almost certain that Norway and Sweden would declare war on Russia during the next few days; his reason being that whereas Finland had her Mannerheim Line across the Karelian Isthmus, and her chains of lakes further north, which made her eastern frontiers easy to defend with compara-

218

tively small forces, the Scandinavian countries had no such prepared or natural defences. As long as the Finnish front held, Russia's path to the west was barred and the whole peninsula safe, but if Finland were once overrun Norway and Sweden would fall an easy prey; therefore their only hope of salvation from eventual conquest by Russia lay in their throwing in their lot with Finland and fighting now.

On the other hand, he realized the difficult situation in which the Scandinavian countries found themselves owing to Russia's tie-up with Germany. Whereas before, Norway and Sweden would, without hesitation, have come out openly on the side of Finland, the Swedes were now afraid that if they acted Germany, as Russia's new friend, might invade them in the south; so they would be most reluctant to send their best troops right up round the north of the Gulf of Bothnia to Finland.

As Loumkoski talked Gregory was amazed to find what a wide knowledge the chauffeur had of the international situation and it cheered him immensely. It showed so clearly that whereas the masses in Russia could have little idea what they had been ordered to fight for, and the masses in Germany were being deliberately misled, the democratic Finns knew exactly and precisely *why* their Government had called upon them to lay down their lives; which made an immense difference to the morale and fighting power of any nation.

Loumkoski went on to say that the Finns had always looked to Germany as their natural protector but, since Germany had let down Lithuania, Latvia and Estonia, Finland could hardly expect any assistance from the Nazis. Did Gregory think that Britain and France might send Finland aid?

"The trouble is that the Baltic's closed to us," Gregory replied, "so it wouldn't be easy to bring you military support."

"There is our ice-free port of Petsamo in the north," suggested Loumkoski; "they could land troops there."

"But that's the best part of a thousand miles away from the main theatre of operations," Gregory objected, "and conditions up there in the Arctic would make it very difficult to move large numbers of troops south over indifferent communications during the winter."

"Perhaps Norway and Sweden would allow them free passage?"

"Yes," Angela put in. "They certainly would if they come

219

in with you, but not if they stay out through fear of Germany. To do so would lose them their neutral status."

"Not at all, Miss," the Finn disagreed politely. "Finland is a member of the League of Nations. Russia's attack on us is the clearest possible case of unprovoked agression which could ever be put before any court. Naturally, we shall appeal to the League. If the League gives its verdict in our favour—as it must—we shall be entitled to call upon all other states that are members of the League for armed support. If Britain and France decide to give us that support any other League state may permit the passage of armed forces coming to our assistance through their territories without contravening their own neutrality."

Gregory nodded. "Yes. That *is* part of the League Covenant. If Sweden and Norway feel that they daren't risk coming in themselves they can still let British and French troops through without giving any legal cause for Germany to make war on them. The trouble is, though, that Germany is not a member of the League and the Nazis are the last people to bother about legal causes if it suits their book to go to war with anyone."

Erika lit a cigarette and said slowly: "I'm afraid that's true, Mr. Loumkoski. You see, Germany is so largely dependent on Sweden for her supplies of iron ore and if the Western Powers landed troops in Scandinavia they would probably choose the Norwegian port of Narvik as a base and come right down the railway through Northern Sweden to the head of the Gulf of Bothnia. That would be their quickest route to Finland and at the same time it would cut Germany off from the Swedish iron mines at Kiruna."

"With Sweden still neutral we could hardly pinch the mines, however much we might like to have them," Freddie laughed.

"No," Erika smiled. "You could hardly do that; but the British are very clever at managing things when they want to. You see, there's only the one railway line up there; and over it the ore goes north-west for transport from Narvik by sea in winter and south to Lulea for transport by ship across the Gulf of Bothnia when it is free of ice during the summer. It would be found that the Western Powers needed every truck on that railway for transporting their troops and ammunitions to the Finnish front; so, while offering to compensate the Swedes for their loss of business, they would point out that it was quite impossible for them to spare the rolling-stock for transporting the ore in either direction."

"Yes, that's typical of our methods," Gregory grinned. "I'm afraid there's no doubt about it that, law or no law, Germany would invade Sweden in an attempt to reach those mines first if an Allied Expeditionary Force were landed in Norway."

"But if the Scandinavian countries do not support us themselves, and refuse to allow other countries to support us by sending troops through them, they will be signing their own death warrants," Loumkoski argued. "Finland can hold out for a month or two but without help we must eventually be crushed by the weight of the Russian masses. Once we are defeated Russia will push West and seize the iron mines for herself with those ice-free Atlantic ports on the Norwegian coast that she is so anxious to acquire and the whole of Northern Scandinavia. Surely the Norwegians and the Swedes would rather risk trouble with Germany than allow that to happen?"

"Perhaps. I only hope so, for your sake," Gregory replied.

"If the Scandinavians let troops through, how soon do you think military aid from the Western Powers could reach us?"

"It's difficult to say and it greatly depends on the state of the railway from Narvik, but presumably that's in good condition, and if the Allies acted at once their first troops might be arriving in the battle-line in about a month."

Loumkoski sighed with the satisfaction of wish fulfilment. "In that case we'll be all right."

Gregory's forecast had been given entirely with a view to cheering their new friend. His private opinion was very different. The greater part of Britain's Army was still untrained and her Air Force was as yet a long way from having caught up with Germany's so it might well be that however sympathetically the Western Powers regarded Finland's cause they could not possibly afford to decentralize their own war effort by dispatching men and planes to Scandinavia. In having taken on Germany they had as much as they could tackle for the moment and at any time it would be a terrible responsibility to add to their burden by taking on Russia as well. Germany had been brought to her knees before and could doubtless be brought to her knees again even if it meant a long war of attrition; but Russia was a very different matter. Even Napoleon had found Russia too tough a nut to crack owing to the vast area of her territory and almost limitless resources. If the Western Powers once declared war on the Bolsheviks where could such a war

221

possibly be expected to end? And what a triumph such a declaration would be for Germany. It would be playing von Ribbentrop's game with a vengeance to bring in Russia, with her inexhaustible man-power, openly on the side of Germany.

Also, regarded purely as a local operation, the sending of an Expeditionary Force to Scandinavia presented immense difficulties. The British Navy was doing magnificent work but it was already strained to the utmost in tackling the menace of German mines and submarines and in protecting convoys. Russia was known to have a fleet of ninety submarines up at Murmansk in the Arctic—a greater under-sea fleet even than that with which Germany had entered the war. Once those ninety submarines were loosed against Allied and neutral shipping they might do inestimable damage before they could all be accounted for; and in winter conditions it would be doubly difficult for Britain's Navy and Air Force to cope with them. In consequence, any Allied Expeditionary Force dispatched to Narvik would be faced with this under-sea menace to the troopships and almost certainly with terrific bombing attacks from the German air fleets in addition. It would be one thing to run in a small striking force for the sole purpose of seizing the port and the iron mines, which are only a hundred miles up-country, just over the Swedish border; but quite another to attempt sending an army of a size to be of any use to the Finns, along the thousand miles of railway that linked Narvik with the Mannerheim Line.

Narvik was only a small port; much too small to accommodate at one time more than a fraction of the armada of ships necessary to transport a modern army of any size with tanks, guns, lorries and the vast quantities of supplies required to keep it in the field; so the disembarkation would be a slow process. The enemy bombers would have time to blow the docks and railway to pieces at their leisure and, in the face of combined Russo-German opposition, the landing might well prove another Gallipoli.

In Gregory's opinion, if the Western Powers were asked for aid by Finland, and decided to send it, they would not do so until the spring. Submarines are slow-moving vessels and as long as Russia's under-sea fleet was concentrated at Murmansk it might be dealt with in better weather. An aircraft-carrier and flotillas of submarine chasers could be sent up there which would probably account for a considerable portion of it before the Expeditionary Force sailed. By the spring, too, it was said that the Allies' aircraft production would have caught up with that of Germany, which would better enable the Western Powers to protect their troops from aerial attack while disembarking.

It was a sad business, but, apart from volunteers such as had gone out to the Spanish war, Gregory did not feel that the Finns could really count on any military aid for the present—unless Norway and Sweden decided that their own fate was linked with that of Finland.

Madame Loumkoski came in with coffee and sweet cakes but they had barely received cups of the steaming brew when the air-raid sirens sounded once again.

Although the Finns had been working desperately hard these last weeks to provide air-raid shelters they had had to concentrate their efforts in the more populous parts of the city; so when Gregory suggested that they should all go to the nearest, Loumkoski told him that there was no proper shelter less than half a mile distant. The deep booming of the Russian planes could already be heard, so their host said swiftly that they might easily be killed on their way through the streets and that it would be less risky for them to take refuge in a trench which he had dug in his back garden.

They hurried out through the snow and found it to be a long, narrow ditch about four feet wide partially covered with planking and a few sand-bags. Some rubble had been thrown into its bottom to drain away the water but the sides were damp, cold, virgin earth, and there were no seats, so having scrambled down, they had to crouch uncomfortably in it.

They were hardly inside the trench before the bombs began to fall; but it seemed that the Russians were directing their main attack upon the port, which was some miles away. The distant thudding continued for about ten minutes then a few crashes sounded nearer. Suddenly there sounded the sharp "rat-tat-tat" of machine-gun fire ʾead. Loumkoski poked his head out frᵒm underneath ʾ ʾs and gave a whoop of joy. "It's one urs," he shoutᵉ one of ours!"

They had ᵢ ₙ aᵗ ᵒut to pull him back but his excitement was so infectious that ᵥₑn Gregory temporarily lost the extreme caution which had so often been the means of saving his life. He had seen dog-fights in the air before and knew that it was a senseless risk to expose oneself to possible death for the sake of seeing the fun; but there was something so very gallant about that solitary Finnish airman up there in the midst of the Red air-armada that for once he felt bound to take a chance and see the result of the fight.

The small Finnish plane had just circled under a big black bomber and come up on its tail. There was another burst of machine-gun fire; a wisp of smoke streamed out behind the Russian plane, then it seemed to falter. Next moment it was hurtling earthwards with red flames spurting from it and a great tail of oily black smoke smearing the blue sky in its track; while the little Finnish plane streaked away to northwards to attack another enemy.

It seemed that the whole neighbourhood had also come out from their shelters to watch the fight, as the sound of cheering began on every side from the moment the Russian was hit and swelled to a roar as it crashed like a box of lighted fireworks about a quarter of a mile away.

The cheering continued for a moment but was cut short by a fresh series of crashes quite close at hand; another Red plane was unloading its cargo. The earth shook and trembled as each of the great bombs burst with the roar of thunder somewhere on the far side of the house. Stones, earth, and pieces of red tile from the roof-tops came sailing through the air to fall with a clatter upon the boards of the trench under which they had once more taken refuge. For another quarter of an hour they crouched there until the detonations ceased. A few moments later the "All-Clear" signal sounded for the third time in five hours.

It was only a little after three when they climbed out of the trench but the early winter dusk was already falling and Gregory felt that in another half-hour or so they might make their attempt to secure the Sabina. In the little sitting-room of the Loumkoskis' house they found the coffee which Madame had provided, and which they had had to abandon on account of the air-raid, still fairly warm. She wanted to re-heat it for them but they would not let her, as they knew that she was anxious to find out what had happened to her neighbours and give them any help she could.

While they drank the tepid coffee they stood looking out of the window at the sad spectacle the street now presented. Three air-raids in five hours had shaken even the courage of the Finns and—very wisely, Gregory thought—all those who had no duties which detained them in the city had apparently decided to evacuate it.

In front of the small, wooden, workers' houses, sleighs and

carts were drawn up and on to them men, women and children were hastily piling their bedding and their most precious belongings. Already a continuous stream of evacuees was passing down the street from the direction of the centre of the city towards the open countryside. Many of them had no conveyances and carried huge bundles on their backs while they led small children by the hand. It was a sight which filled the watching party at the window with a bitter anger against the Russians and the deepest pity for these poor people who had been driven from their homes.

The hearts of the girls were wrung more than those of the men, because they had already been some weeks in Finland and so appreciated more fully the horror of such an evacuation in mid-winter up in that northern land. They knew that, unlike the country round London, Paris, and Berlin, where hundreds of thousands of houses could be used for billets in such an emergency, the Finnish countryside outside Helsinki was very little built over. Only a very few of these poor refugees who were being driven forth by the terror of mutilation and death would find accommodation in the farms and barns; the vast majority would have to camp out in the woods where the snow was already two feet deep upon the ground. Thousands of them who were fleeing without even bedding would be frozen to death during the night or get frost-bite which would injure them for life.

Gregory, too, felt particularly badly about it, because he knew that he had been to a large extent responsible for the last-minute decision of the Finnish Government to defy the might of Russia, but he tried to comfort himself with the thought that the Finns were at least still free men; whereas, if they had surrendered without firing a shot a month or two would have found thousands of them marching through the Russian snows in forced labour gangs.

Madame Loumkoski returned after about twenty minutes to tell a harrowing tale of the havoc wrought by the bombs that had fallen in the next street. A whole row of workmen's dwellings had been blown down and many more were in flames through fires caused by the explosions. The fire-fighters and ambulance people were at work there so there was nothing she could do except—as she told them—render thanks to God that, whereas she had thought that He had cursed her all these years with barrenness she now knew that He had blessed her by preventing her from having any children of her own.

225

Gregory took out his wad of Finnish notes and peeling off three large ones said to her: "Madame, there is very little that we can do to help but I should be glad if you would take this money. It will buy you a railway-ticket to Sweden and keep you there for a few weeks without want, at least; and I'm sure that your husband would rather have you safely out of all these horrors than that you should risk your life to stay with him. If you're lucky you may be able to get one of the trains leaving to-morrow morning."

She shook her head. "It is mos' kine of you, sir, but I not leave 'im at zis time, no, no."

Her husband and the others all tried to persuade her to do so but she was quite adamant in her refusal. The best that they could do was to make her take the money to put aside so that when her husband was called up—which would mean separation for them in any case—she would then be able to use it to leave the country; which he said would be a great comfort to him while he was serving with his unit.

At a quarter to four they said good-bye to Madame Loumkoski and set off in the car again, back to the aerodrome. It was slow going, as the road was now crowded with an army of refugees who were pouring out of Helsinki to face the bitter cold of the woods rather than spend another night in what appeared to be a doomed city. It was quite dark when they reached the aerodrome and Gregory asked Loumkoski to drive them along a road at its side for about half a mile; then he signalled to him to halt and they all got out. Before taking leave of the friendly chauffeur Gregory asked him if he could spare a spanner with which request he willingly obliged, and they then parted from him with many expressions of goodwill on both sides.

Crossing a ditch Gregory's party began to tramp through the thick snow of the open fields. After ten minutes' laboured going they came up against a wire fence which they knew, from what they had seen in daylight, marked the boundary of the aerodrome. Slipping through it they ploughed on through the snow on its far side. In spite of the darkness they could see for quite a distance owing to the light which the snow reflected, but on this night of death and terror it was not the pale, white light normally reflected from snow, by which, it is said Confucius, as a boy, learned to read on winter evenings because he was too poor to buy candles. It was tinged with a sinister crimson from the blood-red glow shot with fiery orange that hung like a devil's pall above the burning buildings of the city. The light had a horrid, eerie quality about it yet, as they advanced, it served to show them the line of the hangars in one of which the Sabina plane was housed.

At a muttered word from Gregory they made a slight detour in order to get round to the back of the hangars. He meant to approach them from the rear so that if there was a watchman about they could take him by surprise and overpower him before he had the chance to raise an alarm and bring the air-port police on the scene. Ten minutes later they had completed their slow, laborious trek and passing through a narrow corridor between two of the hangars came level with their fronts.

Gregory whispered to his companions to halt and peered out into the evil red twilight, first round one corner, then round the other. In normal times there would certainly have been a watchman on duty who would walk round the whole block of hangars at intervals, but they had seen nobody at the back of the row and there was nobody pacing up and down in front of it. There was quite enough light to see some way across the open, but the watchman might be crouching over some hidden brazier inside one of the hangars, and Gregory thought it best for them to wait where they were for a little, as if there was a watchman there he would almost certainly come out to have a look round from time to time.

It was very cold but with that crisp, dry cold which is exhilarating, and in their excitement at the prospect of getting safely away from Helsinki they did not particularly notice it; although they instinctively kept their faces buried deep in their big fur collars and stamped their feet every now and then.

After a quarter of an hour it seemed that they had been waiting there for an age and Gregory began to hope that, after all, there was no watchman on duty. The first day of war in Helsinki must have thrown all ordinary routine right out of gear. The watchman must have been wounded in an air-raid or called up for military service, and the people responsible for the safe-guarding of the hangars had quite possibly been so frantically busy on more urgent matters that they had had no time to replace him. At last Gregory decided to have a cautious look round and whispering to the others to remain where they were he slid out as noiselessly as a shadow along the front of the hangars.

Ten minutes later he returned to inform them cheerfully that he had examined every likely place and that quite definitely

227

there was no watchman on duty. They followed him out into the open and along to the third hangar from the left-hand end of the row. The doors were padlocked but Gregory produced the heavy spanner he had begged of Loumkoski and in two swift wrenches tore the padlock away from its hinge; after which the double-doors slid smoothly back upon their grooves.

While Gregory shone his shaded torch Freddie climbed into the cockpit of the plane and gave the instrument-board a quick look over. To his joy he found that his orders on landing two days before had been carried out. The plane had been refuelled to capacity, so there seemed nothing to prevent them from making a direct flight to Stockholm. Between them they pushed the plane out of the shed on to the hard, frozen snow and while the two girls and Gregory stood by, Freddie spent five minutes examining the controls to see that they were all in order; then they turned the plane so that it should face the wind.

They had only just finished when Erika gave a gasp of dismay and tugged at Gregory's shoulder. Swinging round he saw coming towards them, from the direction of the air-port buildings, a group of figures.

"Quick!" he shouted. "On board, all of you! Freddie, get her going!"

At the same instant one of the approaching group shouted something in Finnish and they all began to run.

Freddie was in the plane and Angela was scrambling up beside him but Erika and Gregory were still on the ground when the group of men came pounding up to them. One was in pilot's kit; there were five others, armed police and air-port officials. Gregory realized that there was nothing for it but to turn and face them.

"Hullo! What's the excitement?" he said in English.

"What do you do 'ere?" one of the air-port men replied in the same language.

"Getting out while the going's good," replied Gregory calmly.

"But you 'ave not pass the controls and 'ave no permit."

"I'm not going to allow a little thing like that to stand in my way in times like these," said Gregory. "Our passports are all in order and we've come straight from the British Consulate."

"Yes, yes; per'aps. But you cannot take this plane."

"Why not? It's mine."

The official shrugged. "All planes 'ave been commandeered under an emergency decree we make this morning."

228

"You can't commandeer this one!" Gregory retorted swiftly. "This plane is the property of the British Government."

"I can," replied the official abruptly. "As I 'ave told you, we 'ave powers to commandeer all planes under an emergency decree."

"But this is flagrant interference with the rights of neutrals."

"That I cannot 'elp. Compensation will be pay to you for et but Finland makes war and every plane in Helsinki is needed." The official glanced up at Freddie. "You, there—in the pilot's seat—please to come down!"

Gregory could hardly contain his cold, fierce wrath. In another five minutes they would have been on their way out of Finland to Stockholm and perhaps twenty-four hours later safely home in England. Now they were stuck again with no means of getting out of the country. Worse still, by now the names of Freddie and himself had probably been circulated as those of men wanted for murder and at any moment the airport police might demand to see their passports.

For a second he played with the idea of putting up a fight. Freddie was still in the plane and had only to press the self-starter. Gregory would have risked being shot by drawing his own gun and leaping up into the cockpit, but he had the two girls to consider. In a shooting affray they might easily be wounded or killed and Erika was still standing beside him. Before they could both get up into the plane they would be dragged back. There were six Finns against Freddie and himself so the odds were much too heavy and he dismissed the idea as soon as it came to him.

Grimly he nodded to Freddie, who had been waiting for some sign from him whether to obey the order to get out or not. The airman reluctantly climbed down and Angela jumped out after him.

"There's going to be trouble about this," she announced sharply. "I'm Miss Fordyce, and my father is a special assistant to the British Consul here. He would have made other arrangements to get me to a place of safety if this gentleman had not offered to fly me home. If you detain me my father will make things jolly hot for you with your Government."

The official bowed. "I am mos' sorry, Madame; but 'ow can we let private matters interfere with the necessities of our country?"

"But this isn't a private matter," Freddie put in rashly. "I'm a Royal Air Force pilot and this is a British plane. If you're not darned careful you'll have a diplomatic incident on your hands, and you'd be penny wise and pound foolish to start even a minor quarrel with the British Government at this juncture."

The Finn who was dressed in pilot's kit spoke in halting English. "We should have great regret, sir, to offend your Government in any way but this is an urgency. Our so few military planes are all needed; our civil planes are took also for many purposes. I introduce myself. Staff-Captain Helijarvi. I have urgent orders that I must take with no delays to our forces at Petsamo. Please be reasonable. You see how great is our necessity."

In the face of such an appeal they all felt how impossible it was to place what the Finns, not knowing that two of them were wanted for murder, could only regard as their temporary safety before such a vital matter as conveying Marshal Mannerheim's orders to his troops in the far north.

For a moment they all stood there in silence, then Gregory asked: "Do you intend to bring the plane back here and, if so, will it be free then, or will you require it for further service?"

"I shall make return in it," replied Captain Helijarvi, "immediately I 'ave deliver my dispatches, but after—who can say? I fear that all aeroplane in Finland will be required for the duties until more aeroplane come to our 'elp from neutral countries."

It had occurred to Gregory that if there was a chance of their regaining possession of the plane they might have found their way back to Loumkoski's and lain doggo there for twenty-four hours until the plane was back and they could get away in it; but evidently this was the most slender thread upon which to pin their hopes. Clearly, too, even if they could persuade the Staff-Captain to take them with him to Petsamo, as he meant to return at once he would not release the plane there so that they could fly on with it into neutral Norway. But another possibility suddenly occurred to Gregory, and he turned to Charlton.

"Look here, Freddie, Petsamo, as you probably know, is an ice-free port in the Arctic. If we could get there we might have to wait a week or so but we should almost certainly be able to secure a passage in a British or neutral ship and go home that way. How about it?"

"That would suit Angela and myself," Freddie nodded; "but how about Erika?"

230

Erika shrugged. "Almost any ship sailing from Petsamo would call at one of the Norwegian ports before going on to England or America, so you could drop me off in Norway. The point is, though, would Captain Helijarvi be willing to take us?"

"Madame," said the Finn at once. "I only regrets that I 'ave to take your plane at all. In any other way please make your command to me. If it is 'elpful to you that I fly you to Petsamo it will be big pleasure for me to take you."

"This is mos' irregular," cut in the air-port official. "These peoples have not pass the controls, Captain. They mus' 'ave known that we would not allow them to take their plane."

For a second their fate seemed to hang again in the balance, then Helijarvi laughed—a rich, deep chuckle. "There is a war on, friend. 'Ow can you blame two gentlemens for not observing regulation when they wish to get their ladies to safe places? Let us 'ave no more delays."

Gregory felt that his star was once more in the ascendant as the thick-set Finnish Staff-Captain climbed into the plane and began to examine the controls. Freddie got in beside him and swiftly explained the more subtle idiosyncrasies of the plane which his own flight from Germany had shown him. It was a four-seater but none of them were heavy-weights; the two girls weighed only sixteen stone between them and their two dressing-cases were the only luggage; so Helijarvi and Freddie agreed that the plane would not be overloaded. Gregory and the girls wedged themselves into the back while the two pilots sat in front. One of the air-port men blew a whistle; a light flickered for a moment in the distance to give Helijarvi his direction; the engine roared and they were off.

Freddie had offered to fly the plane if Helijarvi would act as his navigator but the Finn had replied that he preferred to fly it himself and knew the route to Petsamo so well that he could manage without assistance; so for once the ace British pilot experienced the, to him, rather dubious joy of being a passenger. Apart from Angela none of the fugitives had had their full ration of sleep for the past two nights and, from nodding drowsily to the engine's monotonous hum, after about twenty minutes they all dropped off to sleep.

The first part of the journey lay over Central Finland, so there was little danger of encountering the Soviet war-planes; which, if their pilots were not tired out after their long day of murder, would be operating against either the towns of the

231

South or the fortifications on the frontier. Helijarvi's only anxiety was that they might run into a blizzard; but the weather had been good all day and the calm of the early night suggested a peace which no longer existed in the stricken land. The Soviet bombers had not confined their attention to Helsinki but had raided many towns and villages that day, so as the plane flew on its pilot picked up the glare of still burning homesteads from time to time and knew that in the dark forests below him a million homeless people were striving to keep the warmth of life in their shivering bodies.

At seven o'clock Freddie roused up, upon which Helijarvi told him that they had accomplished about two-thirds of their journey and were now approaching a part of the country where the Russian frontier juts out like a big cape into Northern Finland. To remain on the direct route to Petsamo he would have had to fly over Soviet territory for about a hundred miles; so he altered course slightly to keep inside the Finnish border, but they were near enough to the frontier to see here and there far below them some evidence of the fighting that was still in progress.

The main battle-fronts were hundreds of miles away to the South, on the Karelian Isthmus and north of Lake Ladoga. Up here the fighting consisted only of encounters between small detached units who occasionally came up against one another in their endeavours either to penetrate or to defend the frontier. At one point a battery was shelling some unseen target but in all the hundred and fifty miles of their detour they saw only three other local engagements and in these the sporadic spurts of fire and individual flashes showed that nothing heavier than machine-guns and rifles were in action.

Soon after they passed away from the frontier they ran into cloud and, coming down to a thousand feet, encountered snow. It was not a blizzard but the gentle, drifting snow that falls so frequently in the Arctic and which pilots must always anticipate there when flying below the lower cloud-levels. Helijarvi said that Petsamo must now lie somewhere beneath them and switching on his navigation lights he began to send out radio signals in anticipation that the air-port would give him a beam to guide him in. After several minutes' tapping they received no response; which looked as though the air-port people were not operating their wireless, for fear of giving guidance to Soviet bombing-planes which might quite possibly be in the area.

232

Without radio assistance it would prove difficult to find the landing-ground but Helijarvi felt confident he could do so.

Circling round he slowly began to bring the plane much lower until after circling six times they picked up some flashes of light. A moment later they were flying over the lights and were able to see that there were two distinct groups of them, about a mile apart. The snow blanket seemed to be less solid down here and they suddenly realized that instead of a uniform greyness below them the cloud-like landscape was rent into two jagged halves, one of which was much darker than the other. As Helijarvi circled again they saw that one group of flashes came from the edge of a prominence in the whiter part while the other was out in the darker, and the explanation flashed upon the two airmen simultaneously. The first group of flashes came from shore batteries on the harbour and the second from Soviet warships which were shelling them from the sea.

As Helijarvi knew Petsamo well the flashes from the forts of the harbour gave him a good idea of his position. Turning inland again he sailed low over them and a moment later was flying only fifty feet above the roof-tops of the town.

They could spot scattered lights below them now, as the black-out was anything but perfect. It was impossible to see the people who were down there but the glow from the snow which was broken by black patches, enabled them to pick up the principal buildings. For a second Freddie's heart was in his mouth as they narrowly missed a church spire, but that gave Helijarvi the final key to his direction and almost immediately afterwards he pointed at a light ahead which he declared came from the air-port.

As they passed over it they saw that the light did not come from the control tower but from a window in the air-port buildings and Helijarvi began to radio again for the landing-lights to be switched on. Twice more they circled but no fresh lights appeared, so they decided that the air-port wireless must have been put out of action by an air-raid earlier in the day and that the only thing to do was to risk a landing without guidance. Zooming up again Helijarvi banked to get into the wind, flattened out and came down on the snow-covered ground.

Owing to the difficulty of such a landing at night they bumped heavily, which woke Gregory and the two girls; but after three more bumps Helijarvi steadied the plane and managed to halt it about two hundred yards from the dark control tower. Directly the plane was at rest they opened the cabin-door and all climbed out, gaily congratulating Helijarvi on his successful flight.

They could now hear the dull rumble of the guns in the distant harbour, but as the town was quiet it seemed a little strange that no air-port people had come out to meet them, since they must have heard the plane droning overhead. There was little wind but it was snowing quite fast, the large flakes coming down silently and steadily. Through the snow they could just make out the glow from the lighted window. With his satchel of papers tucked under his arm Helijarvi led the way towards it. As they approached they heard the muffled sound of singing coming through the double-windows of the building and striding to a door through which he had often passed on completing his flights to Petsamo Helijarvi pushed it open.

It gave on to the Petsamo Air Club smoking-room where, in peace-time, in- and out-going pilots usually had drinks together. After the intense cold of the air outside the heat of the place seemed to hit the newcomers in the face and it was thick with smoke and the smell of spilt beer. The room was occupied by about twenty soldiers who were lolling about on the chairs and settees bawling a raucous chorus as one of their number hammered at the piano. Some of them were very drunk indeed, but that was not the only thing which Gregory noticed in his first swift glance over Helijarvi's shoulder. The soldiers were wearing pointed, gnome-like caps. They were not Finns; they were Russians.

CHAPTER XX

HELL IN THE ARCTIC

In a flash Gregory realized that although the Finns were still holding out in the forts on the harbour their small garrison must have been driven from the town by a massed Soviet attack that afternoon.

From the open door a flurry of snow driven on an icy blast swept into the room. The singing quavered out; the brutish, drunken faces turned towards the door and the nearest soldiers jumped to their feet. As they recognized Helijarvi for a Finnish officer they grabbed up their rifles. One pulled an automatic from its holster and swaying unsteadily yelled something in Russian which clearly meant "Put your hands up!" Before he could pull the door shut again the thick-set Finn was covered from a dozen different directions.

But he had seen instantly the trap into which he had walked; even before they had him covered his hand jerked to his own pistol. Although he knew it was death to do so his choice was instantaneous. Better to kill a few Russians if he could than be ignominiously captured on the first day of the war. Whipping out his gun he pressed its trigger and sent a stream of lead into the crowd of soldiers. The screams of the wounded were half-drowned in the crash of shots that followed and, his pistol slipping from his hand, Helijarvi fell in the doorway riddled with bullets.

Gregory grasped the situation at the same instant as Helijarvi's hand had jumped to his gun. Leaping back he nearly knocked over the two girls who were behind him. As the bullets aimed at the Finn sprayed the open doorway one passed within an inch of Gregory's ear, another zipped through the thick fur on his shoulder, and a third thudded into the dressing-case he was holding in his hand. The Russians were now almost hidden by the drifting blue smoke from the barrels of their

235

rifles; before they had time to aim again he had turned and thrusting his friends back yelled: "Run! Run for your lives!"

Freddie had been bringing up the rear of the party; seizing Angela he wrenched her round and almost dragging her off her feet scampered with her along the side of the building. Lowering her head Erika plunged along in their track until Gregory caught her up and, grabbing her arm, ran with her.

Orders, counter-orders, drunken shouts came from the open doorway behind them as the soldiers tumbled out of it and the horrid fear of bullets in the back lent added speed to the fugitives' flying feet. Freddie and Angela reached the corner of the building and dashed round it into the temporary safety of a narrow passage. A rifle cracked when Erika and Gregory were still some five yards from it, but the bullet went wide and Erika raced after the others.

Gregory had dropped her case and drawn his gun as he was running. He did not want to fire. He and his friends had no quarrel with Russia and it was the most evil luck that at the sight of Helijarvi the troops should have taken the whole party for Finns. Yet he knew that in the darkness and confusion, and lacking any common language, any attempt at explanation was impossible. The Russians, furious at the casualties they had already suffered and half-stupid with liquor, were shooting to kill on sight. Unless they could be checked his whole party would be massacred so, flattening himself against the wall, he sent three rounds of rapid fire into the dark crowd of figures which was pouring from the club-room; a scream of pain told him that at least one of his bullets had found a billet in flesh or bone. His shots halted their pursuers for a moment, and in it he slipped round the corner. Ahead of him he could see his friends running; behind him came the stamping feet and drunken shouts of the Russians.

Freddie was still leading. On reaching the far end of the passage he saw that it gave on to a wide sweep where in normal times people drove up to the air-port. As he charged out into the open a ragged volley sounded in their rear. Some of the bullets whizzed harmlessly overhead and others spattered into the snow. The Russians were shooting wildly as they ran and were too drunk to take proper aim but none the less their shots carried possible agony and death.

When the fugitives were half-way across the open space a tall wooden fence loomed up through the drifting snowflakes in front of them. They had hardly reached it when the Russians

236

came streaming out from between the buildings in hot pursuit.

The fence was too tall and difficult to attempt to scramble over at such a moment and Freddie did not know in which direction the gateway through it lay. Trusting to luck he turned blindly to his left; and luck was with him. Twenty yards further on two big stone pillars flanking a gate appeared. It was open and there was no sentry on it. But the Russians, instinctively assuming that they would make for it, were taking a short cut across the carriage sweep and so had considerably decreased their distance. Yelling and shouting they came pounding over the snow as Freddie and Angela dived through the gate with Gregory and Erika hard on their heels.

Just as they reached the street one of the Russians paused to fire. Gregory gave a cry, staggered and pitched forward on his face. Erika stopped in her tracks and pulling out the little pistol which she had pushed into her pocket after packing her dressing-case opened fire with it.

"Gregory! Gregory!" she cried imploringly, as she prayed with all her might that he would stagger to his feet and run on; but he did not stir.

At the sound of shots so close behind them Freddie and Angela turned. Seeing what had happened, Freddie let go of Angela's arm and running back seized Gregory by the shoulders. He was quite limp and either unconscious or dead.

In all his life Freddie had never had a more difficult decision to make. The two girls were now dependent on him as their only protector, and to try to carry Gregory would enormously increase their chances of capture. If he were dead the added risk would serve no useful purpose; but the young airman felt that he could not possibly leave the companion with whom he had spent so many weeks of difficulty and danger, in case there was still life in him. Seizing Gregory in his strong arms he hoisted him up in a fireman's lift across his shoulders and turning, began to run again.

Erika had taken cover behind one of the stone pillars to which the gate was hinged and stood there peering round it. Her first shots had checked the drunken soldiers for a moment. Instead of turning with Freddie she remained half-crouching there waiting for the Russians to come on. They sent a burst of fire through the now empty gateway and then came plunging forward in a body. Erika aimed carefully as they loomed up out of the drifting snow then pressed the trigger of her pistol twice.

237

There was a shriek as the leading man slumped in his tracks; another staggered sideways and went down in a heap. Several more tripped sprawling across their comrades' bodies, but Erika had barely glimpsed the result of her shooting before she sprang to her feet and was running for her life. She could no longer see her friends but she knew the direction they had taken and fled over the crisp white carpet in their tracks.

She had barely covered a hundred yards when shots came whipping after her; the soldiers had gathered in the gateway and were firing down the street. The gauzy veil of drifting snow now hid her from them and she felt certain that she could outdistance them owing to the lightness with which she could skim over the ground; yet a ghastly fear tore at her heart-strings as she ran. Her adored Gregory might be dead.

Another twenty yards and she caught sight of Freddie. He was plunging along with Gregory's limp body slung over his back and Angela beside him. Putting on a spurt Erika came level with them. In spite of the icy cold, rivulets of sweat were running down Freddie's face. His breath was coming in awful sobbing gasps and each gulp of the freezing air that he drew into his aching lungs hissed out again like a cloud of steam. He had made a supreme effort and covered the first hundred yards in remarkable time considering that he was carrying the dead weight of a fully-grown man; but he could not possibly keep up such a pace. Now, he was stumbling as he ran and his heart was hammering against his ribs as though it would burst with the strain. He knew that he must soon set his burden down or his legs would give way under him.

The firing had ceased but a fresh chorus of drunken shouts told them that the troops had not given up the chase; they were coming down the street after them. As they ran both the girls kept glancing over their shoulders. The dancing snowflakes still hid them from the pursuing soldiers but now that Freddie's pace was flagging they knew that they must be losing their lead and they expected to see the troops emerge through the curtain of whiteness at any moment.

Erika was at her wits' end. She still had two or three bullets left in the magazine of her pistol. But even if she could again manage to pick off their foremost pursuers she knew that she would never be able to hold the others up long enough to give Freddie a new lead that would be of any use now. He was almost done and from his reeling gait she could see that he was due to collapse within another thirty paces.

238

The collosal physical effort that Freddie was making took every ounce of his energy so that he could not use his brain at all but only stagger blindly on to the limit of his endurance. Every second the weight of Gregory's body seemed to grow heavier and now he felt as though he were crushed under the bodies of five men instead of one. This time it was Angela who once more temporarily saved the situation.

They had passed the limits of the air-port and were no longer running along beside the fence but had entered a street with small houses on either side. Between two of them Angela spotted a narrow alleyway. Seizing Freddie by the arm she pulled him with all her force so that he swung round into it. Losing his balance he fell with Gregory just inside its entrance. Erika came sprawling on top of them but in an instant she was up and helping Angela to drag Gregory's body from on top of Freddie and further into the ally. By the time they had pulled the body four or five yards Freddie lurched to his feet and came lumbering after them, only to collapse again just as he caught them up.

While he sprawled there panting as though his lungs would burst, Gregory lay inert and silent. Erika *had* to know if he was alive or dead. Wrenching off her right glove she fumbled franticaly at the furs about his neck and thrust her hand down under his clothing. He was alive. His heart was still beating. Her unspoken relief lasted only for a second. The blank walls of the houses rose steeply on either side of the alley and it was pitch-dark in there except for a faint, greyish oblong which showed where it entered the street. It was impossible for her to ascertain where, or how badly, he was wounded. Perhaps he was dying. Her brain reeled under a fresh spate of agony as she realized that he might be bleeding to death, yet she was power-less to stop it.

Crouching beside their men the girls peered with wide, anxious eyes towards the faintly light patch as they strove to get back their breath and still the beating of their hearts. Erika had dropped her gun when she tripped over Freddie but, although she was less than twenty feet from the place where she had fallen, she dared not go back to look for it. The snow had deadened the sound of their footsteps but it also deadened the sound of their pursuers. The Russians might reach the entrance of the alleyway before she could get her gun and slip back into the darkness. Everything depended now upon the soldiers' not noticing the entrance and believing that their quarry was still ahead of them, further down the gloomy, snow-swept street.

She had been crouching beside Gregory for barely forty seconds when the sound of muffled footfalls and heavy breathing reached her. Angela laid a quick hand on Freddie's shoulder to try and quiet him in case his awful gasping should be heard and he made an agonizing effort to control the hoarse gulps that came spasmodically from his tortured lungs.

Another ten seconds and the troops had passed, ploughing heavily on down the road; but there was not an instant to be lost. When the Russians failed to sight the fugitives they would turn back and might notice the tracks in the freshly-fallen snow that led into the entrance of the alley. Erika had Gregory's head pillowed on her lap. Half-crazed by fear that he was dying she stroked his face and in soft whispers implored him to speak to her; but he remained absolutely limp. She could feel that his mouth was hanging open but he did not utter even a moan or sigh. Angela was the first on her feet and she shook Freddie by the shoulder. "Come on, darling! Come on!" she whispered. "They may be back here in a moment."

Still panting, Freddie struggled to his knees. The two girls hauled Gregory across his back and assisted him to rise; with a lurch he began to plod heavily along, deeper into the darkness of the alley. Erika was already following when she suddenly remembered her pistol and turned back to look for it. She knew within a few feet where she must have dropped it but the uncertain light made it impossible to see the pistol at a glance so she had to grope about on her hands and knees in the snow for a good minute before she found the deadly little weapon. Its safety-catch was still off and only the soft snow had prevented its exploding after it had fallen from her hand. Quickly pushing the safety-catch down she rammed the gun into her pocket and ran after the others.

They had passed out of the black gulf made by the two houses but wooden fences hedged them in on either side for some distance and the only light was the greyish, snow-filled murk above. At last they reached the further entrance to the alley and Freddie set Gregory down again while they held a quick consultation as to which way to go. Their only knowledge of the geography of Petsamo came from their brief flight in the semi-darkness above it but they felt that the town lay towards their left and that it would be best to make in that direction; so Freddie hoisted Gregory on to his shoulders again and they set off along a dreary-looking road.

It seemed that they had managed to evade the soldiers but the thought that the Russians had taken Petsamo filled them all with the gravest forebodings. From the little they could make out, encompassed as they were by darkness and snow, they were passing down a street which consisted of back gardens interspersed with empty lots and they felt that since none of them could speak Finnish it would be a risky business to knock up a house, even when they found one. As the Russians had fought their way into Petsamo that day everything would be in confusion; they might easily walk into a trap, as they had done at the air-port, and find that the building they knocked up had been taken over as a billet for Russian soldiers; or, if it still held Finns the Finns might take them for Russians—as they could not speak Finnish—and set about them. Even the fact of heading for the town seemed a policy of dubious wisdom. The main body of Soviet troops would certainly be quartered there and the sort of fate that might overtake them as prisoners of the Russians was too grim to contemplate; yet they could not stay out all night with the thermometer at thirty degrees below zero.

They had covered about a quarter of a mile at a slow, plodding pace when the bulk of a house loomed up through the snow; before it stood a huge sleigh to which were harnessed three horses. Erika halted the party with a swift whisper. "Wait! If we can get hold of that *troika* we could get away."

"Where to?" Freddie muttered anxiously.

"God knows. But away from the Russians, anyhow."

"Yes," Angela added quickly. "Erika's right. Anything would be better than falling into the hands of those soldiers."

"Right," said Freddie. "Let's take it, then. It's no time to bother ourselves about private ownership."

As they stepped forward a man emerged from the shadows on the far side of the horses. They had no idea if he was a Russian or a Finn but Erika felt now that their very lives depended upon getting possession of the sleigh. Drawing her pistol she advanced on the man, crying sharply in German: "Put your hands up!"

The man stood there, evidently not understanding. In the uncertain light she could not see the expression on his face but she stepped forward another couple of paces and thrust out her automatic so that he could see it. Apparently taken

241

completely by surprise he jumped back a pace and pulling his hands from his pockets lifted them quickly above his head.

Freddie ran to the near side of the sleigh and lowered Gregory into it. Angela scrambled up on to the box and grabbed the reins. The sleigh-bells on the harness jingled and the three small wiry horses began to paw the ground impatiently. Erika waved her pistol, motioning the owner of the sleigh to retreat. He began to curse in some unknown language but gave back a few paces. Then, suddenly regaining his courage, he made a rush at her.

Her pistol flashed as she sent a shot over his shoulder. It brought him up short and she lowered her gun with a determined gesture which showed him that she meant to put her next shot into his body; he hesitated, then still cursing, he began to back away again.

"All aboard !" called Angela, passing the reins to Freddie. With a swift turn Erika grabbed the off side of the sleigh and jumped. Freddie cracked the whip and as Erika half-fell into the body of the *troika* the horses plunged their way into the snow-flaked darkness leaving their unfortunate owner shouting and cursing in the middle of the road.

The three horses were as much as Freddie could handle but he soon had them under control. Although they were still rugged up against the piercing cold they cantered down the street at a fine pace and he let them have their heads for the first mile, until they were clear of the town and somewhere out behind the air-port on a road that had only a line of trees at one side to mark it. Pulling up, he un-rugged the horses and with the reins still over the crook of his arm came round to the side of the sleigh to find out how badly Gregory was wounded.

Erika and Angela had both lost their dressing-cases but they had found a torch in one of Gregory's pockets and were examining him by it. He was still unconscious but the light showed that the fur collar of his coat was glistening with wet blood and on removing his fur cap they found that he had been wounded in the back of the head. At first they feared that a bullet had smashed his skull and was lodged in the bone there, but as Angela held the light and Erika probed the wound gently with her fingers they discovered that it was only a deep cut through his hair and the back of his scalp; upon which Freddie declared that the wound must have been made by a spent bullet which had ricocheted off the brickwork of the air-port building.

As Erika probed the deep cut Gregory began to moan and

242

soon afterwards came round but he was unable to talk coherently. The girls bandaged the wound as well as they could by making a wad of their handkerchiefs and keeping it in place by pulling his fur *papenka* over it; then they made him as comfortable as possible between them in the back of the sleigh and drew the rugs, with which it was well provided, over them.

If the man from whom they had stolen the sleigh had roused his neighbours there was still danger of pursuit so, jumping on to the box, Freddie drove on again. There would have been considerable risk of his driving off the road had it not been that the way was now dead straight and lay between two solid blocks of forest which they had entered within a few hundred yards of their first halt, and even through the gently-falling snow he could see the black blur of the massed tree-trunks on either side.

After they had been going for nearly an hour he pulled up and turned towards the others to ask a little doubtfully: "D'you think we ought to go on? I haven't the faintest idea where this road leads to."

"Never mind," said Angela decisively. "Give the horses another breather, then drive on again. We must get as far as we possibly can from Petsamo now it's been captured by the Russians."

"Yes. I'm with you there," he agreed; "but the devil of it is that we don't know where we're going."

"We can't help that," said Erika; "anything is better than falling into the hands of the soldiers. One look at their faces as they were in that mess-room drinking like hogs was quite enough to show what brutes they are."

After resting the horses they continued their journey into the unknown at an easier pace, halting once more after another half-hour had passed. The snow was still falling so they could not see the stars and Freddie was uneasy about their direction; but the girls continued to insist that they must get as far as they could from Petsamo by morning and Angela volunteered to drive the next stage.

When they went on she found the three horses a heavy strain upon her arms but the vigour she had to exert to control them kept her warm; and it was a pleasant change from sitting inactive in the back of the sleigh where the cold was bitter even under the pile of fur rugs.

Freddie took over again after the next halt and they went on and on down the long, straight road which they had had no

243

difficulty at all in following as it was still bordered in either side by grim, silent forests.

When they halted for the fifth time they estimated that they must be well over twenty miles from Petsamo; yet they had not seen a single traveller on the road or passed through any village. As they drove on again the snow began to lighten. After a little it ceased altogether and they were able to see the moon, which was only four days past full, and the stars gleaming overhead in a pale, frosty sky. Freddie halted the sleigh once more and remained peering up at them for a moment; then he said in an uneasy voice:

"That's the North Star up there on our left. We've been driving into Russia."

"Petsamo is only about fifteen miles from the Russian frontier," said Erika, "so we must have crossed it by now."

"I don't know," Freddie replied. "This road doesn't run due east but about south-east by south, so we may still be somewhere on the Finnish side of the frontier."

"Oh, hell!" exclaimed Angela. "What *are* we going to do? I haven't noticed a single turning for the last ten miles or more and the last thing we want to do is to drive on into enemy territory; yet we can't go back."

Gregory had fallen into a troubled sleep so they could not consult him. Freddie glanced at the dial of his luminous watch. It was not yet midnight and so still November the 30th, the first day of the Russo-Finnish War. It seemed incredible that so much should have happened to them in so short a space of time, yet they had woken that morning in the comfortable room at the Helsinki police headquarters with Finland still at peace; reasonably confident that they would soon be free again and, having completed their mission successfully, be on their way to England. Since then, they had been charged with murder, had passed through three devastating air-raids, had flown seven hundred miles, had made a most dangerous night-landing in a snow-storm, had narrowly escaped being killed or captured by drunken Russian soldiers and had driven twenty-five miles in a stolen *troika* to find themselves lost and stranded in the desolate Arctic.

The seemingly endless forests on either side of them were utterly still with a terrifying silence that could almost be felt. For many miles they had seen no sign of life; they were foodless and shelterless and from the agonizing cold they knew that the thermometer must stand at many degrees below zero.

244

The two men were wanted for murder in Finland; all four of them would be arrested and shot for firing on the soldiers if they fell into the hands of the Russians, and if they did not return to Petsamo they must drive on into Russia, for if they remained where they were they would freeze to death before morning. As all of them silently considered this desperate situation they felt that they were faced with an insoluble problem.

CHAPTER XXI

THE MAN WITHOUT A MEMORY

"Well, we can't stay here," said Freddie, flapping his arms across his chest, "otherwise we'll get frost-bite. This cold is absolutely shattering and the only antidote to it is to keep moving."

"But where to?" said Angela desperately. "If we go on until we reach a village we'll probably find ourselves in Russia."

"For all practical purposes we're in Russia already," Erika remarked slowly; "as the Russians took Petsamo some time to-day they must have driven in the Finnish frontier guards round here; so we're behind the Russian lines now in any case."

"That's true," Freddie agreed, and Erika went on:

"We'll be no worse off if we go forward than if we go back—in fact, we'll almost certainly receive better treatment if we strike a new lot of Russians further along the road than we should if we returned to Petsamo and fell into the hands of the crowd we fired on. They'd never believe we only did it in self-defence."

Angela made an effort to stop her teeth chattering and added: "Ye-ye-es. They'd sh-shoot us if they caught us, so we must go on. I'm going to drive again."

Right oh!" Freddie handed her the reins. "There must be a village somewhere along this road and maybe the peasants will give us shelter whether they're Finns or Russians."

They drove on for what seemed an interminable time through the dark, menacing forest, which now looked even more sinister in the bright moonlight, halting occasionally to rest the horses and change the drivers. Erika remained with Gregory's head pillowed on her shoulder although she was cramped and terribly cold. Angela tried to persuade her to change places and take a turn with the reins but she refused for, brave as she was in other ways, she was frightened of anything to do with horses.

Freddie could not understand how any main road, such as this obviously was, could continue for so many miles without a single village upon it, until Erika said: "I don't think people like ourselves who live in the more highly-populated parts of Europe ever quite realize how sparsely countries bordering on the Arctic are peopled. Sometimes, I believe, there's as much as a hundred miles between settlements, and then they are inhabited only by miners or trappers."

It was nearly two o'clock in the morning when Angela, who was standing up in the sleigh driving again, gave a cry of exultation and pointed with her whip. A solitary light showed clearly through a break in the trees on the left-hand side of the road.

Halting the sleigh, she and Freddie got out and ran towards a track which wound between the trees. It was only just perceptible in the glow from the snow but they soon realized that the light was much further away than they had at first imagined; so they walked back to the sleigh and climbing in again drove along the track towards it.

The track was about a quarter of a mile in length and as they advanced they saw that the light came from the window of quite a large, one-storeyed building. Pulling up in front of it Freddie gave a shout, but no answer came from the lighted room or from the doorway in the log wall which stood ajar. Tying the reins to a near-by post Freddie stamped his feet to try to get some warmth into them, kicked aside a little drift of recently fallen snow outside the door and pushed it open. Catching his breath he paused there for a moment staring at the ghastly sight that confronted him.

A single oil-lamp burned upon a stout, wood table in the centre of the room; its light shone upon four human figures and all of them were unquestionably dead.

Under the window, two panes of which Freddie now saw had been shattered, an elderly bearded man lay clutching a rifle. Near-by a younger man sprawled on his back staring with blinded eyes at the raftered roof. On the far side of the room, beyond the table, a middle-aged woman was huddled with her arms round a boy of thirteen as though in a last effort to protect him.

Blood stained the white scrubbed floor but the large room was not in serious disorder and it was well equipped for a squatter's home. A row of burnished pots and pans hung beside the stove; the table-cloth, curtains and chair-coverings were of decent material. In one corner there were some home-made shelves, containing at least a couple of hundred books, and a wireless stood on a small side-table. Freddie realized at once that such luxuries would never be found in a Russian peasant's shack, so the dead people must be Finns. Perhaps the man and his eldest son had fired upon a body of Soviet troops that they had seen moving along the road earlier in the day. In any case the cottage had been attacked some time after sundown when the lamp had already been lit. It looked as though the two men had been shot while defending it, and the woman and boy brutally murdered afterwards.

The flat-topped stove, a feature of all Arctic dwellings, consisting of cooking range and brick baking oven—in this case a huge affair nearly ten feet square—was still going. But owing to the fact that the door of the house had been left partly open for several hours, the room was little warmer than the climate outside; and as Freddie examined the bodies he found that they were already frozen stiff. Going out to the two girls he told them what he had found and asked them to remain where they were while he disposed of the corpses. He then returned to the cottage and one by one carried the poor dead Finns from their home to deposit them round the corner of the building, since he was far too done up to think of burying them before he had slept.

While Freddie was busy with the bodies Angela took the torch and scouted round the house until she found a large stable in its rear. There were no horses there but one end of it was piled high with roughly-made trusses of sweet-smelling hay, and as the place backed on to the stove in the living-room its temperature was not unbearably cold. Stumbling with weariness she went back to the sleigh, unharnessed the horses, rugged them up and turned them loose in the stable to munch mouthfuls of hay from the trusses.

Erika had meanwhile roused Gregory and found to her joy that he was now able to walk without assistance; but he complained that he had a most frightful headache and that it hurt him to talk. She led him into the house and made him sit down in an arm-chair where she brushed the frost from his eye-brows and chafed his half-frozen hands and feet.

By the time they had finished protecting the room from the cold and had warmed themselves at the stove they could hardly stand from fatigue. Since morning they had sustained eighteen hours of almost constant anxiety and exertion and they felt much too tired even to look round the cottage in search of food. Having stoked up the stove they climbed wearily on top of the oven and drew their furs over them; Freddie put out the light and within ten minutes all four of them were sound asleep.

When Freddie awoke it was still pitch-dark and on looking at the luminous dial of his watch he saw that it was a quarter to three. Knowing that it must have been just about that hour when they turned in he jumped to the conclusion that they must have slept the clock round twice, but it seemed rather extraordinary that all of them should have done so, even allowing for the terrific strain of the previous day. Then the explanation flashed upon him. Up here in the Arctic, now that it was close on mid-winter, the sun did not rise until ten o'clock and it would set again soon after two. They had slept once round the clock but the short four-hour day was already over; although they were encompassed again in pitch-black night it was actually only a quarter to three in the afternoon.

His stirring had roused the others and while he lit the lamp they climbed down off the big, flat top of the oven. Erika's first concern was for Gregory but when she asked him how his head was he looked at her in a puzzled way.

"My head? Yes; it's aching like blazes. I—I wonder why?"

"You were hit on the back of it last night by a spent bullet and passed out. You gave us the most awful shock. We thought you were dead."

He smiled at her. "That's strange. I don't remember the least thing about it and—er—" he looked round the big living-room, "where the devil are we?"

"In some woodman's or trapper's home that we were lucky enough to find—about forty or fifty miles south-east by south of Petsamo," said Freddie.

"Petsamo?" Gregory murmured vaguely. "Petsamo? Where's that?"

"Wake up, man!" Freddie laughed. "It's the Finnish port in the Arctic Circle."

A look dawned in Gregory's eyes that none of them had ever seen there before; a frightened, hunted look. "But, but—" he stammered, "the Arctic! What am I doing up in the Arctic?"

They all stood there in silence for a moment regarding him anxiously until, in a very small voice, Erika said suddenly: "You do *know* me, darling, don't you?"

"Of course I do," he laughed uneasily. "As though I could forget your lovely face in a million years! But wait a minute—that's very queer—I can't remember your name."

"I'm Erika," she said softly.

"Erika," he repeated. "That's a pretty name, isn't it—and marvellously suitable." He looked at the others. "Of course I know both of you, too, but somehow—it's quite extraordinary —I can't place either of you for the moment."

"I'm Freddie, and this is Angela," Charlton announced. "It looks as though that crack on the back of your head last night has caused you to lose your memory, old chap," he added with a worried frown.

Gregory passed a hand across his forehead and nodded slowly. Then he laughed—rather uncertainly. "Yes, I suppose that's it. What a damnable thing to happen! My mind seems to have gone completely blank. I—I haven't the faintest idea who I am or what we're all doing here."

It was a strange and rather alarming situation but the practical Angela pulled them out of the sudden gloom that had descended upon them, by saying: "I expect when we tell you all we know about your past things'll soon come back. In the meantime I'm jolly hungry. What about seeing if we can find some breakfast?"

"That's the idea," Freddie supported her, and the two of them began to poke into the cupboards to see what supplies they could find while Erika examined Gregory's wound. The bullet had cut a furrow about two inches long through the hair at the back of his cranium, exposing a jagged red weal where the torn scalp had bled. He felt no pain from the wound itself; the whole area had gone dull so that he could not feel anything even when Erika pressed quite hard with her fingers, so she washed it carefully and left it unbandaged so that the air could get at the abrasion and heal it more quickly.

In a cupboard near the stove Angela had found a small stock of coffee, sugar, tinned milk, some slices of dried meat on a plate and two flat loaves like small, thick motor tyres. Erika said that as it was too cold to grow wheat in Finland white bread was procurable only in the towns, where it was made from stocks of imported corn, and that this was rye-bread upon which the bulk of the population lived. She had often seen the peasant women carrying a dozen or more such loaves by a string threaded through the holes in the centre, and had heard it said that they went as hard as brick when they were stale but kept almost indefinitely, and that the people made great stocks of them in the autumn to last through the winter.

Angela made some coffee and breaking up a part of one of the brick-like loaves they soaked the pieces in it to soften them; which, with the cold meat, made a not particularly palatable but satisfying meal. Over it they gave Gregory particulars as to who he was and a rough outline of his doings—as far as they knew them—since Erika had first met him on the road between Coblenz and Cologne three months before.

He was naturally extraordinarily interested in this recital but at certain parts of it they had great difficulty in persuading him that they were telling the truth. At first he refused to believe that he was a secret agent and said that such an incredible series of adventures could never have happened to anyone in real life; but he had to admit that they could hardly have invented such a story on the spur of the moment. He seemed to take everything in but he said very little and they were greatly distressed to see that his loss of memory had robbed him of his mental agility to such an extent that he was almost a different personality.

While rummaging for food they had pulled open a low door beside the stove which led into a small lightless chamber that had a drain in the centre of its sloping concrete floor and was empty except for a pile of large stones. Erika said that it was a *Suma*, or Finnish steam bath, and that to use it the stones should first be heated in the fire then have buckets of cold water poured over them which created clouds of steam in the small, almost airtight chamber making it like the steam room in a Turkish Bath.

But the supply of food they had found in the cupboards was very limited so Freddie was still greatly concerned about their situation. If there was not a larger stock somewhere about they would have to move on again; a thought that presented a score of difficult problems. In discussing their prospects it was Freddie who now took the lead while Gregory meekly agreed to everything that was said. Angela declared that she must go and look after the horses and Freddie said that he would make a full inspection of the premises; upon which, in silent acquiescence Gregory followed them out of the house like an eager but meek-looking spaniel.

When they drove up to the building the night before they had been vaguely puzzled by the fact that although from the outside it appeared to be quite a sizable place it seemed to consist of only the stable and one large living-room; but they had been too exhausted to bother about that at the time.

On going round the house they found that there were three other rooms in it, although none of these led into the room where they had slept; which Erika, who had followed the men out, remarked, was probably to prevent the intense cold seeping into the living-room through the cracks round a number of doorways.

The first room they entered was a fur store. It was very nearly empty, as the trapping season had only just begun, but its use was obvious from three bundles of pelts lying on the floor and a dozen skins which were hanging up to dry from rafters in the roof.

To their delight they found that the second room was a food store and, evidently, the trapper had laid in his supplies for the winter. No refrigerating apparatus was needed in that climate and there was a great pile of skinned and gutted carcases with the antlered heads still attached, showing that they were reindeer. Two or three dozen joints which hung from the beams they took to be haunches of either bear or venison; and filling almost half the floor-space was a stack of cases. They set to work opening these with a jemmy which lay handy on a shelf and found them to contain tinned stores—milk, coffee, the cheaper varieties of jams and fruits, pork-and-beans, soups, sausages, sweet corn and other vegetables; there was also a pile of about a hundred of the cart-wheel rye-bread loaves and twenty crocks of pickled eggs. Altogether it was a most satisfactory supply which, although containing few luxuries, would have been ample to see the trapper and his family comfortably through the winter and, if necessary, would serve a similar purpose for the party that had taken over his home.

The third room was a general store. It contained half a dozen sets of skis and ski-sticks of varying sizes, several pairs of big snow-shoes, three small sledges of a size to be pulled by dogs or men and all the family's spare clothing, which included several sets of furs and two trunks full of other garments; the whole of the far end of the room was stacked with a huge pile of logs and a number of drums of paraffin.

Angela rejoined them while they were still examining the packing-cases in the food store to report that the stable was equally well-equipped. The trapper had evidently owned two or three horses, although these must have been driven off by the Russians; but that the horses had been stabled there was obvious from the sleigh-harness that was still hanging on the hooks, a big *troika* that occupied one corner of the stable and a good stock of corn and hay that had also been left intact.

The examination of the cases, trunks and other items had occupied them for over three hours so it was close on seven o'clock by the time they returned to the living-room. Erika had brought with her from the store a tin of sweet corn, a tin of fruit and half a dozen eggs upon which, with another boiling of coffee, they made their evening meal. While they were eating it, and afterwards, they gave Gregory a more detailed account of the recent adventures in which they had all been involved, but they were still tired from the excitements and anxieties of the previous day so at nine o'clock, having banked-up the stove, they put out the lamp and climbed on to the warm top of the brick oven again.

They awoke the following morning at seven o'clock. It was still pitch-dark and it now seemed to them that they had not seen daylight for several days, but they got up and prepared breakfast. When they had finished Freddie said that he thought they ought to give some sort of burial to the owners of the place, who were still lying round the corner of the house where he had carried them, warped and frozen, in the attitudes in which they had died.

With Gregory as his meek, willing helper he went outside. Having retrieved the bodies from the previous night's fall of snow they carried them about a hundred yards to a group of trees. Digging through the snow—which was already several feet deep—they laid the four bodies on the iron-hard ground. Freddie could not remember the burial service—apart from the phrase "Ashes to ashes and dust to dust", but rather self-consciously he said a short prayer over the grave, recommending the Finnish family to the mercy of Almighty God, while Gregory looked on with child-like interest. They then shovelled the snow back on top of the bodies, just as the late dawn was filtering through the silent, snow-covered forest.

Directly they were back in the house Freddie called a Council of War. The one and only item on his agenda was: should they stay where they were or re-harness the horses to the *troika* and try to break through the scattered Russian lines, which lay somewhere to the west, in an attempt to get back to the territory that was still held by the civilized Finns?

Erika pointed out that if they did get back to Finland both he and Gregory were wanted for murder there; at which

Gregory began to giggle. Pulling up short he apologized and said he found that awfully difficult to believe, because he was really a most harmless person and had never raised a finger against anybody in his life.

The others looked at one another and smiled with pained discretion but they forbore to argue with him and Freddie admitted the point that Erika had made. The last thing he wished to do was to expose himself to re-arrest and the possibility of being hanged for murder by the terrifyingly law-conscious Finns.

"The only alternative, then, as far as I can see," he said, "is for us to strike north towards the coast. It can't be more than forty or fifty miles distant and we ought to be able to find a fishing village somewhere along it where they won't know anything about us. Gregory has plenty of money . . ."

"Have I?" interrupted Gregory. "But how nice."

"Yes," Freddie continued. "From what I remember, you've still got over £500 in your pockets and your boots."

"Then if we could get home I could buy a cottage somewhere and a lot of books—I'm sure I used to like books," Gregory remarked with considerable interest.

"You could, but you wouldn't, darling," Erika assured him. "You'd be much more likely to blow the lot on taking me to Paris if there wasn't a war on, and hiring the Royal suite at the Ritz."

"The Ritz . . ." echoed Gregory thoughtfully. "I believe I used to stay there sometimes. I seem to remember a long, long corridor with show-cases on each side of it."

"Go on," said Angela, her blue eyes laughing, "go on. What else?"

"There was a foyer as one came in from the square . . ."

"That's it. The *Place Vendôme.*"

Gregory nodded. "And one went through the long corridor to the bar. It was run by a great character—a fellow who would always cash everybody's cheques. I can't remember his name—wait a minute, though—it was Frank—yes, Frank. He was a grand man, and you could never go into the place without meeting somebody you knew."

Erika sighed with relief. If he could remember that sort of thing it showed that his past was not a complete blank and that gradually he might recover his memory entirely.

"That's right, old chap," Freddie encouraged him. "But as I was saying, you've got plenty of money so we could hire some of the fishermen to take us out in a boat along the coast until we sighted a neutral or British ship; then we'd go aboard and pay our passage back to civilization."

Erika lighted one of her few remaining cigarettes. "I think you're underestimating the difficulties, Freddie. You're thinking of the Arctic as though it was the South Coast of England, with towns and villages along it every few miles; but it isn't like that at all. Between Petsamo and Murmansk I doubt if there are more than half a dozen scattered fishing settlements and those will be inhabited only by Lapps. We can't talk their language and, even if we could explain to them what we wanted, the only sort of boat they'd have is the Eskimo *kayak*—a little canoe affair the top of which is covered with skin. We'd need one apiece with an oarsman to propel us and I don't suppose their maximum range is more than twenty miles. The whole world to such people consists of their village and the nearest trading station, and for them to sight a steamer up in those parts is an event which may not happen once in two or three years. If we did as you suggest our chances of picking up a vessel which would take us to a civilized port are unbelievably remote; and on our way to the coast we might easily get lost and die of cold in this accursed snow."

"If that's the case," said Freddie gloomily, "it looks as though we'll have to stay here the whole winter and wait to make our attempt to break back to civilization until the spring."

Angela smiled at him; she was looking very well and very pretty now that she had recovered from the strain of their flight from Helsinki. "Would you mind having to stay here the whole winter—very much, darling?"

He looked up quickly and a slow smile lit his face. "I suppose it's my duty to get home as soon as I can, since there's a war on, but if it isn't possible that lets me out. There's masses of food and fuel here so we haven't got to worry how we're going to keep alive. Since you're with me, and I've got a perfectly good excuse for staying, nothing else matters as far as I'm concerned."

"How do you feel about it, darling?" Erika asked Gregory.

He laughed. "Perhaps my loss of memory is a blessing in disguise. If all you tell me about myself is true I suppose I ought to be busy assassinating Hitler or kidnapping President Roosevelt to induce him to come into the war on our side; but as I can't for the life of me remember what I'm supposed to be up to, there doesn't seem much sense in my risking being frozen

255

to death in order to get myself back into the middle of this scrap that's going on. If you'd like to go somewhere I'll go with you; but if not, I'm perfectly content to stay here."

She laid her hand gently over his. "I'm so glad you feel like that, dearest. I was afraid you'd want to take all sorts of mad risks to try and get home . . ."

"Oh, but I never take risks," said Gregory. "I'm a very cautious person."

"I'm sure you are," she smiled. "But I was afraid that you might be anxious to get back to your own country. That would have meant our separating again and, you see, as I now have no country to go to I would much rather stay here with you and rough it than live in a little more comfort in some dreary hotel in Norway or Sweden without you."

She glanced at the others. "Let's forget the war. If only we can do that we'll cheat the gods, and at least snatch a few months' happiness out of our lives, until the spring."

As they were apparently safe and well-found where they were, yet could not leave the place while the winter lasted without endangering their lives, Erika's reasoning seemed sound common sense. All four of them were in love and loved by their opposite members in the party. Their duties would be light, as the girls, between them could easily do the cooking and keep the one room tidy while the men looked after the stove and bath-house, tended the horses and cut fresh fuel when required.

The others nodded, smiling their agreement; but it did not prove so easy to forget the war.

CHAPTER XXII

OUT INTO THE SNOW

IT was all very well to decide lightly on taking all the happiness they could while hibernating for the winter and on making their retreat a snow-bound Arcady where they could forget the new madness that had come upon the world; but each of them had friends or relatives who were involved in the struggle and, although they could not hope to secure news of individuals, they had a natural anxiety to know how their countries were faring.

Their conference was hardly over when Angela noticed the little wireless set in the far corner of the room which had been half hidden since their arrival by some furs that Gregory had inconsequently tossed across it. Running over with a cry of delight at finding a radio which could give her dance-music, of which she was passionately fond, she pulled away the furs and switched on. The set buzzed and crackled as she turned the knob, then a foreign voice came through which was speaking English.

"Leave it! Leave it!" said Freddie quickly. "We may hear what's happened to the Finns."

As they had cut in almost at the begining of a news bulletin they were able to do so. Apparently, *Monsieur* Errko's Government had resigned at midnight on the first day of the war to make way for an all-party Government, under *Monsieur* Risto Ryti, Governor of the Bank of Finland, which was to seek a truce. Their efforts so far had proved unavailing and the Finns had withdrawn a few miles from their actual frontier on the Karelian Isthmus to their most forward posts in the Mannerheim Line, leaving a few small evacuated villages in the hands of the advancing Russians. In one of these Stalin had set up a puppet Government under the Bolshevik, Kuusinen, who had taken refuge in Moscow after the Finnish revolution was suppressed by Marshal Mannerheim in 1918 and had since acted

257

as secretary to the Comintern. A pact between the Soviet and this Puppet Government was now in the course of negotiation while Soviet troops were hurling themselves against the Finnish lines only a few miles away. So far the only success reported by the Russians during the three days' fighting was the capture of Petsamo, the harbour and fortifications of which had fallen the previous night. On all other fronts the Finns were holding their ground.

After the actual news the commentator gave extracts from the world Press which clearly showed the general horror and indignation which was felt at Russia's unprovoked attack on Finland, and when he signed off they learnt that they had been listening to one of the Swedish broadcasts in English from Stockholm.

"D'you think the Swedes and Norwegians will go in with the Finns?" Freddie asked Gregory; but evidently Gregory's mind was now almost entirely blank on the subject of international politics, as he just shook his head in a puzzled way and said:

"I—I'm afraid I don't even know what they're fighting about."

Erika suppressed an exclamation of distress. It seemed utterly tragic to her that his fine brain and brilliant reasoning powers should have been wiped out as though they had never existed. In an attempt to cover his lapse from the others she said quickly:

"It all depends on the Nazis' attitude. If it's part of their devil's pact with Butcher Stalin that Russia should have Finland von Ribbentrop will exercise pressure on the Scandinavian countries to prevent their going to the assistance of the Finns. He may even threaten them that Germany would invade them in the south if they do. On the other hand, you can be quite certain that the Nazis don't mean the Bolsheviks to walk right through Finland to the Swedish iron-ore mines, so there's just a chance that they may encourage the Swedes and Norwegians to go to the Finns' support."

During the afternoon and evening they further explored the resources of their new home. The books, unfortunately, all proved to be in Finnish or Swedish and they could find no games or other diversions in the house, so it looked as though they were going to be entirely dependent upon the radio and their own conversation for amusements during the many weeks ahead of them before the thaw was due to set in. But they soon found that Gregory's loss of memory provided them with an unusual occupation.

All his previous life, all history, all knowledge except the simple, instinctive things, such as helping to lay the table for a meal and stoking up the fire, seemed to have left him. Every few hours he suffered a bout of acute headache and at times his eyes troubled him, as he found it difficult to focus them properly; but his brain was perfectly sound and once given any piece of information it registered again for good. Moreover, as each subject was broached it seemed to unlock a few cerebral cells here and there so that after he had heard them talking about any matter for a little time he was able to join in the conversation quite normally. Yet the sum of knowledge acquired casually in the active life of an educated man is so vast that, once lost, it is an extraordinarily long business to get even a considerable portion of it back, however quick the learner, and during the process the person who is reacquiring his education appears to have almost endless blanks in his mental make-up. If Freddie said "William the Conqueror, 1066", Gregory would promptly say, "William II, 1087", and find himself perfectly well aware that William Rufus met his death while out hunting; but that did not give him the slightest clue to any other period of English history. In consequence, they began to employ themselves with his re-education and, as all they had to do was to talk of a variety of subjects for him to regain his knowledge of them, they were amazed at the almost endless interesting discussions which arose as a result of their efforts to help him to get his memory back.

There were no razors in the house so the two men had to grow beards and the girls agreed that during the process they both looked most unattractive; but after a week their bristles began to soften and Freddie had a silky, golden halo round his chin while Gregory's was black with grey hairs in it, although he had not a single grey hair on his head.

At first Angela had kept the wireless on almost constantly to pick up dance-music as well as news, until Freddie suddenly realized that as they were many miles from a town the set was not run from an electric main but was one of the old-fashioned battery variety and that once the batteries ran down the instrument would be out of action for good. In consequence, he decreed that they must use the radio only to get the news every other evening and for an hour of dance-music as a treat on Saturday nights.

259

The set was not strong enough to pick up any English station, except very faintly, so they had to content themselves with the English broadcasts of neutral commentators on the Continent and the German broadcasts, which came over very clearly. During their first week Freddie whooped with joy when he learned that on December the 3rd R.A.F. planes had scored direct hits on German warships in the Heligoland Bight and that during the week the British had sunk three submarines and captured a fourth.

A few days later they learned that the King had gone to France and that the franc had been linked with sterling. Rather surprisingly, Gregory seemed to know what this meant and said that the one good thing which so far seemed to have come out of the war was the way in which the British were getting together with the French. By pooling the resources of both nations and making the two great empires one for the duration of the war it looked as though the two groups of countries might continue on those lines afterwards, which might be the first glimmer of a new world order where many, and eventually all, nations would remove their trade barriers and hold their assets in common for the good of mankind.

The Finns appeared to be putting up a magnificent show on the Mannerheim Line, but the Russians were trying desperately hard to break through the chain of lakes that guarded the Finnish frontier further north, and this was a grave danger for, if they succeeded, they would be able to cut through the narrow waist-line of Finland to the Gulf of Bothnia where lay the only railway by which the Finns could get supplies and volunteers from Norway and Sweden.

Russia was now threatening Rumania again, but that was more than offset by the news that Churchill had knocked the bottom out of the Nazi lies about Germany's success in her ruthless war at sea. The great First Lord had announced that 150 merchant ships were entering or leaving British ports each day, that over 2000 were on the high seas and that the loss of British ships in convoy was only one in seven hundred and fifty. By the end of the week Hitler was busy waging another "nerve" war with threats to both Scandinavia and Holland, while his co-murderer, Stalin, was attempting to blackmail the Turks.

It was on December the 9th—ten days after they left Helsinki—that during the incredibly short morning, when the silent forest was revealed for a little in full daylight, Erika saw through the only remaining glass panes in the window of the house three figures approaching out of the wood with a dog-team and a sleigh. She quickly called to the others and Gregory and Freddie snatched up the rifles which had been left by the Finnish father and son who had died defending their home. But the use of weapons proved quite unnecessary.

The dog-sleigh drove up before the doorway and on going out they saw three strange little figures confronting them. The newcomers were so muffled in furs that it was impossible to tell their sex, as what little could be seen of their brown, wrinkled faces gave no indication of it. Their speech was incomprehensible but by smiles and gestures they indicated that they wished to come into the house, and as in such desolate countries hospitality is always freely offered to strangers Freddie immediately beckoned them inside.

Unharnessing their dogs they came in and sat down in a row, cross-legged on the floor, like three little Chinese mandarins. They did not say anything at all but just sat there waiting. It seemed obvious that they expected to be fed so Erika cooked them a meal. When the food was ready they took some out to their dogs and ate the rest with their fingers, displaying happy, abandoned greed and relish, but they gave no sign of leaving when they had finished. All attempts to converse with them proved quite fruitless and after sitting there belching cheerfully for a little they moved over to the corner beside the stove and curling up in a complicated ball went to sleep.

"Well, what d'you make of that?" Gregory inquired.

"They're Lapps or Eskimos, I expect," Freddie said. "When they've had their sleep out and another meal they'll probably go off just as they arrived. But how the poor little devils live in this ghastly wilderness, God only knows."

The Lapps woke late in the afternoon and going outside took their dogs into the stable; they then returned to the living-room and sat down on the floor in a row again, where they remained until the evening meal was cooked. Having gleefully participated in it, after many appreciative grins and belchings they moved over to the corner and once more went to sleep.

"I wonder if they'll go off to-morrow morning or if they've decided to stay here for keeps," Freddie remarked.

"Well, if they do stay it doesn't matter," Angela replied. "We've got plenty of food and they're nice, harmless little people. It would be a shame to send them packing into the snow."

When they woke the following morning the Lapps had

261

disappeared, having made off without a sound, but an hour later it transpired that they had not gone for good. They all arrived back in time for a hearty late breakfast; then one of them, who was slightly taller than the other two, beckoned Freddie out of the house. He went obediently and followed his visitor across the clearing some distance into the woods, where the Lapp halted and pointed at the snow. Freddie saw that there were some heavy tracks in it; the Lapp raised his arms as though he were holding a rifle and about to shoot.

Freddie got the idea at once and returning to the house he and Gregory put on snow-shoes, collected the rifles and went back into the forest with their queer little companion. For an hour they followed the tracks, then the Lapp motioned them to halt and went forward himself for about a hundred yards on his hands and knees. After a short interval he beckoned to them to follow and, crawling up, they saw through the trees a fine brown bear.

It seemed a rotten business to shoot that harmless Bruin which was so reminiscent of a large teddy in a children's toy-shop, but they had not tasted fresh meat for nearly a fortnight so, sighting their rifles carefully and aiming just behind the bear's left foreleg, they fired almost together. The animal reared up on its hind legs, gave a loud grunt and toppled over, dead.

Instantly the Lapp rushed forward brandishing a long knife and fell upon it screeching with delight. In a few moments with swift, skilful cuts he had skinned the bear and, with uncanny suddenness, his two companions appeared, leading their dog-sleigh. The carcase was loaded on to it and the triumphant hunters retraced their steps to the house, reaching it with their kill just as the short afternoon was done and twilight was falling once more. Erika roasted some of the fresh bear's meat in the oven that evening and after the dried reindeer, to which they had now become accustomed, it tasted delicious; so they all felt that their uninvited guests had more than earned their keep.

As they did not know the Lapps' names Angela christened the taller one Bimbo and the two shorter ones, who followed him about wherever he went and whose job appeared to be to look after the dogs, Mutt and Jeff. The habits of all three were extremely primitive and after their feast of bear's meat the gleeful chuckles and other sounds which issued from their corner, once the light had been put out, made it clear that at least one of them was a woman. The following day Freddie definitely ascertained that Bimbo was the man of the party while Mutt and Jeff were his two wives.

In the days that followed it became clear that the Lapps had decided to winter with them, but far from interfering with the comfort of their hosts they added considerably to it. Bimbo seemed to know instinctively where game was to be found in the trackless forest and he had not been with them long before he added fresh fish to their table. To their amazement he arrived back from one of his expeditions late one evening carrying a large pike in his arms. It is true that most of the tail end of the fish was missing, but the girls cooked the body and it proved a most welcome change to their meat diet.

As they could not ask him where he had caught it, next morning Freddie drew in the snow a picture of a fish, demonstrating that they would like to get another. Bimbo remained unresponsive until the early afternoon, then led them nearly three miles through the forest to a large clearing which looked at first sight to be only a great treeless dip in the snow-covered ground; but on going down into it they found that it was a frozen lake in which at one spot Bimbo had cleared away the snow and hacked a hole through the ice. As twilight fell he lit a lamp that he had brought with him and lowered it on a string to the bottom of the hole, kneeling above it with a thin barbed spear clutched tightly in his hand.

For twenty minutes they waited. The surface of the water rippled and Bimbo struck. Jerking out his spear he produced a fair-sized perch wriggling upon it. His little, black, boot-button eyes flashing with eagerness, he tore the fish from the harpoon and, having knocked its head on the ice to stun it, proceed to tear great mouthfuls of the flesh out of its body, gobbling them down with huge enjoyment; upon which his companions realized what had happened to the tail end of the pike.

They remained there for two hours, during which they bagged a trout, another perch and three fish that Freddie thought might be fresh-water herrings. It was now night and Freddie was worried that they might not be able to find their way home; but his anxiety was quite needless. Bimbo led them back through the seemingly impenetrable darkness with an unerring sense of direction and they all enjoyed an excellent fish supper.

The news over the wireless contained no events of startling importance. During the first week after the Lapps' arrival

Russia had been formally expelled from the League of Nations and Italy also ceased to be a member, leaving Britain and France as the only Great Powers remaining in it. So it had come openly at last to what, in fact, it had been for a long time past; not a League of Nations at all, but an association of states under the leadership of the Western Powers used as an instrument by them in their losing struggle to maintain by diplomacy alone the Peace of Vengeance which they had dictated after the last Great War.

It was on December the 15th that the exiles first learned of the Battle of the River Plate, although it had taken place two days before. On the face of it the British appeared to have put up an excellent show, but the full significance of the action was not brought home to them until it had been explained to Gregory what sort of ships the *Graf Spee* and the cruisers *Ajax*, *Achilles* and *Exeter* were when, quite suddenly, his memory about naval matters, gun calibres, speeds and weight of shells flooded back.

"But don't you understand?" he cried, his eyes glowing. "It's magnificent! An epic fight that will go down to history beside the exploits of Drake and Frobisher, and Sir Richard Grenville taking on the seven great Spanish galleons in the *Revenge*. Just think of it! Those little cruisers, out-gunned, out-ranged, and infinitely more vulnerable with their much lighter armour, going straight in against the pocket battleship instead of waiting for one of their own big ships to come up. Why, one salvo apiece from the *Graf Spee's* eleven-inch guns might have sunk the lot of them before they could even get into range. It's the real Nelson touch, and it makes one incredibly proud to think one's of the same race as those splendid sailor-men."

Freddie and Angela caught his enthusiasm and they had all momentarily forgotten that Erika was a German, until she said: "Hans Langsdorf, who commands the *Graf Spee*, is an old friend of mine. He's a fine fellow, I can't bear to think of him sitting there with his crippled ship in Montevideo Harbour. But he'll come out and fight, of course, even if one of your big ships with fifteen-inch guns arrives on the scene. When he has completed his repairs he'll show you that German sailors are every bit as brave as the British. I'm going for a walk on my own, I think."

They waited anxiously for further news and two days later

learned that at Hitler's orders Captain Langsdorf had scuttled the pride of the German Navy.

At first Erika refused to believe it but when she was fully convinced that the news was true she burst into a storm of bitter weeping. "The humiliation of it!" she cried. "How dare that swine, Hitler, give such an order and make us appear cowards before the whole world. If anything could make all decent Germans loathe him more than they do at present, this thing will. It's enough to start a mutiny."

It was all the others could do to comfort her, but as by this time Gregory had got back a few of his memories about the last war he was able to persuade her that Hitler alone would be regarded with contempt as a result of the scuttling; since everybody knew that innumerable gallant actions had been performed by German soldiers and sailors in the past. There was one particular example which he wished to give her but, rack his brain as he would, he could not recall it until he had made Freddie tell him the names of the principal battles in the Great War. When Cambrai was mentioned it unlocked the closed door that he sought and brought back to him a whole series of events.

"That's it!" he cried, "Cambrai; the great Tank battle. Previous to that, before each big attack we used to do a seven-days' preparatory bombardment. Our Generals had so little imagination that the drill was always just the same and, naturally, the Germans got quite used to it. When the strafing started in earnest they used to say to one another: 'There are the British giving us seven days' notice that they mean to attack in this sector', and they all went down to play *vingt-et-un* in their dug-outs for the next week, until the bombardment was over; then they popped up fresh as daisies to receive our men when at last the assault took place.

"But Cambrai was planned by Fuller. He was only a Major then, and Heaven knows how he got his plan passed by the Generals; but he did, and this was his idea. On the morning of November the 20th, 1917, at the same moment as the guns opened fire every man in the British Third Army was to move forward, from the Infantry in the front-line trenches to the last A.S.C. waggon miles away in the rear. Our tanks, which were then a new weapon and had only been tried out in one or two side-shows, advanced with the Infantry, and the chap who commanded them sat on the top of one as it went over, with a miniature flag-staff flying the signal:" 'England expects that every man this day will do his damnedest.'

"Directly the balloon went up the Germans all went down into their dug-outs anticipating the usual seven days' rest. Before they even had any idea that an attack was in progress our men were bombing them out. The tanks went slap through the front-line, second-line, and reserve trenches. When they did encounter a few Germans the poor chaps simply ran for their lives at the sight of those iron monsters spitting fire and machine-gun bullets; because, you must remember, none of them had even seen a tank before, and there were no such things as anti-tank guns or anti-tank rifles in those days.

"The tanks began to penetrate the German artillery positions and directly the German gunners saw them approaching they just abandoned their guns and fled as though all the devils in Hell were after them. There was one German field-battery outside a village called Flequiers and all the gunners there took to their heels, just like the rest, officers as well as men —but with one exception—the Major.

"When his men started to run he ordered and implored them to stay; but as they ignored his pleas and commands he remained there alone. All by himself he loaded, sighted and fired one of his guns at the nearest tank, blowing it to Jericho. Would you believe it, that German Major took nine tanks to his own gun, single-handed, and held up our attack in that sector for over two hours, which delayed the whole British advance.

"Eventually our tank people had to throw their hand in. They simply could not get past him. So the attack was called off while a couple of tanks were sent on a long detour to take him in the rear; and only then did he surrender. Nine tanks to his own gun—I reckon that's the biggest bag in history, and how's that for a hero?"

"Thank you, darling." Erika placed her hand over his. "It was sweet of you to tell me that, and how wonderfully your memory is improving. You see, I've heard the story before, and you're right in every detail."

He laughed. "Oh, details don't bother me once I can get the lead to any subject. It's just that there are so many subjects on which I'm still completely blank; but I suppose they'll all come back in time."

But such bursts of coherence were rare, and although he was not mentally apathetic the effort to connect facts tired his brain, so that he was often silent for long periods. His headaches had ceased but his eyes still bothered him a little. In many ways he remained simple, almost like a child, but his affliction did not seem to worry him and from having been incurably lazy, to his friends' surprise, he appeared to enjoy physical exertion. The horses had to be rubbed down three times a day to keep their circulation going, even in the temperate stable, and he was happy at such work if Erika would sit watching him at it. He picked up ski-ing in a remarkably short time and was the only one among them who, during the first days, did not feel an awful craving for cigarettes; which drove the others nearly crazy.

On December the 20th, Captain Hans Langsdorf shot himself; a sad and futile end to one whom all the prisoners he had taken in the South Atlantic during the early months of war agreed to be a brave and gallant gentleman; and one more death to be laid at Hitler's door, for which he must answer in time to come.

Erika heard the news with mingled feelings; sorrow for the loss of an old friend, but pride that having carried out the orders of the blackguard who ruled Germany, as was his duty, he had by this personal act saved the honour of the German Navy.

In the meantime the news of the Finnish War was excellent. For three weeks of ceaseless battle the Russians had hurled division after division against the Mannerheim Line but had failed to make the least impression upon it; and the attack on the narrow waist-line of Middle Finland had ended in a major defeat. The Finns had not only checked it but had surrounded and destroyed two whole Russion divisions numbering 36,000 men.

During all the time they had been in their refuge they had seen movement on the road less than half a dozen times. Perhaps that was partly because the winter days were so brief that most of the infrequent traffic upon it passed either before the sun was up in the morning or after sunset in the afternoon. Having taken Petsamo in the first days of the war there were no other strategic points of value to tempt the Russians in the extreme north of Finland; and it was so unbelievably cold up there that, to begin with at all events, they probably considered the objectives to be gained in that sector by any major thrust insufficient to justify the difficulties of maintaining an army of any size in such adverse climatic conditions.

Two detachments of Soviet cavalry had passed north-west-wards along the road, doubtless to support a line of pickets further west which was presumably carrying on a guerilla war-fare with similar bodies of Finnish pickets in that area. They had also seen one column of light tanks, a company of infantry on skis and a civilian driving a sleigh.

Each time they saw anyone passing they immediately con-cealed themselves and at night they kept the single window of the house heavily curtained so that it should not attract unwel-come callers. For twenty out of each twenty-four hours the house was hidden from the road by darkness and as it stood well back among the trees it was not easily noticeable even in daylight. They attributed their escape from unwelcome visitors to passers-by either not having noticed the house or being too anxious to get to their destinations to waste time by going a quarter of a mile out of their way to see if the place was occupied.

They had gradually come to regard themselves as reason-ably immune from any likelihood of trouble, until they woke on the shortest day of the year to hear sounds of singing. It was eight o'clock in the morning and still dark; since the moon, which was now in its first quarter, had set hours before. While the girls heated the coffee for breakfast Freddie and Gregory went out to investigate. They were now so used to finding their way through the trees in the murky half-light when there was neither sun nor moon, but only the faint reflection of the snow, that they had no difficulty in keeping away from the open track and cutting through the woods direct to the road. On reaching a snow-bank from which they could overlook it they saw, as they expected, that the plaintive soulful singing came from Russian soldiers on the march towards Petsamo.

Crouching there in the semi-darkness the two watchers could vaguely make out the bulk of tanks, numbers of horse-drawn waggons and heavy, lumbering guns. They remained there for three-quarters of an hour and although the column was still passing when they retired to the house they felt reason-ably confident that the whole contingent of troops would have gone by before daylight; so they sat down to breakfast with unusual relish, after their exposure to the keen frosty air.

At ten o'clock they went out again and found to their dismay that the Russians were still passing. It looked as though, having failed to break the Finnish front on the Karelian Isthmus or cut through Finland's waist-line, it had now been

268

decided to send heavy reinforcements north with a view to attempting a break-through there.

As it was the shortest day in the year the sun was not due to rise until nearly eleven o'clock and would set again shortly after one; but if troops were still marching by during those two hours it seemed that there was real danger that when the column made one of its periodical halts to give the men and horses a breather some of the troops would see the house and come over to it in the hope of a free meal. They might be content with a meal but, on the other hand, they might not; and Freddie had very vivid memories of the fate that had overtaken the unfortunate Finnish family, probably in very similar circumstances, on the first day of the war; so he decided to evacuate.

Putting out the fire, they harnessed the horses and dogs to the sleighs, filled them with their most treasured possessions, including all their furs and a supply of food, and drove half a mile further from the road, deep in the obscurity of the surrounding woods. Freddie then returned to within a hundred yards of the house to see if any of the troops paid it a visit.

By the time he had taken up his position daylight was filtering through the snow-covered larches. After waiting there for half an hour he moved nearer to the road so that he could get another look at the passing column. The soldiers were all clad in the ordinary Soviet uniform greatcoats and the pointed caps; only a few of the officers were wearing furs; so it looked as if the men were in for a pretty tough time of it with nothing but indifferent quality cloth to protect them from the Arctic cold. Freddie noted too that they were not even wearing white overalls so, unless they had them in their kit, they would present a very easy target against the snow for the Finnish sharp-shooters.

As he studied the passing faces more intently, however, he saw that the men were not European Russians but, apparently, all Asiatics; so it seemed that the Soviet Generals were bringing divisions from their far-eastern provinces to fight upon this northern front where they would be no more handicapped by the rigours of the climate than the local inhabitants, as the villages from which these Asiatic Russians came must lie under snow for half the year.

It was about twelve o'clock when his fears of a visitation materialized; and it did not prove to be just a few soldiers casually taking advantage of a halt to go to the house in the hope of a warm by the fire and a hot drink. Leaving the road where the track joined it an officer led the way towards the clearing, followed by about half a company of troops and six heavily loaded wagons, as though by arrangement. While the officer and some of his men went into the house the waggons drew up outside it and the rest of the party began to unload them. Some of them contained machines which Freddie made out to be petrol engines and large circular saws. In considerable dismay he returned to the others to report what he had seen.

"I'm afraid I've got bad news," he said. "They're in the house—and it's no casual visit. About eighty of them have deliberately taken the place over. It may have been marked on their maps or noted down by somebody who's been along the road on a reconnaissance. Anyhow, it looks as if they mean to use the clearing as a lumber camp for cutting pit-props to use in their dug-outs and gun-emplacements on this new front they're forming."

"That sounds pretty bad," said Angela. "It means that we won't be able to get back into the house to-night, as we'd planned."

"If Freddie's right we won't be able to go back at all," said Erika gloomily. "It means we're orphans of the storm once more."

"Let's all go and have a look what they're up to," Angela suggested. "Perhaps Freddie's wrong, and when they've cut enough fuel to supply their regiment for the night they'll move on again."

Returning like ghosts flitting through the silent trees they soon reached a position where they could observe the Russians and, as they lay there watching, their spirits sank to zero. Eight tents had now been erected in the clearing; the fire in the house had been got going again, as they could see by the smoke coming from its chimney. Four petrol engines had been hauled into position and the big circular saws were adjusted to them. Three squads of men with axes were already at work chopping down the nearest trees; and while some hacked away at the branches with machetes others hauled the tree-trunks towards the saws for cutting into suitable lengths.

When darkness fell the little party was still gloomily watching, although all of them had realized that there was no hope of the Russians moving on that night. They were once more homeless and fireless in the great frozen north. They had the sleigh and their furs, but to sleep in the open meant risking frost-bite; and if they moved on, where in those grim endless forests could they hope to find shelter?

CHAPTER XXIII

THE WOMEN'S WAR

Erika was already shivering with cold. "Come on," she said despondently, "let's get back to the sleigh."

Without a word the others followed her through the gathering darkness in miserable dejection.

Among the things which they had brought with them was a hay-box containing a big stoppered can full of hot coffee. It was still warm when they broached it and after a drink they all felt a little more physical well-being but no less depressed. During the three weeks they had lived in the house they had made many expeditions with Bimbo, which had given them an opportunity to explore the surrounding country, but on none of them had they found any sign of human habitation. They were faced once more with the same horrible dilemma that they had come up against a few hours before they had first found their refuge. Should they drive back towards Petsamo, where they would now be quite certain to fall into the hands of the Soviet troops? Or should they follow the road south-east which would take them into Russia, where they would just as certainly be arrested and thrown into the local jail when they reached the first Russian village?

Angela's deep blue eyes sparkled angrily in her pale face. "What I couldn't do to these filthy Russians!" she exclaimed. "Surely there's some way in which we could turn them out of our little home. We've all been so happy there."

Freddie shook his head. "We've got our rifles, darling, and I daresay Gregory and I could pot a few; but that would only be like stirring up a hornets' nest. Two of us couldn't possibly tackle eighty of them."

"Nobody but a lunatic would expect you to, my hero," she said sarcastically. "I meant that you should use that marvellous brain of yours to think up some way of getting rid of them."

271

Freddie remained quite unruffled by her taunt. He knew perfectly well that brains were not his long suit and he did not mind admitting it. "You've got a better head than I have," he replied at once, "so you do the thinking and I'll carry out any plan you like to suggest."

Erika looked hopefully at Gregory for a second, then quickly away again. She felt certain that if his brain had been functioning properly he would have hatched some clever scheme in no time but, although he had got back scores of pieces of miscellaneous knowledge since he had lost his memory, his brain was still incapable of constructive thought.

He was just standing there with a look of childish interest in his eyes; obviously willing to accept anything that anybody else might plan but totally unable to plan anything himself. His face, which so openly portrayed the crippled state of that once swift and brilliant mind, wrung her heart with pity to such an extent that she could think of nothing else just then. She found it impossible to focus her own mind on the problem of producing any scheme which might save them from freezing to death that night or, at best, a terrible journey through the snows which would end in their capture.

"I know!" Angela suddenly exclaimed. "The Russians are a superstitious lot, aren't they?"

"Not the tough eggs in the Kremlin," replied Freddie. "They're all atheists; but I expect these chaps here believe in all sorts of things—certain to, as they're mostly Asiatics."

"Right, then; let's play ghosts," Angela went on excitedly.

"Ghosts!" repeated Erika.

"Yes. They won't place any sentries round a camp like this, as it's miles from anywhere. When they've all gone to sleep we could dance round the place waving lights and emitting the most blood-curdling yells."

"It's good, that! Darned good," Freddie exclaimed. "Worth trying, anyhow. With luck they might think the place is haunted and take to their heels."

Although it had been dark for some time it was still before five in the afternoon. The glimmer of lights through the trees and an occasional faint shout showed that the Russians were still busy at their tree-cutting under arc-lamps which they had erected; so it looked as though the party would have to wait for several hours before they could put their plan into operation, but they started their preparations at once.

Erika got behind the sleigh. With the chattering teeth of a

272

swimmer who is about to plunge into icy water she undid her furs and lower garments so that she could pull off her suspender belt. When she produced it the others stared in amazement but she smiled and said: "The best ghosts always give the death-rap before they put in a personal appearance. I mean to use the elastic on this belt to make a catapult."

"I don't get you, darling," Gregory murmured.

"Go and cut me a nice forked branch, not too thick, but strong and springy. Then trim it down and you'll soon see."

Freddie, meanwhile, was delving into the contents of the sleigh for any tins or cardboard boxes he could find; with the intention of punching holes in them which, when a light was placed inside, would show eyes, nostrils and a mouth like grinning death's heads.

It took them two hours' hard work but by the end of that time Erika and Gregory had made four good catapults and by rummaging in the snow at the base of the trees had collected enough small, hard fir-cones for ammunition; while Angela and Freddie had an assortment of seven ghost-masks into each of which they had fitted a candle from a box that was among the most precious stores taken from the house. At half-past seven they drank the rest of the lukewarm coffee and ate a scratch meal from some of the supplies, which were so cold that, at first, they could hardly bear them in their mouths. Soon after eight Freddie went off to make a reconnaissance. Half an hour later he returned to say that the men occupying the tents had turned in but that a light was still burning in the house.

They huddled under the rugs in the sleigh for an hour, then went forward again together. The light was now out and the moon was not yet up; the whole camp was wrapped in the stillness of the Arctic night so they proceeded to arrange their dispositions. Freddie and Angela were to go round to the far side of the clearing and take on the tents while Erika and Gregory attended to the house. They reckoned that their supply of fir-cones would last them for about half an hour, if they used them two at a time with short intervals between, and by then they hoped to have the soldiers badly rattled. The death-masks were then to be lit for a few minutes, blown out and carried to another place, then re-lit and blown out again and so on, moving in circles round the camp. Lastly, when Freddie held one of the masks aloft in the air, that was to be the signal upon which they would all give tongue to the most banshee-like screeches they could manage.

273

It was with tense expectancy that Erika and Gregory first loosed their catapults, directing their aim at the darkened window of the living-room, and they distinctly heard the sharp "rap-rap" as the cones struck the window one after the other. They waited a little and as nothing happened loosed off two more. Still nothing happened; but after the third "rap-rap" the lamp was lit and somebody came to the door of the house to peer out.

Seeing no-one the man went in again, the light was put out and, presumably, he climbed back on to the top of the oven. They gave him a few minutes to settle down then started to shoot again.

In the meantime Angela and Freddie's fir-cones had been thudding on to the tents. They were taking two at the end of the row by turns. First a man came out of one, then a man came out of the other. They saw each other, had a short angry argument and returned to their respective tents.

Erika and Gregory's second series of shots next had effect. The light went on in the house again and this time the officer came right outside to shout something to his men. Several soldiers came out of the tents that Angela and Freddie had been attacking and advancing to the middle of the clearing held a short consultation with their commander.

While they were talking, Angela and Freddie started shooting at the two tents at the other end of the row and soon several men appeared out of each of those to join the group in front of the house. The whole party then walked round the house and round the tents but, finding nothing, went in again, with the exception of two men whom the officer had apparently ordered to remain outside on watch.

As soon as the camp had settled down again the ghostly attackers recommenced their shooting and almost at once got results. The officer came stamping and cursing out of the house; the soldiers ran from their tents to meet him. Soon every man in the camp was up and about, arguing with his comrades as to what could be causing the uncanny rapping which by this time nearly all of them had heard.

The moment had now come to light the death-masks. No sooner had Freddie lit the first than two of the soldiers spotted it and letting out a yell of terror dived back into their tent. As the other masks were lit up general pandemonium broke loose; but it proved a dangerous business. Several of the soldiers blazed off with their rifles and Angela very nearly paid for her brilliant idea with her life. A bullet struck her fur cap from her head just as she was stooping to blow out the candle in one of the masks before moving it.

Freddie ordered her back among the trees and lifting the still-lighted mask on high at arm's length gave a blood-curdling wail. Its echo, even more fearsome, came from the far side of the clearing as Gregory and Erika gave tongue. The Asiatic Russians waited for no more. They had had their fill of terror. With the officer running as hard as any of them the whole party of eighty men took to their heels and fled blindly down the track with the screeches of the demons still ringing in their ears.

Having given the terrified soldiers a few minutes to get well clear of the encampment the two couples advanced and met in front of the house where, striking an attitude, Freddie and Gregory shook hands like Wellington and Blücher after Waterloo.

"Well I'm damned!" Angela appealed indignantly to Erika. "Did you ever see such impudence? Here are our two privates giving themselves the airs of Generals when it was I who planned the campaign and you who invented the secret weapon with which we won it; and it isn't even as though we had scored a complete victory yet."

"But they've gone," said Gregory simply.

"I know, dear"—Erika laid a hand on his arm—"but they'll come back. By morning they will have come to the conclusion that they were only imagining things. We've got to put in a lot of hard work yet before we can hope to scare them away for good. You go along to the road now and act as sentry until one of us relieves you. I doubt if any of them will venture near the camp till daylight, but they just *might* when the moon rises. If you see anybody approaching you can easily warn us by starting to scream like a banshee again."

"That's right." Angela agreed, "and Freddie had better go and fetch in the Lapps and the horses before they are all frozen to death, while you and I prepare a hot meal."

The two men went off obediently about their appointed tasks and as the girls busied themselves with the cooking they discussed further measures for putting the fear of the devil into the Asiatics. The soldiers would certainly recommence their wood-cutting operations as soon as daylight came and to wait until the following night to stage another ghostly attack, even if they drove the men out of the camp again, simply meant that they would return once more the following day. To be really effective the next attack must take place in daylight, to convince the troops that the site they had chosen for their camp was haunted by day as well as by night, and it was Erika who thought of the poltergeist.

There was a good quantity of crockery in the house and the peculiarity of a poltergeist is that it has a passion for hurling china about. The plan entailed the sacrifice of a number of plates and dishes but they considered this would be well worth it if they could devise a means of making them fall from the shelves of the dresser and crash on the floor, apparently without human aid.

The dresser backed on to the stable and in the store-room there were several reels of wire which the trapper had used for making snares. Angela suggested that if they bored tiny holes through the partition wall they might run wires underneath some of the crockery so that when the wires were jerked away the crockery would fall; then, even if the officer got up on to a chair to see what was causing these apparently inexplicable accidents, by the time he did so there would be no evidence for him to find as the wires would have been pulled away through the holes.

When Freddie came in he told them that he had duly stabled and fed the horses but that Bimbo, Mutt and Jeff with their dog-sleigh had entirely disappeared; so they could only suppose that the Lapps would turn up again in due course. Immediately the girls had outlined their plan to him he set to work with a gimlet from the tool-chest, boring holes through the partition wall. They then sat down to the meal which was now ready.

After they had eaten Freddie went out to relieve Gregory, who came back and ate his belated supper while the girls went on boring the holes that Freddie had started and arranging their less valued pieces of crockery in the right positions near them. When Gregory had finished they explained to him what they wanted done with the wire. Going round to the stable, he pushed the loose ends from the reels through the holes to the girls in the living-room where they adjusted them under the china. He then unreeled the lengths of wire, laying them under the stable doors and burying them in a shallow trench which he made with his boot in the snow as he went along, until all their extremities lay with the empty reels near a tree about a hundred and twenty yards from the back of the house.

Erika, who had read much more about black-magic than any of the others, had made further plans by the time he had

276

finished it. She declared that they must make the clearing appear as though a witches' sabbath had been held in it, as that was better calculated to prevent the superstitious Asiatics from spending another night there than anything else. First they went to the soldiers' tents. Taking all they could find there they smashed everything smashable and scattered the things and pieces in every direction except in the centre of the clearing, which Erika said must be left free for the witches' circle. Gregory was then set to run round a central point, kicking up the snow right and left as he went and stamping it down in the middle of his track as though a crowd of mad people had danced round and round in a ring there. While he was occupied with this Erika asked Angela to take over the job of sentry for Freddie because she wanted a man's strength to help her to make a big snow effigy of a goat in the centre of the circle. When Freddie arrived she had already fetched a couple of shovels and started work.

To have made an ordinary snow-man would have been an easy matter, but to make anything that looked like a goat was far more difficult, even though they now had a bright moon to work by; so first they built a large, square base with a solid back to serve as a throne for the snow-animal to sit on. Then they piled up a pillar of the hard, frozen snow out of which Erika sculptured with a carving-knife the figure of the animal. When she had finished it did not look particularly like a goat, but its long pear-shaped head and hoof-like extremities definitely gave it the appearance of some sort of large beast and the slanting eye-sockets, into which two fir-cones had been stuck for pupils, gave it a most menacing and sinister expression.

Gregory was standing admiring her handiwork when, to their surprise, he announced: "I know that the Devil is supposed to appear in the form of a goat in Central Europe, but they don't have goats in these parts. The nature myths of the Arctic all make him take the form of a reindeer or a moose."

"Fine, darling, fine," Erika laughed. "That's all the better. We've got lots of reindeer antlers in the meat store. If you'll get me a pair I'll fix them on its head. I think, too, it would be more effective if we could blacken the brute a bit. What about some soot?"

Gregory fetched the antlers and Freddie succeeded in raking down half a bucket of soot from the flue in the chimney with which they black-powdered the snow-devil. By the time they had finished the moon was high above the trees and in its eerie, silver light the totem of age-old evil seemed to radiate malignance even to its creators.

They spent another half-hour in acting like demons themselves by pulling down the tents, ripping them to pieces, blunting the edges of the circular saws and smashing in the sides of the lorries with axes; but they did not interfere with the engines, as the last thing they wished to do was to rob the Russians of the means of making a speedy departure, and occult forces although at times mischievous and dangerous would hardly be likely to sabotage machinery hidden under the bonnets of the lorries. It was one o'clock in the morning when, chilled to the bone and exhausted with their labours but highly satisfied, they gathered again in the house.

When they were all thoroughly warmed up once more it was decided that the two girls should sleep the night through while the men took turns to watch at the entrance to the camp; but they agreed that they must be clear of the house again by seven o'clock, although there would still be over three hours of darkness to go, in case the Russians plucked up courage to return first thing in the morning.

At six they were all up again. After a good, solid, hot breakfast they took great pains to dispose of any evidence that they had spent the night there but threw the officer's things all over the floor and turned the heavy table over on its side as though the poltergeist had been at work. Gregory fed the horses and led them back to the sleigh while Freddie dug a pit in the snow by the extremity of the wires which led into the house. Angela took up her position some distance to his right where she could see the front of the building and could signal to him without being seen from the camp. When Gregory returned all four of them settled down to wait.

It was half-past ten before the Russians put in an appearance and then, even from a distance, Angela could see that the poor wretches were in an extremity of misery, from having had to spend the night out on the open road. Some of them were limping as though affected by frost-bite in the feet; four of them were being carried by their comrades and all of them were bowed as though they no longer had the vitality to walk erect. Shambling through the snow they reached the edge of the clearing and halted there in a scared, silent huddle as they took in the devastated state of their camp and the grim, black figure that stood out so clearly against the dead whiteness of the ground.

Several of them turned to run again; but the officer gave a sharp order which halted the men, and they all stood there jabbering excitedly for several moments before plucking up the courage to advance. In wonder and fear they approached the witches' circle, those behind pushing forward the ones in front. For a time they stood staring at the malignant-looking beast, but none of them had the courage to cross the trodden track where they obviously thought that snow-demons had danced the night before. Then they split up into little groups and began to collect their broken, scattered belongings.

The officer and two of the men walked resolutely over to the house. Angela gave them a couple of minutes to take in the overturned furniture and the equipment which had been strewn about then she signalled to Freddie. He pulled hard on one of the wires and in the deep stillness of the forest they heard quite clearly the crash that followed.

With yells of fright the officer and his men came bounding out of the door and it was a good five minutes before they mustered the pluck to go in again. Angela signalled. Freddie pulled another wire. There was another crash; and out came the frightened men again as though an enraged lion were after them. This time they made no further attempt to enter the house but, getting a long pole, proceeded to fish the officer's belongings out of the room, through the open doorway, without crossing the accursed threshold.

When they had rescued the things from the poltergeist's lair the officer gave a shout and his half-frozen men came straggling towards him through the snow. He addressed them for a few moments then, apparently inspired by some new impetus, they scattered and quickly began to load up their six lorries.

Angela's stratagem had succeeded and her victory was complete. Three-quarters of an hour later, except for a little scattered rubbish, there was not a trace of the Russians in the clearing. Bag and baggage they had moved on further north to form a new camp in a more congenial atmosphere; and it was a safe bet that they would not select a place within several miles of that devil-ridden spot.

Freddie brought the horses and sleigh back and after clearing up the smashed crockery they were able to settle down in their refuge as though they had never been driven out of it. Nevertheless, after their midday meal Freddie and Gregory went out and felled two tall trees on either side of the track so that they fell across it. Then they cut the lower branches from

279

many others and fixed these firmly among the boughs of the fallen trees; thereby forming a screen which would prevent any other troops that passed along the road seeing the house from it even in daylight.

That night they were able to get the news over the wireless again and from an English commentary on the past week's events—by a neutral—learned of the terrible earthquake in Turkey which was said to have killed 20,000 people and to have wrecked a score of towns and hundreds of villages, many of which were still in flames; while their unfortunate inhabitants who had survived the quake were suffering acutely from having to camp out in the Anatolian snows. Two German cruisers had been sunk by British submarines right in the mouth of the Elbe —another splendid feat of naval daring—and the first Canadian troops had arrived in England without a single casualty.

Nearer home the Soviet Generals had been hurling division after division of their troops against the Mannerheim Line in a new offensive. It was reported that the Russians were ill-equipped, ill-led, and abysmally ignorant creatures who had not the least idea what the war they were waging was about. Many hundreds of them among the thousands of prisoners taken said that they had never even heard of Finland, that they fought only because they were ordered to, and that Communist Party members drove them on to the Finnish lines by keeping machine-guns trained upon their backs. Yet that did not affect the fact of their overwhelming superiority in numbers in spite of which the Finns had broken every attack, and the great offensive was said to be weakening.

No trace of Bimbo and his wives, Mutt and Jeff, had been seen since they had taken refuge in the forest with the rest of the party on the arrival of the Russians. They had stood near that evening watching the preparations for the first ghost attack; but it had been impossible to explain to them what was being planned and their intelligence, apart from matters pertaining to the wild life of the woods, was of such a low standard that they evidently had not associated the making of the catapults and the cutting of the devil masks with the dancing lights and horrid screaming later in the evening; and so had been just as terrified as the soldiers. In any case, they had disappeared into the great forest as unexpectedly as they had come out of it and the party at the trapper's house never saw them again.

Yet their fortnight's stay had proved an invaluable blessing for, during it, they had taught their hosts their method of fishing

and how to recognize the spoor of certain animals—bear, reindeer, wolf, lynx, hare and fox, several of which were fit for
human consumption. After the Lapps' departure Freddie and
Gregory used to go out most days on their own and often
brought back some animal or fresh fish, the supply of which
from the frozen lake appeared quite inexhaustible.

Among the trapper's stores there were few luxuries but such
as there were had been set aside for special occasions; so on
Christmas Day they were able to have a gala dinner although
not a single course of it was in any way similar to the fare they
would have had at home. They felt confident that the King
would be making a personal broadcast, as usual; so, remembering that such broadcasts took place at about three o'clock,
Greenwich "mean time", and knowing their own longtitude to
be roughly 30° West, Freddie began to tune in at a few minutes
before four. With bent heads they sat round the radio, listening
intently. After a little while they heard a faint, indistinct mutter,
not a word of which could they catch, but it went on for about
ten minutes and they felt certain that it had been the King of
England speaking to the people of his Empire and all those of
British race and sympathies who were scattered over the five
continents and the seven seas, which filled the English members of the party with a strange satisfaction.

For the rest of the evening they got dance-music from nearer
stations and amused themselves with a Christmas-tree which
Erika had dressed with some of the store of candles, cut into
small pieces, and hung with presents. Their gifts to one another
were little things that they had made in secret during the past
week and brought all the more joy to their recipients in that
they were the product of time and thought instead of easily
made purchases.

By December the 30th, when Finland had been at war for a
month, not only was the Mannerheim Line still intact, as Loumkoski had said it would be, but a Finnish Suicide Squad of two
hundred and fifty ace skiers had penetrated into Russia and cut
the Leningrad-Murmansk Railway; which magnificent achieve-
ment was immediately followed by a smashing Finnish victory
on the Suomussalmi front where two more divisions of Soviet
troops had been surrounded and cut to pieces.

Over Christmas they had used the wireless extravagantly
and by New Year's Eve they found to their distress that it was
growing fainter. Even the nearest stations became difficult to
pick up, so they decided to conserve it as much as possible by

only listening to the news twice a week. Yet by January the 6th it had faded out entirely. The batteries were dead and although they had searched through all the stores they had failed to find any replacements.

For the last week snow had been falling in greater quantities every day. The barricade of felled trees and branches across the track now appeared as a solid barrier of snow, twenty feet in height, shutting them completely away from the road. Fresh falls of snow had long since obliterated the rubbish left by the Russians and the Satanic snow-god which Erika had fashioned was now a cone-shaped pillar; the only landmark which broke the smooth, crystal-white carpet of the clearing. On cloudless days when the sun shone for an hour or two low over the tree-tops there was a temporary thaw. The monotonous patter of drips would start about one o'clock, only to cease again shortly after two as the melted snow froze into icicles which got longer and longer as the days passed, until by early January the trapper's domain was like a fairy scene in a pantomime portraying the Ice King's realm. The cold was so intense that they never went out except on the necessary business of visiting the stores in the block or tending the horses, and occasionally on longer expeditions to secure fresh food.

The icy air seemed to have driven even the Arctic animals into some secret shelter of their own. Only the wolves still evinced their presence by their dismal howling at night; and even Freddie, who was the hardiest of the party, found that he could not remain out long enough to follow the occasional spoor they saw for a sufficient distance to get a shot at a bear or reindeer; so they had to content themselves with fish.

But each expedition to the lake became more hazardous as although they knew the way there well now there was always the danger of being caught in a heavy snow-storm. When returning from the lake on January the 18th Freddie and Gregory were surprised by a blizzard in which they lost themselves for an hour while they could not see more than two yards ahead. They only found the house again by sheer good luck, and decided that to make further fishing expeditions would be courting death.

Their inability to hunt or fish any longer explained why the Finnish trapper had laid in such a large stock of dried meat and tinned stores; for without these things any family in that region would have starved to death long before the thaw set in.

By the end of January they were completely snow-bound and the radio which had kept them in touch with the outer world had been silent for three weeks. In all that utter stillness no sound had reached them except the occasional howl of a wolf or the dripping of the trees, and that of their own voices and movements in the one big room where they lived and slept.

They knew that they had at least three months to go before the thaw would start in that high latitude. In the meantime two wars were raging; one, with bitter intensity, only a few hundred miles away; the other a strange, unusual sort of war which had so far consisted of ceaseless naval vigilance and tip-and-run aircraft raids, but a war upon which hung the fate of their countries and the future of all civilization. Yet they could learn nothing of them since they were cut off from the world just as surely as though they had been dead.

But the Timeless Ones who fashion for all mankind their trials and opportunities decreed that they should leave their refuge long before the thaw set in.

CHAPTER XXIV

BURIED ALIVE

IN the long dark days, when the grey light filtered through the remaining panes of window for such a little time that it seemed as though they were living in perpetual night, their only occupation was telling stories and seeking to improve Gregory's memory, as there were no books in any language that they could read, no games to play or radio to listen to.

By the end of January he had reacquired quite a considerable stock of miscellaneous knowledge but countless facts and many episodes in his own life about which the others could not inform him still remained a closed book. For instance, although he had eight scars from old wounds on his body he did not know how he had acquired any of them, except the cut on the back of his head which had caused him to lose his memory and the wound on his shoulder which he had received on the night of November the 8th during the Army *Putsch* in Berlin. He talked intelligently again about the subjects he had mastered, but rather in the manner of a bright schoolboy than in that of an extraordinarily well-informed man and, while he entered cheerfully into any pastime or job that was suggested, he seemed entirely to have lost his initiative and to be incapable of producing any new ideas as to how they might wile away the endless hours.

For going out in the snow he used a pair of the trapper's snow-boots but he still retained most of his money in the false soles of his shoes, which he used in the house, and one of the soles had worn a little thin, so Erika suggested that he should turn cobbler and resole it with a piece of untanned leather cut from the thickest pelt they could find in the almost empty fur-store, nailing the piece of tough, dry skin on with some brads, of which there were plenty in the trapper's tool-chest.

Before he started on the job he removed the false sole inside the shoe and took out the wad of high denomination German bank-notes. With them were a few folded sheets of thin paper, almost filled with close typescript, which he glanced at casually and threw aside.

"What's this?" Erika asked, picking them up and smoothing them out.

"Something out of my dead past, I expect," he laughed. "Anyhow, I have no secrets from you, my sweet, so read it and see."

"It's in German," she said, "and obviously typed by an amateur."

He smiled. "I'm afraid that means nothing to me. What's it say?"

She read for a few moments in silence, then replied: "Heaven knows; it seems to be somebody's plans to hold a *Familie Tag*."

"What's that?" asked Freddie.

"It's a type of reunion, very popular in Germany. The head of a family selects a certain day in the year—generally in the summer—and he issues invitations to every member of the family wherever they may be, with their wives and husbands if they have them, and even to their relatives by marriage. The whole lot gather together—sometimes as many as two or three hundred people if the head of the family is a rich man; even his relatives abroad attend if they can. Although they call it a Family-day it's generally an affair lasting a whole week, and during it they have picnics and dances and dinners with speeches and lots to drink."

"I see," said Angela; "the idea is to keep the members of the family in touch with one another, I suppose?"

"That's it," Erika nodded; "and at the same time profitable business often results. It gives the men an opportunity to discuss their affairs and if they have similar types of undertakings in different cities they're able to get in quite a lot of good work at the same time as they are having a week's holiday with their relatives and friends."

"Yes, I remember the custom," said Gregory, "but I can't think where I could have got hold of such a thing. If it gives the names of any of the people, read them out; that might give me a clue."

"Great-Aunt Wilhelmina, Cousin Julia, Jacob Bauer—(he's a Jew and doesn't seem to be at all popular with the rest of the crowd)—the Engels branch of the family, Ernst, Mr. Saxe, Mrs.

285

Klein—aslo referred to as Aunt Marta—Uncle Rudolf, Uncle Ulrich, Cousin Vicki, the Müllers, Mitzi, Gerta, Paula, August, little Paul . . ." Erika suddenly broke off. "There are dozens of them mentioned here."

Gregory shook his head. "No, none of those names mean anything special to me."

"Read it to us," Angela suggested, and Erika began, translating slowly into English as she read:

" 'ARRANGEMENTS FOR THE NEXT FAMILY-DAY

" 'Our last Family Reunion was not the success it should have been, owing to lack of forethought and careful preparation. As a result of over-eagerness Great-Aunt Wilhelmina arrived before we were ready, so we lost the telling effect of the old lady's entrance. Mother let us down very badly at the last moment by refusing to come at all; and, through neglect, other important members of the family did not receive their invitations or, having done so, did not accept because insufficient fuss was made about the importance of their presence in our midst. Our main mistake, however, was to quarrel openly with Cousin Julia, since this resulted in throwing her into the arms of that unspeakable Jew, Jacob Bauer, who immediately became engaged to her and who, through the power of his money and his hatred for us, has always striven to keep the family apart for his own benefit.

" 'As you will remember, they threw a rival party to our own to which many outsiders, as well as certain members of the family, went instead of to ours. Even Mother was induced to desert us because she was very hard-up at the time and, as usual, Jacob used his money-bags, advancing her a big loan on condition that she put in a belated appearance at his party.

" 'The failure of our last Family Reunion was all the more disastrous in that we had already decided that the time had come when the family must co-operate and amalgamate their various business interests if our central firm was to increase and prosper in the way that a flourishing business should; but the attendance at the Reunion was so poor that it proved impracticable to put such a suggestion forward. The death of Great-Aunt Wilhelmina, which followed, was a sad blow to us as it meant the splitting-up of the Engels branch of the family; and an even more serious setback was the publication of Grandmother's Will which so wickedly deprived us of many assets.

" 'So serious were our firm's losses as a result of these unfor-

286

tunate events that many people thought we should be compelled to go out of business altogether; but since the appointment of Ernst as managing director of our firm the business has regained much lost ground and under his able guidance has become solvent again. It is, however, still under-capitalized and owing to the restriction of markets finds difficulty in competing with its two principal rivals, the Jew, Jacob Bauer, whose bitter enmity, hypocrisy and cunning are used without respite in an attempt to strangle every enterprise which we start, and the firm of Saxe & Co., whose products compete with ours in many markets but whose major interests lie outside our sphere.

" 'Competition has recently become so intense that it is more necessary than ever that members of the family should be induced to pool their resources instead of struggling on independently; otherwise each member will tend to become poorer and poorer until they fall entirely into the octopus-like tentacles of Jacob, who will mercilessly exploit them as he has exploited the members of so many other families.' "

"Whoever meant to throw this party is evidently a big business man," Freddie interrupted.

"Yes. He seems much more concerned with the possibilities of amalgamating all the family interests than with the social side of the gathering," Erika agreed; and read on:

" 'The time has come, therefore, when it is imperative to hold another Family Reunion and use every means in our power to induce all members to accept the propositions which we shall place before them. It is suggested that the arangements should be made by gradual stages, with careful preparation between each, so as not to alarm Cousin Julia and her Jew fiancé and cause them to work against us before we come out into the open and actualy isssue the invitations to our Reunion.

" 'Jacob knew quite well what our intentions were if we had been sucessful with our last Reunion, and as these constitute a grave threat to the prosperity of his own business he will naturally do everything in his power to prevent our holding another. But he is by no means so virile as he was, and if we go to work skilfully we might even succeed in persuading Julia to break off her engagement to him. She is, after all, a member of the family, and apart from her predilection for this blackguardly Jew we have no differences of opinion with her which cannot be surmounted. It would, therefore, be a great triumph for us if we

287

could bring her back into the family fold; and nothing should be neglected which might lead towards this end.' "

"Gracious! How he hates this Jewish business rival of his," Angela laughed. "And what a lark that the Jew is marrying into the family."

Erika smiled. "Apparently the family is by no means united. Father and Mother seem to have been living apart. Listen to this!

" 'In one respect we start off with much better prospects this time, because Father and Mother have made up their differences. Mother has taken a new lease of life and has at last been fully persuaded that she can do better for herself by coming in with the family than by dragging out a penurious old age as a pensioner of Cousin Julia and her Jewish fiancé.

" 'The amount of active help which she can be expected to give us is still debatable as Jacob is certain to exercise financial pressure upon her to restrain her as far as he is able. Therefore she must not be unduly pressed to come to the party during the first days of our Family-week but must be persuaded to work behind the scenes wherever possible in getting our more distant relatives together; particularly the Müller branch of the family as she has great influence with her nephews and nieces.

" 'Apart from Jacob, the two people who might most seriously menace our plan for securing complete family unity are Mr. Saxe and Mrs. Klein—or Aunt Marta, as we have always known her—although she cannot really be considered as a member of the family.

" 'As well as being our competitor in some respects Mr. Saxe is immensely rich and, as money gravitates to money, he was persuaded to give his support to Jacob when our interests last clashed. But it cost him a considerable amount and, as usual, Jacob took all the credit to Julia and himself for the success of his operations; so Mr. Saxe was far from pleased and is much less likely to give Jacob his assistance this time when we eventually come into the open market against him. However, it is too much to hope that Mr. Saxe would support an amalgamation of the family interests to the detriment of Jacob—to whom he is allied by ties of blood. The probability is that he will sit back and reap what advantage he can for his own firm while we are endeavouring to reconstruct ours and Jacob is occupied in endeavouring to check our expansion. Our objective, so far as Mr. Saxe is concerned, should therefore be to promote as much

bad feeling between him and Jacob as possible so that he will
reject any fresh advances that Jacob may make to him and,
lulled by a false sense of security for his own concerns, be glad
rather than sorry to see us putting a check upon the insatiable
ambitions of the Jew.'"

"He seems to be a proper crook, doesn't he?" Angela broke
in.

"No," Erika shrugged. "Just a very shrewd business man,"
and she continued:

"'Mrs. Klein presents a very different and particularly
knotty problem. Her firm cannot be considered as a competitor
to ours or Jacob's, and she has no particular love for either
of us; yet, potentially, she could prove an immense asset to
either of our rival concerns.

"'The half-derelict chain of stores which she inherited is
still incredibly badly run but they cover a huge area; and while
for some years Aunt Marta's firm has failed to pay a dividend,
it is quite certain that if the chain were taken over and placed
under proper management it could be made to show handsome
profits.

"'Any suggestion of an amalgamation with Mrs. Klein may
seem extremely revolutionary from many points of view.
Mother positively loathes her, while Uncle Rudolf and Uncle
Ulrich—with both of whom we are on the best of terms at the
moment—dislike her as much as does Mother; in addition,
Aunt Marta has a long-standing quarrel with our managing
director, Ernst.

"'Can all these difficulties be overcome? Aunt Marta's dislike of Ernst is not so much a personal one, as in many ways
they think alike, but is mainly due to fear. Knowing Ernst's
ability and enterprise she is always frightened that one day he
may decide that our firm should launch out in a new direction
which would jeopardize her own rickety business. If she could
be persuaded that Ernst has no such intention and, in fact, that
she has much to gain from settling her quarrel with him, since
he could then offer to reorganize her business and put it on a
sound footing, and possibly help her in other directions too, she
might well consider an amalgamation with us; in which case it
would certainly be worth our while to invite her to our Family
Reunion.

"'It is inevitable that Uncle Rudolf and Uncle Ulrich will
take offence if Mrs. Klein is asked to our Reunion; but that

need not give us any immediate concern, because Uncle Rudolf is so far removed from the family sphere and Uncle Ulrich has been so ill recently that it is very doubtful if either of them will appear—at least until the end of the week during which the party is held—and they need know nothing of any overtures which we may make to Mrs. Klein until the whole matter is settled. They will be very annoyed when we have to inform them of it, but if we get satisfactory results from Mrs. Klein's attendance they will realize that we had good reason for our decision to ask her—and, in any case, their interests are too closely allied to ours for there to be any danger of their going in with Jacob.' "

"Is there much more of it?" Angela asked, stifling a yawn.

"Reams of it, my dear," Erika replied. "Would you like me to stop?"

"No, no," said Freddie. "Go on, do."

"All right, then."

" 'Mother is the remaining difficulty, and by far the greatest; but, whereas it would be a major triumph to get Mrs. Klein to appear early in our Reunion Week, we have no intention of asking Mother to join us until the party is properly under way. Her function will be to gather in the Müller family in secret and to allow Jacob to believe, until the very last moment, that he still has her under his thumb. Her appearance will then be all the greater triumph for us, and by the time we wish her to arrive we shall have had an opportunity to explain to her how wise we were in our decision to amalgamate; and that she will participate, just as much as any other member of the family, in the benefits to be derived from Mrs. Klein's chain of stores.

" 'It is of the first importance that as much work as possible should be put in before the invitations are issued, in order to ensure as great a number of acceptances to the Reunion as possible. Our first concern should be to link up with Cousin Vicki; our next to rope in those members of the family, such as Greta and Paula, who own small firms which were originally part of *our* business but were severed from us by Grandmother's iniquitous Will.

" 'It is also of the first importance that we should absorb as many of these small firms as possible on plausible excuses such as our excellent case for being granted the legal guardianship of Little August and Little Paul—so as to postpone arousing Jacob's open antagonism as long as we can. At any stage of our

arangements he may realize that our firm is once more becoming a serious threat to his and he may decide to take active
counter-measures against us; but Mother must be used to quiet
his suspicions. The longer we can prevent his endeavouring to
wreck us by an open price-cutting campaign the more likely we
are to succeed in undermining his business to such an extent
that when he wakes up to what we have been doing it will be
too late to save himself from bankruptcy.

" 'The following are the stages in which it is proposed eventually to bring about a complete Reunion with all interests
amalgamated under the head of the family.' "

"Erika darling," Angela interrupted, "must we really hear
the stages by which this awful man proposes to blackmail all
his relatives into letting him make a combine of their
businesses?"

"Not if you don't wish to," Erika smiled. "As we don't know
any of these people his schemes aren't of the least interest to
us. I must say, though, that I should like to know how the thing
came into Gregory's possession."

Freddie frowned. "Yes, it's hardly likely that you would
have kept a thing like this in a secret hiding-place on your
person if it wasn't of some importance. Perhaps we can help
you recall where you got it if we go back over the last few times
you've taken money out of your shoes."

"I don't even remember when I took out the money last,"
said Gregory despondently, "let alone ever having seen these
sheets of flimsy before."

"Well, you changed some German money into Finnish the
day we arrived in Helsinki."

"That's right—with that fair-haired, half-German chap in
the hotel who did us down; but that was part of the money that
Goering gave me and I was carrying it in my pocket."

"Right, then. Did you take off your shoes for any purpose
while we were at Karinhall? Didn't you have a bath in the
morning?"

"I've got it!" Gregory suddenly snapped his fingers. "That's
when I put the papers with the money. Those bits of typescript
came out of Goering's safe."

"Out of Goering's safe?" echoed Erika. "Then they *must*
be something important."

"I remember now"—Gregory stood up and began to pace
quickly up and down; "I did have one look at them in Helsinki;

when I was up in that room we took at the hotel, Freddie, just before you came in with the invitation to lunch with Angela and her father. I read the first few paragraphs, and as I couldn't make head or tail of them I put the sheets back to study when I had more leisure."

"But how on earth did you get hold of them?" Erika asked.

'I stole them," Gregory replied promptly. "It was while Goering was getting me the money. He had just taken a big packet of bank-notes out of his safe when the telephone rang. Thrusting the bundle into my hand he said: 'Here! Count yourself out three thousand marks,' then he turned his back on me to answer the call.

"They were one-hundred-mark notes so I peeled off thirty, then I noticed that those flimsies had got wedged underneath the packet, in the rubber-band that held the notes together. I suppose it was a crazy risk to take but it seemed to me at the time that any typescript out of Goering's private safe might contain some terrific secret; so I acted on impulse, pulled the sheets from under the rubber-band and slipped them in my pocket. Later, when I undressed to have a bath, I took the opportunity to transfer the flimsies to my boot. It looks now, though, as if I risked my neck for an extract from his family album."

Erika glanced at a few further passages in the closely-typed sheets. "Goodness knows! I've met most of Hermann's relatives at one time or another but I don't recognize any of these surnames and the Christian names don't seem to fit, either. It looks to me as though this has been sent to Goering because he is the commercial dictator of Germany and would naturally be interested in any amalgamation of big business interests that was projected; but how he could be expected to know all the ramifications of somebody else's family, I can't think."

"Perhaps it isn't what it appears to be at all," Freddie suggested, "but particulars of something quite different, set out in secret code. I'm jolly good at crossword puzzles; let me have a look at it."

"What is a crossword puzzle?" Gregory asked.

While the girls explained to him Freddie studied the latter part of the document; his German was just good enough to make out the general sense. At last he looked up and said:

"The chap who compiled this seems a most awful thug and means to go to any lengths. In one place he suggests that his mother should forcibly remove a girl named Marlene from the

Schwartz's because they didn't look after her properly; and in another that they should get Mrs. Klein's daughter, Paula, certified as insane if she refuses to come into the ring. There's a lot, too, about the careful preparation of cases for the courts by which it's proposed to try to secure the custody of several children with a view, apparently, to influencing the parents through them afterwards."

"Big business is often as dirty as politics," Angela shrugged. "Many a rich man has made his millions by taking for his motto the saying: 'The end justifies the means'."

Freddie nodded. "I expect you're right. It's just a very carefully worked out plan to amalgamate a whole lot of commercial interests which are under the control of different branches of two or three families, and to break the rival concern of this Jew chap, Jacob Bauer, whom the writer seems to dislike so much. Still, as it came 'out of Goering's safe there's just a chance that it might contain some hidden meaning; and it will amuse me to see if one could possibly read any other interpretation into all this blather about uncles and cousins and aunts."

He slipped the papers into his pocket and pulling on his furs went out to give the horses their afternoon feed and rub-down.

In the days that followed even the joy which the two couples derived from being together was a little marred by their extreme boredom. All four of them had hitherto led very active lives with many friends and interests, whereas now there were no papers, no posts, no radio, no parties, no cinemas, no shopping-expeditions, no business to transact, no minor family worries or joys to engage their thoughts. They had not even the pleasurable anticipation of looking forward to seeing their respective lovers from day to day, or receiving letters from them, as for twenty-three out of each twenty-four hours they were cooped up together in the same room; and the spells of wintry daylight were so short that, in that room, it almost seemed that they were living in eternal night. There was not even enough blank paper in the house for any of them to contemplate writing some short stories or a book, and when Angela decided to make a pack of cards she had to use the crudest materials; moreover, as Erika loathed cards the experiment did not prove much of a success.

Freddie spent a lot of time poring over the flimsy papers that had been found in Gregory's shoe. He ran all the words together then separated the letters into blocks of five and placed differently-arranged alphabets over them. He gave a different number to each letter, added them up and turned the resulting numerals back into letters again, reaching various conclusions none of which made the least sense. He then got Erika to translate the typed pages for him into both French and English and once again set to work with his groups of five letters and innumerable alphabets; but that did not get him anywhere either. Yet he could not let the thing alone.

Perhaps it was lack of any other occupation, but the perfectly straightforward account of somebody's plans to hold a Family Reunion and amalgamate various business interests seemed to have become an obsession with him, and the more the others chaffed him about his efforts the more mulish he became in his assertion that since the papers had come out of Goering's safe they must contain information of importance, if only some clue to their real subject could be found.

Now that the risk of being caught in a blizzard made it impossible for them to go on long hunting expeditions or journeys to the lake the only exercise they could get, apart from work in the house and rubbing down the horses three times a day, was an hour or so each midday playing games in the clearing.

Freddie and Angela had always been winter-sport enthusiasts so they loved romping together out in the crisp air; Erika had never been interested in outdoor games and only joined in to oblige the others; but Gregory surprised them all. In his normal wits he would never have set foot outside the house, except when he positively had to do so, even if he had been confined there for a twelve-month. Physically, he was bone-lazy and loathed any form of unnecessary activity; so he would have slept a lot, talked a lot and made love to Erika whenever the other two were out of the way, and in the meantime would probably have taught himself to read Finnish with the aid of the Finnish-German dictionary which was among the books.

As it was, his loss of memory seemed to have thrown him back to the period of his life when, as a very small boy, his animal spirits had not been submerged in the joy of mental pleasure and he had not yet developed that contempt for "hearties" which became apparent soon after he went to his public school. Somewhat to Erika's annoyance, he entered with incredible gusto into snowball fights, games of leap-frog, tip-and-run, hide-and-seek among the trees and other childish pastimes. Not content with this, he made himself a long slide out of the frozen snow at which, from a slight eminence, he took a long run to come hurtling down it with loud, boyish cries of glee.

It was, curiously enough, this harmless if infantile amusement which on February the 17th resulted in an accident that had far-reaching results.

He was careering down his slide for the fifth time that morning when he tripped on a little freshly-fallen snow which he had failed to brush away sufficiently far to the side of his ice-run. His feet flew from under him. Crashing backwards his head hit the ice a blow that could be heard; then he skidded on for about fifteen feet and remained there, lying quite still.

The others ran to him and finding him unconscious carried him to the house. A few minutes later he came round, groaning, and complained of frightful pains in the back of the head. They gave him a hot drink and tucked him up on top of the oven where, after a little while, he went to sleep.

When he awoke that evening he sat up and stared in astonishment at the others and round the room. It then transpired that he had got his memory back; that is, he could remember perfectly the whole of his previous life up to the point when he had been wounded in the head by a spent bullet, outside the Petsamo aerodrome, on the night of November the 30th; but things that had happened since seemed to him like the disconnected episodes in a dream.

They were overjoyed at his recovery and it did not take them very long to run over with him the few excitements which had broken the pleasant routine of the two and a half months they had spent in the trapper's house. He laughed a lot when they recalled to him how they had driven the Russians away by pretending to be ghosts and even more when he realized that he owed the recovery of his memory to his favourite occupation of sliding like a schoolboy on an ice-track that he had made with considerable labour for himself. Next day they had great fun in taking him round their small domain and showing him all the arrangements they had made to continue there in as much comfort as possible until the coming of the thaw.

Two nights later Freddie was sitting up as he often did—long after the others had tucked up on the oven—straining his not very brilliant wits to find a hidden meaning in the now thumbed and crumpled typescript. Regardless of time, he worked on and on. It was past three o'clock in the morning when he suddenly stood up from the table, marched over to the oven and roughly roused the others from their slumber to declare with shining eyes that he had at last solved his puzzle.

CHAPTER XXV

THE DIABOLICAL PLAN

"Oh, that damned letter!" murmured Angela sleepily. "But couldn't you have waited until to-morrow morning, darling, to tell us about it?"

"Certainly not," said Freddie brusquely. "The explanation flashed on me quite suddenly, soon after you turned in, and I've spent the last five hours working the whole thing out. Every single piece fits into place quite perfectly, and it's really awfully interesting. Get up, you lazy little pig, and I'll read it to you."

Grumbling a little the other three crawled from under the thick layer of furs which constituted their bedding; none of them displaying any particular enthusiasm, owing to the fact that they had become distinctly bored with Freddie's efforts and were still half asleep. As they gathered round the table and Angela poured some cups of hot coffee from a pot which they always kept simmering on the hob Gregory inquired:

"What's all this about a letter? I thought you were working on some damn-fool puzzle."

"It's the letter you stole from Goering," Freddie explained. "It was in code and I've been . . ."

"Good God!" Gregory sprang to his feet. "Why on earth didn't you tell me about this before?"

"But we did!" Freddie protested. "Still, perhaps none of us has said anything about it in the last two days, since you've been your old self again."

"Of course! I remember now. Quick—let's hear what you've made of it?"

"The whole thing is frightfully simple, really, once you get the hang of it," Freddie replied, as they all settled down. "You see; the family is really the German nation and the other branches of it include the rest of Europe. The Balkan countries are the Müllers, the Scandinavian countries the Heins, Mrs.

Klein is Russia and Mr. Saxe the United States. Every name in the whole thing represents some country or other and the wicked Jew, Jacob Bauer, who runs the rival business, is poor old Britain."

"But how thrilling!" Angela exclaimed, her blue eyes shining. "Freddie darling, I *do* believe you're a genius, after all."

He almost purred with satisfaction as he threw her a loving and triumphant glance. "The whole of the first part explains why Germany failed in her 1914-1918 attempt at world dominion. Apparently, Austria-Hungary precipitated the Great War before the Germans were ready for it and, later of course, Italy ratted on them. All the stuff about holding another Family Reunion is their plan for a second attempt to become masters of the world—or, at all events, to coerce all the other European countries, with the one exception of Britain, into a sort of United States of Europe under German leadership. It was drafted about 1936 or 1937, I should think, and it's extraordinarily interesting to see how many stages of their plan have already been carried out by peaceful means before the war even started."

"Interesting!" Gregory echoed. "My God, it is! What else does the thing say?"

"It proposes what must have then been the revolutionary idea of a German tie-up with Russia. The Germans foresaw that such a step would offend their Axis partner, Italy, and the other anti-Comintern nations, Japan and Spain, but they didn't mean to let them know anything about it until it was a *fait accompli*. Anyhow, they never intended to drag Italy into the war on their side during its early stages. Her rôle is to gather the Balkan nations under her wing, then it will be an even greater blow for the Allies when she does come in."

"That's counting their chickens before they are hatched, with a vengeance," Gregory broke in. "Italy is basicly pro-British and would never have been anything else, even superficially, if Baldwin and Eden hadn't stabbed 'Sam' Hoare in the back over the Hoare-Laval pact. If that had gone through the Italians would have got all they wanted but Haile Selassie would still be living in Addis Abbaba as Emperor of Abyssinia and Britain would be in control of the headwaters of the Nile. Instead Sanctions drove Mussolini into Hitler's arms and resulted in the Rome-Berlin Axis. But Mussolini's a much cleverer man than Hitler and he's only been using Germany for what he can get out of her in the way of backing. It's all Lombard Street to a china orange that he'll remain neutral, unless we offer him British Somaliland and a slice of Tunisia to come in with us."

"Wait a minute," said Freddie. "This thing makes it quite clear that 'Musso' is not a party to the German plan. He's only to be let into it a bit at a time. Italy may remain neutral for the present; in fact the Germans want her to. But if they succeed in gobbling up half Europe it wouldn't be so easy for her to keep out. Anyhow, the writer of this reckoned that by the time they wanted Italy to join them they would have been able to justify their Russian tie-up by results already achieved. The idea of trying to split the Anglo-French alliance is mentioned here too, as apparently they decided that France could not be left out of a European confederation whereas Britain could, and the grand design of the whole thing is the smashing-up of the British Empire."

"How jolly," said Angela. "Go on."

"It particularly stresses the importance of getting as much territory as possible under German control by diplomatic pressure so as to stall off an armed conflict until absolutely unavoidable. The really interesting part, though, is the seventeen stages in which Germany planned to become master of Europe with Russian and Italian aid. Apparently they were very nervous about Stage 2, which was the Czech business, but they thought that if they could get over that without having to fight they'd be all right down to Stage 8, which involves walking into Holland and Belgium. 13 was a sticky corner for them, too, as the Russians were to collar the oil-fields in Irak; but they had the sublime self-confidence to think that they might even get away with it right up to Stage 17, when they meant to rope in France; but I suppose they felt that we'd darned well have to fight then."

Gregory had been studying the document and he looked up quickly. "Have you de-coded the whole of this thing, Freddie?"

"No; but I've got a list here of all the names and the countries they represent."

"Let's have a look at it."

Freddie handed over the sheet and Gregory read:

Britain	...	Jacob Bauer	Germany		Father
France	...	Cousin Julia	Italy	...	Mother

U.S.A. ... Mr. Saxe	Japan ... Uncle Rudolf
Russia ... Mrs. Klein	Spain ... Uncle Ulrich

The old Austro-Hungarian Empire Great-Aunt Wilhelmina
The Mediterranean ... ... Mother's estate
The North Sea ... ... Father's estate
The Baltic ... ... The property for which
Ernst and Aunt Marta
are joint trustees
The Versailles Treaty ... ... Grandmother's iniquitous
Will

Ernst ... Adolf Hitler   Aunt Marta...Joseph Stalin

Austria	Cousin Vicki	
Czecho-	Greta	
Slovakia	Gretchen	The Engels branch of the
Sudetenland	Little August	family
Ruthenia	Little Caspar	
Hungary	Mitzi	

Yugo-	Marie	
Slavia	Mara	
Greece	Mansi	The Müller branch of the
Albania	Marlene	family
Bulgaria	Oscar	
Rumania	Otto	

Bessarabia	Fritz	
The Dobruja	Franz	Otto Müller's adopted
Transylvania	Friedricka	children

Portugal	Berthold	Uncle Ulrich's son

Belgium	Siegsmund	
Holland	Siegfried	The Schwartz branch of the
Switzerland	Siebald	family

Sweden	Hermann	
Norway	Heinrich	The Hein branch of the
Denmark	Hilda	family

Finland	Hans	
Lithuania	Karl	
Latvia	Kurt	Mrs. Klein's children
Estonia	Konrad	
Poland	Paula	

| Little Paul | The Polish Corridor | } Paula's children |
| Little Peta | Danzig | |

Irak	Liese	⎫
Turkey	Leopold	⎪
Palestine	Ludwig	⎪
Egypt	Lenchen	⎪
Africa	Johannes	⎬ Unrelated to the family
India	Julius	⎪
Libya	Georg	⎪
Tunisia	Erika	⎪
Algeria	Elfrida	⎪
Morocco	Erna	⎭

"You see how they run in series," Freddie went on. "The Christian names of all the Schwartz's begin with 'S' and those of the Heins with 'H'. That's what enabled me to tumble to it. No members of any real family would all have the same initials or, anyhow, the practice wouldn't extend to a whole group of families connected by marriage. Whoever devised the code arranged for overlapping, too, in the most important cases. Mitzi is Hungary and, although one of the Mid-European 'Engels', her name ties her with the Balkan 'Müllers'. Finland is Hans and one of the Russian Mrs. Klein's sons but his first name connects him with the Scandinavian 'Heins'. I expect it was arranged like that so that these dozens of names could be remembered easily from alphabetical association with various parts of the map. That would have enabled the Nazi leaders to mention the countries guardedly in the presence of people who weren't in the know, without much risk of giving anything away."

Gregory nodded. "You've done a grand job of work, Freddie, in puzzling all this out; but you're looking pretty done-up now. I should go to bed if I were you and we'll talk some more about it in the morning."

Freddie smiled his acknowledgements and climbed on to the oven with the two girls; but Gregory remained seated at the table. He was immensely intrigued at Freddie's discovery and wanted to run through the whole document with the key that Freddie had provided. When his friends woke again after a four hours' sleep he was still working on it.

That day the others went about their occupations much as usual, rubbing down the horses, thawing out the strips of dried

300

reindeer meat so that they should be ready for cooking in due course, and taking their hour's exercise in the crisp, crystal-white snow; but Gregory left all the work to them for once and seemed extremely preoccupied. In the afternoon he made a detour round the snow-covered barrier of trees to go and look at the empty road. That night after they had finished their evening meal he suddenly announced:

"I'm afraid you may not like what I've got to say but I want you to listen to me patiently for a while. I spent the early hours of the morning translating the famous document into ordinary language. I won't bother you with the early part of it but I think you ought to hear the last part, which consists of the stages by which Germany plans to dominate the world. I say *plans* rather than *planned* because the plan is still in active operation."

With an uneasy feeling of foreboding they settled down to listen as he read:

" 'STEPS IN THE WORLD PROGRAMME TO ACHIEVE WORLD DOMINION

" '1. The Austrians are a part of the German race although their country formed part of the old Austro-Hungarian Empire. Therefore an *Anschluss* by which we must absorb Austria should arouse little opposition.

" '2. With regard to the rest of the old Austro-Hungarian Empire, Hungary values her independence but once Austria has been absorbed into Germany we can move troops up to the Hungarian border upon which Hungary will be in no position to resist us. She can, therefore, be invaded at any time so it would be preferable to settle matters first with Czechoslovakia. The Czecho-Slovaks also value their independence, particularly the Czechs, who are extremely anti-German, but they are rich people and the Skoda arms-works are essential to us early in the game. Pressure can be brought to bear upon the Czechs and the Slovaks through the Sudetenland and Ruthenia respectively. The Czechs ill-treat the Sudeten Germans, who are a part of the German race, so it should not be difficult to present a case for the return of Sudetenland to Germany. The Ruthenians are also ill-treated by the Czecho-Slovaks and Hungary regards Ruthenia as one of her lost provinces. In order to divert Britain's attention from our own operations we should incite Hungary to claim Ruthenia. The Czechs will appeal to their ally, France, which may precipitate a crisis, but the French will have great difficulty in giving military support to Czechoslovakia and the crisis must be faced. Unless Britain agrees to give France her aid there will be no war. Once the Sudetenland has been cut off Czechoslovakia will prove an easy prey.

" '3. Albania is very badly governed and none of the Balkan countries give her any assistance. Here is an excellent pretext for involving Italy. She must be persuaded to take over Albania, by force of arms if necessary. It is a poor country but an excellent base for operations against the Balkans. Once Italian troops are stationed there Italy would be in a much stronger position to exert pressure upon Yugoslavia and Greece.

" '4. Some inducement will have to be offered to Russia to bring her into a Russo-German alliance. Germany has considerable interests in the three Baltic States, Lithuania, Latvia and Estonia. It is proposed that we should sacrifice these interests to Russia, upon which she would have no difficulty in regaining possession of these three ex-Russian provinces.

" '5. Poland should be dealt with next. Parts of Poland are by right German and other parts by right Russian. Danzig and the Polish Corridor are definitely a part of Germany. The Poles persecute their German citizens in these territories which gives us every justification for reabsorbing them into the Reich. Poland may go to war rather than agree to surrender them peaceably, but if she does she will have such a bad case that we shall be able to brand her as a warmonger before the world. Russia and Germany will then act in concert, invade Poland and divide the country between them.

" '6. Finland is another portion of the old Tsarist Empire which should be reabsorbed into it. The Finns are an independent people who are making a success of their small country and they may give Russia a certain amount of trouble; but Finland has always relied on German support. If we cut that off, Finland will go the same way as Lithuania, Latvia and Estonia.

" '7. While Russia deals with Finland we must exert pressure upon the Scandinavian countries to prevent their going to Finland's assistance. When the Russians have advanced their frontier across the Mannerheim Line there will no longer be any danger of the Scandinavians combining against us, as they can be threatened by Russia and ourselves simultaneously. Sweden is strong enough to require a separate operation so she should be left for the time being, but Norway and Denmark can be taken over together. Sweden will then be entirely isolated, and so in no position to resist us whenever we consider it convenient to take control there.

" '8. Before going down into the Balkans it is essential that our right flank should be secured on the North Sea, otherwise Holland and Belgium may become alarmed at our operations and for their own protection invite Britain and France to attack us through their territories while we are occupied elsewhere. This reasoning also applies to any suggestion of attempting to absorb Holland separately. The Low Countries must, therefore, be overrun in one operation. At this point we must certainly anticipate a conflict with Britain and France, but having already established ourselves in Austria, Czechoslovakia, Poland, Norway, Denmark, Sweden, Holland and Belgium, we should have ample resources and nothing to fear.

" '9. Switzerland, like Sweden, having been almost encircled by the powers of the Pan-German Federation, can be absorbed at any time, but should a major war eventuate at Stage 8, Switzerland should be next on the list so that we can outflank the Franco-British front and drive straight down towards the Mediterranean.

" '10. A sufficient interval will now have elapsed since our take-over of Austria and Czechoslovakia for us to have properly established ourselves in those countries; so our next move should be to exert pressure on Hungary and to absorb her also.

" '11. If over a period of five or six years we have succeeded in absorbing Austria, Czechoslovakia, Norway, Denmark, Sweden, Hungary and a part of Poland, and Italy has absorbed Albania, either without provoking war or through a series of short wars, Britain will not fight again until directly threatened. However, our next stage, being Yugoslavia and Greece, involves our coming down into the Mediterranean, so it is highly prob-able that this will provoke Britain, for the first or second time, to conflict, but as the masters of the whole of Northern and Central Europe our position will then be very strong. Yugoslavia will be sandwiched between German-Austria and Italian-Albania and Italy must now be forced into the open. With Yugoslavia in Italo-German hands, Greece will fall to the Federation naturally by pressure from Yugoslavia and Italy.

" '12. Our advance into Hungary will bring us to the borders of Rumania. Bulgaria is already a Russo-German sphere of influence. She will be instructed to demand the return of the Dobruja. Russia will put forward her equally good claim to Bessarabia and on behalf of Hungary we shall claim the last province of Transylvania. Entirely encircled and threatened on all sides, Rumainia must succumb and join the Federation, of which Bulgaria will also automatically become a part.

" '13. To secure ourselves in Europe the Near East should also be brought under our domination. If our advance to the Mediterranean provoked Britain to conflict Russia must attack Irak to draw pressure from us if we are waging a major war in the West. If we have accomplished Stages 8 and 11 by peaceful means Stage 13 is another step in which we shall probably encounter armed resistance, as in Irak we shall *for the first time* be attacking a territory which can be considered as a part of the British Empire. Hence, for this operation we must provoke trouble in India simultaneously. India is ripe for revolt and German propaganda must ensure a rising there which will occupy a large portion of the British forces. Should a major war eventuate in the Near East Turkey should either be persuaded to come in with us or be overrun by attacks from Russia and Bulgaria in the same operation.

" '14. Supported by Italy, Spain will now take over Portugal and by entering the Federation close the Western end of the Mediterranean.

" '15. Pressure from us exerted through Turkey and Irak, and by Italy through Libya, should now secure Palestine and Egypt, closing the Eastern End of the Mediterranean.

" '16. France must now be cut off from her sources of strength in Africa by the taking over of Morocco, Algeria and Tunisia from bases in Spain, Italy and Libya.

" '17. France will now be the only remaining European country outside the German Federation. If we have succeeded in separating her from Britain she may surrender peaceably. If we have not done so, however. war is bound to result at this stage; but by that time our resources will be so great that the destruction of the British Empire is certain.

" 'It is impossible to forecast at which stage of these operations Britain will decide to fight, but if we can negotiate No. 2 successfully there is good reason to suppose that she will not feel herself forced to declare war until we go into Holland and Belgium at Stage 8 or even until her interests in the Mediterranean are directly threatened by Stage 11.

" 'If at any stage before the last Britain does decide to fight every effort must be made to prevent other countries from becoming involved, so as to limit the area of hostilities. Immediately we have subdued whichever of the smaller nations has refused to be peaceably absorbed, and whose resistance has caused Britain to declare war upon us, our next objective must be to secure a peace by negotiation which will leave the remainder of Europe as far as possible unaltered from what it was at the cessation of hostilities. Then, after an interval for recuperation the next stage must be undertaken; until all stages have been successfully completed either by diplomatic pressure or, if necessary, by a series of short wars.

" 'It is impossible to forecast the dates for any of these stages as some may merge into others and shorter or longer periods be required for recuperation between stages, according to the intensity and duration of the series of short wars Germany may be called on to wage before the major conflict, but it should be possible to complete the whole series of operations in from ten to twelve years. Whatever the time taken, five years will be required for reconstruction after the defeat of the British Empire and the whole of Europe having been united under German leadership. The German Federation and Japan will then launch a joint attack on the United States of America in order to subjugate that distant but dangerous English-speaking people. This final campaign will, within twenty years, leave the German race dominant throughout the world.' "

Gregory laid down the paper and looked round at the others. "You see how immensely important this document is."

"I see that it would have been important if we'd discovered it before the war," Angela answered, "because if the British Government had had it they would have known what Hitler's intentions were; and that every time he declared he had no more territorial ambitions in Europe he was lying in his dirty teeth. But fortunately they got on to his game quite early in the programme and decided to fight when he'd only got as far as Stage 5—wasn't it? Anyhow, the partitioning of Poland."

"That's right; Stage 5," Gregory nodded.

"Well, then," she continued, "now the war is on, that's all that matters. The rest of the plan can be considered as a wash-out."

"They have got as far as Stage 6, really," Erika put in: "since the Russians have carried out the next move allotted to them and attacked Finland. Gods knows what has happened to the Finns since the beginning of January, but I should think the Red Army must have forced the Mannerheim Line by now from sheer weight of numbers. If so, the principal crook is probably preparing for the next step in the programme."

"That's it," Gregory agreed. "Number 7 is the absorption of Norway and Denmark. If Stalin has done his stuff the Germans may have arrived in Copenhagen and Oslo while we've been sleeping our heads off here."

"Britain and France won't be sitting still doing nothing, though," Freddie put in. "If Germany has moved into Norway and Denmark the Allies will establish a Scandinavian front."

Gregory's thin mouth twitched in his old cynical smile which had returned to him with his memory. "Yes. *If* the countries attacked *ask* us to come to their assistance and *after* the Germans have seized every port, railhead and air-base worth having."

"If we are not invited in, then, we'll just have to sit and watch the Nazis putting two more countries, with all their resources, in the bag."

"That's it. And if the neutrals do ask for help we'll send it—of course. But our Expeditionary Force will have to land at miserable little fishing villages with only one rickety, wooden pier apiece and totally unfitted for military bases, while the German planes bomb them to Hell."

"That puts the Allies in a pretty nasty fix, then."

"It certainly does; since they're still mugs enough to observe the law of nations. If I had my way I'd scrap every pre-war treaty in existence until the war is over and go into these places before the Germans can get there, whether the neutrals liked it or not."

"But we couldn't do that," Freddie exclaimed in horror.

"Couldn't we!" Gregory's cynical laugh echoed through the room. "By God we could! And if we had the guts to do it we'd soon put paid to Hitler and all his crew. Regard Europe as a village, the nations as its householders and Britain and France as its two strongest and wealthiest inhabitants. What would they do if one of the villagers went mad? They would appoint themselves sheriffs and issue a declaration on the following lines:

" 'A homicidal maniac is at large and we have taken on the extremely dangerous and expensive job of catching him, for the safety of all concerned. As he is breaking into people's houses, damaging their property and murdering their occupants, to facilitate our catching him we hereby assume the right to enter

306

any house without a warrant and give notice that we will prose-
cute anybody who supplies him with food or shelter with the
utmost rigour of the law.' "

"That would be ratting on all we've said about entering
this war to protect the rights of small nations," Freddie said
dubiously, "and we'd lose the sympathy of all the neutrals."

"Not at all! We should only be suspending international
law for the duration of the conflict. Directly it was over we
would restore every country's independence and respect their
rights just as we have always done in the past. As for the
sympathy of the neutrals, what is it really worth? Nearly all
the small European nations are under Germany's thumb
already; and the United States is not going to enter the war
against us because we take the law into our own hands. As a
matter of fact they would all become very much more pro-
British if only we showed some guts and that we really meant
to get down the bully of whom they're all so terrified. They all
want to keep their liberties but they kow-tow to Germany
because they think we're weak and effete; and they're scared stiff
that we might make a negotiated peace which would leave
Germany free to give them a dusting up after the war, if they
don't do just what she tells them now."

"I don't see how such a declaration would help you to win
the war, though," Erika remarked.

"Don't you?" Gregory laughed, "I do. The Siegfried Line
is too strong for us to attack it across the French frontier without appalling losses; but they're still only digging it along the
Luxembourg and Belgian borders. If we chose to walk into
the Low Countries one fine night we might outflank the main
line and carry the war into the enemy's country. They would
only put up a formal show of resistance, then join us, because
they hate the Nazis as much as we do. We could scrap this childish nonsense about territorial waters and put British destroyers
into the Norwegian fjords. where the strain on the crews would
be much less in bad weather, and we could cut off the iron-ore
supplies which come down to Germany through Norwegian
waters. We could do the same thing along the coast of Yugoslavia and stop the supplies of bauxite coming up the Adriatic
from Dubrovnik to Trieste. With the Turks' consent we could
send a part of the Mediterranean Fleet through the Dardanelles
into the Black Sea and cut off the oil-tankers that bring supplies
from Batum to Constanta and Varna before they go through
to Germany—and believe you me, it's oil that is going to win

307

this war. That's why perhaps years hence it will be fought out in the Near East. There are a thousand and one things which we could do to give the Nazis hell, if only we went into this thing with knuckledusters instead of kid gloves."

"Do you think they'll stick to their programme now Britain and France have come in?" Freddie asked.

"As far as Scandinavia and Holland and Belgium are concerned, yes. A German landing in Norway would be a clever move to draw a big proportion of our troops away from the central theatre of war, so let's hope we don't fall into the trap. But once they invade Holland and Belgium we'll have a real chance to get at them, so they may be compelled to alter their plans. It's going to be awkward if they follow it to Stage 9 and drive through Switzerland while Italy attacks France from the south; but the need for oil may force them to attack Roumania first."

"Perhaps," said Angela. "But where is all this speculation getting us?"

"Nowhere," Gregory grinned. "So let's get back to the business. This document is of immense significance for two reasons. Firstly, although the Allies declared war on Germany when she had reached only Stage 5 of her programme, it shows her true intentions. I'm prepared to swear that I got it direct from Hermann Goering. Copies of it, with my affidavit of that fact, ought to be sent to every neutral Government to inform them that Germany had deliberately planned to enslave the whole of Europe. Even if some of them doubt its authenticity it may cause them to take steps against the Nazi fifth columns which are undermining their powers of resistance and to reconsider their position a bit more carefully. Secondly, it is the penultimate paragraph which is of such vital importance. I'll read it to you again.

" 'If at any stage before the last Britain does decide to fight every effort must be made to prevent other countries from becoming involved, so as to limit the area of hostilities. Immediately we have subdued whichever of the smaller nations has refused to be peaceably absorbed, and whose resistance has caused Britain to declare war upon us, our next objective must be to secure a peace by negotiation which will leave the remainder of Europe as far as possible unaltered from what it was at the cessation of hostilities. Then, after an interval for recuperation, the next stage must be undertaken; until all stages have been successfully completed either by diplomatic pressure or, if necessary, by a series of short wars.'

"Now do you see what I'm driving at?" Gregory said grimly. "This is not only the outline of the German plan to put the whole of Europe in her pocket; and having achieved that, to secure world dominion; it shows how she intends to do it. She does not mean to exhaust herself by another giant effort such as she made in 1914-1918, and to exhaust other nations by dragging as many of them as she can in as her allies. It is a far cleverer and much more dangerous scheme. It has worked, too, in four stages out of five, as the Russo-German-Italian bloc have already conquered Austria, Czechoslovakia, Albania, Lithuania, Latvia and Estonia without having had to fire a single shot. For Poland Germany has had to fight but, as we all know, as soon as Poland had been overrun Hitler opened a peace offensive. He didn't pull it off, but if a stalemate continues in the West as time goes on everybody will get bored and dispirited; among the people of France and Britain there will be a growing feeling of resentment at having had their lives thrown out of gear for a war that isn't a war at all."

"That won't be the case if Hitler goes into Holland and Belgium," Freddie remarked. "It will be war with a vengeance, then."

"True; and if Goering is overruled this plan may be abandoned for an attempt to force a quick decision. But say they do attack the Low Countries, what happens next? The great Armies will clash on the Yssel and the Maas. There will probably be a few weeks' terrific fighting and the Allies will stem the German advance on the Albert Canal and the Meuse. They'll dig in there and unless the Germans drive through Switzerland there will be another stalemate, perhaps for years as there was in the last war. Then, after a time, Hitler will start another peace offensive. People will be bored and war-weary. His fifth column in London will get busy among the cranks and idealists that support organizations like the Nordic League and the Peace Pledge Union and an agitation will be started on the lines that Hitler isn't such a bad fellow really. They will be saying: 'He would never have attacked Poland if the Poles had let him have Danzig back. Now that he has rectified the wrongs—and they *were* wrongs—done to Germany by the Versailles Treaty he's not asking anything else and he's quite prepared to make peace. So why should our young men have to spend the best years of their lives in battle-dress, and why should we be burdened with this incredible taxation which is sending us all bankrupt, when we could quite well make a decent peace by negotiation?' "

Freddie nodded. "Yes. Lots of people will come to feel like that if this war drags on for years without any sign that there may ever be a finish to it; but even if we did make that sort of peace Europe would remain an armed camp, so the Germans wouldn't dare to proceed with their plans any further."

'That's where you're utterly wrong," Gregory declared. "We had riots in our Army after the last war because the men were anxious to get home and they couldn't be demobilized quickly enough. The same thing would happen again and all the business people would start pressing for a reduction of taxation. Our Army, Navy and Air Force would dwindle and we should cease to manufacture the latest types of planes and munitions. Everybody would say that we had all we needed and our types would become obsolete, because Germany would not react in the same way at all. Hitler would be training another generation of German youth for the battlefield; Goebbels would be stuffing them with his propaganda; Goering would be improving his aeroplane designs and turning out better models than ours as hard as he could go.

"Within a year Hitler would be ahead of us again and ready to make his next move with impunity or, if need be, to fight another nine-months' war. That is why this document has got to be placed in the hands of my old friend, Sir Pellinore Gwaine-Cust, who will put it before the Cabinet and the Allied War Council. He will vouch to them for my integrity; that if I say I got it from Goering's safe I *did* get it from Goering's safe. As it is irrefutable proof of Germany's intentions it may be the means of checking any move towards peace until Germany is *down and out and split up into little pieces once and for all.* It must reach them at the earliest possible moment. Therefore, I intend to leave for England to-morrow."

Had a Russian plane dropped a bomb in the clearing at that moment it could not have caused a greater consternation among Gregory's listeners.

"But you can't, darling!" Erika exclaimed. "We're snowed up here."

"Of course he can't!" Angela supported her. "We dont even know the way to the nearest village and it may be fifty miles away. He'd be frozen to death long before he got there."

Freddie sat silent with a strained look on his face. The

310

girls continued their chorus of protest, but it was clear that their arguments were not having the least effect on Gregory and when at last they petered out in a miserable silence Freddie said:

"I do understand now, old chap, how important this thing is. From what you said it's quite clear that by making any premature peace we should only be falling into Hitler's trap, and it's got to be a fight to the finish. I doubt if one of us could get through alone, but two of us might, and I'd willingly come with you if only there was some way in which we could leave the girls with a reasonable hope that they could remain here in safety."

There was an awful silence as Angela stared at him wide-eyed, but Gregory said at once: "I'll manage somehow, Freddie; you must stay and look after them."

Erika sighed. "You know, we've been very happy here; but fate didn't mean our happiness to continue. It couldn't with everything which we hold dear in the world at stake; and when the thaw came we should have felt drawn back anyhow. I don't believe that Gregory could get through alone, either, and I think I should be tempted to kill myself if I had to stay on here not knowing what had happened to him. But if we all went we could take the sleigh, drive and sleep by turns, collect wood to make fires when we have to halt and cook meals."

Angela nodded. "I know that Freddie feels he ought to go; and although I suppose we could manage for ourselves I'm not staying without him. Besides, it's up to us as much as the men to stop the Nazi terror bringing misery to countless people all over the world; and we've learnt to do so much in these last two months that I'm sure we should be a help rather than a hindrance."

"Very well, then," Gregory said quietly. "I wouldn't allow any of you to budge from here if I didn't know that your coming with me would enormously increase my chances of getting back to civilization with these grimy bits of paper. But as you're game to risk death with me I accept your offer. We start to-morrow."

Once the decision had been taken they began their preparations immediately. It was important that the sleigh should be kept as light as possible, in order not to overburden the horses, so they made out a list of things they might require, carefully assessing the value of each item before deciding to take it with them. Fur rugs to keep out the devastating cold, spades for digging the sleigh out if it got stuck in a snowdrift, hatchets for

311

chopping wood to make fires, paraffin with which to light them easily, and arms for their protection, were all essential. The rest of the load was to consist of various utensils and food and fodder enough to last them a week.

Having completed their list they turned in and went to sleep wondering uneasily where the following night would find them; but they were all up early the next morning and, concealing the anxiety which they could not help feeling under a rather forced gaiety, they set to loading the sleigh.

Over breakfast their light small talk petered out and it was a very silent party that harnessed the horses to the *troika* half an hour later. They had many regrets at leaving their Arctic refuge and little elation at the prospect that in a few days they might be back in civilization again. Between them and safety lay the possibility of capture by the Russians or—worse—of their getting lost in the limitless forests and dying from cold and hunger.

It was still dark when they started and Freddie, who had taken the reins for the first spell, drove the *troika* in a zigzag course between the trees to avoid the great snow-covered barrier they had erected across the track. The road was now only a big snow-filled gully between the two masses of trees, but in its centre, where there were no drifts, the surface was even and hard enough for the horses to trot on without burying their hooves further than the fetlocks.

Freddie turned the sleigh to the right on reaching the road as it had been decided to head towards Petsamo until they could find a side-road leading west, in the direction of the frontier. Apart from losing their way their main danger lay in the possibility of running into Russian detachments which might be patrolling that section of the broken battle-front, but owing to the rigours of the climate such detachments must be rare, so they hoped to get through unchallenged.

If they managed to get back into Finnish territory there was still a risk that the two men might be arrested for murder, but over two months had elapsed since the charge had been brought against them and the Finnish police must since have had a multitude of more urgent matters to attend to. Unless they had the unlikely misfortune of running into *Monsieur* Wuolijoki, or the Chief of Police himself, they did not feel that they had to worry very much on that score; particularly as they had no intention or trying to get back to Helsinki but meant to strike across Northern Finland into Norway.

312

Resting the horses for ten minutes in each hour they drove for three hours but during all that time they saw no sign of a side-road leading to the west; so Gregory decided that they had better enter the next wide break among the trees where they could strike west across country. Half an hour later they turned left along a clearing which penetrated the forest as far as they could see, finding little difference between the snow-covered grassland and the snow-covered surface of the road.

As they advanced the clearing widened until the trees had fallen back a mile or more on either side of them; but after another hour the ground became broken and uneven, which slowed up the pace of the horses. Ten minutes later they became stuck in a snowdrift. They soon had the sleigh free and the work of digging it out warmed them; but they were not so pleased at having to exert themselves when it got stuck again a hundred yards further on.

In the next hour they had to dig the sleigh out of snowdrifts six times and in their heavy furs it was a wearing business, but at last they struck hard snow and were able to move on again at a decent pace.

The short day was now over and full dusk had come when they reached a barrier of forest lying right across their path, where the trees were so thick that it was impossible for the sleigh to be driven between them. Gregory said that they must turn south but that as long as it was dark they might pass another gap in the trees by which they could get further westward; whereas they would later have the moon—which would be full that night—to light their way; so their best course was to eat and afterwards sleep for a few hours.

Having put on the horses' nosebags and rugged them up they made a meal of a portion of the cooked food they had brought with them; then snuggled down together under the furs in the sleigh, burying themselves under the great heap to keep in the warmth as much as possible.

At ten o'clock they roused up and set off again, driving south along the edge of the forest until a clearing opened in it. Turning west they drove on in a zigzag course from clearing to clearing, or sometimes across broad stretches of open land, until one o'clock in the morning.

They had reached another impasse and Gregory felt that, even allowing for the evening halt, enough had been asked of the horses in one day. In the clear Arctic night with a moon only occasionally hidden by scudding clouds they proceeded to form a camp. The men collected and cut branches while the girls got a fire going and it was soon blazing well enough for them to melt snow in saucepans for drinking-water for themselves and the horses. They had to wait a little until part of it had died down sufficiently for them cook on, but by making a separate pile of part of the red embers Angela was able to heat up some tins of soup and warm up some coffee. After they had eaten they piled the fire high with all the branches they could find and, curling up in the sleigh, went to sleep.

When they awoke next morning their vitality was very low. The frightful cold had penetrated even their heavy coverings and immediately they crawled out from beneath the rugs frost from their breath rimed their eyebrows. Their sleep had not refreshed them for they felt drowsy and their extremities were numb. While they tried to warm themselves by violent exercise they wondered miserably if after another night like the last they would fail to wake in the morning and remain frozen in their sleigh, with the snow for a canopy, until someone found them in the spring. Angela, forgetting that it was dangerous to touch metal when the thermometer was so many degrees below zero, burnt her fingers through removing her glove to open a tin; Erika was crying from the cold and her tears froze as they ran down her blue cheeks.

Snow was falling gently but, urged by an instinctive effort of self-preservation, they managed to get another fire going and cook themselves some breakfast. After they had eaten they felt a little restored. The hardy Arctic ponies had taken less harm from the cruel night than the humans and, having harnessed them to the sleigh, the party set off once more.

All through the short day they continued their journey, often having to turn south but sooner or later always finding an opening that led them further to the west. The girls were dumb from the agony they felt and Freddie, who loved winter sports and exercise, had been reduced to a state of despondency in which he was too dejected even to blaspheme each time they had to dig the sleigh out of deep snow. It was the indomitable spirit in Gregory's lean body that kept them all going as he mocked or cussed them into making a fresh effort whenever they got stuck and encouraged them with the belief that they must sight a village in another mile or two. He was feeling the cold as acutely as any of them but he would not show it and it seemed as if he was made of steel.

314

The days were lengthening slightly but dusk still fell before four o'clock, an when it came they halted once more, to eat again and rest before making the second daily stage of their journey, by moonlight.

It was about eleven o'clock and their last camp was an hour behind them when Erika caught the first distant howl of a wolf. A moment later it came again and the others heard it. Gregory was driving and he cast an uneasy glance over his shoulder. A lone wolf was nothing to be frightened of as it would never dare to attack them; but even he was not proof against a spasm of fear at the thought that they might be hunted by a pack.

The howling came again, this time from a slightly different direction—another wolf had taken it up. Within five minutes the forest, from being dead with an unearthly silence, was filled with a horrid baying in their rear.

The horses had heard the threatening note before the humans. Gregory had no need to urge them on. They were straining at the harness. For ten minutes the sleigh was carried across the snow at a faster pace than any they had made since leaving the trapper's house.

Suddenly another barrier of trees loomed up before them in the moonlight and Gregory had to swerve south along it. Churning up the snow, which glistened in the moonlight like two sheets of spray as it flew out on either side of them, the sleigh sped on for another five minutes. But the howling of the wolves was nearer now—much nearer. They had decreased their distance by cutting across the corner formed by the sleigh's track.

Freddie and the girls had crawled out from underneath the rugs and were straining their eyes through the semi-darkness in their wake. Another moment and they could just make out a black shadow that seemed to dance upon the snow in the distance. It was the pack that now had them in sight and was in full cry after them.

Another gap opened in the woods. Straining at the reins Gregory cornered it at such speed that the sleigh nearly overturned. A breathless second and they had straightened out again to continue their wild career.

Not one of them had spoken, but a ghastly fear filled all their hearts. They were miles from any form of help or shelter. If they struck another snow-drift, or the wolves once caught up with them, the horses would be torn to pieces and they, in turn, would suffer a frightful death as they fell fighting under the tearing fangs of the ravenous pack.

315

HUNTED BY WOLVES

GREGORY dared not look behind again; it was all he could do to control the sweating, terror-maddened horses. The *troika* was flying over the ground at such speed that in spite of his fears he felt all the exhilaration which he would have got out of driving a Roman racing chariot; but it needed iron muscles to guide the three stampeded beasts and an unswerving eye for the ground ahead. Any hummock in the snow might conceal a tree-stump and overturn the whole outfit, leaving them a defenceless prey to the famished beasts which were hunting them so relentlessly.

The others had got out the arms they had brought and Freddie was lying with a rifle over the back of the sleigh. The wolves were now less than two hundred yards behind; a dark, undulating patch that seemed to streak along the white carpet of snow. It was impossible to count them but he reckoned that there were anything from seventy to a hundred. Another few minutes and he could distinguish the leaders; see their fiery eyes gleaming in the moonlight.

Still no-one spoke. Driver and passengers were all frantically racking their wits for some way to escape the terrible death that menaced them. It was useless to drive in among the scattered trees on the fringe of the forest in the hope of throwing the pack off. Wherever the sleigh could go the wolves would follow. For a second the idea came to Gregory that they might pull up and climb a tree. But even if in their mad flight he could have selected a tree which it would have been easy for them to climb they had not sufficient lead to do so now before the wolves would be upon them; and if they could have fought them off long enough to scramble up to safety it would have meant sacrificing the horses.

That thought gave him an idea which he was horribly

reluctant to carry out; but their lives were at stake and it might mean a temporary respite during which he could perform the seemingly impossible and think of some other plan to save them. Now that he had his full mental capabilities back, to think was, once again, to act.

Rolling the reins round his left hand, with his right he drew the trapper's sharp hunting-knife from his belt and, stooping, swiftly severed the leather thongs by which the breast harness of the off-side horse was attached to the sleigh. Directly it felt itself free of the weight it was dragging it bounded forward with a new spurt of energy nearly jerking Gregory out of the sleigh by the single rein which was all that now held it. But he had been expecting such a movement and had thrown himself backwards at the same instant, partially counteracting the pull. The other horses reared and the sleigh was almost brought to a standstill. Sheathing his knife he eased the reins and, as the sleigh started forward again, released the rein of the off horse altogether. As it broke away, outdistancing the others, he pulled his gun. For a moment the horse streaked ahead of them, its harness flapping wildly. Gregory swerved the sleigh a little to the left and did the horrible thing he had to do. Aiming his pistol at the horse he had freed he put three rounds into its buttocks.

An almost human scream of pain went up from the wounded animal. It faltered slightly in its gallop, its pace lessened. As they raced past Gregory put another bullet into its head in the hope that his last flying shot might kill it. He could not turn to see what happened; but the others saw. The horse plunged on, reeling from side to side for fifty yards, then fell. A howl of exultation went up from the pack and the poor beast was submerged under them.

For a few minutes it seemed as though the sacrifice had saved them so Gregory hauled on the reins of the two remaining horses to ease their pace and conserve their flagging energy. The evil baying of the wolves fell away in the distance; but it was never quite lost and soon they realized that it was drawing nearer again. For a pack of seventy to a hundred wolves a single horse was far from sufficient to satiate their ravenous appetites. The carcase had been picked clean and the pack was now hunting further prey.

Ahead another barrier of thick, impassable forest loomed up and Gregory knew that they must turn again; so he swerved to the south a few hundred yards before they reached it. Once more the others, peering out of the back of the sleigh, could see that sinister black patch undulating across the snow in their rear. The speed of the sleigh had diminished now that it had only two horses to draw it and they had already spent their best efforts; but the raw flesh that the wolves had just devoured did not seem to have lessened their pace. Very soon they were near enough again for their gleaming eyes to be seen sprinkling the black patch they formed as they loped swiftly forward.

Gregory had been driving along the side of the forest for several moments before he realized that the surface they were now on was harder than that over which they had been moving before. Instead of being crisp and uneven it was solid and beaten flat. By pure chance they had struck a road and troops with lorries or tanks must have passed that way recently. The new hope that came to him with the discovery was killed almost instantly. Villages were so incredibly few and far between up there in the far north, and the fact that troops had used the road that day did not mean that they were necessarily encamped in that area. They might be a dozen miles away by this time and in the almost static war that was being fought in the Arctic one convoy might move along a road without its following that a second would do so for another week or more.

Freddie had his rifle trained again. The girls were crouching on either side of him; the wolves had ceased to bay and were running, a sinister, silent mass, no more than a hundred yards behind the sleigh. Now that they were on a road, with little risk of being overturned by crashing into some unseen obstacle in their headlong flight, Gregory was able to glance over his shoulder from time to time. The wolves were gaining upon them every moment. He thought of sacrificing the near-side horse as the only means of securing further respite but after a moment's reflection he knew that he dared not do it. Both horses were flagging and if he cut free the near-side horse the centre one, which carried the heavy arch of the *troika*, would not have sufficient strength to pull the fully-loaded sleigh much further. In its terror it would go on until it dropped; but the strain the horses had undergone in the last hour was already terrific. As it was, either of them might burst blood-vessels or die from a heart attack at any moment.

The silence was broken only by the hoof-beats of the horses. Not a sound or whisper of wind disturbed the illimitable forests and the pack ran on, a little tired now but silent, relentless and still making a better pace than the horses. The wolves crept up

318

and up until the white breath of the leaders formed a little cloud above the dark, heaving mass of furry bodies.

Freddie waited, staring into the fiery eyes of the pursuing pack. He did not mean to waste a single bullet. But at last the leader of the pack was within five yards of the end of his rifle. He took careful aim and fired.

The big beast turned a complete somersault and vanished under the swarm of lean, dark forms that leapt across him. A few wolves at the rear of the pack stopped to worry the carcase, but the others, feeling their prey almost within their grasp, did not swerve from their course or even hesitate an instant.

Within a minute Freddie had to fire again; then he settled down to the job in earnest. It was easy enough to pick off the wolves one by one as they came up to within a few yards of the back of the sleigh; but there seemed so many of them, and ammunition was limited. As Freddie emptied one rifle Angela passed him the other and reloaded the first. Soon he had to shoot more rapidly. The wolves spread out a little on to a frontage of about thirty feet and those at each extremity of the line were constantly creeping right up to the level of the sleigh in an attempt to pass it. He had to fire first to one side and then to the others as well as picking off the more courageous brutes that were still following in the sleigh's track.

The road lay clear before Gregory now as another thick belt of trees loomed up on their left-hand side and the way entered the depths of the forest. But a mile further on he suddenly saw that the road seemed to end; there were trees ahead of him as well. Turning, he glanced back. The wolves, now spread out across the whole width of the road, seemed hardly to have decreased in numbers for all the execution that Freddie had done among them.

With anxious eyes Gregory stared ahead, then the moonlight showed him that the road did not end but took a sharp bend to the left. As he cornered, it was just the opportunity the wolves had been waiting for. Those on the off-side of the road fell behind but those on the near-side cut off the corner and streaked ahead.

Freddie had just exhausted the magazine of one of the rifles. Grabbing the other from Angela he opened rapid fire with it but there was no time to take careful aim. Two wolves leapt and fell in their tracks. Erika came into action with her pistol, firing over his shoulder, and killed a third; but the other bullets went wide and half a dozen of the brutes were now running level with the horses.

Next instant their leader, a great, grey beast with slavering jaws, leapt at the throat of the near horse. It screeched and reared, jerking the sleigh violently to one side; but Gregory had out his knife again and in two swift strokes severed the harness.

With a neigh of fear the centre horse plunged forward just as Gregory released the near horse's rein. The terrified beast had hardly broken free when another wolf buried its fangs in the wounded animal's flank and the sleigh had not covered another ten yards before a dozen wolves had pulled the poor brute, screaming, to the ground.

Gregory knew that their lives could now be measured by minutes. Crazy with terror the centre horse was galloping blindly on, but now that it had to drag the full weight of the sleigh it could not possibly continue much further. The near-side horse would be devoured before they could cover another half-mile; then the pack would be after them again and all hope of outdistancing them gone.

Suddenly, ahead of him, he saw a change in the dim land-scape. The forests on either side of the road ended abruptly but they did not give way to another open space. The snow was broken here and there by the black bulk of buildings. Glancing back he saw that the wolves were already on the move behind them. A black heap in the moonlight showed where about a third of their number were still tearing the remnants of the dead horse; but the rest had abandoned the fight with their comrades for a mouthful of the easier prey and were once more in full pursuit.

Even now Gregory feared that they might not reach the village in time. At this hour nobody would be about. The wolves would follow them into the village street and they might be pulled down before they could rouse the peasants to their assistance. Their only chance seemed to be that they might secure shelter in the nearest house. Freddie and Erika were now firing again as the nearest wolves gained once more upon the sleigh. The house was only a hundred yards ahead now. Using his whip for the first time Gregory drew the last spurt out of the beaten horse.

Suddenly the door of the house was flung open and a light appeared. The inmates had been aroused by the sound of firing. A group of men came out and in the bright moonlight one glance was enough for them to take in the situation. Some of

them ran back into the house. As the sleigh drew level with them they tumbled out again; next moment there was the crash and rattle of machine-gun fire. There was no need to pull up the sleigh; the remaining horse tottered to a halt and fell dead at that moment, and as the party it had carried to safety stepped into the road they saw that their rescuers were soldiers.

Their burst of fire had scattered the wolves, which were running up and down baying again now, but not daring to approach any nearer. In a few moments they were driven off and the survivors, still howling dismally at being cheated of their prey, disappeared into the edge of the forest.

No sooner had the last shots been fired than the soldiers turned with cheerful exclamations of congratulation to the people whom they had saved; but it soon became apparent that none of them could understand what was said. All Gregory and his friends could do to express their gratitude was to shake hands, smile and pat the soldiers on the back. A very tall, black-bearded, dark-eyed officer motioned Gregory's party into the house which was evidently used as an out-post. The fug in the low room was frightful but they hardly noticed it in their relief at their miraculous escape and sank down, with their hearts still pounding, on a long bench by the wall.

They had eaten only a few hours before so they were not particularly hungry but after a little while some of the soldiers brought them bowls of hot stew and mugs of coffee substitute which Gregory thought was probably made from acorns. A quarter of an hour after their arrival the street door opened and the officer entered with another man who came over and greeted them in a language which was different from that of the soldiers. They guessed then that they had been taken for Finns and that the officer had brought a Finnish prisoner who could speak Russian from the local lock-up to question them and act as an interpreter.

This having proved a failure the officer stroked his long, black beard and regarded them with increased interest. Gregory attempted to open communications with him by using German, English, French and Italian, but apparently none of the Russians or the Finn had even a smattering of any of these languages, so the deadlock continued.

When they had finished their not very appetizing meal—out of politeness rather than because they wanted it—the officer spoke to one of his men, who led them through a short passage and up a narrow stairway to an attic under the rafters of the house. With a broken-toothed grin the man pointed to the rugs from the sleigh which had been thrown down on the floor there, handed to Freddie a tallow candle that he was carrying and closed the door behind him; but he did not lock it. The Russians were evidently not bothering to take any precautions to prevent the party from leaving without permission because they knew quite well that now they no longer had horses, the deadly cold, the isolated position of the village and the wolves in the forest would be a better deterrent to any attempt at escape than iron bars, steel doors and sentries with loaded rifles.

"What d'you think they'll do with us?" Angela asked in a low voice.

"Send us for questioning to some place where there are people who can speak our language, I expect," Gregory replied.

"I wish we had been able to grow beards like you," Erika said uneasily.

Gregory knew what she was thinking. The hair of both girls was hidden under their fur *papenkas* and they were quite as tall as many of the smaller Russian soldiers; so in their thick furs, which concealed their clothes and figures, they might quite well have been taken for men, except for the tell-tale smoothness of the lower parts of their faces.

He stroked his own black-and-grey imperial. "I'm afraid there's no hiding the fact that you're women and you might have had a nasty time if you'd fallen into the hands of those drunks at Petsamo; but I don't think you've got anything to fear here. Women are *really* treated as the equals of men in Russia and there's quite a lot of them in the Soviet Army, so the troops are used to having women among them. They won't make a pass at you unless you show any inclination that way yourselves."

He was by no means certain that things would be as easy as all that, since no outlandish clothes could disguise Erika's loveliness and Angela's good looks. but it was no good meeting trouble half-way and he wished to reassure them as far as possible. On his old axiom that in any difficult situation one should always get as much sleep as possible when there was nothing else that one could do, he added: "Our best line at the moment is to follow a masterly policy of inactivity; so let's turn in."

The soldier who had shown them up to the room roused them before it was light. As they had slept in their furs they were already dressed and apparently their hosts considered any form of toilet quite unnecessary, so they were led straight downstairs to join the soldiers at a breakfast which did not differ in any way

322

from the meal they had had the night before. Afterwards they sat by the stove for about an hour while the Russians eyed them with a curious but not unfriendly stare; then the street door opened and the officer appeared in it, beckoning them to follow him outside.

Two sleighs were standing there in the pale dawn light, each with a soldier sitting in it and another on the box. Gregory and Erika entered one sleigh and Freddie and Angela the other. The big officer gave them a wave and both sleighs drove off. Any form of communication with their respective guards was impossible and it would have been completely pointless to attempt either to overpower them or to get away, so they resigned themselves to being driven south-eastward through the crisp, frosty air.

They halted every few miles to give the horses a breather and to restore their own circulation by flapping their arms and stamping their feet. At midday they made a longer halt during which the soldiers provided a picnic meal of coarse bread and iron rations. All through the afternoon they drove on again, making, Gregory estimated, a steady twelve miles an hour, and just as dusk was falling they pulled up at another village. The prisoners assumed that they were to spend the night there but after having been given mugs of very weak hot tea and a bowl of stew apiece, in a large, log building where there were a number of other soldiers, their guards led them out again and with fresh teams of horses they took the road once more.

At six o'clock the road emerged from the forest and they saw that the carpet of snow ahead was broken by some scattered buildings. These soon grew more numerous. They passed a railway-station, then the houses merged into the street of a small town where other sleighs and people were moving in the semi-darkness, which was broken here and there by street lamps and the lighted windows of a few poor-looking general shops. On reaching a small square the sleighs turned right and mounted a steep incline at the end of which there loomed up the bulk of a great building that seemed to tower above the town. Two minutes later they were halted by a sentry who, after a brief exchange with their escort, passed them through a high, arched gateway and from lights fixed to the walls they saw that they were in the courtyard of an ancient castle.

The drivers of the sleighs remained with their horses while the two other soldiers led their charges through a low door. A non-commissioned officer who was writing at a desk in a small

323

room took the guard's report, then he shouted for an orderly who took the whole party along a gloomy, vaulted corridor and left them in a large room with some benches in it and a stove at one end. Having loosened their furs they waited there for three-quarters of an hour, after which the orderly reappeared to conduct them through several more long, echoing passages and up a broad flight of stairs. Their guide then unceremoniously threw open a large door in the upper hallway and motioned to them to pass in.

The room they entered was large and lofty but its furniture presented some queer contrasts. Much of it revealed the splendour of bygone days when the castle was a Tsarist stronghold. There were bearskin rugs on the now unpolished parquet floor; a fine array of antlers and heads interspersed with a collection of ancient arms decorated the walls; several settees and chairs, from which the brocade was worn and the gilt rubbed, looked like genuine *Louis Seize* pieces and might still have fetched a good price at Christie's, but the room had now been converted for use as a modern office. Incongruously a row of steel filing-cabinets lined a part of one wall under a piece of fine *Gobelin* tapestry, while in the very centre of the apartment there stood a cheap pinewood desk on which were littered cardboard files and wire letter-trays.

Behind the desk a clean-shaven, grey-haired officer with several stars on his collar was sitting smoking a cheroot. His eyebrows were still black and ran thin and pointed towards the temples of his smooth, white forehead. Under them were a pair of rather lazy blue eyes of which Gregory took quick note. He had met that lazy look before in other people and knew that it nearly always boded a shrewd intelligence. At a word from the man behind the desk the two soldiers told their story, helping each other in a friendly, conversational way as they went along and showing none of the trepidation which is usual in privates who are addressing an officer of high rank.

When they had done the officer looked at the prisoners and said: *"Parlez-vous français?"*

"Oui, mon Général," replied Gregory at once, giving him the benefit of General's rank although he was not sufficiently well acquainted with Soviet badges to know the Russian's actual status.

"Good," said the officer, continuing in French. "I should be glad, then, if you will give some account of yourselves."

Gregory had had ample time to think out what he meant to

say when they had to face an examination and he had realized that, short of telling the truth, which would certainly land them in serious trouble owing to the Russians they had shot at Petsamo, only two lines were open to them. Angela had a British passport, Erika had a German passport, he had a faked British passport in his own name and a German passport in the name of Colonel-Baron von Lutz, but Freddie had no passport at all. With the two countries at war such a mixed bag was sure to arouse unwelcome suspicion so they must either all pose as Germans or all pose as British and, since Germany was now Russia's ally, it seemed that Germans would be likely to meet with a much better reception.

Having informed the others early that morning of what he intended to do he produced the two German passports, and announcing himself as Colonel-Baron von Lutz, introduced Erika as the Countess von Osterberg and Freddie and Angela as Oscar and Fredeline von Kobenthal.

The officer glanced at the passports and asked for the other two.

"They were lost, unfortunately, with our baggage," smiled Gregory.

"Indeed?" The Russian told the soldiers to bring up chairs for their charges and went on: "Remove your furs and be seated, please; then continue."

Gregory acknowledged the courtesy and proceeded to the much more difficult task of explaining what his party had been doing up in the Arctic.

"Von Kobenthal and I," he said, "are members of the German Military Intelligence and these two ladies were acting as our assistants. Before the war broke out we were naturally able to move about Finland with much more freedom than would have been accorded to any Soviet subjects, and we were allotted the duty of assisting your attack on Petsamo. We lived in the town for a couple of weeks during which we were able to gather considerable information about the Finnish plans for resisting a Soviet invasion and it was our job, immediately upon the declaration of war, to cross the frontier, contact the Russian Military Intelligence and pass over to them such data as we had gained.

"We left Petsamo in our aeroplane on the morning the war broke out, ostensibly for Helsinki, but fifty miles south of the town we turned east intending to cross the frontier and land at your Arctic base of Murmansk. Unfortunately, we ran into a

325

terrible blizzard, ice formed on the wings of our plane while we were still somewhere over the frontier and we were compelled to make a forced landing. The snow was so thick that we could see nothing, but luckily for us we came down in a clearing instead of crashing among the trees.

"I will not describe to you, General, the incredible hardships which we suffered during the next twenty hours. The undercarriage of our plane had been ripped away on landing so it was impossible for us to take off again, and if we had not made a bonfire of the wreckage we should have frozen to death during the night. We should certainly have died in the forest if we had not been lucky enough to find on the following day a trapper's shack which had been provisioned for the winter. As we had no means of getting back to civilization the only thing we could do was to remain there until the coming of spring or until help reached us."

"A most interesting and exciting adventure, *Monsieur le Baron*," commented the Russian. "So you have been out of everything for nearly three months. And how did you manage to make a break from your snow-bound prison after all?"

"A sleigh and horses were virtually sent to us as a gift of Fate," Gregory lied affably. "Four days ago we were gathering kindling in the woods when we saw three horses drawing a *troika* come galloping down a long clearing in the forest on a most eccentric course. They did not appear to have any driver but we managed to head them off and halt them. We found that there was a driver in the sleigh but, as far as we could judge, he had been dead for some hours; probably he had refused to halt when challenged by some sentry. In any case, he had a bullet through his heart and evidently the horses had bolted. The following day we packed the sleigh full of provisions and set off eastward into Soviet territory. As no doubt the soldiers who brought us here will have told you, we narrowly escaped being devoured by wolves two nights later. But all's well that ends well. I can assure you that it's a great joy to myself and my friends to meet someone who can speak some other language than Russian and to find ourselves in comfortable surroundings once again."

"It is a pleasure for me to receive you here," the Russian said. "I am General Kuporovitch, the Military Governor of Kandalaksha, and I shall do my best to make you comfortable during your stay here."

"General, you are most kind," Gregory smiled, "but I was

hoping that you would provide us with facilities to proceed on our journey."

"Certainly," said the General. "Certainly, *Monsieur le Baron*. But we took Petsamo on the first day of the war, so your mission has long since lost its purpose. As you have been out of everything for nearly three months a few extra days will surely make no difference to any new plans which you may have formed. I see so few people here—I mean, of course, people who know anything of what is going on outside the Soviet Union. It will be a great treat for me to have you as my guests."

"I can assure you, General, there is nothing that we should like better," Gregory replied most cordially; "but unfortunately my country is at war and as a serving officer it is my duty to report there as soon as possible. The families of myself and my friends probably fear that we are dead by this time, too, so while we should be most grateful for your hospitality to-night I trust that you will find it convenient to help us proceed on our way south to-morrow morning."

"Forgive me, *mon cher Baron*, if I remark that as yet I have only your word for your somewhat extraordinary story."

"But, Comrade General, you have seen the passports of *Madame la Comtess* and myself," Gregory protested quickly.

The Russian stubbed out the end of his thin cheroot and a smile creased the wrinkles at the corners of his lazy blue eyes. "Passports can be forged, you know, and in a frontier command like this we have to be constantly on the watch for—er—spies. I endeavoured to put the matter as tactfully as possible but I'm afraid that you and your friends will not be able to leave the castle until I have had an opportunity to make full inquiries about you."

CHAPTER XXVI

THE GENERAL WITH A PAST

GREGORY knew that any check-up would prove fatal to them all. The Russian Military Intelligence in both Murmansk and Moscow would deny that any Colonel-Baron von Lutz and his companions had been expected to report to the H.Q. of the Northern Soviet Army on the first day of the war. The matter would then be referred to the German Embassy in Moscow and the Military Attaché would communicate with Berlin. The War Office there would know that Colonel-Baron von Lutz had been shot dead on his estate on the night of November the 26th and would consult the Gestapo. As the inquiry concerned German subjects outside Germany it would then be passed to the Foreign Department U.A.—1, and would come before Grauber. He would instantly realize that his old enemies had turned up again at Kandalaksha and apply to Moscow for their extradition. They would then be sent under armed guard back to Germany and woe betide them when Grauber had them in the Gestapo torture cell.

Now, too, there was something far more important than their lives at stake. By hook or by crook the typescript from Goering's safe had to be got back to England.

Concealing the consternation that he felt Gregory said smoothly: "How long d'you think it will take for you to satisfy yourself about us?"

General Kuporovitch shrugged. "In winter we are very isolated here. The heavy falls of snow often interrupt our telephone and telegraphic communications with Leningrad. Since the war, too, they are sometimes cut by raiding parties of Finns and our Air Mail has been stopped because we need all our best pilots for service at the front; so I send all my dispatches by courier. However, I should receive a reply in a week or, at the utmost, ten days."

He rang the old-fashioned hand-bell on his desk and went on: "But, as I mentioned before, it is not often that I have the opportunity of talking to intelligent foreigners and I shall accept your story—strange as it is—until it is proved to be false; so I have no intention of throwing you into the castle dungeons. On the contrary; since you cannot possibly escape from the castle I will put you in some of the guest-rooms that overlook the inner courtyards and I hope that we may enjoy some pleasant evenings together."

"That is most kind," Gregory murmured tactfully, as the orderly appeared in answer to the bell.

The General spoke to him in Russian, then turned back to the others. "I expect you'd like to wash after your journey. The orderly will take you to your rooms; then we will sup together. You will probably find his manners a little uncouth compared to those of the servants to which you are accustomed, but as long as people do what they're told we are all equals in my country now. You will observe that he talks to me with a cigarette in his mouth and if he had a mind to do so he would certainly spit on the floor. That gives him a delightful illusion of freedom and equality but he knows perfectly well that if he didn't obey me I should have him shot without trial."

Gregory grinned. The cynical humour of the lazy-eyed Russian appealed to him tremendously and with a further word of thanks for the General's courtesy in providing them with bedrooms instead of cells he followed the others out of the room.

The orderly led them down a long corridor and throwing open two doors side by side, tapped first Erika then Gregory on the shoulder, indicating that they should go in and remove their furs. The rooms had the same lingering flavour of past glories that they had noticed in the General's office, so evidently the castle had not been sacked in the Revolution but had been taken over with its furnishings complete. The beds were large and looked comfortable but the sheets were of the poorest quality cotton and pale grey in colour. There were no fixed basins in the rooms or water in the jugs, so having taken off their furs they both came out into the corridor again.

A door on its far side stood open and looking in they saw that it was a big room with a huge four-poster double-bed. Freddie was standing near it, blushing furiously, while Angela was taking off her furs, and the orderly leaned against the wall near the door smoking a cigarette. Erika caught Angela's eye, then

Gregory's, and all three of them had difficulty in suppressing their mirth. They had forgotten for the moment that Angela and Freddie were supposed to be the von Kobenthals; their host was naturally treating them as man and wife.

With a muttered word the orderly took them to the far end of the corridor and showed them a big, old-fashioned bathroom where they all took turns to wash. He then escorted them back to the main hall on the first floor of the castle and threw open another door next to that of the General's office.

Kuporovitch was there standing with his back to a big fire of logs. Another orderly was laying a mahogany table for five people. Moving over to a sideboard the General poured out five glasses of vodka.

The fiery spirit made Angela choke but Gregory took his down in one gulp, as he knew he was expected to do, and was poured a second ration as they sat down to table where, to start off with, they were given helpings of caviar which would have cost a pound a portion in London.

It was their first opportunity for nearly two months to learn anything of the progress of the war and the General spoke quite freely about it when they questioned him.

The Finns had put up a much stronger resistance than had been expected. It seemed that the Soviet Political Commissars had been grossly misinformed. They had believed that they had only to create a Finnish Communist Government under Kuusinen for the Finnish workers to arise and revolt against the brigand, Mannerheim; but that had not proved the case at all. Instead of a walkover the war was proving an expensive business for the Soviet. The early attacks on the Mannerheim Line had failed completely so many more troops had been brought up and another onslaught launched between January the 22nd and 28th; but that had failed also. It had not been until a third great offensive, at the end of the first week in February, that the line had even been dented at its coastal extremity to the south and the Finns were still holding their first-line positions in the north, at Taipale, where the line ended on Lake Ladoga.

The Soviet attacks had proved equally disastrous against the Finnish waistline further north and owing to the incredibly bad communications several Russian divisions had been very badly mauled. The General attributed these reverses to the fact that, against the advice of the military commanders, the politicals had insisted that second-rate troops were quite good enough to use in the easy victory they anticipated over Finland; but he said

330

he thought that things would be different now as Marshal Budenny had brought some of his crack divisions up to be employed on the Karelian Isthmus, and the Russian War Lord, Marshal Voroshilov, had taken command of operations there in person.

As a dish of venison was served they passed to the war between Germany and England and France; but about this the General had little to tell. He said that all over Europe it had proved the severest winter for the best part of a century. Even England was reported to have been under snow for several weeks at a stretch and Central Europe had been entirely frozen up; which probably accounted for the continued delay in the launching of the threatened Nazi *Blitzkrieg*.

The Germans had been making continuous air-attacks on British shipping and, if their reports were to be believed, half the British Navy and countless British cargo ships had been sunk; but then . . . he smiled a cynical apology to his guests . . . nobody outside Germany *did* believe the German reports. It was quite clear from bulletins issued in the United States and other neutral countries that the British convoy system was working with almost miraculous effect and the British Air Force was continuing to drop leaflets with impunity all over Germany. The raids on both sides were, however, no more than tip-and-run affairs and the war in the West seemed to have reached a stalemate.

"No other countries became involved, then, during the time that we were out of the world?" asked Erika.

The General shook his head. "No. *Herr* Hitler continues to exercise pressure on the Balkans and it looks as though he is gaining ground there. At the end of January the Rumanian Government took over the control of all the oil concerns, in order to ensure Germany a good supply, but Italy is the dominating factor in the Balkans now. Mussolini is straining every nerve to keep the peace there, but he continues to be very antagonistic towards us. He has sent quite a number of planes to Finland."

"How about the Scandinavian countries?" Gregory inquired. "Do you think they will continue to keep out?"

"Yes. Sweden and Norway are helping Finland with military supplies and they have sent many volunteers. Without them I doubt if the Finns could have held out for so long; but they dare not openly declare war on us—much as they would like to do so, They are much too frightened of being attacked by Germany in

331

the south. There was great excitement in Norway last week, though. A German cargo ship with three or four hundred British prisoners on board who had been captured during the actions of the *Graf Spee* in the South Atlantic sought refuge in Norwegian territorial waters and was creeping down the coast on her way home. For once the British took the bull by the horns and sent a destroyer right up the fjord where this ship, the *Altmark,* was lying up. The British sailors boarded her with cutlasses and took their compatriots off. It was a direct contravention of Norwegian neutrality, of course, and set every Embassy in Europe humming with activity."

Freddie's French was not very good but he had been managing to follow the conversation with a word of help from Angela here and there. Having gathered the gist of the General's remarks he began to grin with delight at this grand, old-fashioned naval action; Gregory caught his expression before he could speak and, giving him a hard kick under the table to remind him that he was supposed to be a German, launched out into a bitterly hostile attack against Britain's cunning, injustice and hypocrisy.

Some very sticky sweet cakes completed the meal and with them Caucasian champagne was served—at least, strictly speaking, it was not *served,* for the orderlies just opened a couple of bottles and dumped them on the table.

As they drank the rich, sweet wine the General turned the conversation and refused to discuss the war any further, saying that he was much more interested in other developments outside Russia, of which he had been able to gather very little for a long time past owing to the strictness of the Soviet censorship. Erika and Gregory willingly gave him many details about conditions in Germany at the time they had left it and the state of things in other European countries which they had visited before the war; all of which their host lapped up with the eagerness of a child who is let loose in a sweet shop after having long been denied sweets.

While they talked they drank. There appeared to be an inexhaustible supply of the Muscat-flavoured champagne which, since the orderlies had left the room after stacking the dirty plates together while the diners were still at table, the General fetched, bottle by bottle as it was required, from a case under the sideboard. By midnight Angela and Erika were so tired that they had great difficulty in suppressing their yawns, while Freddie looked extremely bored; he could only follow the

332

conversation with great difficulty and had long since given up any attempt to do so. At length, as the General showed not the least inclination to go to bed, Erika asked if he would excuse them since they were all terribly tired after their ninety-mile sleigh-drive.

He stood up at once and apologized for his thoughtlessness but expressed his hope that the men would not leave him yet as he had not enjoyed himself so much for ages. Gregory expressed his willingness to make a night of it but he noted with some concern the look of almost comical indecision on Freddie's face.

Having lived within earshot of Freddie and Angela for weeks at a stretch he knew that they were as amorously inclined as most healthy engaged couples, but Freddie would never have admitted such a thing to a third party and his embarrassment upon being shown into a double bedroom with Angela earlier that evening arose from his desire to continue to shield Angela's reputation even before their friends. Gregory did not care two hoots if Freddie took what the gods and Angela seemed prepared to give him or slept in his clothes on the sofa in her room; the one thing he did *not* want was any fuss about their *sharing* a room, which might cause the General to suspect the particulars he had been given about the party even more than he obviously did at the moment.

To Gregory's joy Angela stepped into the breach by gamely relieving Freddie of any responsibilty. Smiling at the General she said sweetly in her best French: "As the Baron is going to remain up with you I'm sure that you won't object to my taking my husband with me, because I never sleep well without him."

Picking up the old silver candelabra the General personally lighted his guests to their rooms and a few minutes later returned to Gregory.

Having polished off the current bottle of champagne Kuporovitch fetched a bottle of *sleivowitz* from the sideboard, remarking: "That fizzy stuff's all right for a change but I only had it up for the women. I expect that, like myself, you prefer a man's drink, eh, Baron?"

"Thanks." Gregory kicked the logs into a blaze before settling down beside the fire. "I'm all for something with a kick in it."

Putting the bottle of plum brandy on a small table between them, the General sat down again and they began to talk once more upon many topics which are a closed book to Russia's millions: the possibility of German and Austrian restorations; the part still played by the British monarchy in the affairs of the Empire; the truth behind the headlines about the Civil War in Spain; the purchasing power of the mark in Germany, the franc in France, the pound in England and the dollar in America; the development of the film industry outside Soviet Russia with the part that ballet and the theatre played in the Western world; the price of stalls and gallery in terms of roubles; the cost of good food in the best restaurants in capitalist countries; the price of apartments, steamship travel and clothes.

It was quite clear to Gregory that General Kuporovitch was not an ordinary Bolshevik leader who had started his life as one of the ignorant Russian masses, but a man of considerable culture who was rusty on his subjects only because he had so little opportunity to talk of them, and when they were half-way through the second bottle of *sleivowitz* the General's story began to emerge.

He was not an aristocrat of sufficient prominence for his name alone to have brought disaster on him in the Revolution, but he came of a good family and had been a captain, aged twenty-nine, in a cavalry regiment when the Revolution had broken out. As he said: "All thinking Russians were atheists and Liberals in those days. We knew that the monarchy was rotten and it disgusted us to think that the Little Father, weak fool that he was, should allow himself to be made a dupe by that dirty villainous priest, Rasputin. We officers who had to fight the war had plenty of evidence of the corruption that was rife in high places. The soles of the boots issued to our men were made of paper. They were sent to the front with only one rifle between three men and there was never enough ammunition for the guns. The country was long overdue for a proper clean-up; so when the Social Democrat Revolution took place, and the Tsar was forced to abdicate, we officers hailed the news with every bit as much joy as our men.

"When the Bolsheviks seized power, six months later, that meant very little to us down on the lower Volga until a movement started among the men to shoot all their officers. But we had been fighting the Turks most of the time and I had had the luck to save the life of one of my sergeants—a chap called Budenny."

"*The* Budenny?" Gregory asked with interest.

"That's it. All the world knows him as Marshal Budenny to-day; but *then* he was just Sergeant Budenny, of the Dragoons;

a great strapping fellow with a moustache like a couple of horses' tails. He protected me when some of the others wanted to put me up against a brick wall.

"Someone—God knows who—ordered us away from the front and we went to Tsaritsyn—they call it Stalingrad now. They would have shot me if I'd tried to leave them, so I went with my regiment. A few weeks later Voroshilov arrived there after his amazing retreat from the Ukraine and was elected to defend the town. It was Voroshilov who picked Budenny out of the rut and Budenny took me with him. Horses were his speciality and he hadn't got much of a brain—but enough to know that my military education would be useful.

"Tsaritsyn was right at the apex of the triangle held by the Bolsheviks. They called it the Salient of Death, you know—the Red Verdun. The odds against us were tremendous; but if the Reds hadn't managed to hang on there the grain barges would no longer have been able to get up the Volga. Moscow would have starved and the Revolution would have collapsed. By the time I had been fighting there for a few weeks it became a matter of professional honour to me and lots of other regular soldiers who were with the Reds that the town should not be allowed to fall. I don't think we cared much whom we were fighting, but by the time it was all over I was looked on as a dyed-in the-wool Bolshevik."

"Queer, the tricks Fate plays with men, isn't it?" Gregory commented.

Kuporovitch refilled the glasses; his hand was steady as a rock but his voice had begun to slur just a trifle as he went on:

"Yes. Fate served me well, though, to put me where it did. I'd probably have done the same if I'd been with the Army commanded by Tukachevsky—been made a Red General afterwards too—but I'd be dead by now. As it was, I was a Voroshilov man and no soldier ever served under a finer leader. He was just a mechanic—never handled a rifle until the Revolution broke out; but he held Tsaritsyn for six months against all comers. He wasn't afraid of God or the Devil. He even told War Lord Trotsky to go to hell when Trotsky wanted to relieve him of his command because he wasn't a professional soldier." The General leaned forward and banged the table. "D'you know what Clim Voroshilov said to Trotsky?"

"No," said Gregory.

"I'll tell you," said the General a little thickly. "Trotsky threatened to arrest him for insubordination, so Clim turned round and said: *'You* arrest *me,* a Russian working man, one of the oldest members of the Bolshevik Party and an active revolutionary of twenty years' standing? You—who only sneaked back from Canada after the Revolution was all over to join the Party six months ago? Get to hell out of here—you dirty, snivelling Jew journalist, or I'll throw you out—and you can tell Lenin what I said!' "

"Good for him!" laughed Gregory. "Of course, Tukachevsky was Trotsky's pet, wasn't he, while Voroshilov was backed by Stalin; who wasn't such a big noise in those days?"

Kuporovitch paused with the bottle in his hand and replied in a lowered voice: "It's all right to mention Stalin here—these old walls have no dictaphones—but wiser not to talk about him where you're liable to be overheard. He was with us down at Tsaritsyn, as Clim's Political Commissar. Clim's a decent sort and never soiled his hands with murder; but the other one—well, sometimes I think he's the Fiend in person."

Gregory nodded. "He must have bumped off a good few people in his time."

"You'd never believe what's been going on these last three years." The General raised his eyebrows to heaven. "It started with the Tukachevsky *Putsch* in 1937. They executed him and eight other leading Generals; then the Ogpu began to trace the ramifications of the whole conspiracy. Thirty Army Corps commanders disappeared and hundreds of other Generals—yes, *hundreds* I said. Staff after staff was wiped out. They did the same thing in the Navy and the Air Force. There was hardly an officer over the rank of Captain left in the Soviet Army. That's the inside story of this colossal mess they've made in Finland. Fellows commanding the battalions there have been jumped up from platoon leaders. Not one out of ten of the staff officers has ever seen the inside of a military college for as much as a month's course. At a rough estimate—judged by the divisions I know about—Koba Stalin must have executed between 30,000 and 40,000 senior officers in the last two and a half years."

Gregory had heard the same tale of wholesale murder from a very different source but he forebore to comment and asked:

"How did you manage to escape?"

The General laughed, a little drunkenly. "Because I'm an old friend of Clim's. After Tsaritsyn I was with him when we formed the First Cavalry Army, which took Rostov, and I was with him all through the Polish campaign. *Sacré nom,* those were the days! We thought we were going to Paris! Luckily

336

for me, Clim Voroshilov doesn't forget his old friends. All the same, they won't trust me with a command and I have to put up with a damned Political Commissar who pries into everything I do. Thank God his wife's ill, so he's down in the town to-night, otherwise I'd never risk talking to you like this; but it's the first chance that I've had for years to talk to anyone intelligent without fear of being reported."

"I'm very flattered, General," Gregory smiled, "but don't you think it's a risk to talk to me? Say I repeated what you've said?"

The Russian's lazy blue eyes narrowed. "There's no fear of that. In the first place, you're one of my own kind, so you wouldn't let me down. In the second, if you *did* nobody would believe you. I haven't kept my head on my shoulders for all these years without learning a thing or two. I'm so pro-Stalin that the Pope of Rome is a heathen by comparison and although old Oggie—that's my Political Commissar—is a nuisance, he's more frightened of me than I am of him."

"That's the spirit!" Gregory laughed, filling up the glasses yet again. "But since we're being frank, don't you get damned sick of it? I shouldn't think it's much fun being a Soviet General and always having to mind your p's and q's."

"Fun!" The General waved an arm. "It's a godforsaken life and this is a godforsaken country. There's *nothing* here— *nothing*, d'you understand?—which could appeal to any civilized human being. It's drab, dreary, poverty-stricken, and it gets worse instead of better with every year that passes. What wouldn't I give to see Paris again?"

"You used to go there as a young man?"

"Mon Dieu, yes! Every year. And what a place it was in those days! Girls—scores of them—real girls—in silk and feathers—not animals, which are all we have left here. Beautiful women—exquisitely gowned and perfumed. Did you know Paris in those days? But no; you're not old enough."

"I'm old enough to remember the original Moulin Rouge," Gregory smiled.

"Ah; the Moulin Rouge—and the Abbaye Thélème; where the girls danced on the tables without any drawers and we drank champagne out of their slippers."

"That's it. And the Rat Mort—and the Café de l'Enfer."

"And the Bal Tabarin. What nights I had in those places! But it wasn't only that. There's something about Paris. The flower-women outside the Madeleine. Lobster washed down

337

with that fresh *pétillant* Touraine wine for lunch at Pruniers, the paintings in the Louvre, taking one's *apéritif* on the pavement outside the Taverne Wagner, the bookshops in the arcade of the Palais Royal, the Sacré Cœur by moonlight, the Latin Quarter, the students in the Luxembourg Gardens, and . . . and the trees, when they're just budding in the Bois. Yes, that's it! Paris in the springtime—Paris in May. Shall I tell you something?" The grey-haired but still immensely virile-looking Russian leaned forward suddenly. "I'm damned well going there again before I die."

"You'll find it pretty difficult to get out of Russia, won't you?'

"Oh, it *can* be done. Quite a lot of people manage to get themselves appointed to Soviet Embassies abroad, and once they're out of this lousy country they never come back."

"Doesn't the Kremlin usually hold the wife and children of people sent abroad, as hostages?"

"Ah! But I'm all right there. I haven't got any wife or children."

"In that case, they'd never attach you to an Embassy."

"Perhaps not. But I might manage to slip over the frontier one dark night."

"In that case, what's kept you here so long?"

"Valuta—foreign exchange—my boy. I'd rather teach Russian in Paris than be a General here; but I've got to have the money for the journey and I want to take a good-sized nest egg so that I don't starve in my old age. I've been saving up and secreting foreign currency for years. I should think another twelve months ought to do it."

Gregory glanced at the clock. It was half-past three and they were attacking the third bottle of *slievowitz*. He was a little tight himself now but he could drink most people under the table and for some time past plans had been forming again in his agile brain. "I suppose," he said casually, "if you fail to get any information about us from your Military Intelligence people you'll send my friends and myself under escort to the German Embassy in Moscow?"

"That's it," the General nodded.

"Well, to be honest with you, that wouldn't suit our book at all."

"Why?" asked the Russian suspiciously, and he suddenly seemed to become quite sober again.

"Because I and my friends are not very popular with the

Gestapo—that's why we arranged to get ourselves given special work in Finland. 'Out of sight, out of mind', you know; and since we've failed to do the job we were given, we're going to be even more unpopular when we get home."

"Will they shoot you?" asked Kuporovitch with interest.

"I don't think they'll go as far as that; but we'd much rather remain out of Germany until the war's over. I suppose—as between friends—you couldn't fix it for us to be sent to some neutral country, like Estonia, for example?"

The General raised his dark, pencilled eyebrows which contrasted so strangely with his grey hair. "*Sacré Tonnerre*, no! Oggie will be back to-morrow morning. I call him that because he's a member of the Ogpu. When he arrives he'll want to know all about you. If I failed to put in a report to the proper quarter afterwards it would probably cost me my life."

"In that case, what about letting us go to-night?"

"Help yourself to some more *slievowitz*, my friend, and try to talk sense. Those two crétins who serve me as orderlies will report to Oggie that you all dined with me this evening; so I've got to produce either the four of you or your bodies, haven't I? Otherwise, what would Oggie say?"

"I see," said Gregory thoughtfully. "Still, if it could be arranged, may I take it that you would have no personal objection to our leaving Kandalaksha?"

"None at all. None whatever, now I know that you're not spies," the General said suddenly.

"How d'you know?" Gregory asked with quick curiosity.

"Because of what you just told me. And, anyhow, there's nothing worth spying on up in the Arctic, since Petsamo fell. You and your friends are just a party of Germans who managed to get out of Germany and want to keep out of it because the Gestapo's after you."

Gregory grinned. "You've hit it, General. Now, how are we going to work this thing? If you can't get us out of Russia into a neutral country, and you must report us if you keep us here, who *could* get us out of the country?"

"Stalin could, if he wanted to—or Molotov or Krassin or Voroshilov; but I don't see why they should, do you?"

"If only I could get to one of them I believe I'd manage to persuade him to, all right."

"Well, you can't, so I'm afraid that's the end of it," said the General thickly.

"Saying I could," Gregory persisted, "which of them d'you think would be likely to prove the most reasonable?"

"Oh Clim—Clim Voroshilov every time. He may be a red-hot Communist but he's not like these mealy-mouthed politicians. He wanted a fair deal—a fair deal for all; but he's not like the other fellows—he's human; used to like his drink and a pretty girl when he was younger. *Nom d'un nom!* The scandal there was after one of our victories at Tsaritsyn, when Clim and all his staff drove through the streets as drunk as hell with a whole lot of girls and danced the *trepka* in a restaurant. All the seedy intellectuals in Moscow said we were a disgrace to the Party but Clim didn't care. Their bally revolution would have gone to blazes if he hadn't held Tsaritsyn. D'you know what we called him? The Organizer of Victories. *Mon Dieu! What* a man! Did I ever tell you how he threw the Chief of the Leningrad Ogpu down his own stairs?"

"No," said Gregory.

"Well, he did. Found out that the fellow had bribed one of his mistresses to spy on him. Anyone else would have had ten fits—but not Clim. He walked straight round into that den of assassins and beat the fellow up with his bare fists. God! It makes me cold to think of it. There isn't another man in Russia who would have dared to do that. Have some more *slievowitz.*"

"Then, if I could get to Voroshilov he might be sympathetic when he hears that the Gestapo are after myself and my friends?"

"He might; but he won't; because you can't get to him. No-one has ever escaped out of this old castle since I've been here. It's no good your trying; and in this country a man is either above suspicion or else he's dead. I haven't managed to keep alive among these blackguards for twenty-three years by taking any chances, so don't imagine that because I'm a bit tight I'm taking any now. If I let you go Oggie would be on the war-path to-morrow and I might receive an invitation to Moscow. Then I'd never get to Paris again before I die."

The General was certainly tight—very tight indeed—but Gregory knew the type of man with whom he was dealing too well to set any great hopes on that. The Russian was one of the old school who could take any amount of liquor and might show it by a slight slurring of his speech but would keep all his mental faculties about him until he suddenly passed out. The fact that he had managed to keep alive so long, although he liked his liquor and loathed the Soviet régime, was ample evidence that he was an efficient officer and never made a serious slip. Since he said that it would be impossible for his prisoners to escape Gregory accepted that as a fact; but he felt that to-night was his one big chance. From to-morrow onwards the little "filth" referred to as Oggie would be snooping round and, in consequence, the General would have become ten times more difficult. If the all-important schedule for the Nazi "Family Reunion" was ever to reach London it must be got out of the castle that night.

Russians, Gregory knew, were notoriously open to graft and it had already occurred to him to try to bribe Kuporovitch; but he wondered desperately if he dared to risk it. The fact that the General had been collecting valuta for years with a view to shaking the dust of the Soviet off his feet would make him eager to acquire foreign currency that he could secure without risk of being reported. But if he were offered a large bribe he would know that his prisoner had had no opportunity to secrete the money since he had arrived at the castle; so he must be carrying it on him. Having played a lone hand successfully against murderers and bandits for so long it was heavy odds in favour of the General's being a most unscrupulous man. Once he learned that there was money to be had for the taking what was there to prevent him from having his prisoner shot and acquiring the cash without any risk to himself? Yet how else, except by taking this desperate chance, was there any hope of getting out of the castle?

Drawing a long breath Gregory said: "You were talking about valuta just now. If it could be arranged for me to try to reach Voroshilov I should want some Russian roubles. Make your own rate of exchange. I'm prepared to pay four times the normal value if you like—in German or Finnish marks—and I've got a big sum on me." He had played his ace, but for all he knew it might be the Ace of Spades—the death card.

341

CHAPTER XXVIII

GREGORY GAMBLES WITH DEATH

For a moment the Russian's face remained absolutely impassive, then he asked sharply: "How much have you got?"

"About six thousand five hundred marks."

"A nice sum." Kuporovitch's eyes narrowed and he stared at Gregory with a thoughtful expression on his face.

"Enough to keep you in moderate comfort in Paris for the best part of a year," Gregory said slowly.

The General did not reply. He stood up, walked to the door with a slightly unsteady gait and left the room without a word.

Gregory helped himself to another ration of *slievowitz*. He was pretty tight himself but he had a head like a rock and was a very long way from passing out. As he might be dead within the next quarter of an hour he didn't feel that it would make very much difference if he got slightly tighter; but he could not keep himself from wondering why the General had left him. The most likely answer to that all-important question was that he had gone down to the guard-room to fetch a couple of soldiers. These Russians were quite used to shooting people without a trial. It was all in the day's work to them and they would think nothing of it if they were told to take a prisoner down to the castle execution chamber in the middle of the night; then good-bye to Gregory Sallust.

'Well,' he thought, 'I haven't had a particularly short life and I have had an extremely gay one; and, after all, death *is* the greatest adventure upon which any man can set out!' He had been near death on too many occasions for the thought of it to worry him; but he *was* worried about Erika and the others. Those hectic nights that he had spent with her in Munich and Berlin had been very marvellous; but recently, since he had got his memory back, he had grown to feel a far deeper and more profound love for her. In his life he had known many women

342

and it seemed hard that now he had found the one whose presence gave him such utter satisfaction and contentment their ways should be parted after a few brief weeks of happiness and —worse—that he should have to leave her as a prisoner, menaced by the grim prospect of being handed over to the Gestapo, which he could do nothing to avert.

The door opened again and the General came in—alone. His gait was brisker and Gregory noticed that his hair was slightly damp. Evidently he had been to his room and poured a jug of cold water over his head to bring himself back to a complete state of sobriety before taking any decision. Such an act was typical of the man and Gregory did not yet allow himself to hope. It might be that the Russian wanted all his wits about him so as to trick his prisoner out of the money before he had him shot, in order that the execution squad should not see him take it from the body and report the fact to Oggie.

With a steady hand Kuporovitch collected the three empty *slievowitz* bottles from the small table, replaced them on the sideboard and said abruptly: "Say I give you a quarter of the value of your marks in roubles, what d'you wish me to do?"

Gregory breathed again. Although he might have soiled his hands in all sorts of dirty business for nearly a quarter of a century, the Russian was, at the rock-bottom, still the man of honour that he had been as a young officer in pre-Revolution days.

"Since your Political Commissar is bound to hear about us to-morrow," Gregory replied, "fix it so that it looks as if we had escaped during the night."

Kuporovitch shook his head. "Four of you—including two women? No. Oggie would never believe that. Besides, only a strong and resolute man could leave the castle, even with my aid, in a way which would enable me to avoid all suspicion of complicity. The best I can do is to arrange matters so that it appears that *you* have escaped. My record is so good that no-one will hold the escape of one prisoner against me; but your friends must remain and the report about them will have to go in to-morrow morning through the usual channels. If you can reach Voroshilov within a week or ten days and get an order for your friend's release, with permission for all of you to leave the country, you'll have cheated the Gestapo. If not, your friends must take their chance."

Gregory was thinking swiftly. Nothing would have induced him to desert his friends in ordinary circumstances but if he could get away himself it would at least offer him some chance to save them; and—above all—there was the typescript. That must be put before everything. He nodded slowly.

"In that case it's imperative that I should get to Voroshilov's headquarters at the earliest possible moment. I can't speak Russian and I may have difficulty with the railway people. Are you willing to throw in a railway voucher for my journey, faked in any name you like?"

"Yes, I'll do that." The General moved towards the door again.

"All right. That's a deal, and I'm eternally grateful to you."

Gregory removed his boots and took out all his bank-notes except five hundred German *Reichmarks*. The General was away about a quarter of an hour and when he returned he was carrying Gregory's furs as well as the railway voucher.

The money was changed and the voucher handed over. Kuporovitch said that he had made it out for a mythical Vassily Stetin and that it was signed by Imitroff, one of his clerks whose name he had forged; but as the man was in hospital even if the paper were ever traced the clerk could not be held responsible for its issue and it would be impossible to find out who had forged his signature.

Gregory drew on his furs and said: "I'll just go along and tell the others what I propose to do; so that they'll know what's happened to me and at least have something on which to pin their hopes during the coming week."

"Oh, no, you don't!" The Russian shook his head. "Oggie will question them all to-morrow and I'm not going to risk their giving anything away. They mustn't know that I've had any hand in this, or even that you've escaped until they learn it for themselves. That's why I collected your furs from your room on my way back from the office."

It was a bitter blow to Gregory that he had to leave without even being able to say good-bye to Erika and the others but he saw the soundness of Kuporovitch's dictum.

"Very well," he said reluctantly. "I'd better get off, then. But I shall want the Russian for 'railway-station', in case I get lost in the town, and the name of the place at which I'm most likely to find Voroshilov."

"'Railway-station' is *Vogzal Borzair*," replied the General, and went on: "The Supreme Command is at Nykyrka, in captured Finnish territory, on the south of the Isthmus. Would you like one for the road?"

"Thanks." Gregory nodded, so they moved over to the sideboard to empty the remains of a bottle of vodka into glasses.

"Good luck, *mon cher Baron*!" The Soviet General winked.

"Good luck—and a thousand thanks, Comrade General," the impostor Nazi Colonel smiled back, and they emptied the glasses.

Outside on the landing it seemed that the whole of the ancient castle was sunk in grim, foreboding silence. No sentries were about and although they trod as softly as they could their footfalls echoed on the stone steps of the grand staircase. Down on the ground-floor the General turned along a narrow passage. At its end he produced a large bunch of keys, shone a torch and unlocked a door; then they tiptoed down two more long, chill corridors till they reached a heavy postern. The bolts creaked a little as they drew them back, but no other sound disturbed the stillness. Kuporovitch unlocked the door with another large key and swung it open as he put out his torch; the cold, night air struck their faces.

As Gregory stepped out into the snow the Russian said: "Keep along this wall as far as the corner then turn left for a hundred paces; that will take you past the sentry. Ahead of you, you will find a shed that is used as a wood store. If you get on to its roof you'll be able to climb to the top of the outer wall of the castle. It's a nasty drop—about twenty feet—but the snow will break your fall. Go straight ahead again and youll reach the nearest buildings of the town."

Gregory gripped his hand and slipped away into the darkness. He was free again; but he had only seven days—or ten at the most—to save his friends from being sent back into Nazi Germany to face a Gestapo execution squad.

It was nearly five o'clock in the morning so the moon had set and he was almost invisible against the blackness of the castle. Gaining the corner he paused for a moment to peer ahead in case the sentry was patrolling there; but he could detect no trace of movement in the shadows so turned left and crossed the open space. The store of wood had overflowed and at one side of the shed was a great heap of logs which made an easy way up to its roof; but as he scrambled up the pile some of the loosely-stacked logs rumbled down under his feet. Fearing that the noise, which sounded like hammer-blows in the silence, might attract the attention of the sentry he crouched on the roof's edge for a moment holding his breath.

Nothing stirred so he pulled himself up to the apex of the

345

roof and, by balancing himself upon it, found that he was just
able to grasp the edge of the castle wall. With a heave he
wriggled up on to its broad surface and lay there, flat, so that
even in the dim light his silhouette would not be conspicuous
against the fainter darkness of the sky-line. The next stage was
a tricky one, as twenty feet is a nasty height from which to have
to drop. Had there been no snow on the ground he would have
had to risk injuring himself seriously and, even as it was, he
feared that if he let himself drop feet-first he might break a leg,
which would put an inglorious finish to his enterprise. But
Gregory was an old escaper and knew a trick or two. Wrapping
his arms round his head to protect his face he just rolled off the
wall. The act required much more courage than jumping but
it distributed his weight over a greater surface. He struck the
snow full-length and suffered no ill effects apart from a hard
jolt as his body buried itself in the soft cushion of whiteness.

Picking himself up he went forward until some buildings
loomed in his path and, skirting round the nearest, entered a
narrow street, down which he proceeded at a rapid pace, to keep
his circulation going. The houses were all shuttered and silent,
the infrequent street-lights dim and the road deserted.

He had a vague idea that Kandalaksha was at the head of a
gulf running westwards from the White Sea. From what he had
seen the previous evening it was quite a small place and dreary
in the extreme. There were a certain number of brick and stone
buildings in the centre of the town but most of the houses were
made of wood. There were no tramways or buses. But the
important thing was that it lay on the Murmansk-Leningrad
railway. Five minutes' walk downhill brought him to the little
square and, turning left out of it, he reached the railway-station
ten minutes later.

In peace-time it would certainly have been shut at this hour
as it is doubtful if more than one train each way passed through
it per day, but the war had caused a big increase in traffic. The
line was Russia's only link with her northern forces operating
round Petsamo and trains were coming through at all sorts of
odd hours, so the station was open day and night. Marching into
the booking-hall he handed his railway warrant to an official
who, after examining it, said something to him in Russian.

Gregory tapped his lips and ears and shrugged his shoulders,
conveying that he had the misfortune to be a deaf-mute. He
then pointed to himself, to the voucher and to the door on to
the platform; upon which the official nodded kindly and indi-

cated by signs that Gregory should go into the waiting-room and that he would fetch him when the next train for Leningrad came in.

The waiting-room was incredibly stuffy and already full of people. Most of them were soldiers but there were a certain number of peasants and townsfolk who had evidently gathered there not knowing when the next train was likely to come in and, for fear of missing it, had parked themselves at the station for the night. All the benches were occupied, and a good portion of the floor, where dirty, smelly people lay sprawled, looking extremely repulsive in their sleep. Gregory found a corner and, as he had not slept for nearly twenty-four hours, dropped off almost as soon as he had stretched himself out.

When he awoke daylight was filtering through the grimy window, so picking himself up he left the waiting-room to see if he could find some breakfast. There was a small buffet on the other side of the booking-hall and after doing his deaf-mute act again he secured a huge doorstep sandwich, which contained some sort of sausage between the thick layers of greyish bread, and a steaming cup of substitute coffee. As he had had a good dinner the night before he did not want the sandwich and forced himself to eat it only because he did not know when he would be able to feed again; but the boiling-hot coffee substitute was extremely welcome, since the amount of vodka, Caucasian champagne and *slievowitz* that he had had to drink the night before had given him a most frightful hangover and he felt like death. While paying for his snack he also bought some biscuits rather like stale sponge-cakes—which were the only kind available—and a packet of chocolate that cost him about ten times as much as it would have done in England.

He then showed himself to the official again so that the man should not forget about him and went back to the waiting-room to nurse his splitting head. The fug and smell there were quite revolting but it was the only warm place available. A sharp wind was coming up the frozen gulf across the harbour, which lay on the far side of the station, and the cold outside was bitter.

Two trains going north rolled in during the morning and both waited in the station for the best part of an hour before proceeding further, while the troops with which they were packed got out to stretch their legs and crowd the little buffet. Gregory's awful state, the pain behind his eyes and the evil taste in his mouth to some extent took his mind off his impatience to get started on his journey; which was just as well, since it was

347

nearly midday when the official came to fetch him. Many of the other people in the waiting-room went out on to the platform with them and a long train slowly chugged its way in.

Only one coach was allocated to the civilian passengers so there was a free fight among them for seats and many had to stand in the corridor, although some of them were proceeding upon journeys which would occupy a day and a night—or more. As Gregory had a military voucher he was able to get in with the soldiers. No sleepers were available but he considered himself lucky to secure a corner seat in one of the roomy carriages, which, owing to the broader gauge of the Russian railroads, were much larger than those on the railways in Western Europe. An hour passed before the train started and when it did it chugged out in such a hesitant manner that it seemed as though the driver had really not made up his mind if he intended to take it any further.

Gregory's companions were a mixed lot. A few of them had pleasant, open faces but the majority were almost brutish types and obviously conscripted from among the totally uneducated land-workers. They did not seem unhappy and apparently the simplest witticism could raise a laugh among them. It soon transpired that Gregory was deaf and dumb; a fact that provided matter for some crude fun, as he could judge from the way they looked at him. But it was not meant unkindly and after a few minutes they soon left him to himself, which was all that he desired.

The early coming of night soon shut out the dreary, snow-covered landscape. The train rumbled on, its top speed being not more than thirty miles an hour, and it halted from time to time for periods of from twenty minutes to an hour and a half without any apparent reason. Gregory made a snack meal with the soldiers, who exchanged some of their iron rations for a part of his biscuits and chocolate, then he dozed for a good portion of the night.

Twice during the following day the train stopped at stations where they were able to get hot soup or the substitute coffee and other food from buffets in addition to the meagre rations issued to the troops; and as Gregory had enough money to stand treat he became extremely popular with his companions. Since he had now slept as much as he was able the second night proved much worse than the first, particularly as he was intolerably tired of sitting in one position hour after hour in the crowded, smelly carriage; but early next morning the train at last steamed into Leningrad. It had taken him forty-two hours to accomplish the seven-hundred-and-fifty-mile journey which, including the many halts, worked out at an average speed of eighteen miles per hour. Although it had proved a dreary and wearisome experience he felt that that was not at all bad going for a Russian train and that the railway people probably considered they were doing wonders to help on the Soviet war effort.

Gregory could not read the signs on the platform but he had no doubt at all that it was Leningrad since the station was a great terminus with a dozen or more platforms, where everyone left the train. Having arrived there he felt considerably easier in his mind. Britain was not at war with the Soviet Union so for an hour or two he could reassume his own identity without fear of running into immediate trouble. It is true that he had no Soviet visa on the British passport which had been faked for him by the German Foreign Office, but he did not propose to try to cross any frontiers for the time being so there was no purpose for which he was likely to be called upon to produce it.

He was just one inconspicuous person among two or three million who thronged the streets of the capital of the old Russian empire. Every other person that he could see was clad in some sort of fur—lamb, goat, seal, pony or rabbit—so there was nothing in his appearance to mark him as a foreigner and, as he was both extremely dirty and still wearing a beard, he did not look the least like an Englishman who normally wore clothes cut in Savile Row.

His first job was to find the British Consulate but he was much too wary to make his inquiries at the Intourist Bureau in the station, which was there for the convenience of foreign travellers. Instead he walked straight out of the station and along a broad boulevard.

It was only just after six o'clock in the morning so the streets were still dark, but there were plenty of people moving in them. Gregory waited for a few moments under a big lamp-standard, watching the passing crowd, until he saw a man who was better-dressed than the rest coming along. He then tackled him in French, German and English. The man did not understand any of these languages, so this first attempt was a failure, but at his third trial a tall young man in a smart black-leather jerkin responded with a cheerful smile and answered him in halting German. Gregory explained what he wanted. The young man did not know the whereabouts of the British Consulate but he led Gregory down the street to a rank which contained three

349

ancient taxis and, after a voluble discussion in which all the drivers took part, he was put in the leading vehicle and driven away.

He knew quite well that, as a British Secret Agent, he had no right whatever to involve the Consul in his affairs but, strictly speaking, he was no longer a British Secret Agent. His original mission had been given him through an unofficial channel and he had completed it early in November, so for the best part of three months he had been off the record. That was to some extent begging the question, but as he could not speak Russian and did not know a soul in Leningrad he felt that he had a very adequate excuse for going to the Consul.

The taxi pulled up in front of an old, stone-faced building in the Krasnaya Ulitza. Gregory got out and, displaying some loose change in the palm of his hand, trusted to the honesty of the cabman to take the fare due.

A Russian dvornik who was standing at the door eyed Gregory suspiciously as he entered the building and went up-stairs to the first-floor flat in which the Consulate was situated. His ring at the door was answered by a Russian maid, who smiled brightly at him but informed him in hesitant English that the Consul did not live there and the Vice-Consul, Mr. Hills, was not yet up.

On Gregory's asking if he could write a note she led him across a small hall straight into an office, where he scribbled a few lines which ran:

"In return for breakfast this morning I can only offer you lunch at Boodle's on some future date, but as I have a train to catch we must do our business over the eggs and bacon."

This cryptic message gave nothing away but it conveyed two facts. One, that the writer had urgent business to transact. Two, that as he was a member of one of London's most exclusive clubs he was a person of some standing and therefore his business was presumably of importance.

A few minutes later the maid returned and led him along to a sitting-room, where a tall, beaky-nosed, fair-haired man was standing in a dressing-gown. He had evidently only just got out of bed and he regarded his dirty, bearded visitor with a by no means friendly eye; but Gregory apologized with his most charming smile for having got him up so early and without waiting for an invitation to do so began to remove his furs.

350

"In the ordinary way I should have sent the girl to tell you to wait until the office opens," Mr. Hills confessed, "but, quite frankly, your note intrigued me. One doesn't often receive an invitation to lunch at Boodle's in this godforsaken city. Not that I am likely to be able to accept it until the war is over, but it was a clever way of making me curious to find out what you want at once."

"As you've probably guessed," Gregory said, "I'm a British Agent."

Hills frowned. "Then you know quite well that you ought not to be here."

"Dont worry. I'm not being hunted by the Ogpu—at least, not for the moment—and I don't want you to hide me, or anything of that kind, but I had to come to you because several people's lives are hanging on my time and I can't afford to waste a moment. I want to get rid of this beard and I'd be immensely grateful for a bath. Will you be a good chap and save me a precious half-hour by listening to my story while I'm shaving and tidying up?"

"Well if it's as urgent as all that . . ." Hills smiled, and leading Gregory to the bathroom he produced clean towels, scissors and a razor.

As Gregory went to work to make himself a little more presentable he gave the Vice-Consul an outline of his doings in the last few months, then he passed him the pencilled translation of the typescript that had come out of Goering's safe.

"Amazing!" muttered the beaky-nosed Vice-Consul when he had finished reading. "And you're quite right about this thing. It proves up to the hilt just what so many of us have been afraid of. Germany never meant to fight over Czechoslovakia or Poland but, if she had to, her game was to make the war as short as possible, and localize the conflict; get a negotiated peace as soon as she could, then gobble up another slice of Europe a few months later."

"That's it," Gregory agreed, "and the devil of it is, the plan still holds. There's a strong party among the Nazi leaders who're for changing it now that a major war is actually on. They want to overrun Belgium and Holland in order to have a slap at Britain, or to go down into Rumania and collar the oil; but the really clever boys are for keeping a stalemate going and their Army and Air Force virtually intact. Goering himself told me that and, although he didn't say it, there's no doubt now that he's hoping that Britain and France will get bored with the war

351

and worried by its financial strain; so that through the mediation of Roosevelt or Mussolini they'll agree to a round-table
conference. Hitler will just give way a little bit but hang on to
most of what he's got and after a nice breather be all ready to
jump a new and bigger claim this time next year."

"Well, what d'you want me to do?" Hills asked.

"As time is such a vital factor and I can't speak Russian
there are several ways in which you can help me," Gregory
replied and, over breakfast, he went into details.

When they had finished the meal they went into Hills' office
and Gregory sat down to a typewriter on which he drafted a
letter in German. It was headed: "Karinhall, 27.11.39,"
addressed to Marshal Voroshilov, Commissar for Defence of the
Union of Soviet Socialist Republics, and ran:

"My dear Marshal,

*"This is to introduce to you Colonel-Baron von Lutz.
The Colonel-Baron is not a member of the Nazi Party and
unfortunately some of his criticisms have given great offence to
certain of our Party Chiefs, particularly Herr Himmler. The
affair will, I hope, blow over in due course but it is most
desirable that the Colonel-Baron and three friends of his should
leave Germany for a time.*

*"As he is an old war comrade of mine, and a very dear
personal friend, I should naturally afford him my protection;
since there is no question at all of his being a traitor to the
Fatherland; but I do not wish to enter into a quarrel with my
colleagues if this can be avoided.*

*"He is a most able officer so it occurred to me to send him
to you as he may prove of assistance should the Finns maintain
their resistance to the Soviet demands and it becomes necessary
to launch a campaign against them.*

*"If you would receive him kindly and enable him to arrange
accommodation in the Soviet Union for the other members of
his party, which includes two ladies—or, if they wish, give them
facilities to travel to one of the Scandinavian States—I should
consider it a personal kindness.*

*"Heartfelt greetings and, in the event of a campaign, all
success to your Arms."*

Having addressed an envelope for the letter Gregory took
from his pocket Goering's original letter of introduction to
Wuolijoki.

With great care he proceeded to trace the signature, Hermann Goering, in pencil, again and again upon a thin sheet of paper. Then taking a pen he wrote over each signature until, after a hundred or more trials, he was satisfied that he could do this with a bold, flowing hand. He next traced one more signature on a clean piece of paper, blacked its back with his pencil and, writing over the name, got a faint rubbing of it at the bottom of the letter. When he had inked this in it would have taken an expert in caligraphy to tell that it was a forgery.

Having completed his preparations he asked Hills to accompany him to the station for Helsinki, as the line to Finland now terminated at the Russian rail-head on the Karelian Isthmus, and the Vice-Consul would be able to inquire about trains for him and see him off. It was still only nine o'clock in the morning when they left the house and Gregory, bathed and clean-shaven once more, felt that in the last two and a half hours he had accomplished some most satisfactory work.

They visited several shops, in which Hills purchased a fibre suitcase, shaving-tackle and other necessities for Gregory, then proceeded to the station, where no difficulties arose. Gregory's railway warrant was made out to carry him to the Soviet G.H.Q. and as the Karelian Isthmus was the major front of the war, which was raging less than seventy miles away, trains were leaving for it with troops or supplies every half-hour. After seeing Gregory into his carriage and having received his heartiest thanks Hills departed. Ten minutes later, just as day was breaking, the train moved out.

For the first few miles there was little of interest to be seen; the creeks around which Leningrad is built were frozen over and once they had left the city behind the panorama was the same snow-covered landscape that Gregory had known for many days, except that it was broken by many more buildings. The train travelled no faster than the one on which he had come south from Kandalaksha and it halted just as frequently; but after an hour it reached the pre-war Russo-Finnish frontier and half an hour later entered the southern part of the Mannerheim Line from which the Finns had been forced back.

Here, in spite of the snow, there were many evidences of the war that had swept over the land a month or more earlier. Broken-down lorries and limbers lay abandoned at the roadside; here and there a now silent gun still reared its muzzle to the sky out of a concrete emplacement that had been battered to pieces. Every village through which they passed, and every

353

building, not only bore the marks of shell-fire but in most cases had been blasted to the ground by the terrific pounding of the Russian bombardments. In many places tangled heaps of barbed wire straggled up out of the snow, sometimes with a frozen corpse still hanging on them like a scarecrow. As the train puffed on there was more and more evidence of the frightful carnage which had taken place as the Russians had hurled division after division against the Finnish lines. By one o'clock Gregory could hear the distant booming of the guns and at a little before two the train halted in a siding. All the troops got out and Gregory saw from the many trains collected there that they had reached rail-head.

The notice-boards were all lettered in Russian, so he had to ask his way to the Railway Transport Officers' quarters, but he found an officer who could speak German; a tall, fair-faced fellow who obligingly took him along to a block of hutments which housed the R.T.O.

Having explained that he was a German officer who had to report to Marshal Voroshilov he was told that the Marshal had gone forward to Battle Headquarters as he had now taken over the direction of operations in person; but after a short wait Gregory was led out to a car which was taking two other officers up there.

The road was a solid jam of troops moving up and down—lorries, tanks, guns, infantry, ambulances, motor-cycles and horse-drawn vehicles—so, even in the car, they made slow going. One of Gregory's companions spoke a little English but not enough to carry on an intelligent conversation and, after smiling an exchange of greetings, Gregory contented himself with watching the thousand activities that were going forward in the wintry scene.

Soon they had reached the area where the Russian heavies were shelling the Finnish positions ten miles or more away. These monster guns were mostly on railway-sidings to which lines had been specially run for them from rail-head. Their blast was terrific and where the sidings were near the road each round nearly shattered the ear-drums. Flights of great black bombers were roaring overhead as they came up from their bases at Leningrad and Kronstadt to pass over the Finnish line. They saw no Finnish planes and Gregory guessed that owing to their smaller numbers they were having all their work cut out to protect the Finnish towns so were unable to spare aircraft for bombing the Russian back areas.

By three o'clock the road was winding through an area of big, irregular mounds covered with snow, out of which stuck jagged bits of brick wall and occasionally a twisted steel girder. The officer who spoke a little English told Gregory that it was the Finnish town of Nykyrka which had been virtually obliterated by the Russian guns before its capture. Soon afterwards the car left the road and going down a side-track of sleepers which had been laid across the snow, entered a wood. Among the trees there were many lines of hutments and the car drew up before one of these, from which officers and orderlies were constantly coming and going. Gregory's English-speaking companion took him past a sentry and secured him admission to an office where a big, shaven-headed man with a fierce moustache was seated behind a table.

Gregory introduced himself and stated his business, upon which the Russian replied in German:

"As you can imagine, the Marshal is extremely busy. If you will give me the letter I will see that it reaches him."

Presenting the letter, Gregory said: "I should be delighted for you to read it, but I would prefer to hand it to the Marshal in person."

The Russian glanced through it and shrugged as he handed it back. "As you wish, *Herr Oberst-Baron*, but I doubt if the Marshal will be able to see you until next week."

Gregory's throat muscles tightened. He had left Kandalaksha on the morning of Saturday, February the 24th, and it was now Monday afternoon. He had made the journey in just over two days, which was remarkably good considering conditions in Russia in the winter; but he could only count upon his friends remaining out of danger for seven days from the time he had started. After the coming Saturday orders might at any moment reach Kandalaksha for them to be sent under guard to Moscow and the beginning of the following week would be the absolute deadline.

"Surely you can arrange for me to see the Marshal before then?" he said quickly. "I am anxious about those friends of mine who are mentioned in the letter and it is a matter of great urgency."

The Russian shrugged again. "At the moment the greatest offensive of the war is just opening; the battle for Viborg. So for some days, at least, the Marshal will be much too occupied to give time to other people's personal affairs. In the meantime you had better be attached to the German Military Mission which we have here. Even if you are in bad odour with some members of your Government your personal introduction from Marshal Goering will be a recommendation to your brother-officers. General von Geisenheim is the head of the Mission. I will send an orderly with you to his quarters. Report to him and he will arrange for accommodation to be provided for you."

There was nothing that Gregory could do but thank the officer and accompany the orderly, through the twilight that was now gathering in the woodland camp, to another block of hut-ments a quarter of a mile distant; where, after waiting for ten minutes in an ante-room, he was shown in to the German General.

Knowing that ninety per cent. of the German army officers detested Himmler and admired Goering, he had little trepidation about producing his forged letter. Having saluted smartly, he handed it over to the General with the words: "I have been told by the camp commandant to report to you, *Herr General*, and this letter will explain my presence here."

General von Geisenheim was a tall, thin, blue-eyed man with an aristocratic face and greying hair. He read the letter through carefully and replaced it on his desk. Quite casually he picked up his pistol holster from a near-by chair, took the weapon out and waggled it at Gregory.

"This letter is all right," he said with a frosty smile. "I know Marshal Goering's signature well. But I should be interested to hear where you stole it, because *you*, my friend, are not Colonel-Baron von Lutz."

CHAPTER XXIX

THE BATTLE FOR VIBORG

T HE German Army can muster, with its reserves, some 5,000,000 men. Its officers, therefore—including both the active and retired lists with staffs and specialists—must number at least a quarter of a million, so it seemed incredibly bad luck to Gregory that out of 250,000 men he should have run into one of the few hundred—at most—whom the late Colonel-Baron should have known even as a passing acquaintance.

He had realized that he had to take that risk, as it was certain that a number of German officers would be attached to Voroshilov's headquarters, but he had not thought it sufficient for serious concern and he had taken up the imposture of the Colonel-Baron again simply because he had no choice in the matter. It was essential that he should be able to prove his identity to the Russians, if asked, by some other means that the letter and, while he had a perfectly valid passport issued by the German Foreign Office in the name of the Colonel-Baron, it was quite impossible for him to fake another.

"Come along!" snapped the General. "Who are you? And what game has led you to attempt this imposture?"

Gregory sighed. "It's a long story, *Herr General*, and of course you're quite right—I'm not von Lutz; although he was a friend of mine. I'm sorry to say that he died on the night of November the 26th, shot by the Gestapo on his estate in Brandenburg."

"I'm sorry to hear that, as he was also a friend of mine." Von Geisenheim frowned. "But if he died on November the 26th he couldn't possibly have passed this letter on to you himself, since it is dated November the 27th."

"That's right," Gregory said. "It was on that night I had the honour of dining with Field-Marshal Goering."

"How nice for you," the General smiled cynically. "Have you any other tall stories?"

"Plenty," said Gregory, "if you have time to listen to them."

"Unfortunately I have not. Quite obviously you are a spy, so you can tell them to the Gestapo. We have several Gestapo men with us here; they like us so much that they can't bear us to travel without them."

Gregory's brain was working like a dynamo. If von Geisenheim once handed him over to the Gestapo his number was up. But as he studied the lean features before him things were beginning to come back to him and he felt almost certain that he had seen the General's face before. Anyhow, he must chance it.

"There's one story that I could tell the Gestapo, *Herr General*," he said slowly, "but as one gentleman to another I think it would be only fair to let you hear it first. It starts at the Pleisen Palace out at Potsdam on the night of November the 8th."

"Eh, what's that?" The General sat forward suddenly.

"I was present at a great gathering of high German officers there and they were preparing to attend a little party that was to be held at the Hotel Adlon later in the evening. The entertainment was to consist of arresting the three hundred odd members of a dining club called the 'Sons of Siegfried', who were actually the Inner Gestapo, while *Herr* Hitler and his principal supporters were blown to pieces by a bomb in Munich. Are you too busy to hear any more?"

"That's quite enough!" said the General. "If you were at the Pleisen Palace I suppose you saw me there, or afterwards at the Adlon?"

The long shot had come off and at that moment there flashed into Gregory's mind the actual circumstances in which he had seen the General, so he replied: "I saw you shoot the very tall man, near the service entrance to the banqueting room, in the terrific gun-fight that followed von Pleisen's assassination. It would interest me a lot, though, to know how you managed to escape arrest afterwards?"

Von Geisenheim shrugged. "When the *Putsch* faded out most of the others changed into civilian clothes and tried to get out of the country. I didn't like the idea of being hunted like a hare or living concealed in an attic until the war was over, so the following day I went back to my office in the War Ministry just as though nothing had happened. Naturally, I expected to

358

be arrested and executed within an hour of my arrival; but evidently any Nazis who recognized me in that horrible mêlée must have been shot afterwards. Nobody's ever questioned me about the matter from that day to this, so it was a case of a supreme bluff coming off. But I thought I knew most of the officers who took part in the affair, at least by sight, and I don't remember your face. What is your real name and regiment?"

"I have no regiment," Gregory had to admit. But, loosening his furs, he took out the Iron Cross that had served him so well already, and added: "Yet General Count von Pleisen gave me this for the part I played. You will see his name engraved on the back of it."

Von Geisenheim looked at the inscription and handed the Cross back. Lowering his bright eyes he stared thoughtfully at the blotting-pad in front of him.

Gregory waited there in silence. Fate had given him a bad break in facing him with an officer who had known the real von Lutz but she had evened up the scales by making him one of the rebels who had participated in the anti-Nazi conspiracy, and so given Gregory a hold over him; but how slender and fragile that hold was Gregory knew only too well. He could almost see the thoughts racing through von Geisenheim's brain.

'This man is not one of my brother-officers. He may have stolen the Cross just as he stole the letter. He is a spy of some kind and damnably dangerous to me. I thought that I'd got away with murder, but I haven't—not quite. This fellow can denounce me to the Gestapo. They will arrest me on suspicion and send me back to Berlin. Inquiries will be made about my movements on the night of November the 8th. I shall not be able to account for them satisfactorily. That will be quite enough for Himmler. I shall find myself facing a firing-squad. How can I protect myself from that? The best way would be to shoot this impostor dead where he stands and simply say afterwards that he attacked me. A nasty business, but it's a case of his life or mine.'

"Herr General," Gregory broke in upon his thoughts, "I imagine that you're now considering the best way to eliminate me with as little trouble as possible before I have a chance to tell the Gestapo what I know; but I would ask you to remember that von Pleisen gave me this decoration because he considered that I, an Englishman . . ."

"An Englishman!" exclaimed the General. "Well, really! You speak remarkably good German."

359

"Thank you. As I was just saying, I was decorated because I had rendered a great service to all those who had the best interests of Germany at heart. In the past you also have served that cause. The time may come when both of us will have an opportunity to work for it again. Will you not, therefore, regard me as a friend—at least until you have heard what I have to say?"

"Very well. Sit down and tell me about yourself."

As Gregory pulled up a chair he was easier in his mind. He knew that if only he could convince the General that he had not the least intention of betraying him the German would observe his confidence as far as the Russians were concerned and even, perhaps, do much to help him; so he told the truth for once, but not the whole truth, and these were its limitations.

He recounted the failure of his attempt to get out of Germany with Freddie on the night of November the 8th, their meeting with the real von Lutz, their stay with him in Hans Foldar's cottage, the fight that had followed and the manner in which he and Freddie arrived at Karinhall. He cut the reason which had induced Goering to send him to Finland and said only that the Marshal had agreed to do so on compassionate grounds when—as was the fact—he had virtually signed his own death warrant by telling the truth about himself because he was so anxious to learn if Erika were dead or alive.

Von Geisenheim had been regarding Gregory with polite attention yet with a reserve which suggested that it was hardly reasonable to expect him to swallow this incredible story in its entirety. But when Erika's name was mentioned he suddenly laughed. "Come, come! This is too much. You can't honestly expect me to believe that you were having a love affair with the famous *Gräfin* von Osterberg—the most beautiful woman in Germany."

"I am still," Gregory replied seriously. "I left her only two nights ago up at Kandalaksha; you can check that up. And I'm proud to say that if only we can get out of this alive she has promised to divorce von Osterberg—who has never been anything to her but a friend—and marry me."

"*Donnerwetter!* You are lucky then, as well as brave. So the *Frau Gräfin* is here in Russia? Go on, now. This becomes much more interesting."

Gregory then told how he had found Erika in Finland, how his English pilot had run into his ex-fiancée and how the four of them had decided to fly to Sweden on the first day of the Russo-

Finnish War. He refrained from giving any account of their affair with Wuolijoki and Grauber, as to have done so would have necessitated his giving away the part that Goering had played in inducing the Finns to fight, but told how their aeroplane had been commandeered and that rather than remain in Helsinki they had flown with Captain Helijarvi to Petsamo. From that point he told the whole truth, except for suppressing his visit to the British Vice-Consul in Leningrad that morning.

When he had finished the General glanced at the letter again. "But this mentions the other members of your party, and it is addressed to Voroshilov. Why should Marshal Goering have given you such a document when he thought you were going to Finland?"

"Oh—that," Gregory laughed, "I forged it in a hotel in Leningrad only a few hours ago. The ink of the signature is hardly dry and that worried me rather. Somebody might have noticed that it's colour doesn't tally with the fact that it was supposed to have been written nearly three months ago."

"Umph! I missed that; but the signature appears to be genuine. How did you manage to fake it?"

"I was able to copy it from a letter Goering gave me to Erika; which she had fortunately kept and passed on to me before I left Kandalaksha."

"May I see it?"

Gregory shook his head. "I'm sorry; but I destroyed it after having forged the other; I thought it was too dangerous to carry it about any longer."

"It doesn't matter." Von Geisenheim shrugged. "The details of your story hang together too well for me to doubt you further. Now, what am I going to do about you?"

"Both of us are neutrals here and both of us have risked our lives to destroy the Nazi régime," Gregory said slowly, "so I think we should forget for the time being that our countries are at war. And, since you appear to know Erika, I very much hope that you will use all the influence you have to secure me an early interview with Voroshilov, in order that I can prevent her falling once more into the hands of the Gestapo, who are the common enemy of us all."

The General nodded. "I'll do what I can but don't count on that too much. It's the very devil to get these Russians to do anything. Voroshilov himself is a very able man but, as you doubtless know, they've massacred thousands of their best officers in the last two years and most of the present staff are hopelessly incompetent. The mess they have been making of their campaign is almost incredible. I and my colleagues were sent here to help them but they hardly ever consult us and generally ignore our advice on the rare occasions that they ask for it."

"How is the war really going?" Gregory asked. "I have heard little authentic news since it started."

"They thought it would be a walk-over and that the Finnish workers would greet them with open arms, so they made no proper preparations at all before launching their first attacks. In consequence, their only initial success was in the far north. On January the 1st the 163rd Soviet division was trapped and cut to pieces at Suomussalmi and a week later the 164th division was routed with heavy losses in the same area. On January the 10th the Finns won another major victory down here on the Isthmus, but at the end of January Voroshilov left Moscow to take command himself. The Finns managed to annihilate the Soviet 18th division at Kitella on February the 5th, but by the 7th Voroshilov had brought up some 200,000 fresh troops and nearly all of them were Budenny's famous shock battalions. Since then the attack has been continuous. The Finns have put up a wonderful resistance, but by mid-February they had to abandon Suoma and had been driven from all their positions in the southern half of the Mannerheim Line. They are still holding a line outside Viborg but I have no doubt at all that Voroshilov will go right through now, as he is outflanking them by throwing the left wing of his Army across the ice where there are no prepared positions except for the island forts."

Gregory nodded. "That looks bad for the Finns, then."

"Yes. The punishment they are receiving now is terrific; as you will probably see for yourself if you're here for any length of time. They generally let us go up to see a big attack every few days and I propose to consider you as a member of our Mission, on one condition."

"What is it?"

"There are about twenty of us here and we have our own Mess. If you are to continue as von Lutz you will naturally be made a member of it. I want your word that you will not use anything which you may learn in conversing with my brother-officers to the detriment of Germany should you succeed in getting back to England."

Gregory readily gave the undertaking. He felt that the request was only reasonable and, in any case, it was most unlikely that he would learn anything of real importance about projected operations in the West from casual talk of the officers in the German Mission, whose sphere of interest was at present so far removed from their own war with Britain and France.

"Good, then," von Geisenheim went on. "There's one other point. How d'you propose to account for your arrival here and the fact that you are not in uniform?"

"I shall say that I left Germany by plane, that my pilot lost his way and was forced down in desolate country by engine trouble and that I've been snowbound there until I managed to get away a few days ago. As I was leaving Germany on a foreign mission there is nothing very extraordinary about my having departed in civilian clothes and my uniform could have been destroyed with my baggage when the plane crashed."

"That's quite sound. But where will you be if some of the others knew von Lutz and expose you?"

"It's extraordinary long odds against even one out of twenty officers having known the Baron and the fact that you did so makes the odds twenty times longer. Would any of them have known that he was a friend of yours?"

"I don't think so. I only knew him in a social way; we were never in the same regiment or command."

"Then if I am found out you can always say that you didn't know him and so had no idea that I was an impostor."

"All right, we'll risk it. I'll take you to the Mess and arrange for a room and a servant to be given to you."

The Mess consisted of a big ante-room and dining-room, in a neighbouring hut. In the ante-room half a dozen German officers were talking or reading and the General introduced Gregory to them, placing him in charge of a Major Woltat, who gave him a drink and led him to another hutment which contained a long corridor and about a dozen rooms. A German soldier-servant was sent to the Quartermaster for bedding, etc., as Gregory had no equipment of his own, and one of the rooms was made over to him.

He dined in the Mess and would have thoroughly enjoyed the experience if he had not been so worried about the apparent difficulty in securing an interview with the Russian Generalissimo. The Germans were nearly all officers of senior rank and although they were very careful to make no reference to the Nazi Government, on account of the three black-uniformed Gestapo men who were present, they discussed the war with considerable intelligence.

Gregory learned that a few days before R.A.F. planes had made successful leaflet raids over Vienna and Prague. This seemed an extraordinarily fine performance, owing to the great distance over enemy territory that had to be covered, and it perturbed the Germans considerably because Goering had transferred some of his largest aeroplane factories to the neighbourhood of Vienna; believing that they would be out of bombing range there and so not only safe but able to work three shifts a day unhindered by the necessity of black-outs.

That Monday night Gregory went to bed thanking his stars that he had happened to see General von Geisenheim among the conspirators at the Adlon, but extremely worried about his prospects of being able to secure the release of his friends.

He spent most of Tuesday morning sitting about in the Mess, for he had no duties to perform, but the Germans also appeared to have very little to do, so he was never without company. However, in the evening Major Woltat informed him that on the following day the Military Mission was to make one of its periodical visits to the front, as part of Marshal Voroshilov's *entourage,* so Gregory retired to bed hoping that luck might serve him and that he would be able to get a word with the Marshal.

Next morning he was called early with the rest and long before the late dawn they piled into a fleet of cars which left the wood, moving in a westerly direction until they struck a main road running north that led them to the shore of the great bay south of Viborg. There, in a totally ruined village, they left the cars and changing into sleighs drove out for several miles across the ice until the higher ground of the opposite shore of the bay could be seen in the distance.

The sleighs drew up at a small island which rose out of the ice. It had been a Finnish strongpoint until the day before, but its concrete forts had been reduced to rubble and its abandoned guns lay broken and twisted from the Russian shells. The party numbered about fifty people in all and Major Woltat pointed out to Gregory the Russian Generalissimo as he led the way in the short climb to the island's top. He was a square-built man of middle height, with a rather plumpish face but good, open features. Beside him his trusted second-in-command, the old ex-Sergeant of Dragoons, Marshal Budenny, was easily recognizable from his huge moustaches.

Having taken up their positions they began to scan the bay through their field-glasses and to study the maps which some

364

of the officers were holding. To the north, which was now on their immediate right, they could just make out the square tower of the old castle which rose above the shattered roofs of Viborg; but it was directly in front of them and to their left front that the main Russian attack was being launched; its objective being the ten miles of coast-line running south-westward from the city and behind the last positions in the southern flank of the Mannerheim Line.

Major Woltat explained to Gregory that while the weather had favoured the Finns at the outbreak of the campaign by heavy snow-storms which hampered the Russian advance, the severe winter had now reacted in the Russians' favour. Normally the bay would have frozen over but the ice would not have been thick enough to send anything but infantry across it; whereas, owing to the extraordinary degree of cold which had continued for so long, the ice had frozen to such a thickness that the Russians were able to send tanks and guns over it without any fear of these falling through.

Individual men could not be seen at any distance as the crack Russian regiments which were now being flung into the battle were all equipped with snow-shirts; but as wave after wave of them came past the island towards the firing-line the great, flat ice-field seemed to undulate with their perpetual motion. From what Gregory could gather, their morale was good, as they pressed forward in spite of the shells from the Finnish batteries which were exploding among them, and all those who passed near enough to the island to recognize Voroshilov raised a cheer for him, which he acknowledged from time to time with a wave of his hand.

Gregory had seen the bombardment which the Germans had put over on March the 21st, 1918, when they launched their last offensive in the first Great War and broke through between the British and French Armies. That was said to be the most devastating that had ever taken place in the history of the world, but from what he could judge the one that he was now witnessing was even greater.

Major Woltat told him that the Soviet artillery was putting over 300,000 shells a day and, from the sector that Gregory could see, he had little reason to doubt this estimate. The whole Finnish line from Viborg in the north to a point far away in the south-west was one continuous ripple of light from the shellbursts. The hundreds of explosions per minute merged into one unceasing roar that made the air quiver and rocked the senses.

The island on which they stood was in a constant state of vibration as though an earthquake threatened or a concealed volcano was rumbling beneath it, and the Finnish coast, now obscured by a dense pall of smoke which sparkled like a black sequin dress with innumerable shifting flashes, appeared such a veritable hell that it seemed utterly impossible for anything to remain living upon it.

By comparison the Finnish artillery retaliation seemed only like a few batteries doing a practice shoot with all the economy which they would have had to exercise in peace-time; yet it was miraculous that they continued to fire at all, and the Russians were so massed that every Finnish shell did deadly execution. Here and there the Finnish heavies blew holes right through the ice causing men and horses to plunge to their death in the freezing water and scattering a great hail of ice-splinters, as deadly as the steel fragments of the shell itself, to whizz through the air killing and wounding scores of Russians.

They remained on the island watching this incredibly terrible spectacle for just over an hour. Then Voroshilov said something to Budenny, which made the old Dragoon laugh, and, turning, led the way back to the sleighs; the whole party following. This looked to Gregory just the opportunity for which he had been waiting, so hurrying up to von Geisenheim, he asked the German if he could possibly request the Marshal to give him a moment; but von Geisenheim shook his head.

"I'm sorry, but I'm sure it would be useless. You see, he is intensely nationalistic and resents any suggestion that Russia is not capable of concluding this campaign successfully without help from Germany. In consequence, he won't even speak to any of us in public except on ceremonial occasions, in case it is thought that he is seeking our advice. But I'm having an interview with him to-morrow and I'll ask then if I can present you to him."

It was a maddening situation but there was nothing that Gregory could do about it so with bitter disappointment he accompanied the others back to Battle Headquarters.

On Thursday evening he asked von Geisenheim if he had been successful in obtaining an interview with the Marshal for him and the General said: "I'm afraid I haven't managed to fix any definite appointment but he said that he would send for you as soon as he is able to spare a moment," so Gregory could only endeavour to possess his soul in patience.

All through Friday and Saturday he waited in the German

366

Mess hoping for the Marshal's summons; but Voroshilov was away long before dawn on both days visiting various sectors of the front. Unlike most modern Generals who spend nearly all their time in conferences far behind the lines, he maintained his old routine which had won him his brilliant victories twenty years earlier. Utterly fearless of death, he was always to be found in the most dangerous forward areas observing things for himself while daylight lasted, and it was only when he got back to camp at night that he reviewed the general situation with his Staff from the day's reports.

The battle for Viborg raged with unceasing ferocity. By Saturday, March the 2nd, the Russians had fully established themselves on the coast south of the city. The Mannerheim Line was still holding in the north, at Taipale, on Lake Ladoga, but in the south it had now been completely outflanked and nothing except one wing of the small exhausted Finnish Army lay between the Soviet host and an advance direct on Helsinki.

By Sunday morning Gregory was becoming desperate. It was eight days since he had left Kandalaksha. Instructions might be arriving at any time now for the prisoners to be transferred to Moscow. Even when he was allowed to see Voroshilov he had yet to get over the big fence of securing from him an order for their release, and in the desperate conditions of this ghastly weather it might take a considerable time to get the order through. Except by railway, communications with Kandalaksha were most unreliable. Kuporovitch had told him how he always sent his reports by courier as the quickest and surest way during the worst months of the winter. It seemed certain to Gregory now that under the pressure of his own affairs Voroshilov had forgotten his promise to give him an interview; so he made up his mind that, legitimate means of getting to see the Marshal having failed, the time had come when he must resort to desperate measures; he would throw all military regulations overboard and attempt to beard Voroshilov personally on his return to camp that night.

Although Gregory had no uniform his civilian clothes did not make him a conspicuous figure about the camp as everybody there was muffled in fur or leather garments of one kind or another. Having dined with the Germans he went out and took up a position among the trees from which he could observe the front of the long hutment that contained the Marshal's quarters. After a few moments the bitter cold forced him to start walking up and down, but as a number of people were constantly moving about the camp, and he kept at some distance from the building, he did not excite the attention of either of the sentries who were on guard outside it. An hour later his teeth were chattering in his head but at last he heard the note of a musical klaxon horn and the Marshal's fleet of cars came twisting down the woodland road.

As the klaxon sounded Gregory moved swiftly forward. At the same moment the sentries shouted something in Russian and he guessed that they were turning out the guard to receive the Marshal. When the leading car pulled up Gregory was still about thirty yards from the road and he began to run; three fur-clad figures stepped out of the car as he reached a point half-way between them and the hutments. Pulling up in their path he came to attention and saluted smartly; but even as he did so he caught the sound of running footsteps behind him. Before he had time to open his mouth the guard had seized him by the arms and dragged him aside.

"Marshal! Marshal! I have a request," he cried in German; but one of the soldiers clapped a gloved hand over his mouth, muffling his cries, and Voroshilov walked on, followed by his officers who seemed scarcely to have noticed the incident. With kicks and curses the Russians hauled Gregory across the snow towards the end of the long hutment. Two minutes later he was thrown head-foremost into the guard-room.

CHAPTER XXX

VOROSHILOV SIGNS TWO ORDERS

As Gregory lay bruised and panting on the guard-room floor
he realized that his crushing fear for Erika had become such
an obsession that it had led him into making a blunder which
might prove disastrous to them all. If only he had fought down
his impatience a little longer the Marshal might have seen him
in a day or two and, even if his friends had left Kandalaksha by
then, with an order of release from Voroshilov, there might still
have been time to intercept them on their journey south and
prevent them from being handed over to the Germans in
Moscow.

Now that the failure of his plan had sobered Gregory's
anxiety-racked brain he knew that even the Supreme Com-
mander of the Soviet forces would not keep a German officer of
some standing waiting indefinitely for an interview, when he
had a personal letter from Marshal Goering and the backing of
the chief of his own Military Mission; but by to-night's exploit
he might have sabotaged his own chances and be held a prisoner
during these next few all-important days.

When the officer of the guard found that Gregory could not
speak Russian an interpreter was sent for and explanations
ensued. The Russians became slightly more courteous when
they learned that he had not had any intention of attempting
to assasinate the Marshal, but they were still frigid as they left
the guard-room, locking him in.

A quarter of an hour later, to his immense relief, von Geisenheim arrived and, having identified him, vouched for his future
good conduct. Gregory had to give his word that he would not
try to force himself on the Marshal again. He was then released
and, unbelievably thankful at having so swiftly got out of the
mess in which he had landed himself, he listened with a good
grace to a severe ticking-off from von Geisenheim, who privately

369

sympathized with him but had his own position to consider as the responsible head of the German Military Mission.

The whole of Monday Gregory sat fuming in the Mess, hoping for a summons and listening with one ear to the talk which was all of Mr. Sumner Welles' arrival in Berlin on the previous Friday and his interviews with the German leaders on the succeeding days. Von Ribbentrop was on his way to Rome further to strengthen the Berlin-Rome Axis and the British were giving considerable offence to the Italians by detaining their coal-ships; so the officers hoped that Mussolini might be persuaded to give stronger support to Germany. Gregory smiled to himself that evening when the news came through that Britain had spiked von Ribbentrop's guns by releasing the coal-ships at the last moment. Just as he was going to bed he was warned by Major Woltat that the Military Mission was to accompany Voroshilov to the front again on the following morning.

It was now apparent that the Finns could not hold out much longer although they were contesting every inch of ground, and on the Tuesday of this second visit to the front Gregory saw for himself the frightful price that Russia was paying for her victory. This time Voroshilov and his *entourage* went right across the bay to the coast that had been the main Russian objective in the previous week's battle. In front of the now abandoned trenches on the Finnish mainland the Russian dead were piled waist-high in one horrible, frozen tangle which stretched as far as the eye could see on either side. The carnage there had been without precedent in history and those members of the German Military Mission who had been allowed to question Finnish prisoners said that the Finns declared that they had plied their machine-guns upon the massed Russians until their fingers ached to such a degree that they were positively forced to release the triggers. For days on end, until they had lost all hate for the Russians, they had continued the slaughter filled with utter horror at the massacre which duty called upon them to accomplish; then, at last, from sheer exhaustion they had dropped beside their weapons and had been captured in their gun-pits fast asleep.

It was that night they heard the first rumours of peace negotiations and Gregory's immediate thought was as to how an armistice might affect his friends; but as far as he could see, it would not be of any help to them at all. They were being held as German subjects and once they reached the German Embassy in Moscow they would be dispatched to Berlin to be dealt with whether the Russo-Finnish War was still going on or not.

On Wednesday morning they learned that Doctor Svinhufoud, the ex-President of Finland, had accompanied von Ribbentrop to Rome and that Sven Hedin, the pro-Nazi Swedish explorer was on his way to see Hitler in Berlin, as apparently both Italy and Sweden were now concerned in assisting the Russo-Finnish Peace *pourparlers.*

By this time Gregory could barely eat or sleep for the gnawing worry that beset him. It was eleven days since he had left the Arctic and nine of those days had dragged by in fruitless, nerve-racking waiting. He seemed no nearer now to getting ten minutes with Voroshilov than he had been on the first day of his arrival in the camp, and, badger his wits as he would, he could think of no way in which to expedite matters except plaguing von Geisenheim morning, noon and night; which he did without success.

His complete helplessness had driven him to such a state of despair that at first he hardly believed it when, on coming into the Mess for lunch that day, von Geisenheim said to him:

Now that peace is almost certain the Soviet offensive is to be temporarily eased, as Voroshilov does not want his troops to be killed unnecessarily. He did not pay his usual visit to the front this morning so I was able to get hold of him. He has agreed to see you at half-past two this afternoon."

Over the meal the Germans were all talking of the rumoured Soviet peace terms, which seemed extremely harsh and would give Russia even more than she had demanded before the outbreak of hostilities; but Gregory hardly listened, until his attention was caught by a monocled Colonel named von Falkenhausen saying:

"I hear that the British refused to pass on the same terms to Finland three weeks ago, because they considered them brutally excessive, and that they are now talking of coming to the help of the Finns. No Allied Expeditionary Force could possibly reach Finland in time to be of any use, of course, but it will suit us admirably if they try it. They can't make such a move without declaring war on Russia, which would be playing right into our hands. Then they would have to infringe the neutrality of Norway and Sweden or, if the Scandinavians agreed to allow the passage of their troops, give us a perfect excuse for walking into both countries. And, in either case, when they came down that railway from Narvik to Lulea, which is their only line of advance to the head of the Gulf of Bothnia, our bombers would be able to blow their troop trains to merry Hell."

It seemed to Gregory that the German had put the situation in a nutshell and he prayed with all his might that the Allied Governments would not undertake any such futile and suicidal venture.

At twenty-five minutes past two he was with von Geisenheim in the ante-room of Voroshilov's office. At half-past two, with quite exceptional punctuality for Russia, they were shown in, and the interview proved infinitely easier than Gregory had expected.

The Marshal was a bluff, hearty man who stood up to shake Gregory warmly by the hand directly von Geisenheim presented him. The German General, who spoke Russian fluently, stated briefly that the plane in which the Colonel-Baron von Lutz's party had left Germany had run into a blizzard and that, having lost all sense of direction, they had crashed hundreds of miles from their destination to become snow-bound in the Arctic forests for nearly three months. He added that having made a bid to get back to civilization towards the end of February the party had encountered Soviet troops and been arrested on a quite unjustifiable suspicion of espionage; but that the Colonel-Baron had been allowed to come south on parole while his friends had been detained at Kandalaksha as a surety for his good behaviour.

Gregory then handed over the forged letter from Goering. The Marshal put on a pair of pince-nez, glanced at it and passed it to a Major who was with him. The Major gave Voroshilov a swift translation and the Marshal then spoke quickly in Russian for a few moments; after which von Geisenheim said:

"The Marshal condoles with you upon the accident which deprived him of your services for so long but congratulates your ladies on having survived the rigours of the Arctic under such conditions for so many weeks. He says that it is a pleasure for him to give hospitality to any friend of Marshal Goering's. He regrets that you have had trouble with some of the Nazi leaders but assures you of his protection for as long as you choose to remain in the Soviet Union. He is sorry that your friends should have been detained in Kandalaksha and will give an order for their immediate release. He wishes to know now if they would prefer to be given accommodation in Leningrad or travel permits to one of the neutral countries in the Baltic."

372

"If the Marshal could have them sent to a Baltic port where they could get a ship for Sweden I'm sure they would all be extremely grateful," said Gregory. "The trouble is, though, that they may already be on their way to Moscow, because a report will have gone in about the party and, as they are Germans, if nothing is known about them it may have been decided to hand them over to the German Embassy."

When this had been translated Voroshilov said that the question of their whereabouts could easily be ascertained by a telephone inquiry to the War Office at Moscow and, when this had been made, he would let the Colonel-Baron know.

Gregory thanked him and the interview was over.

It seemed that there was nothing more he could do except wait for news, and he could only hope and pray that he would not be called upon to pass through further days of miserable uncertainty while the Russians were making the inquiries with their usual slowness. The only thing that cheered him a little was the fact that Voroshilov did not seem the sort of man who would let the grass grow under his feet; but having at last become aware of Colonel-Baron von Lutz's existence and his anxiety for his friends, would definitely do something about them. This proved the case, as barely an hour later Gregory was to be sent for by von Geisenheim, who told him that Voroshilov wished to see them again. They walked down the slippery, snow-covered track through the woods together, and after a short wait were shown in to the Marshal.

The interpreter-major, who was still with him, said at once: "The department concerned in Moscow has just telephoned a reply to our inquiry. On February the 28th they received a report that your friends were being held on suspicion of espionage at Kandalaksha. Apparently they told some story about having been in Petsamo on the day that war broke out, and having left there in an aeroplane for the purpose of getting in touch with the Military Intelligence section of our Northern Command."

Gregory was ready for that one, and nodded. "We said that, because we hoped to be transferred immediately to Murmansk, as from there my friends could have got a ship to take them along to Norway, once I had got in touch with the Marshal and secured his consent to the arrangement."

When Voroshilov learned what had been said he smiled and made a remark which was translated as: "Evidently your friends feel that they cannot get too far away from the Gestapo." And the interpreter went on:

"Moscow got in touch with Military Intelligence at Murmansk by wireless, but naturally, in view of what you say, Murmansk knew nothing of the prisoners, so the inquiry was refered to the German Embassy, who took the matter up with Berlin. The Embassy replied on March the 2nd that the *Gräfin* von Osterberg is an enemy of the German Reich who has been found guilty of treason, by a court held during her absence, and condemned to death. The German Ambassador requested that in order to save time and expense permission should be granted for Gestapo agents to travel from Moscow to Kandalaksha to examine the other prisoners and carry out the sentence on the *Frau Gräfin* there."

"*What?*" stammered Gregory. "But *good God,* how frightful!"

This bolt from the blue was worse than anything he had feared. He had been comforting himself for the last hour with the thought that the prisoner's journey, *via* Leningrad and Moscow, to the German frontier was bound to occupy several days, so with the Marshal's assistance he might be able to trace them to the place they had reached and secure their release; but if Gestapo agents had already been sent to Kandalaksha to execute Erika this last hope was now gone.

"Was—was the permission granted?" he asked almost in a whisper.

"Yes," replied the interpreter: "on March the 5th."

Voroshilov said something in Russian and von Geisenheim translated. "The Marshal says that he is so sorry to learn that *Herr* Himmler has managed to overreach Marshal Goering in this private vendetta of his against at least one of your friends. However, he remarks upon your good fortune in having managed to reach his headquarters; because you, von Lutz, were reported as being with the *Frau Gräfin* and it seems that in your absence you also were condemned to death by a Nazi court held soon after the November *Putsch,* so if you were still at Kandalaksha you would share the *Frau Gräfin's* fate."

Into Gregory's stricken mind penetrated the fact that the General spoke of Erika as though she was still alive, and a second later he realized that it must be so. It was only March the 6th, so the Gestapo execution squad could not have left Moscow earlier than the previous evening and the night train would have arrived in Leningrad only that morning. Between leaving the one train and catching another for the North they would certainly go to an hotel in the city for a meal and a bath and, after their night sitting up in the train, would probably go to bed for a few hours' sleep before proceeding on the much longer stage of their exhausting journey. In no case would they have left Leningrad until after lunch and it was possible that they did not intend to catch a train north until the evening; so the prisoners at Kandalaksha were as yet ignorant of the menace that was moving slowly but inexorably towards them and Erika had at least another day and a half to live.

With a surge of new hope Gregory asked if the Marshal would arrange for the authorities in Leningrad to be spoken to on the telephone and told to hold the Gestapo men, if they were still there; or, alternatively, issue counter-orders and have the prisoners brought to his headquarters.

Voroshilov's reply was to the effect that the Gestapo agents would be travelling on a Foreign Office permit and he could not interfere with Foreign Office affairs. On the other hand, in military matters he was the supreme authority and, as the prisoners were in the hands of the Military, he would be happy to oblige Marshal Goering by snatching his friends from the clutches of the Gestapo; but the difficulty lay in conveying such an order to the Governor of Kandalaksha in time to save the *Frau Gräfin*. There were many lines from this, the main theatre of war, to Leningrad and Moscow, but to the northern front communications were far from reliable. On several occasions the Finns had even succeeded in cutting the railway just south of Kandalaksha, and heavy falls of snow frequently broke the telephone and telegraph wires. One such blizzard had brought down miles of line only two days ago.

"Why not get in touch by wireless?" Gregory suggested at once.

The interpreter shrugged. "Kandalaksha is only a backwoods town. There is no radio station there."

"What would the Marshal do, then, if he had urgent orders for the Governor of Kandalaksha?" Gregory asked.

"Send a plane. But the Governor does not control our fighting forces up there, which are many miles further west on the Finnish frontier, so there are never any urgent orders to be sent to him."

"Cannot the Marshal send me up there in a plane on this occasion?"

The request was transmitted to Voroshilov and the reply

came back. "The Marshal regrets, but that is impossible. The war with Finland is not yet over and every plane we have is required for military purposes. He begs that you will not think that he has been made cynical by the sight of so much death, but he points out that this is a purely private matter and—willing as he would be to oblige you in other circumstances—he cannot divert a military plane from its duties for your use at such a time."

"Could he have me flown to Leningrad?" asked Gregory desperately. "There must be planes constantly returning there from their advance bases. If he could, I should arrive in time to catch a train leaving this evening; perhaps the same one on which the Gestapo men will travel or, anyway, one that leaves a few hours after theirs; in which case I might manage to reach Kandalaksha before the *Frau Gräfin* is actually led out for execution."

Von Geisenheim put this up to the Marshal and they had a brief discussion in Russian as to how long it would take Gregory to reach the nearest airfield, get to Leningrad by plane, and from the air-port there to the Northern Railway terminus; after which they decided that it was a hundred to one on the Gestapo agents having at least several hours' lead of him, so that the *Frau Gräfin* would almost certainly be dead by the time he arived at Kandalaksha. But at the end of the discussion Voroshilov stood up, looked at Gregory and said something which the interpreter translated as:

"Are you a brave man and are you prepared to undertake a most hazardous journey? If so the Marshal can suggest a way which will give you a much better chance of saving the *Frau Gräfin* than any you would have if he sent you in to Leningrad by plane or car."

"I am prepared to undertake *any* journey," Gregory replied firmly.

Voroshilov moved over to a large map of Western Russia and Finland that was nailed up on the wall. Speaking swiftly he touched Viborg, Lake Ladoga and the great bend in the Leningrad-Murmansk railway. His Staff-Major then interpreted for him.

"The Marshal says that while he cannot spare you a plane he will willingly place at your disposal cars, sleighs and horses. He suggests that you should cross the Karelian Isthmus to the south-western shore of Lake Ladoga, cross the ice of the Lake to Rabaly, on its north-eastern shore, and proceed from there to

Petrozavodsk, on Lake Onega. Cars and racing-sleighs move as fast as trains in Russia. From here to Petrozavodsk by the normal route is over 560 *versts;* but by following the tangent across the arc it is barely 300. The Marshal warns you that in crossing the Lake you will risk capture by the Finns and that, in any case, it will be a most terrible journey; but if you decide to adopt this plan it will give you a real chance actually to get ahead of the Gestapo men and catch a train at Petrazavodsk before any train which left Leningrad this afternoon can reach it."

"If the Marshal will provide me with facilities for such an attempt I shall be eternally grateful," Gregory replied eagerly, "and I cannot thank him enough for his brilliant suggestion."

There was another short conference, then the Major sat down to a typewriter. He tapped out two documents which the Marshal signed. Picking them up the Major handed one of them to Gregory.

"This," he said, "is an order for the release of your friends. It is addressed to the Governor of Kandalaksha or any other military authority who may be holding them in custody, so that it will still be operative should they have been transferred to any other place during your absence. Now, about your journey. The Marshal will place a car at your disposal to take you across the Isthmus to the Headquarters of the division that is holding the south-western shore of Lake Ladoga. I will telephone them at once, instructing them to provide you with a racing-sleigh and guides for crossing the Lake to Rabaly. From there on you will have to make your own arrangements, as communications with the north-western shore of the Lake are difficult and un-reliable."

Handing over the second paper he went on : "However, this is an open order to all officers and officials of the Soviet Union within the *Zone des Armées* to assist the Colonel-Baron von Lutz, by every means in their power, to travel, either alone or with his companions, with the utmost speed wherever he may wish to go. Since it is signed by Marshal Voroshilov as Supreme Com-mander and Commissar for Defence, you may be sure that you will have no difficulty whatever in obtaining the quickest possible means of transport. When will you be ready to start?"

"In a quarter of an hour," Gregory replied, placing the papers carefully in his pocket. He would have said 'at once', but he knew that to keep up his vitality he ought to snatch a quick meal before leaving, and he wanted to collect the few belongings that he had acquired in Leningrad.

"Very good," said the Major. "In a quarter of an hour I will have a car waiting for you outside this office."

The Marshal wished him good luck, asked to be remembered to his old comrade-in-arms, Kuporovitch, and shook hands again. Gregory expressed his most grateful thanks and, with von Geisenheim, withdrew.

"Two hundred miles across country over snow sounds a most ghastly trip," the General said gloomily, as they walked back to the Mess together. "Do you think you'll be able to make it?"

"God knows!" Gregory muttered. "Every moment will be precious, as we can be certain that the Gestapo men won't give Erika even an hour's grace once they get there, so it will be a neck-to-neck race. But I may just beat them to it if I don't meet with any unforeseen delays."

In the Mess he made a hasty meal of soup, *brödchen* and coffee substitute, then having had a large flask filled with vodka he repaired to his own hut to collect his things.

The light was on when he opened the door and he saw a broad, uniformed back bent over a suitcase. The man turned at that moment and he found himself staring into the solitary eye of Gestapo Chief Grauber.

CHAPTER XXXI

GRAUBER INTERVENES

For a moment the two men stared at each other, speechless with surprise, but it took Gregory only a fraction of that time to guess how it had come about that he found Grauber unpacking a suitcase in his room.

He had been so preoccupied over lunch with the thought of his coming interview with Voroshilov that at the time he had hardly taken in something Major Woltat had said to him. It had been to the effect that he had received a wireless message from Berlin that a number of other officers were on their way by plane to join the German Military Mission; mainly engineers who were coming out to examine the undamaged forts in the Mannerheim Line when the Finns surrendered and the Russians took them over. The Major had gone on to say that as accommodation was limited he would have to put one of the new arrivals in Gregory's room. Evidently Grauber had come in on the plane that afternoon and an evil fate had decreed that he should be chosen as Gregory's stable companion.

It took Gregory barely a second to realize what had happened and in another he had answered his own question as to why Grauber should have accompanied a group of engineer officers to the Russian front. As the Chief of the Gestapo Foreign Department U.A.-1 that bird of ill-omen appeared almost automatically at each point outside Germany to which the main interest of the war shifted. The surrender of the Finns appeared imminent, so what was more natural than that the Gestapo Chief should pay a flying visit to the Soviet General Headquarters, where the military side of the negotiations would be conducted?

The instant Grauber swung round from unpacking his suitcase he recognized Gregory. The black patch still hid his left eye-socket but his good eye flashed amazement—then deadly hatred. His gun was lying on a camp table just out of reach and he did not make the mistake of trying to grab it. As Gregory thrust his hand into his furs to draw his pistol the sixteen-stone Gestapo Chief hurled himself at him. The weight and suddenness of the attack carried Gregory right off his feet. They went down together with a frightful crash, Gregory underneath. With a speed which would have done credit to an all-in wrestler Grauber got his hands on the Englishman's throat. Next moment Gregory was fighting for his life.

Wriggling like an eel he twisted himself partly from under the German and bringing up his knee thrust it into his adversary's groin. Grauber let out a harsh grunt and for a second his hold on Gregory's throat slackened. Their faces were within a few inches of each other. As the grip on Gregory's throat relaxed he jerked his head forward and buried his teeth in Grauber's chin.

For two minutes the Gestapo man bore the intense agony, his blood streaming over Gregory's face while they fought with silent ferocity, then Grauber could bear the pain no longer. Withdrawing his right hand he clenched it and lifted it for a sideways blow that would smash Gregory's face away from his own. As the blow came Gregory let go his bulldog grip and flung his head aside so that the German's fist lost most of its force and only hit him a glancing blow on the left ear. But, twist as he would, he could not get out from under the heavy body.

Having freed his chin Grauber jerked himself up and holding Gregory down with his left hand bashed at his face with his right. Gregory dodged two of the blows but the third caught him full in the left eye. The pain was excruciating and for a moment he thought that he was blinded. Gathering all his force he kneed Grauber in the groin again. The German gave another awful grunt and tried to retaliate, but as his body shifted Gregory crossed his legs and stiffened the muscles of his stomach. At the same instant he brought up his right fist with a short-arm hook to the side of Grauber's chin. Grauber's face, as he straddled Gregory, was almost out of reach so the blow was not a heavy one; but it was just sufficient to tip him off his balance and, straining every muscle, Gregory forced him over on to his side.

Grauber kicked out and his heavy boot landed on Gregory's shin, but thrusting the German away from him he managed to wriggle to his knees. Rolling right over, Grauber jumped to his feet with the agility of a huge cat; but Gregory was as quick.

380

Flinging himself at the Gestapo Chief's knees he embraced his legs and pitched him right over his left shoulder to crash, face-foremost, spread-eagled on the floor.

The fall gave Gregory just time to stagger to his feet. He was puffing like a grampus, sweat and blood were streaming down his face, his heart was pounding as though it would burst through his ribs, but he dared not let up for a second. It was no time for Queensberry rules but a matter of life and death, and much more than his own life depended upon his getting out of that room a free man. As Grauber rolled over and came up on his knees again Gregory hit him full in the face.

He swayed there for an instant, rocking on his knees, yet such were his enormous powers of resistance that in spite of the blow he jerked up to his feet and came charging at Gregory like a thunderbolt.

Gregory managed to keep his balance but was forced back against the wall. He landed a right on his enemy's ear just as Grauber drew back his right and swung a terrific punch on his opponent's body. The blow left Gregory gasping and he sagged a little. Half-blinded and sick with pain he lurched sideways; but his right hand brushed the top of the small table and its fingers encountered Grauber's automatic. There was no time to grasp it properly, as Grauber had drawn back and was coming at him again with a hail of blows. Raising his left arm to protect his face Gregory dodged aside and lifting the clubbed automatic struck Grauber with all his remaining force upon the temple. The German collapsed like a pole-axed ox and lay, a limp, still, huddled lump, on the floor.

It was three minutes before Gregory could get back his breath or concentrate his thoughts. Once he could do so he listened for any sound in the passage or the adjoining rooms. It seemed certain that someone must have heard the racket caused by that frightful struggle and come to find out what it was all about; but in spite of its intensity it had occupied only a few moments and at this hour all the other occupants of the line of huts would be gathered in the Mess for their usual afternoon *Kafe-trinken*. As Gregory realized that he breathed a little more easily, locked the door and set about examining Grauber.

Blood was trickling from the German's temple as well as from his chin, but he was not dead, For a moment Gregory toyed with the idea of killing him. He was a murderer many times over and—worse—a blackmailer and a torturer, who had

381

climbed to high office in the Nazi State upon the blood, the misery and the tears of innumerable victims. With Hitler, Himmler, Heidrich, Streicher and all their crew, he deserved a more agonizing end than the human brain has power to devise; yet, while Gregory would have emptied the contents of an automatic into Grauber's stomach with the greatest possible pleasure if he had been conscious, he could not bring himself to crack the man's skull with one more blow from the pistol now that he lay there helpless.

A great thermos containing two quarts of hot water was kept filled in each hut by the soldier-servants for their officers to wash with when they came off duty. Gregory emptied his into the canvas basin and, having cleansed his face and hands of blood, began to bathe his eye; it was horribly inflamed but had not yet started to colour up. He felt extremely shaky but, using all the speed he could command, he collected everything of Grauber's that he thought might be of use to him and rammed the articles into the suitcase. Next he lashed Grauber hand and foot, lifted him on to his camp bed and drew the blankets over him; so that if anybody looked in they would think that, tired after his journey, he had turned in at once and was sound asleep. With luck he would not be discovered until the soldier-servant came to rouse them the following morning.

Gregory had just started to tidy the hut and remove all traces of the struggle when he caught the sound of footsteps. Next moment there came a sharp knock on the door.

For a second his heart stood still but he controlled his breathing and asked in a steady voice: "Who is it?"

"Von Geisenheim," the reply came back. "You said you would be only a quarter of an hour and over half an hour has gone already."

"I'm so sorry. I'll be with you now in one moment," Gregory called out. He felt certain that although von Geisenheim might be secretly anti-Nazi he would never dare to condone a murderous attack upon a Gestapo Chief who had been attached to his Mission. Swiftly righting the remaining things he snatched up the suitcase and opening the door slipped through it before the General had time to get a glimpse of more than a section of the room.

There was a bright, unshaded light in the passage; by it von Geisenheim immediately noticed Gregory's chalk-white face and damaged eye. Before he had time to speak Gregory said:

"I've just had a nasty accident. While I was packing I

382

tripped over my suitcase and fell against the corner of the table.
I was darned lucky not to lose the sight of my left eye and it
hurts abominably. That's what delayed me."

"Hum! It looks as though you've caught it an awful smack,"
von Geisenheim agreed sympathetically as they stepped out of
the hut into the darkness together, but he made no other
comment.

Five minutes later they were outside Voroshilov's office. A
powerful car was waiting in the roadway with a military
chauffeur at its wheel, and beside it stood the Staff-Major. In
the half-light which came from the headlamps of the car he did
not notice the state of Gregory's face as he said that he had made
arrangements for a racing sleigh to be in readiness on the south-
western shore of the Lake and wished him good luck.

Gregory murmured his thanks, shook hands with him and
von Geisenheim, saw from a glance at his watch that it was a
quarter-past five, and got into the car. The chauffeur spoke
German but had already been given his instructions. Next
moment they were off.

Directly they left the cover of the wood it was much easier
to see their surroundings. No moon could be hoped for later
that night, as it was the dark quarter, but for several days past
it had been what had become known as "Molotov weather";
clear, almost cloudless, blue skies from which the Soviet planes
were easily able to pick up their objectives without having to
come right down low as an easy target for the Finnish anti-
aircraft gunners. The nights had been equally fine, with a
million stars gleaming in a frosty sky, and now that the early
darkness had fallen again they were just beginning to twinkle.

Gregory's head was splitting and his body was one mass of
aching bruises, but as they turned on to the main road towards
Nykyrka he rallied himself to ask the chauffeur what he thought
he could get out of the car. The man gave a figure in *versts*,
which Gregory calculated as about eighty miles an hour; but
the chauffeur went on to add that he meant 'given a clear stretch
of good road', and they would be lucky if they could average a
quarter of that speed at night through cross-country lanes only
a few miles from the firing-line where masses of troops were in
constant motion. Gregory knew the journey across the Isthmus
to be nearly sixty miles. If the chauffeur was right it would take
them at least two and a half hours whereas he had hoped to do
it in under two; but they were soon out of the snow-mounds

which were all that was left of the Finnish town and making good going along a road that led almost due east.

Their route lay practically parallel to the battle-front as although the Soviet Armies had forced the south-western end of the Mannerheim Line and made an advance of nearly seventy miles there they had made hardly any impression upon its north-eastern end at all, and the Finns still held Taipale, which lies on Lake Ladoga. That was the nearest point from which to cross the Lake, but to remain within the Soviet lines they would have to keep a little to the south of it.

Fortunately the chauffeur had been driving officers of the Soviet General Staff all over the Isthmus for several weeks past so he knew every road and village on it well. He handled his car admirably, seizing every advantage to accelerate and press ahead whenever there was a free stretch of road or he could slip round a slowly-moving vehicle. This part of Finland had been very highly populated so the roads were good, and after each fall of snow the Russians were clearing them by mechanized snow-sweepers to enable their troops and transport to move about more freely, but the car had constantly to slow down when parties of marching men or guns and tanks showed up in the headlights.

For the first hour of the journey Gregory sat almost comatose while he slowly recovered from his fight for life with Grauber; then, after the terrible strain of inaction and anxiety for so many days, all he could think of were the precious papers in his pocket and the fact that he was at last on the move again. He had become so accustomed to the constant thunder of the guns that he hardly noticed it any longer except when the road passed near one of the concealed Russian batteries which loosed off with an ear-splitting crack, without any warning. Although the Soviet offensive had eased during the last two days and they had not been hurling thousands upon thousands more of their infantry into fresh attacks the artillery bombardment seemed very nearly as devastating as before; the Soviet guns were still battering the Finnish forts night and day without respite.

Rousing himself again he asked the chauffeur: "What is the Russian for 'It is by order of the Marshal and my business is *most* urgent'?"

"*Prikaz Marshala ie srotchnya prikaz,*" said the man, and Gregory repeated the phrase over and over again until he had mastered and memorized it perfectly.

Swerving, darting—down to a crawl—swerving and darting

again, the car nosed its way eastward through farmlands and half-glimpsed ruined villages, gradually drawing a little nearer to the firing-line until, just before seven o'clock, the chauffeur turned off a main road and up a side-track into a coppice that concealed a block of huts which were similar to those they had left at General Headquarters but not so numerous. The car drew up before one of the huts and the chauffeur sounded his horn loudly; the hut door opened and an officer came out who asked in German if it was the Colonel-Baron von Lutz.

As Gregory acknowledged his false identity he took a new grip on himself and prepared for trouble. This was evidently the Divisional Headquarters which was to provide him with a sleigh and horses. If the trussed and battered Grauber had been discovered by a soldier-servant or one of his own people while the car was crossing the Isthmus there would be hell to pay. G.H.Q. would have phoned through ordering the arrest of the Colonel-Baron pending explanations. Even if he could lie his way out of the new tangle vital time would be lost; not moments but hours, or days perhaps, while he was sent back under guard to face his accusers; and Erika's life hung on the ticking of the clock. If he was arrested now the game was up.

"They telephoned us from G.H.Q.," the officer began, but as he went on Gregory allowed himself to breathe again. "In the last two hours I've made all the arrangements and everything possible has been done to assure you a safe crossing of the Lake. It's four miles to the foreshore. The horses are waiting so we will go to them in your car." Getting in, he gave the chauffeur directions and turned again to Gregory. "This is a most unusual journey you are making, *Herr Oberst-Baron*."

"It is a matter of great urgency," Gregory replied.

"So I understand. But it's a most hazardous undertaking to attempt to cross the Lake in such a manner; particularly as there is no proper front upon it and our men are constantly engaging Finnish patrols out there which sometimes slip through behind them in the darkness."

Gregory shrugged. "I'm afraid that's a risk that must be taken."

They ran along a twisting road through the trees until it sloped down to a little village which had been almost pounded to pieces. As the car drew up in an open space among the ruins Gregory could see that they were on the edge of a small, frozen harbour which in peace-time had sheltered the fishing-boats of the villagers. He glanced at his watch and saw that it was 7.20.

385

They had crossed the Isthmus in two hours, five minutes, averaging about twenty-eight miles an hour, which was a magnificent effort considering that for nearly the whole way they had had to pass along troop-congested by-roads.

Having thanked the chauffeur for his excellent driving Gregory picked up his suitcase, left the car and went down a few ice-covered steps to the frozen harbour. A group which consisted of a light *troika*, eight horses and two bearded, fur-muffled soldiers was waiting there.

"It's seventy-two miles from shore to shore," said the officer, "and, as you probably know, it's unusual to drive for more than thirty miles without a change of team. Unfortunately there's nowhere in the middle of the Lake where you can pick up relays, so I'm sending a spare team which will be led with a spare saddle-horse. That will enable you to change teams every hour or so. The horses are all young and fresh, the best that could be picked for such a journey, but I'm afraid you may have to kill some of them if you are to get through. The strain upon them will be frightful."

"I know." Gregory nodded. "It's a pretty desperate venture, but it's got to be done, and I'm more than grateful to you for giving me your best horses for such a ghastly trip."

"The two men have been picked because they both speak German and are well fitted to act as your guides," the officer went on. "They will accompany you right through in order to act as your interpreters with the officials in any villages where you have to get relays on the opposite mainland. This"—he pointed to the taller man who was standing in the sleigh—"is Sergeant Boroski; the other, who is holding the spare team, is Corporal Orloff."

Gregory said a cheery word to the two soldiers, put his suitcase in the sleigh and getting in himself said good-bye to the officer, who had been no more than a shadowy form and a voice in the semi-darkness. Sergeant Boroski cracked his whip and the horses went forward at a canter out of the little harbour.

With a sigh of relief Gregory snuggled down into the sleigh, pulling the thick fur rugs right up to his chin. One great danger was safely past. Grauber's men might get the Russians to telephone till all was blue but they could not stop him now. Communications ended on the south-western shore of the Lake; the very thing which had previously prevented him from getting an order for Erika's release to Kandalaksha was now his protection. They could send a courier after him but they could

386

not catch him, and even a few hours' lead would be enough. If he could reach Kandalaksha before the Gestapo men he could free Erika and leave with her immediately. Now that he had Voroshilov's *carte blanche* order in his pocket for everyone to facilitate the journey of his party he backed himself to get clear before the pursuit with counter-orders could possibly arrive.

Yet he knew that he was still terrifyingly far from succeeding in his bid to rescue Erika and was only now entering upon the most dangerous and difficult stage of his journey. While by no means an impossibility, seventy-two miles is a terrific distance for horses to cover without at least one interval for prolonged rest and recuperation; yet in that bitter cold there could be no question of halting for any length of time, as there was no shelter for the teams and if they were given more than a breather at stated intervals the cold might affect them too severely for them to proceed further. He remembered, too, what he had been told about Finnish patrols often penetrating between the Russian outposts on the Lake. For the first six or eight miles, at least, there was the added risk of being shot or captured, and he could not possibly afford the time to make a wide detour which would have carried him outside the limits of this very definite danger.

Recovered now from his hellish scrap with Grauber, except for dull aches which he knew would not leave him for many hours, he began to calculate times while the sleigh ran smoothly forward, drawn at a fine pace by the fresh, well-fed horses. The distance from Leningrad to Petrozavodsk along the great bend in the railway was just over three hundred miles, and Gregory knew from his own experience that on that line the Russian trains averaged only eighteen miles an hour, so the journey would take the Gestapo agents seventeen hours. If they had not left Leningrad until that evening—say, at eight o'clock—they would not get into Petrozavodsk before one o'clock the following afternoon; in which case, if he succeeded in crossing the Lake and managed to maintain a reasonable speed in doing so, he should arrive well before them.

On the other hand they might have left Leningrad much earlier. It was possible that they had departed as early as two o'clock in the afternoon. If so, they would get into Petrozavodsk at about seven o'clock in the morning.

Gregory asked Boroski what speed he thought they could make over the ice and the Sergeant replied: "Twelve miles an hour in normal conditions; I might do even better with such fine horses, but if we encounter broken ice we may be badly held up. As we have such a great distance to cover I must husband the strength of the horses or we might never get there at all, so we cannot hope to do more than nine or ten miles an hour at the most."

The man spoke of *versts* but Gregory translated the Russian measure into English distances as he listened and began another series of calculations. Nine miles an hour would bring them to Rabaly in eight hours—about half-past two in the morning. They would then have to make arrangements for fresh horses and cover another seventy miles to Petrozavodsk. The going would be better along the road—say fifteen miles an hour with halts—which meant another five hours. It seemed doubtful if they would arrive at Petrozavodsk before eight-thirty at the earliest. He could only pray that the Gestapo men had not left Leningrad until the evening.

Behind them the guns still thundered and, looking over his left shoulder, to the west, Gregory could see a constant flickering in the night sky as shells and Verey lights burst upon the Finnish defences at Taipale, although the rising shore of the lake and the pinewoods which fringed it hid the actual explosions from him. To his front and right the darkness was unbroken, but the snow and stars enabled them to penetrate it for some distance. Orloff had gone ahead with the spare horses to act as an advance guard and give warning if he sighted any detachments of troops out on the ice of the Lake; but Gregory and Boroski also kept their eyes strained to the north-west, as in this first part of the journey there was a constant danger that a white-coated Finnish ski-patrol might suddenly emerge out of the shadows. Twice they caught the flash of rifles out there to the left and heard sharp reports; once a single wailing cry of a man in his death agony echoed over the snow-field.

While keeping alert Gregory began to think about Grauber and wonder if he would die from his injuries in the night. He hoped so, and cursed himself for his weakness in not having killed him when he had the chance. If Grauber survived he would be found, at the latest, when the soldier-servants came to call their officers at seven o'clock in the morning and he would have a fine story to tell von Geisenheim and the Russians. The General already knew that Gregory was an impostor but he could not possibly admit it and would have to press the Russians for the speedy capture of the false Colonel-Baron. That would make things damnably tricky once the hunt was up. But Gregory thought he knew how to cheat them. He would not come south again; that would be running into trouble. He would maintain his lead of it by heading north. Murmansk was only a hundred and seventy miles north of Kandalaksha and from there, with Voroshilov's order, they could get a ship along the coast to Norway. They would be out of Russia before the news that they were wanted reached the Arctic port. If only he arrived in time to save Erika, if only he arrived in time. . . .

Suddenly a challenge rang out right in front of them. Boroski swerved the sleigh to the right with the intention of making off at a gallop towards the east. Gregory snatched up the sub-machine-gun that was part of the sleigh's equipment; but Orloff answered the challenge as he was nearer the point from which it had come and had heard it clearly enough to recognize that the men ahead of them were Russians. Having shouted a pass-word he called to the others that it was all right and Boroski turned the sleigh back towards the north again. A moment later they passed a group of a dozen silent, ghost-like figures on skis, who waved to them before being swallowed up in the darkness.

At the end of the first hour they halted to rest the horses and swap teams. The men changed over duties, too, Sergeant Boroski mounting the spare riding horse to lead his team and Orloff's mount, while the Corporal got into the sleigh as driver. They felt considerably easier now, as it was hardly likely that any Finnish patrols would be so far out on the ice, and Gregory decided to try to get some sleep. His eye was hurting him abominably and his shin ached acutely where Grauber had landed a heavy kick on it; but the mutter of the guns had sunk away to a dull rumble in the distance, which only served to make him drowsy, so after a little time he managed to get off.

When he awoke it was just after ten o'clock and he asked at once how they were going. Boroski was driving again and he replied: "Quite well. We are nearly half-way across the Lake now."

Gregory was surprised and elated. If that were so, as they had been going for about two and three-quarter hours they must be averaging thirteen miles an hour, which was much better than anything he had hoped for; but his jubilance was abruptly checked as Boroski went on.

"There is trouble ahead now, though. It must have been that bad bump that woke you up."

"What was it?" Gregory inquired.

"Broken ice. A ship, or perhaps an ice-breaker, must have

ploughed her way through here just as the ice was forming and churned it all up so that it is hilly and uneven." As he spoke Boroski brought the horses to a walk and strained his eyes into the semi-darkness to catch the signals of Orloff who was riding ahead and picking out the best route for them to follow between the hummocks. For half an hour, while Gregory sat there fretting, impatient and freezing, it was impossible for them to move faster than a walking pace; but at last they got on to smooth ice again and with renewed energy after their change of gait the horses were able to go forward at a trot once more.

They were now over thirty miles from either shore and even the booming of the great guns could no longer be heard. The only sound which broke the stillness was the gentle clopping of the horses' hoofs and the swish of the snow as the sleigh cut into it. The stars overhead were brilliant and enabled the drivers to find their way in this forlorn, white wilderness without reference to the compass which Boroski was carrying.

An hour later they struck another patch of broken ice which delayed them further; by the time they got through it midnight had come and they still had another twenty miles to go. The horses were flagging now as, apart from the distance they had covered, the strain of pulling the sleigh up and down over the big hummocks on this second patch of bad ice seemed to have taken a lot out of them. The drivers were changing teams at shorter intervals and at each halt they were giving the horses a handful of grain soaked in vodka.

By one o'clock, when they pulled up again, the horses stood with splayed legs and their heads were hanging dejectedly down in front of them, breathing heavily. The lead team seemed in little better condition than the one which had just been unharnessed from the sleigh.

"They're in a bad way," Boroski commented, "and, poor beasts, they will be in a worse state before we reach Rabaly; but it cannot be helped, as there are many miles to go yet and we cannot afford the time to walk them."

When Orloff took over he drove the horses at a steady trot, for the first time using his whip to keep them up to their work. Gregory noticed that he did not halt at the half-hour as usual, so some minutes later he asked: "What about giving them another breather?"

Orloff shook his head. "If I do, they will lie down and we may have difficulty in getting them on their legs again. It is

better that we should drive them as far as they will go now and,
if necessary, walk the rest of the distance."

Gregory's heart sank. If they had to abandon the sleigh and
walk in the snow it might be hours yet before he reached the
far shore of the Lake. His only consolation was that the night
continued fine and that there were no signs of approaching
snow; as a heavy fall during the next hour or so would trap them
on the Lake and they might die there. He could now hear the
sound of gunfire once more and for some time there had been a
flicker in the sky, to the north-west, where the Russians were
pounding the Finnish lines before Sortavala.

At ten minutes to two the near-side horse of the *troika*
stumbled and fell, bringing the sleigh to an abrupt standstill.
The other two stood by it moaning for breath, their heads hanging down within a foot of the snow. Orloff got out and unharnessed the dead horse, then he freed the other two while Boroski
brought up the team he had been leading and harnessed them.

For another twenty minutes they drove on, then a second
horse fell dead in its tracks; the other two lay down beside it.
The Russians replaced the dead horse with the fittest from
Orloff's team and, using their whips ruthlessly now, got the
others on to their legs. At a slow amble the sleigh slid over the
snow again.

Ten minutes later a third horse died, upon which both its
companions and the led horses lay down directly they were
halted. It was a nightmare business getting them up again and
Gregory, numbed by the cold as he was, in spite of frequent
pulls at his flask of vodka, had to leave the sleigh and give his
assistance. Both men and beasts were nearly exhausted from
the terrific strain which they had undergone, but somehow the
job was done and, driven by the whips, the horses went forward
once more.

It was with inexpressible relief that a few moments after
the last halt, on Orloff's giving a loud shout, they saw a long,
low patch of deeper darkness ahead of them and knew that they
were in sight of the north shore of the lake. The horses, too,
knew it, and made a last effort. But the course of the sleigh
across the ice had only been plotted roughly, so they still had
to find the little town of Rabaly.

Here luck was with them. They were still scanning the dark,
desolate foreshore for lights when a challenge rang out. By
great good fortune they had run into another Russian patrol
which was able to direct them. The town was only a mile away;

just round a small headland to their left front. Another horse was lost before they reached it and they had to put the spare saddle-horse in to make up the team; but when Gregory stepped ashore in the small harbour he was smiling for the first time that night as he saw from his watch that it was only 2.30. They had made the crossing of the lake in seven hours and ten minutes.

Three soldiers from the patrol had accompanied them on the last lap of their journey, running beside the sleigh, and they roused some of their comrades who were quartered in the houses along the harbour. These took over the remaining horses and the sleigh while with an N.C.O. as guide Gregory, Boroski and Orloff proceeded on foot up the main street of the town to a building which housed the local military headquarters.

It was here, while they were waiting for an officer to be fetched, that Gregory had his first chance to see his two guides properly. The tall Sergeant Boroski was a flaxen-haired, blue-eyed Baltic type, while the shorter Corporal Orloff had a red beard, freckled face and snub nose. They had evidently been specially picked from the Divisional Staff, as they were much above the average Soviet soldier that Gregory had seen during his time in Russia, both for liveliness and smart appearance.

When an officer who was on night duty joined them Boroski acted as interpreter and Gregory produced his chit from Voroshilov with the Russian phrase that he had learnt: "It is by order of the Marshal and my business is *most* urgent."

On the officer's learning that they had just crossed the Lake he expressed great astonishment but agreed at once to provide them with a sleigh and order relays of horses to be ready at every point to get them to Petrozavodsk as quickly as possible. Dispatching two orderlies from the room he sat down to a telephone.

After a few minutes one of the orderlies returned carrying a tray with steaming cups of tea and some hunks of bread and sausage for the half-frozen travellers. They had hardly finished their meal when the second orderly reappeared to say that the sleigh was ready. The officer told Gregory, through Boroski, that he had arranged for a relay at the first village along the road and that directly they had gone he would telephone through to further points with instructions that they were to be given the fastest horses available. Then he took them outside and saw them off.

The magic name of Voroshilov had performed wonders. Instead of the usual Russian delays they had spent barely twenty

392

minutes in Rabaly. Orloff took the reins of the new sleigh while
Boroski sat beside Gregory. The hot tea had not thoroughly
warmed them through but they were in much better spirits now
that they had fast horses again and the really dangerous part
of the journey was over.

The road was long and straight, mainly through forest
country, but as that part of Russia was much more thickly
populated than the far north they passed through villages every
few miles. At nearly every village a fresh relay of horses was
waiting for them as the whole area was under military control
and plenty of horses were available. Whenever possible, while
the horses were being changed, they had further hot drinks
in Russian troop canteens to warm them as the cold was bitter,
and if it had not been for their thick furs they would have got
frost-bite through sitting still for so long in the sleigh. On and
on they drove through the long night, the miles falling away
behind, yet new vistas of tree-lined road ever opening before
them; but now that they constantly had fresh relays that they
could count on they did not spare the horses and were making
far better going than they had done across the Lake.

The stars were paling in the sky when they came out of the
forest to see buildings ahead of them and, from their inquiries
at the last halt, knew that they had reached Petrozavodsk. As
the sleigh drove up before the railway-station Gregory saw from
his watch that it was 7.10; they had done the seventy odd miles
from Rabaly in four hours and twenty minutes, averaging sixteen miles an hour, and he had accomplished the whole, almost
incredible journey from G.H.Q. of nearly two hundred miles in
just under fourteen hours.

Since it was only just after seven in the morning Gregory's
hopes were high. Even if the Gestapo men had left Leningrad
early the previous afternoon they could hardly have reached
Petrozavodsk before him. There was a military guard at the
station and having handed over the horses and sleigh Boroski
and Orloff accompanied him into the building. Thrusting their
way into the station-master's office they inquired at once about
the next train to Kandalaksha.

The sleepy official, who had been on duty all night, shrugged
in the true Russian manner. "There should be another at about
nine o'clock, or perhaps ten."

"Is there no hope of one arriving before nine?' Gregory said,
through Boroski. "We are in a great hurry."

"Then you should have got here earlier," the man grunted,

"and you would have caught the one which left here ten minutes ago."

When Gregory heard that they had just missed a train his language was unprintable; then, producing Voroshilov's order, he demanded to know at what time the train had left Leningrad.

The official suddenly came to life and said that he would do his best to find out. It took him a quarter of an hour to get through on the telephone to Leningrad and while he was speaking Gregory asked that he should also ascertain at what hour the one before the train they had just missed had left.

Boroski interpreted after the man had hung up the receiver. The train they had missed had left Leningrad at 3.45 the previous afternoon, and the one before that at 1.40.

Gregory bit his lip. Although he thought it unlikely that the Gestapo men had caught a train as early as 1.40, there was just a chance that they had. If so, they were two trains ahead of him, and both trains had made a much better speed than he had assumed likely; probably because the permanent way was in better condition at this end of the line than further north; a point that he had left out of his calculation. It was quite definitely on the cards that the Nazis were on the train that had just gone through. If they were, and he had to wait for the next, they would have between two and three hours' start, which he would never be able to make up. Given that much time in Kandalaksha they might execute Erika before he could get there. Somehow or other he had to get on the train he had just missed.

Turning to Boroski he tapped the Marshal's order and said: "Tell the station-master that he is to hold the train at the next station; we will go on by sleigh and catch it there."

Boroski translated. At first the official demurred but Gregory rapped out his solitary phrase of Russian: *"Prikaz Marshala ie srotchnya prikaz."*

The station-master shrugged and got through on the telephone to a place called Baylik, which, it transpired, was about ten miles further north. After an excited conversation arrangements were made for the train to be held there until the Supreme Commander's emissary could join it. Gregory and his two henchmen then hurried outside to reclaim their sleigh and demand another relay of horses, as the ones which had brought them in had just been watered and fed.

A quarter of an hour later they were on the road again. Their conversation with the station-master and military had occupied the best part of three-quarters of an hour but they reached the village of Baylik at 8.25, and found that the train had been waiting for them for only just under an hour; which, as Gregory pointed out to his companions, was nothing abnormal for any train on that railway.

The train was packed, mostly with troops, but as Gregory's warrant conferred almost limitless powers upon him he determined to see to it that his two men had good accommodation. Both of them had alternatively ridden or driven during the seven hours' crossing of the lake, and for a further five hours they had taken turns in driving the eighty miles from Rabaly to Baylik; so, tough, hefty fellows as they were, they were both nearly asleep on their feet. Having tackled an officer he had a carriage cleared of troops and made Boroski and Orloff lie down at full length on the two seats so that they could sleep in such little comfort as it was possible to secure for them.

He was in slightly better trim as, although it was nearly twenty-six hours since he had got out of bed at General Headquarters the previous morning, he had lent a hand with the horses only during the last stages of the terrible journey across the Lake and, not having had to drive at all, he had been able to doze for a good part of the time. Moreover, he yet had work to do. It was essential to his peace of mind that he should ascertain as soon as possible whether the two Gestapo men were on the train, and directly it moved out of the station he set about the job.

The wintry daylight now disclosed the snow-covered landscape. To the left of the track the forest stretched almost unbroken with only a clearing round a village here and there; but to the right there were sometimes gaps between the trees several miles in length as the railway ran alongside the creeks on the west of Lake Onega which stretched, a vast expanse of frozen snow, as far as the eye could see. Slowly but methodically Gregory pushed and bumped his way along the crowded corridor of the train, peering at the sleepy, dirty faces of the occupants of each carriage. The Gestapo men would almost certainly be wearing furs in such a climate but he felt sure that he would have no difficulty in recognizing them both from their appearance and their luggage; yet none of the few civilians that he could see in the crowded compartments looked the least like Germans.

However, the train was not connected by corridors all the way along, so having examined one portion of it he had to wait until it had pulled up, get out, and reboard another portion of it to examine that. The business was a long and tiring one and took him the best part of four hours; but when the train pulled into the town of Perguba, at the head of Lake Onega, he had fully satisfied himself that the Gestapo agents were not on it.

Rousing his two companions he took them to the station buffet to give them a good meal and while they ate he considered the position. It now seemed probable that the Gestapo men had not started until the previous evening, in which case they were one or perhaps more trains behind him; but there was still just a chance that they might have caught the 1.40 from Leningrad. If they had, it would normally have given them a lead of two hours and five minutes over the train he was on, but he himself had held that up at Baylik for just under an hour, whereas in the ordinary way it would probably not have stopped at such a small place for more than twenty minutes. The train ahead, therefore, now had a lead of approximately two hours and forty minutes; five times as long as was necessary to arrange the formalities of the most ceremonious firing-squad. *Somehow* he had *got* to get on the train ahead and make dead certain that the Gestapo agents had not caught it.

When they had finished their meal he got Boroski and Orloff to take him to the station-master and, producing his famous order once again, he demanded that the train ahead should be held until the train in which they were travelling could catch up with it; but here, for the first time, he met with determined opposition.

To hold a train for an hour or so was one thing, said the man, but to hold it for three hours was quite another. In peace-time Perguba was a quiet little town where officials led a pleasant life and were not bothered with such mad requests, and a couple of trains a day were quite sufficient to satisfy every-body. But now that there was a war on things were very diff-erent; everyone had to work night and day; the traffic on the line was chaotic; military officers were always demanding im-possibilities. To do as Gregory suggested would upset all the traffic and make bad infinitely worse.

"It is by the order of the Marshal and my business is *most* urgent," Gregory snapped with a cold authority which he had often found extremely efficacious when forced to browbeat petty officials; but the man was obdurate. He pointed out that the order said that Gregory should be given every assistance to facilitate his journey, but *not* that trains should be held up for him unnecessarily; and that in this case it was *not* necessary to hold up the train ahead, because it would have to wait until Gregory could reach it and, therefore, would not get to Kandalaksha any quicker than the train he was on at the moment.

Seeing that it was useless to argue further Gregory began to insist that his train must put on more speed in order to get him to Kandalaksha as soon after the other train as possible. In consequence, the engine-driver was summoned.

He shrugged his shoulders a great deal and waved his hands, asking if they thought that his engine was an aeroplane. They knew quite well, he said, that it dated from pre-Revolution days and was held together only by bits of wire and his own brilliance as an engineer. Moreover, how could anyone get more than twenty-five miles an hour out of an engine when they had only wood fuel on which to stoke it?—and that was all that was procurable in this part of the country.

Gregory produced his order again and told the driver that whatever his difficulties might be he had got to catch up the other train because, if he did not, Marshal Voroshilov would have him shot as a saboteur and an enemy of the Union of Soviet Socialist Republics.

The engine-driver's mouth fell open in comical dismay and promising to do his best he hurried out to get his ramshackle engine going. Five minutes later they started off at a pace quite unprecedented and with such suddenness that a number of the passengers were left shouting indignantly on the platform.

It was now past one o'clock and Gregory was very nearly all-in. He had done everything conceivable to expedite his journey, so he lay down on one of the seats in his carriage while Boroski took the other and Orloff the floor, and they all went to sleep.

Although the two Russians had had four hours' sleep apiece during the morning they slept like the troopers they were, and Gregory was so fagged-out that he, too, slept heavily, so it was getting on for midnight when they were awakened by a particularly violent series of jolts. The train had come to a halt in another station, which they soon discovered to be Kem.

Directly they had roused up they went along to see the engine-driver to find out how much time he had managed to make up, and they caught him just going off duty. He protested that he had done his very best, but he had succeeded in making up only an hour. His relief arrived while they were still discussing the matter, so the new man was questioned as to whether he thought he could catch the train ahead before it arrived at Kandalaksha. He proved as pessimistic as his colleague but Gregory cut short his complaints about the engine and asked, through Boroski, for a definite answer as to whether or not they could catch up the other train.

The reply was, "No". From Kem to Kandalaksha was under two hundred miles and the new driver said that it was quite impossible to make up the best part of two hours in that distance. Gregory then ordered the whole party to the station-master's office and on the way told Boroski of a new décision he had taken. If the second train could not catch up the first, its engine could; so they were going to abandon the whole string of coaches and proceed on the engine with every ounce of speed that it could muster.

The station-master argued and protested. It would take at least two hours to get another engine out of the yard and ready to carry on the abandoned train; and where, at this time of night, could he be expected to find another driver? But Gregory flung discretion to the winds and sternly pronounced an ultimatum. Either they let him have the engine or he would go straight to the local G.P.U. and have both station-master and driver arrested pending the time when he could see Marshal Voroshilov again and make it his personal business to have them both hanged, drawn and quartered. Under this dire threat, with many gesticulations and expostulations, they at last gave way and Gregory was at last allowed to have his engine.

Once it was going, with only a single coach behind it as ballast to keep it on the rails, their speed was more than doubled and on straight stretches of the line the driver managed to rev. it up to the incredible speed of fifty miles an hour. Gregory rode with Boroski and Orloff in the bunker to make certain that the driver did not slacken in his efforts, and as he sat there on the pile of logs he cursed himself for not having thought of this excellent expedient before; since if he had commandeered the engine to start off with, at Baylik, they would easily have overhauled the train ahead by now.

The glowing furnace of the engine gave them some heat, but the bunker was open to the icy wind so from time to time they took a hand in heaving wood to keep themselves warm, as the solitary engine roared on through the dark night, a cascade of sparks streaming from its funnel.

They had left Kem at half-past twelve and covered the next hundred miles in two and a half hours; so by three o'clock in the morning they were keeping a sharp look-out for the rear lights of the train they were pursuing, expecting to catch it up at any moment. Gregory was now satisfied that even if the Gestapo men were on the train ahead they could not reach Kandalaksha before him; but he was feverish with impatience to board it at its next halt so as to place the matter beyond all possible doubt.

They had been travelling south-west for the last twenty miles, as a creek running inland from the White Sea necessitated the line making a huge hairpin bend and they had just reached its extremity, where the track curved back towards the north, when the engine-driver shouted something to his stoker and grabbed the brake lever. Peering anxiously from the cab Gregory saw that a red light was being waved on the line ahead of them; with a scream of ill-oiled brakes the engine slowed down over the next quarter of a mile and came jerking to a halt within twenty yards of the light.

A man who was holding a red lamp approached and called out to them; upon which Boroski and Orloff, who had now entered into the excitement of the chase with as much enthusiasm as Gregory, exclaimed simultaneously:

"He says the bridge is down."

Gregory used an Italian oath which in the imagination of man has never been exceeded for its blasphemy, and asked them to get details. After an excited conversation, in which Boroski, Orloff, the driver, the stoker and the man with the lamp all joined, his guides told him.

"It is the Finns. Before turning north-east again the railway crosses a bridge at this point, which spans a river running into the creek. The Finnish frontier is only sixty miles from here. This is the fourth time during the war that one of what the Finns call their 'death companies' has come through the forests unknown to us and blown up this bridge in the middle of the night. They creep up so quietly that the sentries cannot see them and they are always cutting the telephone and telegraph wires, because it is impossible for us to keep sentries posted every fifty yards along the line."

"When did this happen?" Gregory asked.

"It has only just occurred. The man with the light is surprised that we did not hear the explosion, but the roar of the engine must have drowned it and we should not have seen the flash because of the curve in the line and the surrounding trees.

The Finns are cunning fellows and they always try to blow the bridges up just as a train is passing over."

"Good God!" exclaimed Gregory. "Do you mean that the train ahead of us has been wrecked and gone crashing headlong on to the ice of the river?"

"No. This time the Finns exploded their dynamite a few minutes too late and the train was almost across; only the two last coaches were wrecked. It was lucky, though, that this man happened to see the sparks flying from our engine; our train is not due here for another two hours yet. If he hadn't pulled us up we should have gone through the broken bridge and all been killed.

The man with the lamp climbed on to the running-board of the engine and the driver turned over the lever. Puffing on slowly for a few hundred yards they rounded the curve and pulled up again. Ahead of them they could now see the silhouette of the bridge and moving lights beyond it where the people from the train were examining the wrecked rear coaches and rescuing their occupants.

Gregory was half-numb with cold and most terribly tired but his brain was still quick enough to realize that, for him, the wrecking of the train ahead was a blessing in disguise. He had only to cross the river to find out whether or not the Nazis were on the train. If they were not, he had got ahead of them by his dash across Lake Ladoga; if they were, it mattered no longer now that they could not possibly reach Kandalaksha before him; but the confirmation of either fact would be a blessed relief after the crushing anxiety that had tortured him for so many hours.

Leaving the engine they walked to the river-bank and scrambled down it on to the ice. Shouts and cries came from ahead and they could now see that it was the furthest of the three spans of the bridge which had been wrecked. The last two coaches of the train had snapped their couplings, run backwards down the collapsed span of the bridge and crashed through the ice, where they lay, half-submerged, one on top of the other.

As Gregory's party mingled with the crowd of people from the train he learned that one of the coaches contained only military stores and that the other was the guard's van in which eight or ten people had been travelling. An officer had taken charge of the proceedings and was directing some of the troops as they tried to rescue the poor, shouting wretches entrapped in

400

the van; while the rest stood on the ice round the great hole which the two coaches and the broken bridgework had made in it.

A number of the men had torches or lanterns so there was quite enough light in which to see people's features, and for ten minutes Gregory moved among them trying to ascertain if the Gestapo agents were anywhere in the crowd; but he could see no-one who looked even remotely like a German S.S. man. Yet there were two or three hundred people standing there in the uncertain light, so having sent Boroski off with his suitcase to secure seats for them in the train, which he assumed would start again when the injured and dead had been got out of the guard's van, he continued his search.

Suddenly a cry of terror went up from a dozen men all round him. The ice upon which they were standing had begun to move. It tilted beneath him quite slowly but he instantly guessed what had happened; the falling coaches had cracked the heavy ice for some distance round the hole that they had made, and the weight of so many people as they all crowded together at the jagged edge of one huge slab that had broken free was causing it to turn over. With screams and shouts the terrified men strove to dash for safety but as the ice tilted more sharply they could not scramble up its slope and slid backwards from it into the water. Swept off his feet in the press, Gregory was carried in with them.

As he went under the cold was so intense that it seemed to pierce his heart like a knife. Striking out blindly he came to the surface; only to be clawed round the neck by a frantic soldier who could not swim. Gregory knew that he would be dead himself in another minute if he could not get out of that deadly, gripping cold which went through his furs as though they were paper and paralysed his muscles. In a fierce determination to live he thrust the man off and grabbed the edge of the ice which, being relieved of its weight, had now fallen back into place. Next moment a man who had managed to retain his balance hauled him to safety and as he crouched, shuddering where he lay, he suddenly realized that it was Orloff who had rescued him.

Half a dozen other men had also been saved but a number of their comrades had died instantly from the shock of the immersion while others, again, had come up under the ice and so were past all aid.

The cold was so intense that the drips from the victims of this new catastrophe were already freezing into icicles as they were hurried away up the far bank towards the train. By the time they got to the engine their clothes were frozen on them; but huddled by the furnace they thawed out and as soon as it was possible began to strip. In spite of the heat from the furnace the cold of the air seemed to burn them as parts of their bodies were exposed to it, but blankets were brought to wrap them in while their clothes were dried. The cab of the engine was only just large enough to hold them all but they huddled up there, with their teeth chattering and their limbs aching, until their clothes, which the driver was holding garment by garment to the engine fire, were dry enough to put on again.

It was an hour before Gregory was able to rejoin his companions. He still felt chilled to the bone and had a splitting headache; but he resisted their attempts to persuade him to lie down as he was determined to make certain whether or not the Gestapo men were on the train. Now that he had succeeded in catching the train it no longer mattered in the least, since he had Voroshilov's order for Erika's release in his pocket and General Kuporovitch would naturally accept that as a higher authority than any document the Gestapo men might produce from the Foreign Office, but to find out if the Nazis had caught the 1.40 from Leningrad on the previous day had now become an obsession with him.

When they had arrived at the bridgehead it had been three o'clock in the morning. It was half-past five before a move was made for the train to proceed again. As the people climbed on board Gregory went from carriage to carriage and he was still at it long after the train was in motion. It was after seven before he had fully convinced himself that the S.S. men were not on this train either. Half-dazed with fatigue, but completely satisfied, he made his way back to Boroski and Orloff and sank down to sleep in the seat they had kept for him for the rest of the way to Kandalaksha.

It was after ten o'clock when they roused him to tell him that they had at last reached their journey's end. When he awoke he felt positively ghastly and knew that he was running a high temperature. He could hardly think for himself any more, except to realize in a dazed way that he had done the job which he had set out to do. He had beaten the Gestapo men and got to Kandalaksha before them. Boroski and Orloff, seeing his state, took charge of him, secured a *drosky* outside the station and drove with him to the castle.

They were kept only for a few moments in the gloomy

vaulted waiting-room that Gregory well remembered; then they were led upstairs to the great chamber with the incongruous furnishings, where Kuporovitch, his dark, slanting eyebrows contrasting so strangely with his grey hair, was seated behind his pinewood desk.

"So you've come back?" the General said, standing up. "But you look in a pretty mess. Whatever have you been doing to yourself?"

Gregory was in an appalling condition. Beads of sweat from a raging fever were standing out on his forehead; the black smuts from the wood fuel of the trains had smeared and run all over his face as a result of his plunge into the river. His left eye was entirely closed and the flesh all round it was a bright purple. His teeth were chattering and he could hardly stand, so that Boroski and Orloff were supporting him by the arms on either side; but he managed to stammer out:

"I've beaten them! I've beaten the Gestapo—I've got the order for release, signed by Voroshilov, in my pocket. Send— send for the Countess von Osterberg."

For a second the General's face went quite blank, then he said slowly: "You are too late. The Countess was taken away by two Gestapo men—in a plane—yesterday."

CHAPTER XXXII

THE ROAD TO BERLIN

On the morning of Saturday, February the 24th, Erika was roused by a sharp double knock. She woke to find herself in pitch darkness and for a moment wondered where she was. In their Arctic home it had never been pitch-dark, as there was always the warm, gentle glow from the cracks of the stove. Then a door opened and a light clicked on.

The glare from the single unshaded bulb lit the worn and ancient furnishings of the bedroom in Kandalaksha Castle and memory returned to her. Apparently there were no women-servants in the castle, as one of the General's shaven-headed orderlies had come into the room carrying a large can of hot water. As he put it down and laid one minute towel beside it she wondered why Gregory had not been in to see her on his way to bed the previous night.

In those hectic days they had spent in Munich and Berlin together early in November they had been the most passionate lovers. When they had met again in Helsinki his absence from her seemed only to have increased his eagerness; but their opportunities for love-making had been lamentably few. Then his injury at Petsamo had changed his mentality in that respect as in all others. On waking on their first morning in the trapper's house he had accepted quite naturally the fact that he was in love with her, but it had been an entirely different kind of love. He was tender and thoughtful for her and followed her every movement with an almost dog-like devotion, but he did not seem to know even the first steps in physical love-making any more.

Erika had known the love of many men but to be treated as a saint and placed upon a pedestal was an entirely new experience to her and she had thoroughly enjoyed it. There was something wonderfully refreshing in Gregory's shy, boyish attempts to hold her hand or steal a kiss on the back of her neck when the others were not looking; and she had known that at any moment she chose she could reawake his passions just as they could open up the cells of his memory upon other matters. But she had deliberately refrained from doing so; feeling that they had many weeks ahead of them and that it would be such a wonderful experience for them both if she allowed him to develop his full physical love for her quite unaided.

During those weeks she had grown to love him more than ever before; but she had been cheated of the consummation of her subtle plan by the sudden flooding back of his memory after his fall upon the ice-run. All his old desire for her had returned with renewed force. But within a few hours of that Freddie had solved his puzzle, Gregory had brought home to them the immense importance of it and they were on their way again in a desperate endeavour to get the German plan for world dominion back to London; so in the last five days there had been no opportuntiy for them to be alone together for more than a few moments.

It was for that reason that she had felt certain that he would come to her the previous night and kiss her into wakefulness directly he succeeded in getting away from General Kuporovitch. But she knew the reputation that Russian officers had for hard drinking and tried to console herself with the thought that their host must have plied Gregory with so much liquor after she had left them, which out of tactfulness he had felt bound to consume, that by the time he got away, hardheaded as he was, he had felt that he would spoil a very perfect moment if he roused her.

When the orderly had left the room she got up to wash and dress. As she looked at her clothes she sighed a little. Her one set of undies had had to do duty with constant washings for twelve weeks and they were in a shocking state. Perhaps she would have been wiser to have availed herself of some of the things belonging to the dead wife of the trapper, but she simply had not been able to bring herself to encase her lovely limbs in those unlovely garments. The tweeds in which she had left Helsinki had weathered their hard wear fairly well, but the soles of her snow-boots were wearing thin and the cold had driven her to make use of the Finnish woman's great, thick, woollen stockings. Fortunately her golden hair had a natural wave so, although to her critical eye it badly needed the attention of a hairdresser, she knew that as far as other people were concerned

405

it still passed muster; but powder, lipstick and face creams had all been abandoned in her dressing-case. Nevertheless, as she studied her face in a cracked Venetian mirror she had to admit that she was looking little worse for the lack of them.

She would have given a lot for a lipstick and some powder for her nose but she had managed to keep her face from chapping and the cold Arctic air had given her back a natural complexion which was better than anything she had had since she was a young girl. As she studied herself she decided that nobody would ever believe she was twenty-eight. She did not look a day over twenty-four and her figure, kept in perfect trim by the work she had had to do in these last few months, was as beautiful as ever.

On going out into the corridor she found the orderly there and Freddie standing beside him. He looked at her, blushed scarlet and looking quickly away again, said:

"Angela won't be a minute."

"Have you seen Gregory?" she asked.

He shook his head. "No. I went into his room a few minutes ago but he wasn't there so I suppose he's already with the General."

"It's rather queer that he didn't look in on me first, to say good morning," she remarked; but her mind was distracted by Angela's appearing at that moment.

Angela had not the good fortune to possess a natural wave so her dark hair was now neatly drawn back and pinned up in a small bun on the nape of her neck; but with her deep-blue eyes and milk-white skin she still looked extremely pretty and Erika, with a knowing eye, took in the fact that she looked prettier than ever this morning. She showed none of Freddie's embarrassment but smiled gaily as she said:

"Wasn't it fun to sleep in a proper bed again after all these weeks of dossing down on the top of the old brick oven? I wish they hadn't got us up, as I should like to have stayed in bed all day."

Erika took her arm affectionately. "Well, darling, let's hope the time is soon coming when you'll be able to, as perhaps Gregory has persuaded the General to release us. I'm sure he wouldn't have sat up all night drinking unless he thought that he could get something out of him."

The orderly beckoned to them and they followed him down the corridor to the room where they had fed the night before. The General was there, looking somewhat bleary-eyed, and his manner was abrupt as he addressed them:

"I regret that I shall have to make a change in your accommodation, since the Colonel-Baron has abused my hospitality."

"Really?" Erika raised her eyebrows. "What has he done?"

"As he can't be found, he must have left the castle in the early hours of the morning; although how he did it is not yet clear. If he had dropped from his window he could not get out that way, as all your rooms overlook interior courtyards; in any case, he couldn't have made the drop without using his bedding as a rope; and his bed is undisturbed."

Their first feeling on learning that Gregory had escaped was one of elation; but it was quickly crushed as the General went on: "I expect he will soon be brought back again. The fact that he cannot speak Russian, together with this godforsaken climate, will prevent him getting very far. In the meantime I intend to see that none of you others plays me any tricks. I am having you transferred to cells downstairs until I receive instructions about you from Moscow."

While they remained silent for a moment Freddie struggled to compose a sentence in French, then said haltingly: "How long do you think that will be; and what sort of orders do you think you will receive about us when they do come in?"

The General frowned. "I should receive instructions about you in a week, or ten days at the most. What they will be I don't know, but in view of what the Colonel-Baron told me last night after you went to bed, I should think that you will be sent to Moscow under guard and handed over to the German Embassy there for transfer to Berlin, as it appears that the Gestapo are most anxious to interview you."

His words were a most frightful blow to them all. It seemed impossible to think that Gregory had betrayed them; yet, on the face of it, that appeared to be what he had done. He had escaped himself without endeavouring to take them with him or even letting them know his intentions, as he obviously could have done if he had gone to his room after leaving his host. Worse; before going, either because he was too drunk to know what he was saying or for some inexplicable reason, he had told the General that they were wanted by the Gestapo.

They had barely taken in this almost unbelievable and very frightening piece of news when the General went on: "You will be treated well while you are here and you have nothing to be afraid of; but in your own interests I advise you to stick to the story that you told me last night until you are out of my keeping. Nobody here speaks French, German or English except myself, so no-one else can question you; but I shall have to do so formally this morning in front of my Political Commissar and I shall naturally translate accurately any answers which you make to my questions. Follow the orderly, please, and he will take you to your new quarters."

The orderly shepherded them downstairs to the ground-floor, where some of the stone-walled rooms of the old castle had been converted into cells. They were given one apiece, each of which was furnished with bare necessities and a stove; but the General had provided them with the additional amenity of a fourth cell in which to take their meals together and sit during the day. As soon as they had been shown their cells a plain but eatable breakfast was served for them in the sitting-room cell and they were locked in there.

At first they were almost too puzzled to discuss the situation. All of them felt that Gregory would never have acted as he had done without good reason; yet whether he had acted wisely was quite another matter. They had no doubt at all that, having escaped, his first concern would be to try to secure their release, but he would have to travel many hundreds of miles as a fugitive himself before he could get in touch with anybody who could possibly assist them, and by the end of the week they might all find themselves on their way to Moscow; after which they would very soon be beyond the aid of Gregory or anyone else.

Later in the morning they were taken upstairs again and questioned by the General in front of a small, fair, ferret-faced man who asked innumerable questions, for which the General acted as translator; but after an hour of this it was found that they were merely going over the same old ground in circles, so they were sent downstairs again.

When they were back in their sitting-room cell they discussed the situation further and decided that they did not at all like the look of it. From their long examination they gathered that the Political Commissar was greatly intrigued that such unusual fish as themselves should have swum into his isolated net and the General's attitude puzzled them greatly. His questions had shown little intelligence, and during the interrogation he had frequently glowered or shouted at them, all of which was in surprising contrast to his behaviour the night before, when he had been extremely courteous and quite clearly a man of considerable astuteness.

Freddie put the change down to the General's annoyance at Gregory's escape, but Erika said she felt that there was more to it than that; otherwise, why should he have gone out of his way first thing that morning to warn them to stick to their original story and say as little as possible in front of his Political Commissar?

Angela agreed with her. She also had felt that Kuporovitch had been pretending to be thick-witted, when they knew him to be nothing of the kind, and that he was therefore hiding some secret of his own which might later prove to be to their advantage. In consequence they hoped that he might come down to see them, or send for them again when he was alone, so that they might talk to him without restraint and perhaps get a clearer view of his true feelings towards them. But the day passed without their seeing any more of him.

On the Sunday morning one of the jailers, who had now taken charge of them, indicated that they should put on their furs and led them out into one of the inner courtyards of the castle for an hour's exercise; after which they were brought back and locked up again. The same thing happened on Monday, Tuesday, Wednesday, Thursday and Friday. This single hour a day was all the respite they had from boredom, which after the first day or two began to outweigh their anxieties. The General neither sent for them nor came to see them; so they decided that a hangover had been responsible for the sudden deterioration in his wits and manners. They had no books, papers or games and, unlike the long spell of voluntary confinement which they had spent in the trapper's house where they had had all sorts of jobs to occupy them, here they had not a stroke of work to do, apart from cleaning out their own cells which occupied only a few moments each morning.

They talked of this and that, but owing to the many weeks they had spent constantly in each other's company each of them already knew the other's views upon practically every subject, so they were reduced to useless speculation as to what had become of Gregory and their own possible fate.

It was on the Friday afternoon that Angela announced: "We shall have been here a week to-night, you know, so our time of grace is nearly up; and if you ask me, we've been counting without any justification at all on the idea that having got away himself Gregory will find some means of helping us."

"I'm quite sure he would if he could," said Erika swiftly.

"Naturally you feel that way, darling," Angela replied, not

409

unkindly, "because you love him; but you know the old saying, 'Love in a man's life is a thing apart; 'tis woman's whole existence'. I believe that applies in this case. If you had escaped, the only thing you'd give a damn about would be trying to save Gregory; although, of course, I'm sure you'd try and get Freddie and me out too, if you could. But Gregory probably views things differently—not because he doesn't love you, but because he's a man; and so would put what he considers his duty before his personal feelings."

Freddie nodded. "Yes. I know what you're driving at. I didn't want to depress either of you by saying so, but I've been thinking on those lines myself from the very beginning."

"On account of the typescript he got from Goering's safe?" said Erika.

"That's it," Angela agreed. "You know how immensely important he considered it was; so much so that he readily risked all our lives in an attempt to get it back to London. We should never have left our refuge in the forest until the spring if it hadn't been for that. Well, the fact that we were arrested hasn't made it less important. Gregory saw a chance to get out so he took it. He may have felt like hell at having to leave us in the lurch but the typescript was the thing that was uppermost in his mind. He's probably resigned himself by now to the fact that we're all as good as dead and is trying to console himself as well as he can with the knowledge that he couldn't have helped us if he had remained a prisoner, whereas, once he was free, it was his definite duty to try to get through with those vitally important papers."

Erika smiled. "I didn't say anything about it either, but I made up my mind long ago that having once escaped that is just what he would have done; and I don't think any of us can blame him."

"Not a bit," Freddie said quickly. "The only thing I don't understand is why he should have given it away to the General that we're wanted by the Gestapo."

"You two are not," replied Erika quietly—"at least, Freddie may be, for that affair in Helsinki, but even that is doubtful; and Angela certainly isn't."

"No," Angela admitted uneasily. "It's you and Gregory they are really after, darling."

"Yes; I realize that, and, of course, once we get to Moscow there is no-one to whom I can appeal, whereas both of you can demand the protection of the British Ambassador."

410

Freddie laughed, a little uncertainly. "I've been keeping that up my sleeve, because I didn't want Angela to count on it. You know what these Bolshies are—they may not allow us to appeal to anybody. I'm afraid all we can do for the moment is to stick together and hope for the best."

That conversation was the last which they were fated to hold on the subject of Gregory's escape and their own gloomy prospects but, afterwards, Erika was glad that they had had it. In the past six days she had been gradually veering towards the opinion that Gregory would not return, and this talk fully confirmed her in it.

For some inexplicable reason he had given away to General Kuporovitch the fact that they were wanted by the Gestapo, so sooner or later she would be handed over to the Nazis and taken back to Berlin to be executed. They were well guarded in the castle and, even if they could have escaped, their inability to speak Russian and the climatic conditions would have made it utterly impossible for them to get away from the Arctic town. She had never shirked facing anything except poverty and dirt in her brilliant but hazardous career. Whatever hopes Freddie and Angela might pin on being allowed to communicate with their own Embassy when they reached Moscow it was better that she should no longer buoy herself up with day-dreams of Gregory's accomplishing her rescue by some brilliant trick or great feat of daring; but make up her mind to endure, with as much dignity and courage as she could muster, the ignominy and death which were in store for her.

It was as well that she made this resolution on the Friday night, because in the middle of Saturday morning two guards came and beckoned to Freddie and Angela; but when Erika made to follow them the soldiers pushed her back and relocking the door left her alone in the cell. Half an hour later the furs and few belongings of the other two, which they had brought from the trapper's house, were collected. Afternoon drew into evening and as they did not come back Erika slowly began to realize that in all probability they had been separated from her for good.

No message was brought to her from them, so evidently they had not been allowed to communicate with her, and she had no means of asking the guards what had happened to them. When breakfast-time came on Sunday morning and they still had not returned, she made up her mind that she must nerve herself to

411

even greater courage, as she would now have to face future eventualities quite alone.

By Wednesday four days' solitary confinement had begun to tell upon her, as with nothing to occupy her the hours in the silent, gloomy fortress seemed to crawl by; but she knew that the period the General had mentioned was already up. At any time now instructions about her might be arriving from Moscow, and on the Thursday, just after she had eaten her midday meal she was sent for.

With the General, upstairs in his room, were the little ferret-faced Political Commissar and two black-uniformed S.S. men. Erika's footsteps faltered as she saw them. She had expected at least the further respite of the journey to Moscow and, although she had tried very hard to put it away from her, there had lingered in her mind the small but persistent hope that even if Gregory could not get her out of the castle he might be planning some attempt to rescue her on her way south. Now, she felt, that hope, too, was shattered. She knew the methods of the Gestapo. They never wasted time or put themselves to unnecessary expense in eliminating their enemies. Evidently, as these two Nazis had come all the way to Kandalaksha, permission had been obtained from their Russian friends for them to execute her there; so her life could now be measured in hours—or perhaps minutes.

One of the S.S. men, a big, fleshy, red-faced young brute, stepped forward and looked at her curiously. "So *you're* the celebrated Erika von Epp? I've often heard of you."

It was pointless for her to deny it as he was holding her passport, which the General had given him, in his hand. Inclining her head she walked, with that regal carriage which Gregory loved so much, to a chair and calmly sat down.

The General, the Commissar and the S.S. men had a short discussion in Russian. The Germans signed some papers, the General bowed politely and said to her in French:

"The courage which you show in such a situation has all my admiration, Countess. I deeply regret that my duty prevents my being of any assistance to you, but I must hand you over to these gentlemen"; and, having thanked him courteously, she was led from the room.

Down in the main hall her furs were brought to her and she was taken out to a large sleigh in which the Gestapo men placed themselves on either side of her. The sleigh drove through the gates and down into the little square of the town, but the driver

412

did not turn towards the railway-station. Instead, he took the opposite direction and after a quarter of an hour, when they had passed beyond the last scattered buildings, it pulled up on a long, flat expanse of snow where a black German plane was waiting.

Erika sighed. When she had found that they did not mean to execute her at once her hopes had risen again, but if she was to be taken back direct to Berlin in a plane, that once more eliminated any lingering possibility that Gregory might succeed in rescuing her on the journey. But she admitted to herself that she had never really thought he would. That typescript he was carrying was of such immense importance. He had been gone twelve days now; with his wit and courage he had probably succeeded in getting out of Russia by this time and was no doubt in Sweden or Norway or, if he had succeeded in getting a plane, perhaps he had even reached London.

Owing to newly-fallen snow they had great difficulty in getting off the ground, but after three unsuccessful attempts the pilot made them all crowd themselves into the tail of the machine and managed to get into the air. It was 'Molotov weather' again, and as the plane roared southwards they could see the frozen lakes and vast forests spread below them. For the first two-thirds of the journey they were well to the east of the Finnish border but the country was very much the same as Eastern Finland.

As Erika watched the countless millions of trees sliding away below them she remembered how Gregory had said that unless the Allies and the Scandinavian countries came to Finland's assistance, making an advance into Russia possible and giving the Finns air superiority, the war must be over by the spring. All Finland's wealth lay in such endless forests, and newly-planted trees took forty years to reach maturity. Once the snow which was protecting them through the long winter had melted, the Russians would be able to start huge forest fires by scattering incendiary bombs. The Finns might hold the Mannerheim Line but they would have to surrender if faced with the destruction of the entire potential wealth of their country for two generations to come.

At last the forests ended and just when dusk was falling a great, white expanse lay before them which Erika knew must be the Gulf of Finland. Far away in the distance there was a streak of colour. It was March the 7th and further south the thaw had already set in; the ice in the Baltic was breaking up and giving place to blue-green water.

Before they reached the coast-line the plane circled and came down on a big military airfield where many Soviet planes were in evidence. At first Erika thought that they had descended only to refuel, but she was told to get out, and was led between the hangars to a car; so she guessed that they were to break their journey here for the night.

The car took them a few miles through the area where the battles of January had raged, until it entered a deep wood in which there were many hutments; to pull up before a block that had bars across each of its long line of windows and a Russian sentry on guard outside it. The Gestapo men got out and shepherded Erika across some duck-boards to the entrance, an N.C.O. was summoned and she was taken inside to one of the row of rooms. It had a stove to warm it but only a palliasse and blankets on the floor. Leaving her there they locked her in.

Twenty minutes later a Russian soldier brought her a meal of stew, rye bread and coffee substitute. It was still quite early—only a little after seven o'clock—but she felt so tired and dispirited that, after eating what she could, she tried to settle down for the night.

She had not been lying still for long before she discovered, to her horror, that the straw of the mattress was alive with bed-bugs and that the blankets held a colony of lice. Abandoning the palliasse in disgust she curled up on the floor, near the stove, but its hardness, together with the irritation of the vermin which had now got under her clothes and were biting her in a score of places, made sleep impossible; all through the long hours of the night she tossed and squirmed in abject misery.

In the morning she attempted to delouse herself but the vermin were so numerous that her slaughter of them seemed hardly to decrease their numbers and, after a time, the job made her physically sick. She expected the Nazis to come for her to continue their journey but, to her surprise, they did not appear, and except for the soldier. who brought her more food, she was left alone until the afternoon.

She had just switched on the electric light when the door was unlocked and Grauber came in. It was a moment before she recognized him. One bandage swathed his head, covering his empty eye socket, another covered his chin and the whole of the lower portion of his face, but his remaining eye glinted at her with evil satisfaction.

"*Guten Tag, Frau Gräfin,*" he said in his thin, piping voice. "So we have run you to earth at last."

Erika did not reply, so he went on with evident enjoyment: "Jawohl; we've got you now, and I had you brought here because long ago I promised myself the pleasure of breaking that aristocratic pride of yours. It will be fun to see you scream and whimper before all that I intend to leave of you is dragged out to the execution yard. And don't imagine that your English boy-friend, Mr. Gregory Sallust, will be able to come to your assistance. We've got him too."

At that Erika was stunned into retort. "You swine!—you filthy swine!" she whispered between closed teeth.

"That makes you sit up, doesn't it?" he laughed in his high falsetto. "He was here two nights ago, posing as von Lutz again, and he had succeeded in wangling an order for your release with which he left for Kandalaksha; but I got on to his game in time and the men whom I sent to fetch you in the plane also took an order to the Governor there to arrest him directly he turns up."

Erika's heart was thudding. Dear Gregory—dear Gregory. So he had risked everything to try to save her, after all; but he was caught this time and—worse—those all-important papers would never get to England now.

"I shall proceed about your extermination slowly, *Frau Gräfin,*" Grauber went on with studied malice. "We have none of the usual aids to questioning prisoners or even an—er—examination room, but I don't need accessories to make little traitors like you go on their knees and beg for death."

Suddenly he struck her a violent blow in the face with his clenched fist. Reeling backwards she fell upon the filthy palliasse, with her mouth cut and bleeding. Having watched her for a moment as she lay there moaning he kicked her twice and, turning away, left the room.

The Russian soldier who brought her evening meal looked at her with round, pitying eyes when he saw the blood on her face and brought her a little lukewarm water with which to bathe her mouth; but that night it seemed to her that she had descended into the depths of hell.

In attempting to save her Gregory had been caught himself. At the very moment of his triumph, after heaven knew what superhuman scheming and endeavour during the last twelve days, he had walked straight into a trap; and been re-arrested the instant he produced the order which was to free her. They would make very certain, too, that he did not escape again. It was the end'for him, and the end for her. In a torment of misery she sobbed herself into an exhausted doze which was constantly broken by the biting of the vermin and nightmare thoughts of Grauber.

He came again the following afternoon, bringing with him a thin, flexible riding switch, and he spent an hour in her cell. Perhaps he did not wish the Russians to hear her screaming, or it may have been that he delighted to start her torment very gently, since he did not apply the switch savagely but struck her on the hands, the hips, the upper arms and the calves of the legs, little stinging blows every few minutes, while he taunted her and told her some of the things that he had in mind to do to Gregory.

On Sunday and Monday he came again and plied his switch each time with increasing vigour until the tender flesh of her whole body was criss-crossed with thin, aching red weals. On the Sunday she fought him, driving her nails deep into his cheek above the bandage and burying her teeth in his hand; but he hit her a blow in the stomach that drove the breath from her body and doubled her up in a writhing heap on the floor. On Monday, with the intention of rousing the guard, she deliberately began to scream the moment her tormentor entered the room; but the soldier who came in response to her screams was not the wide-eyed young peasant who had brought her the water three nights before. He was a sullen-looking lout who, on a sharp word from Grauber, shrugged his shoulders and slammed the door. After that she could only moan and submit to each further vicious little flick which was never hard enough to harm her seriously but which in succession were fraying her nerves to tatters.

The remainder of each twenty-three hours, when Grauber was not with her and she was not drowsing in torpid nightmare-ridden sleep, she spent in an agony of dread anticipating his next visit. She no longer even noticed the lice and bed-bugs that were now swarming on her or cared about her filthy, unwashed condition; and thought only of the fresh torments that were in store for her. But on the the Tuesday afternoon when she shuddered with apprehension at hearing the key turn in the lock of her cell a new figure entered; a tall, thin-faced man in the uniform of a German General.

Scrambling to her feet she ran towards him stretching out her bruised hands and stammering a plea for his protection, but he gently pushed her back and closed the door carefully behind him.

416

"You don't remember me, *Frau Gräfin*?" he said in a low voice.

"Why, yes!" she exclaimed. "You're Rupprecht von Geisenheim."

He nodded. "Yes. I'm the head of the German Military Mission to the Soviet and I don't know if you know it, but this camp is Marshal Voroshilov's Headquarters."

The tears sprang to her eyes as she muttered: "Oh, take me away from that fiend Grauber, he—he's killing me by inches."

Von Geisenheim shook his head sadly. "I can't possibly express how sorry I am for you, but you know the power of these Gestapo chiefs. It's more than my life is worth to try to give you my protection—in fact, I am risking a great deal by coming to see you here today, and I only decided to chance it because Grauber has gone into Leningrad for the night."

"Why have you come, then?" she cried desperately.

"Just to tell you two things which I thought might enable you to die more bravely. Firstly, I wanted you to know that the man you are in love with did not desert you; he moved heaven and earth to get an order for your release and to reach Kandalaksha before the Gestapo."

"I know that," she said quickly. "I know that."

"I'm aware of his real identity," the General went on, lowering his voice to a whisper. "We recognized each other when he arrived here. We were together in the fight that night at the Adlon, but by a miracle none of the Gestapo people who were there appear to have noticed me, so I was not arrested afterwards."

"You—you're one of us, then?" Erika said slowly.

"Yes. And the movement is still going on. As you know, it was only our friends in Berlin who revolted on the night of November the 8th. Since the *Putsch* was a failure the officers who commanded at the battle-fronts and in the garrisons all over Germany did not join in, so there are still many thousands of us who are ready to make a new bid for freedom when the time is ripe. You have been out of things for the last three months so you know nothing of our new plans and therefore can give nothing away however much they may torture you. But I wanted you to know that, although you will not live to see the day, all that is best in Germany will yet rise to overthrow Hitler and make our people great, free and respected again."

"Thank you," she murmured, the tears streaming down her

417

face. "Thank you, *Herr General;* it was good of you to come to me. I shall bear things better now that I know that our country is really to be freed from men like Grauber and all the evil they have brought into the world."

"You see now why I must resist the dictates of all decency and chivalry," Von Geisenheim went on. "By seeking to intervene on your behalf I should jeopardize my life; and it is my duty to live because I have work to do for the salvation of Germany. You will die, I know, with the courage of a true von Epp; in the meantime I can only wish you fortitude." Clicking his heels he bowed low over her swollen, blistered hand and kissed it; then he left the room as quietly as he had come.

That night she tried to fortify herself again with the thought that what she was undergoing was no worse than the sufferings of thousands of other men and women in the German concentration camps who had earned the hatred of individual Nazis or of the countless Czechs and Poles they had enslaved. Yet the knowledge that these brute-beasts, who were now seeking to bring the whole world under the scourge of their whips at the orders of their soulless, power-lusting Leader, would be swept away in due time by the forces of Good which were rallying against them was scant comfort beside the fact that she had yet so much to suffer before she died.

On the Wednesday morning she was shivering with fear again and even the sound of prolonged cheering in the camp about eleven o'clock did not rouse her curiosity. At three o'clock in the afternoon the door of her cell opened once again to admit Grauber.

He was in high good spirits and told her that the Russo-Finnish War was over. As he plied his switch from time to time he gleefully outlined the humiliating terms which the unfortunate Finns had been forced to accept after their magnificent resistance. In a spurt of rage Erika flared at him:

"You laugh too soon, you filthy brute! The Russians and you Nazis can smash these small people at your will, but you yet have Britain and France and America to deal with and they'll get you in the end; then the German people will revolt and crucify every one of you."

He laughed and flicked her across the face with his whip. "You little wild-cat; you're talking nonsense. And, anyhow, if things do go that way you'll never live to crow over us. Now this war's over I'm going back to Berlin and I mean to take you with me. You remember that private cell of mine in my own

418

house? We can have many pleasant little sessions there when I'm off duty. *Auf weidersehen, Frau Gräfin*." He stressed the last word mockingly as he turned and left her.

That night of Wednesday, March the 13th, was the worst of all the ghastly nights that she had spent during the past fortnight. The picture of the cell of which Grauber had spoken was constantly before her eyes; he might keep her there for weeks while satiating his sadistic brutality upon her. All night through she tossed and turned and when morning came she could hardly think coherently. She was afraid now that she would go mad before she died and barely had the strength to wonder what was about to happen; when, long before dawn, her cell was opened, her furs were thrust at her by one of the Russian soldiers and she was led outside to a sleigh.

In the faint light she saw that Grauber was already sitting in it dressed for a journey. He was wearing his eagle-crested peaked cap, instead of the fur *papenka* that he had worn on his visits to her hut, but he had a fur coat over his uniform and its collar was turned up round his ears to protect him from the cold. A Russian soldier was driving the sleigh and another sat on the box beside him. When she got in Grauber grunted at her as he moved over a little to make room, and the sleigh drove off.

Once it was clear of the wood it turned south. A few miles further, having reached the coast-line, it left the shore and drove on, continuing in the same direction over the ice. Erika roused herself for a moment to wonder if they were taking a short cut to the nearest railway-station by crossing a big bay; but she was so cold and utterly wretched that she no longer cared. Grauber, hunched up in his furs beside her, had gone to sleep and, having been roused so early, she tried to follow his example.

A bitter wind was blowing and it was still dark when, after two hours' driving, they reached a break in the ice beyond which blue water could be faintly seen. The sleigh halted and, getting out, Grauber began to flash a torch. His signal was answered. A quarter of an hour elapsed and the sound of oars splashing in the water became perceptible; then a boat drew up alongside the edge of the ice.

Grauber motioned to her to get into the boat and she obeyed while he turned back to talk to the two soldiers for a few minutes. She noticed that in comradely Russian fashion he shook hands with them before he joined her. The boat pushed off and they were rowed away through the gloomy dawn light to a small

419

tramp steamer which was standing out about half a mile away in the bay where the ice had melted. Some sailors helped Erika up the ladder and Grauber followed her. The boat was hoisted in and the ship's engines began to turn over.

Erika had already guessed what was happening. Now that the ice in the Baltic was breaking up it would be quicker and more comfortable to go down by ship to Danzig than to spend two nights sitting up in a railway-carriage on a journey through Russia and Poland. Grauber was standing beside her on the deck as she watched the icy shore of mutilated Finland recede. Suddenly she felt him put his arm through hers and the voice she loved more than anything else in the world said:

"Take it easy, darling."

She swung round with a half-strangled cry. Her companion had taken off his uniform cap and removed the black eye-shade. Next moment she was in Gregory's arms.

"But how—*how* did you do it?" she gasped between her sobs of joy when at last he released her.

His old gay smile lit up his lean, strong face. "I was a day too late when I arrived at Kandalaksha and I reached there in a raging fever that held me up for three days; but I left again on Monday evening. When I heard the Gestapo had sent a plane to fetch you I felt certain that must have been Grauber's work so I hurried back to Voroshilov's headquarters. Von Geisenheim told me what had happened and we planned this coup directly I got in last night."

He paused to kiss the red weal that ran across her cheek, where Grauber had struck her the day before, then hurried on: "I already had Voroshilov's order for your release and when I half-murdered Grauber a week ago I took everything of his that I thought might be useful to me, including his uniform and his eye-patch. With the patch and the bandages he had been wearing it wasn't difficult to get myself up well enough to pass for him in the darkness. The two soldiers on the sleigh were grand fellows who had accompanied me to Kandalaksha and back; but I didn't dare to let you know about my imposture in front of them, because they both speak German."

"But the ship, darling—how did you manage to get a ship? And where are we going?"

"We're going to Norway first, as this is a Norwegian vessel. If only Hitler hasn't walked into it before we get there. You remember the plan. And now the Finnish business is settled Denmark and Norway are the next on the list."

"Angela and Freddie!" Erika exclaimed. "They were taken away just a week after you left. D'you know what's happened to them?"

"They're all right, my sweet. When I first came South I saw the British Vice-Consul in Leningrad and fixed things up with him. No-one will ever know who shot those soldiers in Petsamo so the Russians have nothing against Angela or Freddie and the Consul was going to arrange for the British Embassy to demand their release. It came off all right, too, as Kuporovitch told me when I got back to Kandalaksha. A junior secretary from the British Embassy was sent up there to fetch them, so they're on their way home to a grand honeymoon now."

"Oh, bless them! And you'll be able to get the typescript to London if only we reach Norway safely."

He laughed. "It's been in the hands of the British Government for days. I told the whole story to the Vice-Consul in Leningrad, wrote a letter explaining matters to my old friend Sir Pellinore Gwaine-Cust and swore an affidavit as to how that poisonous plan to brand the Nazi Swastika on every state in Europe, one by one, had come into my possession. He saw at once how damnably dangerous and subtle the whole scheme was and, although he's not supposed to do such things, he agreed to take it himself to Moscow so that it could be flown home in one of the Embassy bags. That was much quicker than my trying to take it myself, and so much more certain."

"But the ship, darling—how did you get the ship?"

Gregory turned to a fur-clad figure that had been standing near them. "You remember our old friend, General Kuporovitch? We left his little friend Oggie locked in a grain store that's only opened once a week; then the General and I came South together. When we reached Leningrad yesterday afternoon I passed over to him my passport as von Lutz and Voroshilov's order. With the order, and his new identity as the Colonel-Baron, he was able to go out to Kronstadt Bay, where the ice is breaking up, and arrange for the Norwegian captain of this ship to steam out and lie off here till we could join him."

Kuporovitch kissed Erika's hand. *"Madame la Comtesse!"* he murmured. "This Gregory of yours is a man in a million and between us we are ten thousand devils. It is I who have left prison and I feel young for the first time in twenty years. How marvellous it will be to see Paris again. The three of us together, eh? We must celebrate our freedom there for at least a month."

Erika shook her head. "You've forgotten, General, that I'm

German. I can't go to either of the Allied countries before the war is over, since I won't go as a refugee. I'm afraid you'll both have to leave me in Norway."

"Perhaps," Gregory said thoughtfully; "but Norway won't be safe for very long. We three know that; and we know, too, that the Allied Governments won't make a patched-up peace after they've seen Goering's typescript. But each time Hitler is compelled to break away from the plan and lash out in a new direction through the pressure of the German people, whom he cannot hold unless he redeems his promise to them of speedy victories, he will weaken himself. Norway, Denmark, Holland, Belgium and the rest—each will take its toll of German lives, planes, steel and petrol. Even if Hitler succeeds in overrunning them he will have to police them afterwards and tie up hundreds of thousands of men to keep them under, just as he has already had to do in Austria, Czechoslovakia and Poland. In the meantime, just as in the last war, the British and French War Cabinets will be reconstructed to bring in more forceful elements, and while Germany exhausts herself the might of the Allies will constantly increase, until under the leadership of Churchill, perhaps, since he is the most dynamic and inveterate enemy the Germans ever had, the full, colossal power of the Free Peoples will stem the Nazi tide of conquest. Once that happens, Hitler's edifice will go to pieces like a house of cards; so the war may be over much sooner than people think."

"Then perhaps we'll be able to celebrate together in Paris by the Spring." Kuporovitch wafted an ironic kiss from his gloved finger-tips to the fading, icy shore of the new territories just acquired at such appalling cost by the Union of Soviet 'Slave' Republics and rolled the words round his tongue.

"Ah! Paris in the Spring!"

"Yes," said Gregory. "Or Berlin."